Gift
20
12603

CW00524176

Daylen of Brunhylde

~ A Tale of FéLorën ~

By

Galemine Gremn

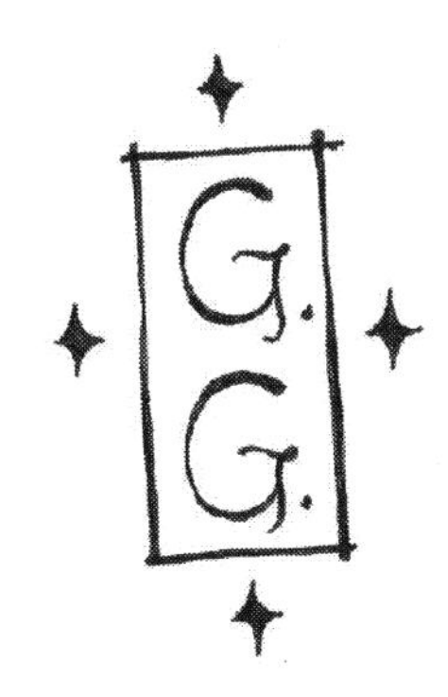

ISBN: 9798482072226

For

Jordan and Jonas

~PROLOGUE~

Memoralice gathered his robe around his frail, dying body. He sat within the corner of his tower chamber, listening to the silence, waiting for Death. Inscribed around him on the floor was a circle of protection, an intricate marking of runes. With arms wrapped around his knees, pressed close to his chest, he rocked back and forth shaking his head. Beyond the iron bars of a solitary window, moonlight penetrated the room, casting shadows across his face. The cold, winter air bit at his shivering skin.

"Tonight..." A whisper rose from the depths of his mind. "Tonight..." the voice reminded, filling Memoralice with fright.

"Tonight..."

"Enough!" Memoralice commanded. He listened to the trailing echo of his voice and felt the creeping fear of madness. He grasped at his head, his fingernails cutting into his skin. Blood gathered at the tips of his fingers and ran down his face. He whimpered aloud, "The insanity must end."

"Tonight..."

Memoralice gave a desperate cry and his voice echoed down a steep flight of stairs. The cry faded, lost to the night, and to the ears of the dead, who lay scattered down the tower steps and across the hillside. It was only moments ago that these soldiers were victim to his spell power, reduced to rotten flesh.

In the company of corpses he waited, like a dragon, guarding his mind, his very soul. He looked to the floor and a spider crawled close to his bare feet. It crossed over the protective ring he had carved around him, mocking him, denying the protection the runes sought to create.

Memoralice smashed the spider's abdomen with his big toe. Thick purple ooze poured out and a scream escaped from the spider remains. The ooze was hot to his touch and steamed. His eyes grew wide with astonishment, as hundreds of little spiders emerged from the ooze and travelled up his legs. He could not swipe them away quick enough. In horror, he produced a scroll and read its inscription, in hopes to invoke a helpful spell.

Wiping a spider from his lip, he began to chant, and energy swelled inside him. The energy was electric and burned in his veins. It shot out of his hands in a blinding light. The room was flooded in a purifying aura that scorched the spiders into flakes of ash. Squinting, and tense with pain, a smile crossed Memoralice's face. The spell brought a wave of serenity. Intoxicated by the strength of the spell, he felt connected to every fabric of life; as if he were part of something greater than himself. He closed his eyes and tried to hold the feeling close to his heart, knowing the feeling would soon be over; knowing it may be the last connection he would ever feel. As fast as the joy came over him, sadness took hold.

Memoralice relaxed his body and opened his eyes. His parched lips parted, and he gave a heavy sigh. The room came into focus, his skin chilled by the cold. He was alone and felt the emptiness of solitude. Weakened by the spell, he lowered his head to the ground. The casting of the spell had etched another scar on his soul, not unlike the thick, etched wrinkles on the contours of his face; a reminder of death, which had never felt more close at hand.

He embraced the silence that followed, until he was jarred by the familiar voice penetrating his mind.

"Tonight."

Weeping, Memoralice raised his head. A presence could be felt in the room.

"Memoralice," a voice whispered from the darkness. It matched the voice that moments ago was only in his mind. He felt a chill at the realization. A figure appeared from the darkness, touched by the light of the moon.

Memoralice saw Death, himself, before him. There was relief that came with the thought that his suffering would soon be over. "Is this the way a Legionnaire will die? Groveling? I was a hero once, but now, why should I pretend? I am old and I am tired and I am ready for Death. Come forth from the shadows, my foe, and let me know you are real."

As if granting Memoralice's wish, the visitor stepped fully into the moonlight. Memoralice squinted, uncertain as to who, or what, he saw. Its face was shifting form, changing features between many faces.

"What is your name, visitor? Tell me the name of one who is able to slip into my chamber undetected, the one worthy to close my legacy into the pages of history. I deserve as much before I accept death."

The presence spoke, its voice was the voice of many voices, speaking in unison. It was as if the visitor was the culmination of many lives, but part of one consciousness. Some voices were nothing more than a whisper, some deep, and other voices were darker still, and tormented. It said, "If only your destination were as rewarding as death." A silver staff was revealed from the folds of the visitor's black robe, which moments before appeared to be nothing more than a cloak of shadow. The haunting voices came forth, "If you need a name to soothe the pain, then know that I am that of the darkest rain. I am the thickest of poisons, a magician's nightmare and creeping bane. Look to the gods, so that you will learn to fear Darkness and his silver cane!"

Memoralice nodded. "I know your presence, Dark One. I have felt it before. I have heard the tales of countless wizards who have fallen to your power and succumbed to your silver cane. You are Death, himself; and from this no magician is safe. Not even a Legionnaire."

The Dark One placed his silver staff upon Memoralice's head. From a shiny onyx stone forged at the tip of the staff a blue light radiated. Inside the stone, milky grey shadows swirled and emitted the moans of wizards who passed, those who had fallen victim to the staff.

Memoralice felt a searing heat upon his forehead and a violent tug originate from within his body. He contorted in convulsions and his veins burst open. Blood poured from his nose, seeped from his ears and gurgled out his mouth. The faint color of his eyes faded, until none remained; leaving clear orbs that stared, vacant, into space. His body swayed a moment and then folded over, lifeless, to the floor.

PART I

HOME

G.G.

Let it be known – the peace between kingdoms was but a foundation. The teachings of FéLorën are explicit in this regard. After The Final War, oppression and inequality still devastated communities throughout the land. While the Great Alliance was significant, let not the marker for modern FéLorën be determined by the year of its forming, but in the year 225 A.F.; when FéLorën, as a way of life, was all but forgotten, reduced to nothing more than a whisper. It was here that the teachings reached the ear of an unlikely young wizard known only, at the time, as Daylen of Brunhylde.

-excerpt from "Modern Histories of FéLorën Vol. I" 1077 A.F.

~CHAPTER 1~

The orange glow of the morning sun rose above steep mountain peaks, soaking the village of Brunhylde with the promise of warmth it had not seen in weeks. Daylen rose, with a sense of excitement. He left his cottage and stepped into the muddy streets. He looked off into the distance, toward a looming mass of dark clouds, all too aware that the warmth would not last. Turning his attention toward the road ahead, he moved silently, careful not to be noticed.

The dirt road led to the manor house, a large stone structure that predated the village, and once served as a fort during the ages of war. The manor loomed above the rundown cottages surrounding it, as an ominous presence, and was home to the tyrant Lord Shyn.

Daylen crossed the path into the overgrown weeds and cautiously stared at the sheer, threatening size of the manor, and feared what transpired behind its ancient walls. He also feared the punishment that would befall him, if Lord Shyn's guards caught him crossing the property.

To Daylen, the shortcut was well worth the danger. Just beyond the border of Brunhylde, behind the manor, was the path toward a steep hill where a lone tree stood. It was the only tree in Brunhylde's surrounding landscape and it had somehow survived for generations, its thick roots buried deep into the dirt. Leafless year round, it was said by the locals to be cursed and was the center of many dark tales. Like all tales, these stories stemmed from an element of truth. There was a history of violence that surrounded the tree, horrors that time could not erase.

Long ago, the tree was used for numerous hangings. It was said, after a revered, innocent woman had been hung, the tree no longer bore leaves. It attracted witches, who set up altars beneath it and hung tokens on its branches. Rumors of the dead buried on the hill rising to seek revenge spread amongst the townsfolk. When the tales were repeated enough times, the truth was no longer discernable from the fiction. Peculiar coincidences and unfortunate incidents fueled the imagination of the townsfolk. Their fear was matched only by their guilt, and blaming ill fortune on the occurrences on the lone tree hill eventually led to the end of the hangings. Witches who flocked to the hill were hunted and slaughtered, one by one, and soon after it was forbidden for anyone to visit.

Despite the tales and the law, the tree was special to Daylen. Thanks to local lore, and the restrictions in place, it was a spot that Daylen was guaranteed solitude, away from the prying eyes of the peasants of Brunhylde. Over the course of the last several years, it provided many treasured memories. The trek toward the hill was not an easy one. The dangerous path through Lord Shyn's property, let alone the fear of ghosts, was only part of the danger. There were sharp overgrown weeds, wildlife and marshes, all the characteristics of an abandoned, overrun landscape. The steep incline and loose gravel terrain could take the wind from any young man. One who was careless enough to step into a deep marsh, fall upon a thorn bush, or get caught up in the prickly vines, could meet their doom. Daylen was not deterred and knew the safest way to his destination.

This did not mean the quest came without his share of scrapes and bruises. A final climb up a rocky ledge always left its mark. A slip or two, and at times a fall, would always send his mother into a fit when she saw his wounds. On this particular trip, he was quick to catch his footing and reached the top, winded, but unscathed.

Daylen stood at the hill's peak and caught his breath beside the lone tree. Below, his village nestled against the surrounding mountain range. It is through the gap in the mountains that he witnessed what was left of the sunrise. The sun made its glorious ascent until it was consumed by storm clouds overhead, blanketing Brunhylde in shadow. Which was to be expected in this region during the Season of Wither. Rains would soon begin, and not let up until the Season of Bloom had come and gone.

Daylen took a moment to reflect on the memories of this sacred place. It was Glazahn who had first shown Daylen this secret, forbidden spot. It was Glazahn who gave him the courage to brave the dangerous path. Glazahn was his only friend. He was more than a friend; he was a fellow wizardborn. Although they were not related, their blood had everything to do with their bond. They were born with the potential to do things that most people could not. Perceived as a threat if left to their own devices, their magical potential meant they would be forced to serve in the king's army; to take their rightful place in servitude.

Growing up in the small town of Brunhylde, they both struggled to understand what none of the peasants of Brunhylde could teach them. They only knew they were different, and had no understanding of their power, or what they were capable of. It would have to wait until they came of age and could enter the Academy of Vixus. Being a year older than Daylen, Glazahn left for service before him, leaving Daylen alone for the last year. He could still recall Glazahn affirming he would see Daylen soon on that final day together, but Daylen knew that it was unlikely he would ever see his friend again.

Daylen thought back to his time with Glazahn, and the moment he discovered Glazahn was a wizard. It was his first trip to the tree on the hill…

*　　　*　　　*

Daylen stood at the top of the hill. Glazahn, slightly taller, placed his arm around Daylen with pride. He pointed to a wound on Daylen's leg, where a thorn plant had sliced open his skin, blood dripping down his calf.

"My mother is going to kill me," Daylen cursed.

"The least of your worries, I'd say."

Daylen looked to Glazahn for an explanation. "How so?"

Glazahn crouched low, his eyes wide. Moving his hand above the dirt he said with a smirk, "When that blood of yours hits the ground it will awaken the undead." He jumped up and yelled, "Who will rise to tear you apart, limb from limb!"

Daylen scowled. "Not true," but his tone lacked confidence.

Glazahn laughed. He motioned to the tree, as if to redirect Daylen's attention from his injury. "This…" his expression turned to one of earnest, "is an amazing tree."

It was, Daylen thought to himself. Its ancient, wrinkled trunk and crooked, winding growth toward the sky, gave it character. He studied the old tree with wonder. He felt small beside it, its limbs reaching like skeletal fingers towards the clouds above, as if clawing their way toward the sun.

Daylen was proud to have faced his fears, and to have joined Glazahn on this adventure. He didn't get out of the house much and to have braved the terrain, to confront the haunted land he now stood on, it seemed right to mark the occasion. It wasn't so scary up here, after all. In fact, it was quite serene. He pulled out a small knife from his pocket and raised it toward the tree. Before he could carve his name in the trunk, Glazahn struck his hand, the knife dropping to the dirt.

Daylen retracted, shaking his stinging hand in the air. "What did you do that for?"

After a moment of hesitation, Glazahn replied, "The tree… is alive. I – I can hear it speak."

Though Daylen could not hear the voice, he believed his friend. This mysterious power Glazahn had was why he was drawn to him. Daylen knew there was something special about him. He was gifted, just like Daylen.

Daylen shared that he, too, was a wizard, although it was clear that he hardly knew what it meant to be one. He knew nothing of magic and did not consider himself wise. What he did know is that he shared the physical traits of all wizards; a thin frail body and eyes which would fade in color with time.

Daylen shared that his mother had seen him levitating in his sleep, but he was unaware of it happening. Without knowing the power he possessed, being wizardborn was a weakness, a trait that simply made him different from others. "What is the tree saying now?"

Glazahn squinted, his boyish face concentrating. His eyes widened, as if receiving a message. "The tree knows what you tried to do, Daylen."

Daylen stepped away from the tree. It apparently was not what it seemed. "Well, what did it say?"

"What you carve in me will be carved in you."

"What does that mean?"

Glazahn shrugged. "I don't know, but I know it is unhappy about it."

Daylen studied the tree, every facet of its being. He brought his hand to the trunk and ran his soft, young fingers across its rough, cracked surface. Moments before, he had thought the tree was lifeless.

Glazahn's voice interrupted Daylen's thoughts. "You are not going to carve something, are you?"

Daylen pulled his hand away and shook his head. "No way."

*　　　*　　　*

The memory of his first trip to the tree faded, but he was left with the thoughts that such an experience afforded. Per Glazahn, the tree shared an uncanny, powerful connection with Daylen. This scared him, at the time. To this day, he did not want to leave a mark on a living thing, or on a world he hardly understood. Though Daylen was deaf to the voice of the tree, Glazahn's interpretation proved he still shared a bond with it. He could sense the tree's loneliness, and in this regard, he felt they were one and the same. Despite having Glazahn as a friend, despite knowing they both carried the gift of magic within them, there were differences that Glazahn didn't know about, secrets he could never know about.

Beside the tree, Daylen reflected upon his life as he had done on past visits. The silence, the solitude, the quality of the air from up high, it always made him reflect on his past and to a time unknown to him. He longed to have known his father, and he wished his mother had been born to a better existence, above poverty and the hardships of peasant life.

Upon coming of age, Glazahn was sent to study at Vixus Academy, like all wizardborn. Saying goodbye was hard for Daylen, because he knew he would not be joining his friend in the academy. Unlike Glazahn, he would run from service, by hiding in place, within the quiet town of Brunhylde. It meant hiding from his duty to the kingdom of Vixus, hiding his gift from those around him, hiding from himself. As long as he avoided Lord Shyn and stayed out of sight, he could at least live his days in peace, no matter how uneventful his life would be. It was days like today, when he stood on the hill watching the sunrise that he would think of the overwhelming isolation that came with his decision to hide. He would never walk the halls of the academy. He would never wield the spells of wizards who came before him. He would live his life in secret, a shadow of a man, forever alone.

There was a sound in the distance. Daylen brought his attention from the clouds to the village below. On the dirt road leading to Brunhylde, warhorses charged through Brunhylde's gates, ridden by fierce knights, clad with black battle armor and helmets shaped like mythological demons. Their crimson capes waved in the wind as did their banners, printed with the seal of Vixus and the symbol of the Knights of Brownstone. The Knights of Brownstone were an elite unit of the Vixus army, Paladins of High Priestess Vamillion, known for their bravery and their equal measure of cruelty. The peasants fled to their homes and barred the doors.

Daylen ran down the hill as fast as his legs would allow. He was oblivious to the pain, as his body brushed against the sharp tall weeds. He stomped through the marsh as he passed the manor house. He saw the paladins come to a shrieking halt in front of the manor, their black horses rearing. He dove into the mud, hiding behind overgrown shrubs.

Lord Shyn waited outside the manor. He shifted his belt and squirmed within his padded armor. His attention was directed to the Knights of Brownstone now standing before him. He did not notice Daylen staring up at him from the shrubbery with prying eyes.

"What is the meaning of this?" Lord Shyn asked, boldly.

A paladin, front and center, removed his helmet. "I am Sir Brundt. I have direct orders from King Averath to relieve you from governing the village of Brunhylde." As he spoke, he leaned forward from his horse and extended a sheet of parchment toward Lord Shyn.

As Lord Shyn grabbed the parchment and began to peruse the document, Sir Brundt continued. "This document certifies our duties here. I have been entrusted to oversee the community's renovation. Brunhylde will no longer be agricultural land, but rather, a stronghold like it once was many glorious days ago, during The Final War.

"The villagers will find new work with us as carpenters and craftsmen, and their women will accept servitude for the training soldiers. The citizens of Brunhylde, in turn, will experience a higher purpose to their lives and glory by the graces of their king. This requires complete cooperation of the villagers, and of you, Lord Shyn. If that requires enslavement to those who defy, then so be it, but I would hate for things to come to that… or worse."

Lord Shyn cursed under his breath.

"As we speak," Sir Brundt continued, "King Averath has deployed two hundred recruits. They will arrive in a week's time. They will help the villagers turn this miserable farmland into a training ground. Let me be direct with you, Lord Shyn, this village is a dire mess, behind on tax and commodity production, you have done nothing worth respect. Cooperation will dissolve all such debt, clear your reputation, and lead to compensation that is far greater than you deserve."

Lord Shyn stared into the eyes of the Vixus knight but said nothing.

"Your experience overseeing the village will prove useful. However, your time as Lord has come to an end. Now, show us to our rooms, and have your maids cook a hearty meal. Our journey was long, and our stomachs are empty."

Lord Shyn paused a moment, as if he contemplated arguing, but reconsidered. "Please, Sir Brundt," Lord Shyn said with a sigh, "You and your knights may follow me." Lord Shyn then promptly waved to an obedient village constable, who stepped forward to escort the horses to the stable.

Daylen watched as the knights dismounted from their horses and followed Lord Shyn through the gates of the manor. Once he was alone, he rose from his place in the bushes, covered in mud. He walked the remaining distance through the village unnoticed. Peasants, who had hidden from sight upon the knights' arrival, slowly gathered in the streets in whispered commotion, fear etched in their eyes.

Daylen shared this fear. He would be enslaved and repressed and knew the quiet life he had grown accustomed to was over. His solitude and secrecy was threatened by the will of his own empire, complicating his future more than ever before.

~CHAPTER 2~

Daylen sat in an old wooden chair and stared out the window of his cottage. His mother, Claudia, moved about in silence behind him, preparing the evening meal with scarce crops and minimal spices. She performed her duties undeterred, despite her poor surroundings, removing the shucks from corn and placing the cobs in a worn, dented pot. Her dinner preparation was more of a meditation, then an act of labor. She was confident and graceful, her fragile frame in stark contrast to the strength of her character.

To Daylen, she was quiet and the keeper of secrets, her opinions and feelings a mystery to him. She lived as a dedicated parent, raising Daylen in a stern fashion, by a code that did not seem to fit their status. She was molding him, as if preparing him for a life of some greater purpose, which he feared would never come to fruition.

Two candles produced meager light as the dark shadows of the night attempted to suffocate the room. The fire light reflected off her dark skin creating rich, auburn highlights, an illusion that made her appear cast in bronze. Daylen could no longer bear her silence of the day's events. "What are we to do, Mother?"

She did not respond, and this did not surprise him. He had learned to be patient with her. Trusting, knowing, that when she spoke, her words would be clear, the message precise. She had grown old, and he worried about this. Her body was thin, her hands; delicate. Her collarbone, accentuated from hunger, was visible beneath a tear in her tattered tunic, which hung loose against her slender frame.

Daylen knew there was little she could do to protect him from the knights that had claimed the village. He felt fear and panic, longing to understand the calm that his mother always possessed. He turned again to the window, through the panes he could see the knights patrol the dirt paths of Brunhylde, the orange glow of their lanterns reflecting off their armor. It would not be long before the troops would see him, recognize his frail frame as one that was wizardborn, and demand his service at the Academy.

Daylen closed his eyes. He would not give his soul away to become a pawn of the king's army. His mother would never allow it, nor did he care to. He would not submit to the empire that killed his father; it was unthinkable.

The sound of the plate touching the table startled him. He stared at the food his mother had prepared, a bowl of corn soup centered on a plate. "I could stay here with you. Couldn't I, Mother? We need each other, now more than ever."

Claudia looked up at him with wide, brown eyes, as if to remind him that he knew better than to suggest such a thing. "If you stay you will risk being caught by the Vixus knights."

"What are you saying? That I should run?"

Claudia placed her hand on Daylen's shoulder. "For you to fulfill your destiny. To live the life you were meant to live."

"What life?" Daylen said. "What destiny do you speak of?" Daylen lowered his head, fearful to raise the question. He fell silent.

"Look at me." Claudia moved in front of him, forcing his attention. "You have your heart to guide you and a soul that is strong. You were meant for more than this."

He remained silent, but met her gaze, searching her eyes, looking for whatever secret she kept there that allowed her to stay vigilant in her hope.

"The knights will need women to work in the manor. I will go to them tomorrow. I will be given food and shelter, and I will be cared for. You need not worry for me. Not ever."

Daylen shook his head in disgust. "You will be their slave."

"I will live in healthier conditions than I ever have. Although I will be working for the ones I despise, I will survive. We must outsmart them, Daylen."

"Outsmart them? If I knew how to cast spells, I would set this village in flames and burn a hole through the hearts of our oppressors!" He jerked from his seat and the chair crashed on the floor behind him. He walked to the window, attempting to settle his anger. Outside, the cold wind of a brewing storm blew through the muddy streets.

Claudia moved beside him and placed her hand on his shoulder. "This is not how I raised you, Daylen. You mustn't act this way."

Daylen felt hatred coursing through his body. He was mindful of this but did not care if the desire for revenge was right or wrong.

"Use your anger, understand its source and act upon it, but not in a way that will jeopardize your future," she advised. "Hate is not the answer."

He could not see past his frustration, but he told his mother what she wanted to hear. "I will go, Mother. I will do as you wish. When I return, I will save you from this place and somehow, someway, I will make sure this place stands no more. Not out of hate," he interjected, "out of justice."

"You have your father's passion, but the angst of a wolf pup in you." Claudia's eyes filled with tears, and she wrapped her arms around him. He held onto her as she whispered, "There is someone who can help you." She pulled away to stare into her son's eyes.

"Tell me, who?"

"Do you remember Rahlen?"

The name struck a chord in his heart, but he struggled to place the memory.

"He used to look after you when you were a small child. He was a dear friend of your father. After your father's passing, he was a loyal friend to me; to us. Rahlen promised he would take care of you, guide you when the time was right."

The image of an adventurer, with a dark green cloak, armor with etched eagle wings, a sword at his side, appeared in Daylen's mind. He shook his head in disbelief. He had believed Rahlen was nothing more than some kind of an imaginary friend from his childhood.

Claudia continued, her voice taking on a strange, curious urgency. "You remember. He came by occasionally, unannounced. He brought food, supplies, and clothing. Then, one day, he came to me and told me that he had an important quest to undertake, something about restoring balance, mumbling historical facts about a time before The Final War. It was a cryptic conversation, with words left unsaid, and I knew better than to pry. I remember him wishing you were old enough to accompany him. I wished the same, but as the days turned to weeks, the weeks to months and then the years passed by, I was grateful he had not taken you. I moved on, for he never returned." She looked upward. "I was grateful for the time he was in our lives."

Daylen started to remember small details. Rahlen had been standing amongst the shadows, watching him. Through his child mind, this guardian had been mistaken for a divine creature, an angel. "I remember… very little. I thought it was a dream, that he wasn't real."

Claudia smiled. "He is real. You were so young; I am surprised you remember anything at all. It was his dream to take you to meet a powerful wizard named Zantigar. He was a rogue wizard, a believer in the ways of FéLorën, and what the world could be; just like your father."

Daylen had heard the wizard's name before. Glazahn had a book about Legionnaire's. The book mentioned Zantigar. It referred to him as a war hero, not as a rogue… not an outlaw.

"Rahlen was determined to help you find Zantigar," Claudia continued, "so that you could learn to use your powers."

Daylen's curiosity grew. "What happened to Rahlen?"

Claudia shrugged. "Honestly, I thought Rahlen died, I- I didn't know what else to think. He abandoned us and it was the only rational explanation." She looked at Daylen with excitement in her eyes. "But he came back. Just four weeks ago." She grabbed hold of Daylen's arms and shook him gently. "Rahlen came back."

"Why didn't you tell me and why did he leave?"

"He arrived late, and you were sleeping. He appeared at the door, standing in silence. I ran to him and hugged him. I had so many questions that he chose not to answer. He told me not to wake you. He walked to your room and checked on you. He stared for a long time, a look on his face like the look your father used to give. I knew he still had plans for you.

"I asked if it was time, if he had come to take you away, and he shook his head. 'Not yet,' he said.

"Rahlen turned to me with compassion and pain in his eyes; Regrets, hardships, the eyes of one who has seen unspeakable horrors. He apologized for his absence. I knew he would have come sooner if he could."

Daylen stepped away. The realization that Rahlen was real and that he was looking after him, gave him the hope he longed for. Rahlen might not have been ready, but it was enough. He was alive and it was enough.

Claudia's eyes got tearful and her voice choked. "There is so much I wish I could teach you. So much I should have taught you, but my faith died when I believed Rahlen was dead. There was no use in filling your head with false hope. The teachings, the wisdom, the way, but it doesn't matter now, none of it matters. There is nothing I could teach you that could compare to the wealth of wisdom you could obtain if Rahlen could lead you to Zantigar."

Daylen saw sadness overwhelm his mother. Everything seemed unreal and the sudden change in perspective made him aware that life was taking him away from his mother sooner than he had expected. There would be nothing left for him at the cottage once she was gone. Out there, beyond the dirt road that led from Brunhylde, out there in the unknown wilderness, beyond the mountain peaks, out there lay an uncertain future, but a chance to have one.

~CHAPTER 3~

Daylen opened his eyes and felt the emptiness that came from solitude. The early dawn was dark and quiet. He rubbed the sleep from his eyes and leaned up from his bed. He walked to the window and saw the village shrouded in the shadow of thick thunderclouds. Several Vixus knights marched by on the muddy street. He caught a shallow, expressionless glance from a knight and ducked from the window.

He wondered if the knights had seen him, if they knew he was alone. He heard a distant laugh from the knight, as if the knight was humored by his fear. When the laughter trailed off into the distance, he raised his head and peeked outside. The knights were gone. They must not have noticed he was wizardborn. However, all it would take is the right amount of attention at the wrong time. If any troop gave notice, his life would be forever changed. His mother was right; it was no longer safe in Brunhylde. Life would not be safe for him as long as it was unlawful for wizardborn to roam free.

He longed for his childhood. He felt he could conquer anything with Glazahn by his side. Now, more than ever, he wished he was normal. He had not been raised like typical boys of his time. Coming to age with his mother, his soul was pure, and his innocent mind was vulnerable. In this world, his imagination had grown wild. Through fantasy he had been able to block out the insanity of a world, the parts he did not understand… until now. Now, he knew he had no choice but to face the unknown.

Life was cruel and unforgiving. Nature brought the harsh storms and the intense heat that destroyed crops every year. It infected the hogs and killed the livestock. It showed no mercy for the weak and the innocent.

A memory rose from his thoughts, a memory he forgot belonged to him.

*   *   *

Claudia was young and vibrant. "Tell me Daylen, who are you?"

"I am a wizard," Daylen said, a mere child.

"Very good, and how does this make you special?"

"It means that the gods have blessed me with an incredible gift."

"What must you remember about this gift?" His mother pressed.

"That there is evil in this world, people who wish to rob me of what makes me special and control me. I must resist them in order to remain free."

* * *

As he surfaced from this memory, Daylen became aware that he was at risk of being noticed and walked away from the window. He moved to the center of the room. A dim light radiated from a solitary candle. It illuminated a wooden box and a short sword resting on the table's wooden surface.

Curiosity took hold and he picked up the sword, handling the weapon he had never before seen. Drawn to accept a challenge greater than he ever imagined, he raised the short sword up to the candlelight. The hilt was colored red and blue, the trademark colors of the Vixus Empire. The sword must have belonged to his father. He stared in awe of its craftsmanship, imagining his father wielding the blade. The thought brought him closer to the father he had never known. He wondered how many had fallen to its sharp edge. There was an inscription on the blade: SYLVER.

He swung the blade through the air. It was short, most likely a secondary weapon, a blade his father strapped to his hip. He set the blade down, his attention diverted by a note adhered to the wooden box.

Have gone to Lord Shyn. In this box is the key to your future.
No goodbye, my son. I shall see you when you have grown.
Good luck to you.

With eager hands, he opened the box. He noticed a plain silver ring. It gleamed, reflecting the candlelight on its smooth surface. He placed it on his finger. It was too big for his frail finger, so he placed it in his pocket.

The box held several coins of copper and a brilliant medallion encased in glass. On the medallion was carved a Vixus royal shield, detailed with crest symbols and the name Donovan Sylver. It was a war medal, given to his father.

He lowered the medallion. "Daylen Sylver," he whispered. Never had he known his last name, his mother has never told him as if to protect him. He looked to the blade, the word "Sylver" confirming his identity. Another memory rose to the surface, of Daylen at ten years of age, sitting with his mother by a warm fire…

*　　　　*　　　　*

"Mother, tell me about my father again."

She leaned forward in her chair, the firelight reflecting in her eyes. "Your father was a great teacher and a caring husband."

"Mother," Daylen beckoned. "Tell me about knighthood!"

She rolled her eyes, smiling. "Yes, my son, your father was a knight. He was honored and respected across the land."

"When will father return?"

"It is not he who will return to us, but us, who will return to him. He loves you very much, Daylen… and he is waiting."

*　　　　*　　　　*

Daylen's mother always had an odd way of describing death. It was not until he was older that he traded the magical beliefs his mother had, for the cold realization that he would not see his father again until he, too, had died. Even in death, he was not certain he would see him.

While the future was clouded in darkness, the past was also a deep void. Several times in the past he had gathered the courage to ask more about his father, curious how the empire killed him and why. But every time he asked questions, he remembered why he shouldn't. It brought too much pain to his mother to speak of the past, and to see his mother struggle with so much sadness was more than he could stand. So, he stopped asking questions.

Standing alone in his cottage, he wondered if he had missed his chance to learn of his father's past. He looked to the wooden box lying open on the table and noticed a folded letter inside, pressed against the bottom of the box. He grabbed the letter, the pages old and faded, and carefully unfolded it. It was a letter to his mother.

Claudia, My Dear,

It is time I leave, once again. Let it be known it is with a heavy heart and a winded spirit that I travel. The days grow colder, the urgency of my mission, ever growing. How I long to take Daylen under my wing, to show him the way, the teachings and the wisdom of FéLorën. There is a town, a secret to most, in the center of the western woodland; a town known as Twilight. Bolinda Lynx is a habitant there, and an ally to our cause. Bolinda is a friend to me, and once a friend to your dear husband. She has found the location of Zantigar. By the blessing of her elven blood, perhaps; I don't know how, but she found him. Zantigar is deep in the heart of the untamed lands. What he is doing there, one can only fathom. I will lead your son to him soon, I promise. When the time is right, when his mind is sharper, his body stronger… I will show him the way. The road ahead is a difficult one, and the trials are demanding. I hope you understand the need for patience in these matters.

The silver ring I left behind is Donovan's. I was with him when he purchased it off a traveling merchant. He bought it upon hearing you were pregnant. He wore it to symbolize his connection, his commitment to you and to his child to be. He was so proud to be a father. If only he lived to see Daylen, if only he knew he would have a wizard as a son. I have not forgotten his dreams, just as I shall never forget my vow to you.

To hold you in my arms, to feel the grace of your kiss again… I will say no more, other than the light of your being grants me strength.

Ever faithful, ever of the way,

Rahlen

~CHAPTER 4~

The moon tower stood toward the southern walls of Vixus castle, rising high as if attempting to conquer the moon, itself. At the top of the tower was a solitary window that opened over the kingdom of Vixus, from which one could survey the kingdom with a watchful eye. From this private study, Vamillion, High Priestess of Vixus, performed her rituals, mixed her potions, and prayed to her god. Nobody in the land knew the lengths she would go to secure the kingdom's strength in the world and to hold onto her own power. She was the keeper of many dark secrets, but none of her secrets compared to the one she had locked away beneath the moon tower. In the dungeon below, lived Beauty, the son of King Averath, the future heir to the throne. He was locked away, like a prisoner, like a monster, never to see the light of day.

Beauty's life was the untold story of the land. The days that followed the night of his birth were filled with tragedy and the inevitable decline of a golden age…

* * *

Never in history had the empire been wealthier, nor the people happier. It is here within Vixus boundaries that King Averath's wife, Queen Liana of Ellindore, was to give birth to Beauty.

Liana held the thriving Vixus Empire together with her love. Her peaceful rule won the hearts of the people. All the citizens of Vixus loved her union with King Averath, so it was no surprise that the birth of Beauty was to be an incredible one.

On the longest night of the year, under a full, brilliant moon, knights and priests gathered in celebration at the royal hall. It was a lovely evening, full of food and drink, dancing and singing, plays and performances. Elaborate decorations and colorful music filled the room. All who attended waited anxiously, aware that Beauty would be born at any moment. The future heir would soon appear, through the doors at the top of the stairs, wrapped in the arms of the king.

However, the hopes and expectations of the gathering crowed were crushed at the sound of a terrible cry, which came from beyond the doors at the top of the stairs. The scream silenced all who waited, and the musicians ceased their merry tunes, and the performers stopped their jubilant dance. A grief-stricken voice could be heard beyond the doors. "The Queen is dead! My beloved Queen is dead!"

Loud cries and gasps filled the hall. The guests began to panic, the festivities on the brink of pandemonium as the crowd shifted restlessly. Vamillion, standing at the top of the stairs, slid through the doors and closed them quietly behind her.

King Averath lay sprawled across Liana's lifeless body. Vamillion searched for the baby, frantic. Beauty was wrapped in the finest silks, oblivious to the devastating outcome of birth. Vamillion ordered the midwives to leave at once and she rushed to the baby's side. With eager, but delicate hands, she grabbed Beauty and brought the baby to her chest. She stared down into his eyes. A boy. Calm, Beauty did not shed a single tear, did not once cry out, but stared up at Vamillion with a blank, unwavering innocence that only a newborn could possess. He was a miracle. Not only was he born on the longest night, under a full moon, but he was born under a unique celestial alignment, one that Vamillion believed to promise incredible power. Vamillion longed for this moment, ever since discovering that Liana had gone into labor. Could it be, Vamillion thought, that Beauty was the one?

She looked at King Averath from the corner of her eyes, clutching Beauty close. King Averath had his face buried against Liana's lifeless body, sobbing. The sight before her only verified that Averath's love was his greatest weakness. It made him weak, and more importantly, it blinded him from seeing the opportunity of each passing moment. It was a mistake that threatened the safety of their people, the very kingdom he was crowned to protect. Before he had met Liana, she thought, he was a brave and valiant warrior, worthy of his title. "My king?" Vamillion whispered. "There is no need to worry. Beauty is safe."

At first, it appeared that King Averath did not hear her speak. After several moments, he raised his head, as if coming to his senses, jolted back to his tainted reality by the mention of Beauty's name. There was a passionate fury in his eyes, a madness, and he focused his glare on Vamillion as he extended his arms. "Give me the boy."

Vamillion turned away from him, her grip tightening around Beauty, protecting the baby from the king's hand.

"Give me the boy!" He screamed. "You defiant, vile priestess! Take heed of my command!"

"Control yourself, my liege," Vamillion urged in a hushed tone. "There are guests beyond these doors. How dare you threaten the safety of your heir."

King Averath stood, his massive frame looming over his queen's body. "Give me that child. Son or not, I will murder the demon who killed my Liana!"

"Have you lost your mind?" Vamillion pleaded. She turned back toward him as she stepped away, revealing Beauty in her clutched arms at the same time that she made distance between them. "Look at him. He is your blood. And look at his face, his serenity, can't you see the power he possesses? He was born under the sign of Agolign, this celestial formation only occurs once in a thousand years!"

King Averath's eyes narrowed with dangerous intent. He stepped forward, clenching his hands in Beauty's direction.

"I will not allow it! This one is special… my king."

King Averath's expression changed from anger to horror. "You… You did this, didn't you?"

She stepped backward, bringing Beauty close to her again. "What are you saying, Averath? Don't you dare come any closer."

King Averath stared into Vamillion's green eyes. His fisted hands relaxed. He could not hurt her. He needed the priestess now, more than ever. His legs trembled and he fell to his knees. He couldn't afford to make an enemy of the priestess, and he feared her powerful magic more than he cared to admit. He wobbled to her on his knees and buried his face into the skirt of her dress. With trembling hands he clutched the fabric in his fingers. "I- I don't know what I am saying anymore. I don't know what to do, how to carry on."

Vamillion looked down on him, unaware of how to help him, unwilling to even care. She loathed the man he had become and could not fathom how he could let himself become so weak, when the kingdom relied on him for their survival. If the guests were to see him in this state, it would cause irreparable damage. "If you will not accept your son, then I will accept him. I will take him to the Moon Tower, where no one will ever have to see him, or know of his existence." She bent down and with her fragile hand under his chin, raised his head so that his lips were next to hers. "I will do everything in my power to help you. Now rise, my king. Rise, and inform the people of Vixus of the death of the Queen, and the death of your son." She brought her lips to his, but he did not engage.

King Averath waited until she pulled away and then stared at his newborn son. He had Liana's eyes. The king's expression darkened; his face sunken with grief. "Never mention his name. In my heart and in my mind, he is dead to me."

Vamillion rose from her kneeled position, while King Averath remained, motionless. "As you wish, my liege."

When at last King Averath had the strength to rise, he opened the doors to greet his guests, who had gathered at the foot of the stairs. He looked out over the crowd of faces, which waited in silence for their king to speak.

Vamillion slipped through a hidden door in the king's chamber and made her way to the Moon Tower. Cradled in her arms, the future king of Vixus squirmed. He was to be hidden from the world, kept under her possessive care as heir to nothing, but a life of imprisonment.

In the years that followed she sought to understand what unique qualities the gods had bestowed upon this rare child. It was not long after Beauty learned to speak that his talent became evident. He was a prophet, and his predictions would never prove false. He could predict the events in a world he would never experience. From the darkness of the dungeon below the Moon Tower, he saw the world of tomorrow as clear as pictures in a book.

Beauty was a miracle, which convinced Vamillion that she had been right about the boy all along.

Over time, Vamillion sought not only to understand, but to control, the power that Beauty possessed. Her life's work depended on it. When methods of extraction failed, she relied on her entrapment of him to ensure he would never be used by another. He was hers to control, so that nothing bad would come to the kingdom of Vixus. She hoped and prayed that in time, King Averath would recognize her and reward her for her hard work and devotion. A recognition she hoped would earn her a seat by his side as the queen. Not out of love, but out of her strong desire to protect her people. A quality her king no longer was capable of.

As Queen Vamillion, there was nothing that could stop Vixus from achieving power over the other kingdoms. Being the king's advisor, she had given him all that she could give. A mighty wizard academy, renowned across the land, was at his disposal thanks to her. Despite this, King Averath replaced any feelings of gratitude with a strong opiate that Vamillion willingly supplied, which kept him under her thumb, devoid of ill feeling, but also devoid of love.

Despite her efforts and her beauty, King Averath would never love Vamillion, and it was the price she was willing to pay to maintain her control.

For a time, in Vamillion's quieter moments, she would reflect upon Queen Liana's death and marvel at how seamlessly her plans unfolded. No one suspected the brutal crime she had committed, since there was no way to trace the small dose of blue liquid that she had mixed in Liana's food on the fateful night of Beauty's birth. She felt guilt for what she had done, but it did not compare to the benefit of the Queen's passing. Beauty was in her possession, and the Queen's throne was empty, just waiting for Vamillion to take her place.

King Averath eventually married a lazy, mindless maiden, whose dull character mirrored his own. It was a persuasion by his advisors that he take up a Queen, for the promise of a future prince. Her name was Abigail, and she had nothing to offer him, but neither did he have a thing to offer her. With all the power of the kingdom at her fingertips, Queen Abigail sat in her filthy wealth, reveling in the simplicity of a luxurious life, not caring if the empire were to fall to pieces around her, so long as she could exist in comfort.

Vamillion would not let her kingdom collapse. She proved she was willing to murder to secure her place on the throne. She would not let her work be for nothing. She spent the next several years manipulating Abigail, taking advantage of her trust and naivety, becoming her secret puppeteer. Vamillion's unrequited dream of the Queen's throne blackened her heart and spoiled her mind as the days turned to years, and the years caught up with the present…

* * *

Tonight, Vamillion had reason to smile. Beauty had spoken. The prophecy unfolded from his lips, sure as the pages of history. Beauty's words were still fresh in her mind and she repeated them in a whisper, as she stared out her study toward the moon. "King Averath will die."

Hearing the boy's words repeat in her mind over and over again, she smiled, preparing the next batch of fluff; the opiate that King Averath had formed his strong addiction to after Liana's death. However, tonight an extra ingredient would be added. Tonight, she brought a thin glass vile over the fluff and allowed a solitary drop of blue liquid to spill onto the narcotic. Everything made perfect sense, she thought to herself. Yes, King Averath would die, because she, herself, would see to it that he did. She was flooded by an overwhelming sensation, a superior satisfaction, as she felt the power of destiny's hand moving her. This, she thought, is what it must feel like to be a god.

~CHAPTER 5~

King Averath sat motionless in his throne, but in his mind, he was sinking. He stared off into space, looking through the golden room around him, past the crystal chandelier, beyond the long, red carpet, unable to recognize the power and potential within his grasp. There was a calm buzzing in his head.

The slow beat of his heart echoed in the chasm of his soul. He concentrated on each monotonous beat. His heart fluttered and his pulse skipped. His serenity was broken. Despair devoured him and the castle walls, with their ornate tapestries, seemed to close in around him. The buzzing in his brain grew louder.

The fluff had worn off, and as the last bit of the drug ran its course, reality came back into view. He was aware of his surroundings and the clarity unnerved him. He was aware of the moment and the power within his reach; it meant nothing to him.

A fly buzzed around his head and landed on his hand, its delicate legs tickling his skin. He squashed the fly with his other hand. The buzzing came to an abrupt end. A servant entered the king's chamber carrying a scroll close to his chest. King Averath watched the servant from the corner of his eyes make his way down the long, red carpet. The servant placed the scroll on a table beside the throne, where King Averath kept a bottle of wine and a silver goblet. The servant bowed, then left the room, the door closing behind him.

Once King Averath was alone, and the hall returned to a stark silence, he grabbed the scroll from the table. With a pull of the string, the scroll unwound. His eyes scanned the document. The words were not registering in his mind until he came across one that evoked an emotion he had not felt since Liana was alive; "Memoralice." He rubbed the tip of his index finger over the name, reminded of a time of deeper purpose.

When Averath was a child, Memoralice had seemed old, already a Legionnaire. Memoralice was a symbol of Vixus Academy's strength, the finest example of what the Academy could produce. It had been a long time since King Averath thought of the wizard and his relationship with him. Too long.

Concentrating, he now read the scroll with intent. His eyes widened in shock and his heart sunk in sadness as he read the news of Memoralice's assassination.

Anger and regret blended and swirled in his troubled heart. The thought of Memoralice's death made him feel a part of himself had been killed. Moments ago he felt nothing, but now he felt anger brewing. He was certain that Vamillion and Queen Abigail were behind this treasonous act. He had suspected that their close allegiance was triggering a chain of catastrophic events, and the pain he now felt made him feel as if their sole purpose was to destroy his will to live and erase every endearing memory he possessed of the past.

King Averath let the scroll fall from his fingers and drift to the floor. He clutched the goblet beside him and downed the wine in a single gulp, letting the goblet fall from his hand to clatter on the marble floor. Rising from his throne, he walked the red carpet with newfound courage.

Without a greeting, King Averath barged into Queen Abigail's study. "It was not wise of you to kill Memoralice."

Abigail was reading a book and was slow to set it down. She finished the sentence with careful attention and then placed the book on her desk before meeting her King's furious eyes. "I heard the news. It was not me, Averath. However, it was for the best. It is law, after all, that any wizard who runs from service is put to death. You, of all people, my king, should be aware of this."

"He was a Legionnaire! He was honored and respected in our kingdom; a status you would know nothing about. He was revered by many important figures beyond our borders as a diplomat. He singlehandedly is credited for the ongoing alliance with our Mullen neighbors."

Queen Abigail waited for King Averath to finish, fiddling with the diamond necklace around her neck. Assuming she had permission to speak she said calmly, "How dare you accuse me of illegal action when-"

King Averath interrupted. "I warn you now, if I find out that you are responsible for this I will personally see to it that you suffer the same fate as he!"

Queen Abigail was expressionless for a moment, a long pause of silence before she suddenly burst into laughter.

King Averath was taken back by her response. "You laugh? All I have to do is command it."

"Command it!" She threatened. "Say it, my King. The power you claim to possess has been stripped from under your feet. Your heart has soured and your will has grown weak since your beloved Liana died..."

"And when Beauty was born," a voice spoke from across the room, finishing Queen Abigail's sentence. The voice was soft, but sliced through the air with a certainty that brought a bitter sting to King Averath's heart.

King Averath turned. "Vamillion; I did not hear you enter."

Vamillion's red lips parted in mischievous smile. "You think I would miss a moment like this? At last, you two are finally speaking to one another… how long has it been? Months, I gather. I wouldn't miss this for anything."

King Averath raised his fist. "I told you to never mention my son's name."

Vamillion would not apologize for her slight. "It is true that Queen Abigail ordered two hundred and thirty well trained soldiers, which included ten paladin trainees for the Knights of Brownstone, to march boldly into certain death against Memoralice. Suicide, you might argue, to advance upon a Legionnaire, and you would be correct in that assessment. I have already lectured your Queen on this point and she has much to learn. But you should not speak so harshly of your queen, nor be so quick to give her credit for the assassination of a Legionnaire. How is she to know that a Legionnaire has the power to combat an entire army? She is naïve, but she is learning."

Vamillion approached King Averath and silenced Queen Abigail, who was about to speak. "It is not she who assassinated Memoralice, despite how hard she tried. It is I who killed Memoralice. Of course, I couldn't do it without the help of your son."

Vamillion was standing beside King Averath and placed her delicate hand upon his chest. "You see, my speculations about Beauty's powers were true, and with his help, I have gained the trust and alliance of a most powerful god."

King Averath grabbed Vamillion's hand on his chest and flung it to her side. "God? What madness do you speak of?"

"I speak of the Dark One; and to feel his power and to embrace it… is to wield the power of creation at your fingertips." Vamillion's eyes widened with excitement. She raised her hand, but this time, it held a small bag of fluff. "I believe you asked for this?"

King Averath struck Vamillion's hand, smacking the bag to the floor, the fluff spilling out in all directions. "You have both gone mad!"

Vamillion watched the powdering remains of the fluff drift through the air, her poisonous plans thwarted.

King Averath shook his head, unaware of Vamillion's devastation. As if waking from a dream, he whispered, "I have been mad. What has become of me? What of this land?" His sorrowful eyes contorted with the anger he felt inside. "I should have killed my son when I had the chance. There is still time for that, but not before I correct the two of you."

Like an old fool, King Averath allowed the power of his empire to fall into the hands of those he had falsely trusted. His past flashed before his eyes. He had once been a mighty warrior who tamed wild regions and expanded the borders of Vixus, brought civilizations together and wealth to his people. He had lived an honorable life, once, living for his god, Glaven, and for his love, Liana.

"Glaven, my liege!" King Averath exclaimed, his eyes burning with fury. "Rid me of my enemies!" He reached out to strangle Vamillion's neck between his strong hands, but a dark cloud was all that he could see in front of him. The cloud shrouded him and the air within this darkness was emptied of oxygen. He dropped to his knees, his hands scratching at his own neck in a desperate attempt for breath, gasping for air. The dark shroud moved with a life of its own, entering his mouth and choking the life from him.

* * *

Vamillion awoke from a short spell. King Averath was dead at her feet. She lay weak and weary, in the arms of Queen Abigail. Her eyes fluttered, stung by the sudden brightness of reality. Attempting to stand, she fell out of the Queen's arms and vomited on the floor. After several deep breaths, she found the strength to rise. Straining to remain upright, the pain she felt did not prevent her from smiling, revealing her blood stained teeth.

Queen Abigail stepped away from her, horrified. "The spells you cast are killing you. You were supposed to poison him."

"I tried," she snapped. "Did you not see him slap the drugs from my hand? I had no choice. Besides, it was a sacrifice worth making. Just as Beauty had predicted, King Averath has died and his power is now mine."

"Don't you mean ours?" After witnessing firsthand the strength of Vamillion's power, her tone was more of a plea, than a threat.

Vamillion was feeling stronger now, the residual effect of the spell fading away. She brushed the dirt from the floor off her dress. "You will benefit from what I have done, my queen. You already have. You are now the ruler of Vixus,

but do not forget it is I who made you ruler, and it is I who can take that away."
Vamillion gave Queen Abigail a look of warning and turned to leave.

~CHAPTER 6~

Daylen's journey began just days before the soldiers arrived in Brunhylde for training. He passed Ludlin, the last Vixus outpost, leaving the kingdom and territory that was familiar to him. Relief came from making it past the empire unnoticed. Although he was filled with courage, each step was made with an element of doubt. It felt like walking along the edge of the world, progressing as if each passing moment was determining the fate of the rest of his life. It was both exhilarating and scary.

He clutched Sylver in his hands, his skill untested. In an old sack, he brought the wooden box his mother had left for him, a blanket, and as much food as he could carry. He had been traveling for five days and his food supply had already dwindled considerably. He did not know how far his travels would take him, only that he would travel west, to the heart of the western woodlands. Unaccustomed to travel, he was ill-prepared for the weather and the conditions of the trails. He faced rains and high winds, his blanket proving to be useless once soaked through. It felt as though Nature was intent on robbing him of any warmth he sought to acquire.

With each day of travel, he felt colder and chills signaled the onset of fever. His throat tightened and his head pounded. Through the rain he could see an eagle soar, but wondered if it was a figment of his febrile imagination. The eagle appeared to be the same one he had spotted days prior. It appeared and then disappeared, throughout the day. It had an extraordinary, expansive wingspan and beautiful spotted feathers. He enjoyed its company when it made its presence known and felt anxious when he lost sight of it. With the eagle as his only company, he focused his attention on its soaring path, believing it was beckoning him onward.

At sundown, the eagle had vanished. He was left to face another cold night, alone and feverish. His fear of what might be lurking in the wild was his sole motivation to find shelter as he made his way to the edge of a deep, dark woodland. He collapsed at the entrance of the woods, sore and tired. He prayed that Twilight would be found somewhere within the dark, mysterious depths of the shadows before him, all too aware that he may succumb to a miserable end, otherwise.

He struggled to make a fire, striking flint to stone repeatedly. When the fire finally started, he sighed in relief, as it was the only thing that would help him live through the night. He scoured the bottom of his pouch for crumbs of bread and flakes of dried meat. He managed to acquire a palm sized pile of scraps and with shaking hands brought it to his lips. Despite his hunger, he was slow to eat. Forcing down the last of his rations, he leaned back against a tree and pulled his wet blanket over his body.

He closed his eyes and for the first time he prayed for a miracle, believing that Nature's cruel and unmerciful ways had gotten the best of him. Tired, but afraid to sleep in fear of not waking, he wondered if his prayers would be answered. The hard evening rain was punishing, and the sound of its forceful descent echoed in his pounding head until he slipped into sleep.

LONELY WOOD

~CHAPTER 7~

Daylen awoke, alarmed to find a scraggly man, with long, unkempt hair standing above him. He jumped to his feet. He had a pulsing headache and the bright morning sun in his face as he staggered backward, struggling to gain balance. With a dry, cracked voice he said, "Wh-who are you? Stay back!" He patted his belt, in an attempt to locate Sylver, but he had taken his sword off during the night and placed it beside the fire.

The woodsman stomped on Daylen's campfire, his large leather boots snuffing out the remaining flames. Thick black smoke rose into the early morning air and the woodsman stared up at it with distaste, his head turning as he followed the smoke's trail overhead with his eyes.

Daylen looked to the ground where Sylver still laid and contemplated making a move for it, but the woodsman's attention turned towards him again. "Don't hurt me, I was just sleeping."

The woodsman leaned forward and grabbed Daylen's chin with his large, thick hands. He turned Daylen's head side to side, studying his features. The strength of the Woodsman's grip was apparent as his hands pressed against Daylen's jaw. It would not take much to crush him, and the woodsman appeared in awe at the sight of this strange traveler. "I see fire from distance," the woodsman spoke in common tongue. "Looking to kill the wanderers who cloud the sky, spoiling hunt for man." The woodsman studied the small pack on the ground, who appeared to realize Daylen was not the type of wanderer he was expecting to find. There weren't even enough supplies for one person who had any intention of surviving the woods ahead. "You are alone."

A cold sweat dripped down Daylen's face. He remained still, at the woodsman's mercy. "I am alone."

The woodsman took a step back, releasing his grip on Daylen's face. "I will not kill you, boy."

"Thank y-"

"But Lonely Wood will!" The woodsman interrupted. He walked away from the camp to a patient mule. The smell of fresh food rose from a leather sack on the mule's side and game was thrown over the mules back, enough to feed a person for weeks if rationed well.

Daylen's empty stomach brought pain and nausea. He felt dizzy and weak. The pounding in his head and the weakness of his limbs made standing almost impossible. "I-I am sick… and I have not eaten."

The woodsman grunted. "I do not care for boys." The woodsman turned from the mule so that Daylen could see his face and the cold, seasoned expression of the wandering survivalist. He pointed to the woods before them. "You no match for Lonely Wood. You will die."

Daylen shuddered. "Please, show some sympathy, I beg you."

"Such is the way of the wild. Only strong live." The woodsman turned to leave.

"Wait! We could trade," Daylen pleaded.

The woodsman paused. He reflected a moment and then shook his head. "No need. You will die in Lonely Wood, and I return to take your things."

"There must be something you could use now. I can pay you. I have several coins in my pouch." He grabbed the pouch from the ground, opening it with eager hands.

The woodsman scowled. "What good is money to me?" He waved his hand around him, as if to imply the land was all he needed. Yet, his eyes brightened as they caught site of one of Daylen's belongings. "The blanket."

"Blanket? You want this?" Daylen dropped the pouch to the dirt and the medallion his father wore, encased in glass, rolled out onto the ground. Daylen picked up the blanket. He swiped leaves and dirt from it and shook it vigorously to provide a better presentation.

The woodsman squinted suspiciously, pondering before nodding his head. "When the wolves devour you in Lonely Wood, they will rip blanket to shreds. I'll take from you now."

"Of course, yes, the wolves." He extended the blanket in offering. "For a meal." Daylen did not care to think of the sleepless nights ahead.

The woodsman caught site of the medallion, as the sun's light reflected off its glass case. His eyes widened with lustful greed. "Let me take Shiny, I give more food."

"The medallion?" Daylen shook his head. "I'm sorry, I can't give you that."

"Shiny!" The woodsman yelled. "What good is shattered Shiny to dead boy?"

"Shattered?" Daylen picked up the medallion and pondered the idea of losing the token which would prove his connection to Bolinda, if he were ever to live long enough to find her. He studied the medallion and shrugged, pondering what good the medallion was if he were dead. He opened the glass case and pulled out the medallion. The woodsman smacked the medallion from Daylen's extended hand. "Shiny!" he yelled, pointing instead to the glass case the medallion came in.

Daylen smiled, raising the case toward him. "Shiny?"

The woodsman nodded. "I will give you medicine."

"For glass?" Daylen questioned.

The woodsman grew irritable. "I take Shiny, so it won't break when the wolves devour you. I give medicine and you have slim chance at survival in Lonely Wood."

Daylen fought his impulse to agree to the proposed trade. "Medicine; and more food. Enough for three meals."

"Yes!" The woodsman grabbed the glass case from Daylen's hand and stormed back to his mule. He slipped the prize into a pouch and fumbled through his belongings. He withdrew a handful of nuts and berries within his large hand and stuffed them into an oversized sack. He threw the sack to Daylen's feet along with a second, smaller pouch. As a final offering, he dropped a dead rabbit on the ground. "Good trade."

Daylen watched the woodsman grab the reins of his mule and walk away without another word, disappearing from view. Daylen collected the bags at his feet and retrieved the medallion from the dirt. His heart pounded from the confrontation, he sighed in relief before collapsing to the woodland floor. When he opened the small pouch, a strong herbal smell filled his nose. He hesitated a moment, thankful for the medicinal recipe, then stuffed the flakey mixture of dried leaves and herbs into his mouth.

He opened the sack of food and picked at the nuts and berries slowly, savoring the nourishment as he propped himself up against a tree. He lay at the outskirts of what the woodsman referred to as Lonely Wood. He dreaded the thought of testing his courage within its dark shadows, his hope resting on the woodland being the same woodland that Rahlen spoke of, home to Twilight, his only salvation.

The morning sun was rising, and although the storm clouds restricted most the sun's light, it was bright enough to brighten his mood. The eagle appeared overhead. It swooped to the edge of the woods and landed on a high tree branch. Daylen kicked what remained of the dead rabbit several feet out in front of him. He looked to the eagle and motioned for it to accept his offering. The eagle ignored him. They stared at each other in silence before Daylen was drowsy again and faded in and out of consciousness.

Daylen opened his eyes, expecting only a short time to have passed. Instead, evening had arrived. The eagle was gone and so was the rabbit. He stood slowly, his mind clear and his balance restored. The medicine had lowered his fever and the food provided much needed strength. He did not wish to wait through another night.

With slow and cautious steps he entered the woods. At home, there had only been the one, lone tree. He sat many days by its side, wishing he were not alone. Amongst the many trees of Lonely Wood, he somehow felt even more isolated. He was a foreign presence in an ancient woodland, out of place and vulnerable. He stared above him, the trees were thick and lush with leaves. Their branches formed a natural ceiling above his head and blocked the last rays of evening sunlight from entering. Daylen did not travel far before finding himself surrounded by darkness. The shadows induced a shiver down his spine. He continued cautiously, lost, exposed to the magical, haunting quality of Lonely Wood.

The sound of howling wolves trailed in the distance. He flinched and jumped side to side in fear of spontaneous woodland sounds. Whistling wind rushed between the trees and tree limbs arched like menacing figures, the ends grasping like ghoulish hands. A breeze lifted fallen leaves from the ground and shook the shrubbery around him as if they encompassed angry spirits. He heard something rustling through the foliage. Terrified, he ran toward a patch of light in a clearing. Before he could gather himself, a sound of trampling feet came rushing toward him. He knelt low to the ground, bracing himself. With sweaty palms, he held his blade out into the darkness, waiting for the advancing horror to reveal itself.

The trampling feet came to a halt. A pair of blood red eyes stared out from the shadows. Daylen was petrified into place, as the unknown beast unleashed a ferocious growl. A flash of gray shot through the darkness before Daylen caught sight of a large, wild wolf lunging toward him. It crashed down upon his chest, pinning him to the ground. Sylver was thrown from his grasp upon impact.

Their eyes met, and Daylen caught a glimpse of intense, wild eyes staring back at him. As the wolf howled. In response, a pack of wolves were heard howling back. Daylen screamed. The wolf bit into him, shaking its head side to side as it buried into his flesh. Beyond his agonizing screams, Daylen could hear the howling wolves circle around him, waiting for an opportunity to feast upon his soon to be lifeless body.

Daylen could not reach his sword, so he grabbed the wolf's head with both hands, attempting to prevent another bite. Clutching tightly to the wolf's hair, he was overwhelmed with the realization of his own demise. He was going to die, and he had no choice but to accept it. In this moment, the pain of his wound disappeared. A sensation unlike any he had felt took hold. From a deep core within his being he felt an energy course through his body and collect in his hands. He watched the wolf's jaw relax under his fingers, and the wolf's growls diminished.

Daylen's hands were radiating with a brilliant glow. The wolf's eyes locked with Daylen and the wild animal's expression changed from aggression to that of recognition. The wolf stepped off of him and lowered its head. It licked at Daylen's wounds before stepping back, as if to observe in silent ceremony. The pack at the wolf's command, followed suit.

Meanwhile, Daylen could not control the powerful energy surging through his hands. Light radiated from his fingers and brightened the dark woods like a powerful lantern light. The pack of wolves were illuminated and for a moment Daylen caught sight of their patient trance, as if witness to a notable ceremony.

Colors danced before his eyes in intricate, puzzling patterns. Bizarre, foreign symbols flashed across his field of vision. The woods appeared to morph and spin, the tree limbs swaying overhead at a dizzying speed. The wolves faded from sight as the burning force in his hands dimmed. Consciousness retreated, his body relaxing and giving way to the darkness. Lonely Wood appeared to swallow him whole, until all discernable shapes disappeared, and everything went black.

~CHAPTER 8~

Floating in darkness, lost to space and time, a sound emerged from the silence and bright fiery colors flashed. The brilliance, in contrast to the dark, left a stain, an impression. Before the after burn could fade, another flash of brightness emerged, revealing another symbol, this time accompanied by a sound, a word, an unfamiliar language.

Confusion shattered the tranquility. Awareness brought a feeling of pain. A ringing came from all around and within. Once the ringing reached a deafening pitch it stopped abruptly, and a voice said, "Daylen."

Daylen felt as though he was trapped, a prisoner of his own mind. He wanted to scream but did not know how.

"Daylen!"

He opened his eyes. He stood in a long, outstretched hallway. Torches burned along marble walls. Before him stood a man surrounded by white. The stranger's face was peaceful and still, his features were warm and inviting. Daylen stared into the stranger's eyes and felt comfort.

"Daylen," the foreign voice spoke again, but the stranger's lips did not move. It was as if their minds were unexplainably linked.

Daylen could hear a fire in the distance. The fire grew louder, and he felt its heat on his skin. It was not until this moment that Daylen became aware of his body. The stranger faded into a transparent shape and then vanished. Daylen tried to call out, but his body prohibited him from speaking. The hallway faded from view and only the sound of the crackling fire and its heat remained.

Daylen screamed, springing forward from a small, soft bed. Sweat dripped from his face and his body was in pain. He hacked a deep, wretched cough and looked around him, alarmed. He was in a small, quaint cottage. Beside him, a warm fire blazed. Daylen wondered if he was still dreaming.

A short, pudgy man wobbled toward him. He was dressed in layers of tattered, warm colored fabric, patched in places with multiple, patterns. Fabric was wrapped around his head, with various flowers, leaves, stems and twigs sticking out from its folds. With an unkempt, bushy white beard and a concerned, compassionate look in his big, round eyes he spoke, "Whoa, whoa, there boy, lie down, lie down, all is okay. You had quite a powerful dream, I should say. You were moaning and twitching from side to side, but rest assured you are safe now."

Daylen was speechless and disoriented, trying to get his bearings. The little man before him was harmless, he realized, once he could gather himself and assess his environment. The little man was no more than four feet tall. He bore a large smile that wrinkled his plump, round nose and stretched his rosy cheeks.

"Don't be frightened. I am Lobire. You must be scared out of your stockings, you poor, poor thing." The man chuckled at his own observation. "If anything, I should be afraid of you, after what I witnessed, after the scene you caused."

"Wh-What?" Daylen attempted to sit up when he noticed the pain. His body was wrapped in bloody bandages.

"Please be still. I am sure you have many questions; which I am prepared to answer, if you just take your time."

The genuine warmth in the little man's words put Daylen at ease and he leaned back down on the bed. "Lobire, you said?"

"Yes, my name is Lobire. I found you in the woods. You made quite a ruckus; the howling wolves led me to you."

"Wolves?" Daylen questioned.

"Yes, my boy, wolves. Tell me, young man, what were you doing out there all alone? Are there others out there?"

Daylen remained silent, unsure as to reveal his mission to a stranger.

"You are a wizard, yes? I am here to help you. Those bandages, the tea at your bedside, I have provided these things for you."

"No…" Daylen said after a long silence. "I am no wizard." He was raised never to let anyone know about his special gift. To deny his power came naturally. Yet his words were not a lie. Struggling to understand the events that led to this moment, he was aware that he had no idea what it meant to be a wizard, and as such, did not see himself as one.

"You have no need to hide from me. I know plenty of wizards, rogue ones like you, and have grown quite fond of them. You could say that I respect them all the more for it. And you, boy oh boy, you are quite an impressive wizard, indeed. Ha," Lobire laughed, joyfully, "if you wish to hide your identity you will have to be far more discreet!"

Daylen lowered his head, as if in shame, but his words carried undeniable pride. "My name is Daylen."

"Ah, now, you see, we are getting somewhere."

Lobire had a likable charm and a compassionate nature, Daylen assessed. He commanded honesty, and Daylen felt comfortable being truthful with him. There was nothing threatening or aggressive in this short, funny looking man. "I am sorry, Lobire, for it has been hard to trust people in this world. Truth is, I am in dire need of help. You have already done more than I could ever expect of another person; you have saved my life and I am indebted to you. However, I am in search of someone and I am afraid I have lost my way."

Daylen told Lobire about his hometown of Brunhylde, and the arrival of Vixus knights. As he retraced his steps and the series of events that led to meeting Lobire, memories of what had transpired in Lonely Wood resurfaced. Daylen held out his thin, delicate hands in front of him. "I have no idea what it was that came from these hands. Whatever it was, it saved my life. The way it possessed me, took control… it scares me."

Lobire nodded in understanding. "I am not a magic wielder, so I won't pretend to understand the burden you bear, but I do know that the very magic a wizard uses will drain his life. It can kill you. That is why wizards are very careful as to what spells they cast and when. If you look closely, you can tell the wizards who have cast many spells, because their eyes have less color than other wizards, as if spells drain their essence. If the eyes are a path to the soul, then a wizard with dull, colorless eyes is wizard with many experiences. You are but a young pup, but a wolf, nonetheless."

"A lone wolf, it would seem." Daylen said, speaking more to himself, than to Lobire.

"You have not told me what brought you to Lonely Wood. Where do you plan to go and what do you plan to do?"

Daylen's face brightened with hope. "I am looking for Zantigar. Have you heard of him?"

Lobire looked to the ceiling, in thought. "No, I don't believe I have."

Daylen nodded. "Have you seen my belongings?"

Lobire wobbled to a small cabinet and retrieved Daylen's small wooden box. "I assume you are speaking of this?"

Daylen opened it and handed him the letter that Rahlen had written to his mother. "This is all I have to live for. This letter is my life, and I trust you to read it."

Lobire unfolded the letter. He retrieved his spectacles from his vest pocket and rested them on the bridge of his nose, looking over the letter with careful concentration. "Hmm," he said, scanning the words. His face twitched, frowned, and then nodded in understanding before handing the letter back to him.

"What?"

"I am not certain how to tell you this, you see, but-" Lobire stopped, as if concerned about the delicacy of what he needed to say. "You are looking for Zantigar Parkn?"

"Why yes, so you do know him!"

"The name rings a bell, alright. Truth is, everyone knows of Zantigar Parkn. It is just when you asked, I never imagined you meant *the* Zantigar." A look of regret filled Lobire's eyes. "Zantigar Parkn is dead, dear boy."

In an instant, Daylen's heart fell. "Then I am dead."

"You mean to tell me that you are serious, that you expected to find this wizard? Have you not heard the legends or read the books?"

"Only what my mother had told me."

"But Daylen," Lobire said with sincerity, "Zantigar lived over two hundred years ago."

Daylen collapsed back into the bed, covering his face with his hands. "But my mother… why would she tell me to find him?"

Lobire placed his stubby hand on Daylen's shoulder. "Maybe she wanted to give you the strength to leave and not look back. There are plenty of rogue wizards who can help you."

Daylen did not want to hear of others. The news was devastating. The story was a lie, and he questioned if any of the childhood stories he had heard were true.

Lobire gave Daylen a gentle shake. "Come now, don't feel discouraged. The woman that was referenced in the letter, a Miss Bolinda Lynx, I know this woman. She is bit of a hero among us simple folk."

Daylen raised his head, giving Lobire his full attention.

"She does not stay far from here, as a matter of fact. Maybe Zantigar is not the answer, but Bolinda Lynx might be able to help you. I will not be of much use to you. I know very little about the great, big world abroad. I have lived in solitude for most my life, and I am just a simple gnome."

Daylen smiled. Until Lobire had spoken, he had no idea what made Lobire so unique. "A gnome, you say? I have never met a gnome before."

Lobire bowed, "Gnome Lobire, at your service."

Daylen laughed. He had not laughed in a very long time.

"Come now, don't be so silly. I am just like you… just a being on FéLorën, trying to live in peace."

Daylen could not contain his sense of wonderment. For this brief moment, the worries of his travels were gone. "If only my mother could have seen this! A real, living gnome!" Daylen laughed again, and Lobire laughed along with him.

When their laughter subsided, Lobire had a remarkable twinkle in his eye. "I am not sure what your life journey is about, or where it leads you, but you have already landed on a small, but significant pebble stone."

"Don't you mean milestone?"

"Milestone? No, smaller than that. More like a pebble, but significant, none the less." Lobire chuckled and then his face became as earnest as his optimistic voice. "Let me be the first to welcome you, young wizard, to Twilight."

~CHAPTER 9~

Daylen awoke in Lobire's cottage, realizing salvation from Lonely Wood had not been a dream. His relief was followed by sadness, remembering that Zantigar was no longer alive and worried about what it meant for his future. The sweet smell of cooked food and steeping tea forced his mind into the present and he looked to stacks of delectable treats arranged on the counter.

Lobire stopped tending a pot of stew and moved toward Daylen. "Good morning, lad." Daylen must have appeared troubled, and if seemingly reading Daylen's mind, he asked, "It is Zantigar, isn't it? You are still troubled by this news."

"There has to be some kind of mistake." Daylen could not imagine that his mother could be lying to him, or be mistaken, considering all that she knows. She was wise and caring and had given him the courage to do what had to be done. He had no choice but to accept that if she had intentionally lied to him, then it was for a good reason, unbeknownst to him. He would just have to have faith in her plans, and in his decision to seek Twilight.

Daylen rose to his feet. "What should I do now?"

Lobire turned to Daylen and handed him a cup of tea. "Drink."

Daylen accepted the mug with a gracious nod. He had not had tea before. He smelled the aroma and the steam on his face. "I mean, what should I do next?"

"After tea?"

Daylen chuckled, amused by Lobire's playfully innocent perspective. "No, what do I do about my future?"

Lobire sat down beside him. "Let me tell you something that I hope you will not forget. I saw what transpired. I saw the pack of wolves surrounding you and saw them change before my eyes. Where once you were mere food, you had become something else. You changed them. They sat with you for a while, as if to make sure you still breathed. When I approached, they turned to stare at me and in their silence they spoke to me. They told me to nurse you back to health and when I nodded in understanding, only then did they leave your side.

"I came forward and saw you lying in a pool of your own blood. Your body was frail and your breath fading. Your magic, however insignificant you may feel, had the power to coerce a ferocious beast. You managed to overcome great adversity in a most astonishing form. The future will be the present, eventually, and I believe you will navigate it with as much courage as all the present moments that came before it."

Daylen listened to Lobire and found wisdom in his perspective. He could not remember what had transpired, just flashes, like in a dream. Lonely Wood was a nightmare and the memory still haunted him. The suffocating experience of the trees spinning and the feeling that overcame him was something he would never forget.

"Rest your worried spirit," Lobire said. "There is a future for someone like you. Perhaps, when you meet Bolinda Lynx, you might see that your place is with us. Here, you would be seen as an equal, not as a king's pawn. You would also have the opportunity to channel your magic and create positive change. But before we find what fate has in store for you, we must eat." Lobire gave a wink and outstretched his arms as if to display results of his cooking expertise. His rosy, chubby cheeks and short, squat nose forced an unwanted, but well needed smile upon Daylen's face.

There was stew and hot, creamy soup and a loaf of warm bread, fruits and nuts and blocks of aged cheeses. Lobire hopped from one food station to another, piling a tall plate of delicacies far bigger than Daylen's starved stomach could ever hope to consume in one sitting.

"All of this food is for us?" Daylen said.

"I didn't know quite what you would be in the mood for, so I gathered a few things."

"It's all about food and drink for you, isn't it?" Daylen remarked.

"What finer life is there, then to eat and drink?" Lobire replied.

Daylen couldn't argue with that. After the replenishing meal, he was led outside for the first time since his recovery. His surroundings suggested he was still in the heart of Lonely Wood. Dense trees and foliage surrounded him and only thin beams of light hit the forest floor through breaks in the leaves. Expecting to see the town of Twilight, he was puzzled to see no signs of townsfolk.

Lobire held a pair of metal hooks in his hands. "Stay right here, Daylen."

Daylen watched as Lobire picked the nearest tree to him and dug the metal hooks into its bark. Lobire scaled the tree with impressive speed and dexterity. It was not long before Lobire disappeared into the leaves high above. "Where are you going?"

"Twilight, of course!" A moment later, a rope fell and dangled at the bottom of the tree. "Climb on up!"

Daylen tugged at the rope. It appeared to be fastened to something beyond his sight. With a shrug, he grabbed the rope and pulled himself up. As his head crested the ceiling of foliage, he stared, wide eyed, at the amazing sight before him. Above the leaves and suspended on strong tree limbs, was a well-crafted village, spanning tree to tree above Lonely Wood. He laughed, amused that he had thought he was alone, when all along a heavenly haven existed overhead.

"Give me your hand," called Lobire, reaching to pull Daylen up from the ladder.

He grabbed Lobire's arm and settled himself on a firm wooden bridge. From this height, he could see the vast sky and the top of Lonely Wood spreading before him as far as his eyes could see. Thick gray clouds drifted overhead, the trees swaying like waves, the sun fading in and out of sight. There was beauty to behold in this world – and Twilight was it.

As they walked across the wooden bridge, Lobire spoke of Twilight's history. The town was quaint, with just a few shops built into the trunks of enormous trees. Fashioned many years ago, by the hands of local wood elves, what it lacked in size was compensated for with fine architecture, blending harmoniously with the natural woodland. It was inspired by contractors from the city of Xyntharia, the famous elven empire far across the continent of Valice, which Daylen had known only through paintings and books in his mother's library.

"Twilight is small," Lobire said, "but by design. It serves more as a meeting place, a place to trade and for debate."

"Debate what?" Daylen said.

Lobire shrugged, seeming uninterested. "Politics, world affairs, things too big for my small way of life. Twilight is the keeper of secrets, and therefore must be hidden from the world below, lest it be destroyed. Those who know of Twilight's existence have discovered it by design and have become its protectors. You should feel blessed that your mother knows of this place and has guided you here."

Daylen's attention was drawn to the locals. As Lobire had suggested, they were unique and moving about with an unknown purpose. He had never met other races, Lobire being the first gnome he had ever encountered. Now, he witnessed elves, humans and gnomes together. He even saw what seemed to be a few dwarves. The thought of these races getting along with each other was unimaginable to Daylen, and he would never have believed a peaceful town like

Twilight could exist. There were elves and dwarves sharing stories and a gnome carving a picture into a sign above one of the shops, while an orc exited and greeted the gnome with a friendly nod and farewell as he passed.

Daylen had seen orcs in pictures and had always believed them to be evil creatures. Stories from home always described them as aggressive beings, but the greeting from the orc as it made its way through town shattered his preconceptions. The very culture of this small community went against everything he had grown to understand.

A loud cry rang out from the gray sky above, grabbing Daylen's attention. It was the eagle that had followed Daylen to Lonely Wood. "Lobire, I don't believe it! I know that eagle."

The eagle swooped into Twilight and perched itself on a tree branch straight overhead. It cried out again, spread its wings as if to show off, before tucking its wings close.

Lobire smiled. "Most peculiar, it has perched itself above the home of Bolinda Lynx," Lobire informed, "Which is right where we are headed."

Like all the other homes and shops, Bolinda's home was cut into the trunk of an enormous tree. Carvings of vines and leaves were made into the surface of the door. Daylen averted his gaze from the artistic craftsmanship of Bolinda's home to the eyes of the eagle above him. There was an elf on either side of the door, faces stern, their bodies tall and still. They held spears in their hands, pointing to the sky, with bows strapped to their backs. They guarded the door in silence and Daylen gathered that Bolinda was a person of great importance to have such security.

Lobire placed a hand on Daylen's arm. "Pardon me, Daylen, for this formality. As I was explaining, it is the secrets of this town, the very knowledge of its existence that causes the citizens to be cautious. You should wait outside while I inform Bolinda of your arrival. You understand, do you not?"

Daylen nodded.

Lobire stepped between the elven guards and knocked on the door in a methodical, distinct rhythm. The elves stayed still and were unalarmed by Lobire's advance. After a moment, Lobire opened the door enough for his body to enter and closed the door behind him.

Daylen stood outside, eager but nervous, feeling awkward to have the fixed attention of the elven guards. He held his wooden box to him, which contained the medallion that would confirm his lineage, and he hoped it would be his ticket of acceptance by the people of Twilight. Looking up, the eagle stared at him.

The door opened, startling Daylen.

Lobire appeared and gave an animated bow. "Bolinda is ready to receive you."

Daylen stepped inside and was greeted by a warm fire. The two elven guards followed him in, taking a place on either side of the exit. He looked back at them, and then at Lobire, who remained on the other side of the door.

Lobire smiled. "I will wait here for you."

A guard closed the door behind him. Daylen walked into the center of the room. Standing behind a cluttered desk was a middle-aged woman. She was a tall and strong human, but her ears were pointed and her eyes almond shaped, like the elven guards that flanked the door.

"Hello Daylen," she proclaimed in a soft tone, with a polite smile. "My name is Bolinda Lynx." Bolinda motioned to a chair opposite her desk. "Please, have a seat."

Daylen did as he was told.

Bolinda lowered herself into the chair opposite him. Her caramel eyes were bright and wise. After appearing to study Daylen for a moment, she spoke. "What brings you to Twilight?"

Daylen sensed that Bolinda already knew the answer. He placed the wooden box on the desk. Opening the lid, he took out the medallion, nervously picking dirt from its crevices and wiping the smudges off its golden surface. It took him a moment before he had the courage to look her in the eye. "My mother," he spoke softly, "said you would want to see this."

Bolinda narrowed her almond-shaped eyes, intrigued, and took the medallion from Daylen's thin hands. Her gaze moved from the medallion to Daylen and back again. She motioned to the elven guards. "Summon Nilderon, immediately."

Daylen glanced back at the elves as they left and felt uneasy at her command. He had not noticed until now that he was under suspicion. Of what, he could not know. He turned back to Bolinda. He studied the dagger on her belt and her weathered tunic. Her sleeves were rolled up, as if deep in her work, exposing her dark forearms, tanned from years in the sun and scarred from unknown labors.

A childlike excitement crossed Bolinda's face. "I see the light of your father in your eyes, young one."

Daylen relaxed in his chair, relieved by Bolinda's words. His mother, it appeared, had not been wrong in sending him to Twilight.

"I must admit," Bolinda said, "I did not know Donovan had a child. Your father was a good friend of mine, Daylen. Having you seated across from me, looking at me with your father's eyes, has me taken aback." She paused, as if to process the feelings that came to her. "And yet, your eyes… a tad dull in color." Averting her gaze to the remaining elven guard in the room she proclaimed, with a smile, "His son is wizardborn."

"Miss Lynx," Daylen said. "My mother sent me to find you. Her name-"

"Is Claudia," Bolinda finished. "I knew of your mother."

Daylen shook his head. "She never spoke of you, or life before Brunhylde."

"We never had the chance to meet. One day, it would be nice to get to know her." Bolinda stood and paced behind her desk until she settled by the fireplace, facing the flames. She appeared troubled by a flurry of difficult memories. "You must have many questions."

"Too many," he said.

Bolinda kept her attention on the fire as she spoke. "I tried to get Donovan to move to Twilight, but he would not do it."

"Why?" Daylen asked. "Twilight seems like a better place to raise a family." Thinking of his childhood, the suffering he had endured growing up, he lowered his eyes.

Bolinda turned to him with surprise. "You don't even know why your father stayed in Brunhylde?"

Daylen raised his head inquisitively. "I hardly know a thing… only that he was a Vixus knight and was murdered by the kingdom he served."

"I see," Bolinda said. "Well, Donovan knew that by moving here he would put Twilight at risk of being discovered by the Vixus army and jeopardized his position. If Twilight were found by the empire, then our very culture would be destroyed. Those of us in Twilight represent a dying way of life."

"Do you know how my father died?"

Bolinda sat down again, restless. Her stare was intense, commanding Daylen's attention. "I met your father in Brunhylde. He arrived one night, in terrible trouble. Assassins were hunting him, and he needed a placed to stay. Because he was a Vixus knight, I did not trust him. When he told me the assassins were working for Vixus, I was more than happy to help. We shared a common mistrust for the empire.

"I gave him a job as a blacksmith. He mostly made farming tools, hardly the life for a knight, but he was grateful. Your father was skilled, but a modest man. It was quickly apparent that he was not like other knights. He kept to himself, mostly. When I was asked to move to twilight, I asked your father to join me, but he refused. It must not have been much longer before he met your mother."

Daylen wondered if Bolinda had feelings for his father, deeper than friendship.

Bolinda breathed a heavy sigh. "I'm just sorry I wasn't there for him when he died. I often thought that there was something I could have done. When word spread of his death I was devastated."

Daylen's heart sank at the news. He sensed that Bolinda was holding back. "Tell me how he died. I must know."

Bolinda nodded. "You deserve to know. His body was mutilated and what was left of it was nailed to the gates of Brunhylde for all to see. His head, however, had been removed and placed on a pole at the side of the road leading to Vixus Castle. It was a common punishment for traitors and served to warn others to not follow in his footsteps."

Daylen leaned back in his chair; the image of his father's dead body stuck in his mind. He could hardly stand the thought of it. Curiosity was stronger than the pain that grew in his stomach. "My father was a traitor?"

Bolinda's focus sharpened; her eyes narrowed. "Any decent person would become traitor to a kingdom as unjust as Vixus has become. Your father was careful not to say much about his past or the situation that brought him to Brunhylde. It was his way of protecting those who he cared about."

"What do you think he did to deserve his fate?" Daylen asked.

Bolinda shook her head. "It doesn't matter. Knowing your father, the truth had to have been skewed by Vixus to rationalize his murder. Why? I can only imagine. He was a just and honorable person. If you knew your father, I have no doubt that you would feel the same."

Bolinda reached out and grabbed Daylen's hand from across the table. Her eyes were misty, and she closed them for a moment to hold back the tears. "I loved your father very much. All of us in Twilight did. Which is why I want you to know that you always have a place here, with us. It is the least we can do."

Daylen heard the conviction in her words and knew it to be true.

Still holding Daylen's hand, Bolinda squeezed it tightly. "I am sorry, Daylen, that you never had the chance to meet him. For what it is worth, it is a real pleasure to make your acquaintance."

Daylen was grateful for her sympathy and for the explanation of his father's character. It was what he always believed deep in his heart to be true. A pain grew in his stomach caused by a festering hatred at the injustice that had been done. He squeezed Bolinda's hand with equal measure, grateful for her hospitality and in support for the town of Twilight.

~CHAPTER 10~

The stone, twin towers of Vixus Academy rose high into the storm clouds. Within their massive structure, the wizards of age, except the select few outlaws who fled from service, studied and practiced the art of magic. Vixus Academy worked much like any academy in the world of FéLorën, its purpose to harness a wizard's power and thereby increase the power of the empire.

An academy was the cornerstone of a kingdom's defense. Academies honed wizards' capabilities, creating nothing short of powerful generals, instruments of war. As a result, kingdoms collected countless spellbooks, hoarding knowledge and spells over generations. The major strength of a kingdom was determined not by gold or land, but by the size of the library of spellbooks they possessed. Within the large stone towers of Vixus Academy lay the largest library of spells on the continent of Valice.

A wizard in training went through twelve stages of development before graduation. Once a member of the military, a wizard strived to become a Master. Masters were exceptional magicians, their spell power, academic excellence, and accomplishments far exceeding the average wizard. Most Masters became political leaders and held seats high in government. Higher still, were the Legionnaires. Legionnaires were either proven heroes in war, or those whose contributions to the Academy library were extraordinary, advancing a kingdom's dominance in the region.

Wizards specialized in specific fields of magic. Not by choice, but by genetic design. A few of these fields included blessed Holy Wizards – who possessed protective and healing spells; Nature Wizards – who could alter and transform the natural world around them; and Mystics – who had the potential to distort the realm of the conscious and unconscious mind through illusions. Yet, since academies were militant by design, there was no field more revered than the destructive, powerful force of Chaos Wizards.

All the academies of FéLorën recognized and categorized their wizards by their specialty. Academics detailed the many fields and sub-fields, and debated the extent of specialties possible. The Academy's on the continent of Oryahn, for example, were known to have identified thirty unique fields of wizardry. One controversial field was that of Necromancy, characterized by the ability to manipulate the dead and conjure power from the afterlife. It was banished by all empires on the continent of Valice, due to its frightful, unnatural implications. Most wizards with such gifts were hung, feared for their ability to tap into the spirit world. Witches, ghouls, or hags were just a few of the names bestowed upon these wizards. Despite being outlawed, Vamillion secretly trained Necromancers as part of an underground institution, kept secret from the citizens of the kingdom, including the king.

After the death of King Averath, Vamillion informed Queen Abigail of the secret school, promising her queen that Necromancy was the key to grant them supremacy over the other kingdoms of the land. Those wizards who had been born with the dark gift of Necromancy, believed to have been sent to their deaths, were living below ground to study their art.

Vamillion was eager to see the students of Necromancy progress and flourish under her careful eye. Her new god, the Dark One, promised her that an unsuspecting Necromancer would create a spell more powerful than she could ever imagine. This very thought excited her and fueled her obsession. She believed that with the discovery of this prophesized Necromancer, she would finally make her kingdom secure. The numerous wizards who walked the halls of the School of Necromancy, in tunnels beneath the School of Mystics, were grateful for her mercy, and their appreciation and love for Vamillion justified the secret and the oftentimes deadly costs involved.

As the Dark One had promised, Vamillion found the wizard she had been searching for all these years. Beauty, the prophet, bastard prince of Vixus, confirmed that the Necromancer she sought, that would change the shape of the kingdom forever, was alive and studying within these very walls. With a word, Beauty spoke, and so it was true… "Glazahn."

*　　　　*　　　　*

Glazahn walked into the large, open courtyard of Castle Vixus. He looked around with a sense of wonderment. He had been underground since his arrival. From the moment he first stepped foot into the dark halls of the School of Necromancy he was under the impression that he would never see the light of day again. The light was a blessing, a gift he was grateful to experience, but it burned his eyes. The underground had a way of making months feel like years, and the light made him feel as though he was not at home amongst the sun's brilliance. He pulled the hood of his cloak far over his face to shade his sensitive eyes.

Like all Initiates, he was naïve to his own potential, anxious to learn from the great Masters of his time. Through the first stage of schooling, he had learned much about the history of the academy and of the different fields of magic. Having heard the voice of the lone tree back home in Brunhylde he assumed he would be accepted in the School of Nature. Therefore, he was surprised to end up studying below ground. He had no idea what his mind was capable of, and did not understand the complexity of his own essence. He could no more control the fate of his gift than he could change the color of his eyes.

Glazahn had undergone a school project that changed his life forever. There was a dead frog, a prop at which he was to focus his magic. In a meditative trance, he saw symbols arise in his mind and had learned to interpret them. Understanding the language, he harnessed the magic that came from within. Eyes closed in deep concentration, the gasps of fellow classmates startled him. He opened his eyes and watched in horror and disbelief as the frog moved as if animated. It was a grotesque scene, the lifeless limbs twitching at Glazahn's command, like a puppeteer manipulating a marionette.

The shrill cry of a classmate caused his concentration to break, the frog plopping limp upon the table several inches from where it first lay. The frog formed infectious black spots on its skin and then decayed from the inside, right before the eyes of his classmates and his teacher. He was approached by Academy guards, graduates from the school, who grabbed him, locked his arms behind his back, and marched him directly to the headmaster of the twelve stages. His fate was clear, he would be sentenced to death for what he could do, for what he was.

The headmaster stood before a council of Masters who with haste, cast judgement and sentenced him to death by decapitation. Doors on the side of the office opened and she appeared… a tall, majestic woman with long black hair that draped over her white robe. She had mercy in her eyes and bore a smile that gave him hope. She took his trembling hand and led him from the council.

"Do you know why you are being decapitated, young wizard?" Vamillion spoke in a soft, inquisitive voice.

"I am sorry, I can change."

She narrowed her eyes. "Never apologize for what you are and never wish to be anything different than what you are. I am the High Priestess of Vixus, and I can offer you life. I can teach you to embrace your power, to make you proud of what you are. Would you be willing to live a life of secrecy, far from the eyes of the world?"

Glazahn looked at the enchanting sorceress. "I would do anything for a chance at life."

"Of course you would, dear boy. Of course you would. Life will come at a price. You will study in dangerous conditions and will most likely never see the light of day again. Are you willing to accept these conditions?"

"Anything, Master."

Glazahn had longed to thank the woman who saved him, the woman in white. She was an angel, his angel, and only knew her as the High Priestess of Vixus. He had not seen her since.

Here he was, now, in the courtyard of Vixus castle, a place he was forbidden to enter. His Master said that the High Priestess of Vixus would like a word with him. He had been waiting for this moment since he had entered the dark dungeons of the School of Necromancy.

Past an extravagant garden maze and a bountiful wall of roses, several royal infantrymen walked toward the courtyard in Glazahn's direction. Behind them, two knights in shining black armor stood at either side of two women, one of which he recognized immediately, and his heart pounded in his chest as they came to stand before him.

Glazahn stared wide eyed at the angel from his past. Her robe was no longer white, but black, black as the hair that fell past her shoulders. Her dress exuded wealth and her presence, power. When her pale, beautiful face bore an expression of joy as her eyes met his, he fell to the ground trembling like the day she first led him from the headmaster office. He kissed her feet.

"Rise, Glazahn, and stand before your queen." Queen Abigail said.

Glazahn had not even noticed the queen was present. He had been so mesmerized by the angel from his past that he looked to her as if looking for permission.

"Rise as your queen instructed," Vamillion spoke, moving her feet away from Glazahn's worshipping grasp.

Glazahn did as he was told and for the first time, looked toward the queen of Vixus. The School of Necromancy taught him that he would never be worthy enough to meet the queen, but here he was, standing face to face with the ruler of Vixus and the High Priestess. He dropped to his knees again. "Your Majesty."

"Is this the young Necromancer that Beauty spoke of?" Queen Abigail said to Vamillion, a hint of dissatisfaction in her tone.

"He must be," Vamillion replied.

"Rise," Queen Abigail said to Glazahn. "Do not force me to ask you again."

Glazahn rose. "I am at your service, my queen." When he looked up he noticed a wizard that had been standing quietly behind Vamillion.

"Glazahn, I would like for you to meet Diamus." Vamillion stepped back allowing Diamus to step forward. His face was etched with wrinkles and his faded blue eyes were distant and dim. He peered, almost lifeless, behind strands of aged white hair.

Glazahn had seen this wizard several times passing through the dungeon halls. He was a Legionnaire, an untouchable, someone the students were forbidden to speak to. It was rumored he was from a distant continent. A foreign land far from Valice, where Necromancy reigned supreme. He was said to carry a spellbook with countless foreign spells, collected from mysterious lands.

Vamillion continued. "Your hard work and devotion to Necromancy has not gone unnoticed. You will play an important part in your kingdom's future. Are you willing to accept this honor and the responsibility that comes with it?"

Glazahn nodded. "I will do anything for you."

"Diamus is going to be your teacher and you are to be his apprentice. Together, you will change the face of this world. Do you understand?"

Glazahn hardly understood why, or what his destiny held, but he nodded nevertheless in servitude.

"Then I will give you and Diamus a chance to get to know each other."

Without delay, Diamus led Glazahn through the garden maze, Glazahn turning back to glimpse the High Priestess and the Queen make their way back to the castle. His attention was captured by the sound of Diamus' raspy, cracked voice.

"Do you know what you are?"

Glazahn had waited his entire life to be able to proclaim his true identity. Ever since he learned what he was, he was forced to hide. "I am a Necromancer."

"You are mine," Diamus corrected. "There are things that I will teach you that will contradict your understanding of the laws of Nature, as well as the teachings of Vixus Academy, itself. You are my student, now. I have travelled to faraway lands of FéLorën and have wisdom that I will bestow upon you, alone. From this day forth, as long as you shall live, my word is law, your obedience is absolute."

"Yes, Master."

"Legionnaire," Diamus corrected.

"Yes, Legionnaire."

Diamus led Glazahn deeper into the garden maze, the hedges towering high over their heads. "Did you know that Valice is the only continent in the world where its kingdoms murder their Necromancers? Some cultures, on distant shores, worship Necromancers. It is because we are able to communicate with the other side.

"You know what I speak of. You feel the closeness of the spirit world. You cannot escape its allure, nor should you try, as it is a part of you. Be proud of what you are, because one day, with the High Priestess' mercy, and my guidance, you will change the world. The people of Vixus and all the races across this vast continent will have no choice but to respect you because of what you are, and more importantly, because of what you will have accomplished."

Glazahn walked beside his teacher, taking in his words, meeting Diamus' powerful gaze with a courage he did not know he possessed. The lesson had just begun and already it woke the warlock spirit within him. "I will give you my all."

~CHAPTER 11~

Daylen could not shake the details of his father's death from his mind. It fueled more questions than answers, and he feared he would never know the truth as to why his father was murdered. Sitting at the desk at Bolinda's home, he pondered upon his quest thus far. Disappointed that Zantigar was dead, he hoped that there were no additional details his mother had been wrong about, especially in regard to Rahlen. "Where is Rahlen?"

"I expect him to arrive very soon," Bolinda replied. "This morning, I saw Ayrowen flying above Twilight."

"Ayrowen?"

"Ayrowen is an eagle, and is Rahlen's loyal companion."

Daylen found it hard to fathom. "I think Ayrowen has followed me on my quest. He is perched outside your door."

"Then Rahlen must not be far behind," she said.

The door opened and an old, tall man walked into the room. He wore a blue robe and a matching blue cap. He removed the cap when he entered, revealing a balding head, surrounded by long wisps of gray hair. His eyes were soft and compassionate, not unlike Lobire's, and he looked toward Bolinda, paying no mind to Daylen. "You called for me?"

Bolinda stood and moved away from her desk. "Nilderon, thank you for coming. She extended her arm to Daylen. "Nilderon, let me introduce you to Daylen, son of Donovan Sylver."

The wizard's eyes widened inquisitively; his attention drawn to the stranger sitting before him. "I had no idea Donovan had a son. It is a pleasure, young man… or shall I say, young wizard?"

Daylen returned an awkward bow. "Yes sir, the pleasure is mine, sir."

Bolinda motioned to Daylen. "He is something of a miracle, isn't he?"

"Indeed," Nilderon replied. "His very existence invigorates our cause." He looked to Daylen. "You listen well to Bolinda. She is a smart half-elf, smart as any human I have met, or elf, for that matter."

Daylen looked at Bolinda closely, her mixed race explained her human build, but pointed ears. Her parents were of mixed race, an uncommon and controversial union.

Nilderon continued. "She was born in the kingdom of Xyntharia."

"My mother was a Wilder; a human who lived with woodsmen," Bolinda said.

"Yes, but she gets her smarts and charm from the High Elves." Nilderon joked, placing his hand on Bolinda's arm.

"Yes, but none of the grace," Bolinda joked, at her own expense.

Nilderon dismissed her observation. "Your grace, my dear, far exceeds any elf I have ever known." He took a seat next to Daylen and gave him a wink.

Daylen was struck by Nilderon's kindness. He spoke to Bolinda like a loving father to a daughter. "I have never seen an Elven city," Daylen remarked.

Bolinda returned to her desk and took her seat. "I lived most of my adult life knowing nothing of elven cities. My father abandoned me. It was my mother who raised me and taught me the ways of the woodland. My parents were ill-fated, because my Elven father had to keep his love for my mother a secret from his family. Their relationship was damned from the start. When this was realized, my mother took me into the forests. I have no memory of Xyntharia, or my father. He chose his kingdom over her, which was no surprise for an elf. He abandoned us, and I never desired to know him."

"Only a fool would dismiss you," Nilderon commented. "And your father would feel the fool if he could see you now. If he had the chance to see who you have become." Nilderon explained to Daylen, "She is selfless, with a heart as pure as gold. A genuine friend to all."

Daylen was struck by Bolinda's tale. He, too, was an outcast. It seemed most people in Twilight were. Perhaps, this is why the people of Twilight appeared to be so accepting and understanding of other people and races.

"Well," Bolinda said, changing the subject, "Nilderon is our sole wizard in Twilight. I thought it would be an excellent idea for you two to get acquainted." Looking to Nilderon she said, "We should discuss what the future holds for our bright new citizen of Twilight."

"Yes, of course," Nilderon said. "So much to catch up on, one wonders where to begin."

Bolinda addressed Nilderon with curious excitement. "Don't you think Daylen is the perfect candidate?"

Daylen did not understand what Bolinda meant, but he was beginning to realize that Nilderon's arrival was for a bigger reason than just an introduction. He looked at Nilderon, only to find the old wizard staring into his eyes, as if searching his soul.

"Rahlen sent you to us, did he not?" Nilderon inquired.

Daylen looked to Bolinda when he answered. "My mother, actually. There was a letter that Rahlen had written to her… I was hoping he would be here."

Nilderon leaned forward in his chair. "Are you and Rahlen acquaintances?"

"Yes, well, no, not really. He was a friend to my mother, I think. Perhaps more. My mother told me that Rahlen was waiting for the right time and then he would take me to see a wizard named-" Daylen paused and lowered his head.

"Go on," Bolinda encouraged.

Nilderon interjected enthusiastically, not waiting for Daylen to explain. "He *must* be the one that Rahlen spoke about."

Daylen didn't want to make a fool of himself. If he mentioned he had hoped to find Zantigar, then they would most likely laugh at his ignorance. Instead, he shuffled through his wooden box and revealed the letter that Rahlen had written to his mother. "Here," he handed the letter to Bolinda. "Go ahead and read this. This letter is what brought me here, it is all I know, and it is only right that you read it."

Bolinda began reading the letter when Daylen added, "I am at a loss as to my purpose. It is important that I speak to Rahlen. I have many questions I need answered."

Bolinda smiled and handed the letter to Nilderon. After Nilderon read the note, he and Bolinda exchanged hopeful glances. Bolinda faced Daylen with a serious, somber expression. "Daylen, what I am about to tell you can never leave this room, do you understand?"

Daylen nodded.

"You are one of a select few who know of Zantigar's existence," Bolinda informed.

Daylen was confused. It couldn't be true. According to Lobire, Zantigar was alive over two hundred years ago. "You mean to tell me that Zantigar is alive?"

Bolinda continued. "He lives far to the south, deep in the heart of a wild region known as the Wanton Lands. He is alone, living in solitude and secrecy. If ever his existence were discovered, he would be hunted by every known Mageslayer in the world."

Nilderon spoke, attempting to explain. "Zantigar fought in The Final War, the war to decide the fate of all living things. The peace that followed was supposed to mark a new era for mankind, a world united. The war to preserve life instilled the ways of FéLorën.

"FéLorën is a way of life, but it is so much more. It existed before our written history. A wizard with no equal, named Erramond the Wise, found the ancient text which proved there was a world before our own. The book was FéLorën, and it was discovered on a desolate island, ten years before The Final War. The discovery changed the world. Not only did the book speak of an ancient society, a culture whose philosophy had, at one time, spread across the globe, it proved that the known history of the world was a lie, designed to hide the truth of our past, as well as the truth of our purpose in this life.

FéLorën means 'One Land,' in the ancient dialect. It was a world united in peace. The book spoke of a way to harmonious, ethical existence. It was the awakening that was required to unite the kingdoms and win The Final War. When the great evil was defeated, our modern world became known as FéLorën, to honor the union of the kingdoms and restore the rightful name of our world."

"However," Bolinda interjected, "despite the sacrifice the heroes of The Final War made for lasting peace, the ways of FéLorën faded with time. People forgot that they were one with each other and connected to all things.

The reasons for losing our way are vast, but those most responsible are those in positions of power. Humans resorted to selfish tendencies brought by the allure of greed, the Dwarves retreated back into the solitude of their mountains, and the Elves resented the other races for their failings, no longer trusting their intentions. The unity of the kingdoms is now only a superficial illusion."

"And Zantigar? What role did he play in all this?" Daylen asked.

"Having endured this injustice," Nilderon explained, "Zantigar had grown bitter. Some believe he went mad over the failings of people and their inability to live up to a higher standard. No longer concerned with worldly affairs, he fled to the hills, leaving his heroic past behind him. A hermit, Zantigar swore never to return to the affairs of mankind; to be free from the confines of a king's corrupt shadow."

Bolinda interjected. "Ending his servitude, he became a rogue, much like yourself. As a result, he was hunted, the bounty on his head greater than any rogue before him. The lucky Mageslayers were the ones who failed to find him. Those that presumably did, were never seen again. Kings had feared that one day Zantigar would return from hiding, that the knowledge he held and the stature he had among the common peasants would be enough to amass an uprising. This was enough to scare them into a relentless search, regardless of the lives that would be lost, just to find him."

"Lucky for those kings of yesterday, and much to the dismay of the poor and the suffering, time proved that Zantigar had no desire to start a rebellion, or to change the world," Nilderon concluded. "He simply disappeared."

Daylen listened, wide-eyed. This was the wizard he was to find? An angry, bitter wizard who wanted nothing to do with the known world? "The Final War… that was over two hundred years ago, correct?"

"Indeed," Nilderon said.

"And he has been in hiding for almost as long?" Daylen asked.

Nilderon reluctantly confirmed this with a nod. "As the years went by, Zantigar was presumed dead from old age. It is the only reason why he has been safe from those who would hunt him. The truth is this - Zantigar is alive and the only person who was present at the founding of modern FéLorën. If any one man has the power to bring the compassionate ways of FéLorën back into the hearts of mankind, it is he."

Bolinda added, "The people of Twilight are dedicated to living as FéLorën has guided, to the best of our ability. There is a long way to go, but Twilight is a town that denounces the ownership of people and land. We accept our strength through freedom, compassion, unity, and love. A love that is infinite and all binding. The ways of FéLorën have not gone away; it merely needs to be nourished and, like a flower, it will blossom in the hearts of people again. Twilight is proof that such a place can be, no matter how small."

Daylen could now understand why Twilight was hidden. It was a threat to the very way of the world, to those in power. It was also clear why his father did not want the Vixus knights to discover Twilight.

Nilderon directed Daylen's attention to the back of the room. A small window high on the wall allowed a solitary beam of light to fall upon a glass case positioned on a wooden pedestal. As Daylen approached, he saw that within the glass case was a large, open book. The glass was preserving its old, fragile pages.

"Is this it? This is the book of FéLorën?" Daylen asked.

"One of only three that were transcribed by Erramond the Wise, himself," Nilderon informed. "As such, it is considered to be the most faithful, pure interpretation of the original text."

Bolinda moved to Daylen's side. "This is what the elven guards protect. It is not I, nor Nilderon or Rahlen. We are of no particular significance. This book, this is the heart of Twilight. We keep it safe. We have pledged in oath to die defending it, so that future generations will not forget."

Daylen stood over the open book. Although the book was large, it was of simplistic construction. Strikingly plain, there was no embroidery or indulgence in its craftsmanship. The binding was strong, impressively holding together the weathered pages it contained. The inscription was in a simple, unassuming font, but was transcribed with the utmost care.

There is no beginning. There is no end.
The eternal eye opened and
Form came into being.
On the surface all is changing.
Within all is the same.
All form is passing, no form remains
The eternal eye is what it perceives
The eye is all. The eye is I.
I am all, and will forever be.

Daylen stepped away from the book. He was searching for the words to express his growing curiosity. Before he could speak, sudden commotion from outside Bolinda's home broke his concentration. He looked at Nilderon, and then to Bolinda.

Bolinda tilted her head, listening intently to the sound of cheers coming from beyond the walls. She turned to Daylen. When she spoke it sent a chill down Daylen's spine. "Rahlen is here."

~CHAPTER 12~

Daylen followed Bolinda and Nilderon outside. In the center of the town, amongst the tops of the trees, a crowd had gathered around Rahlen. He was everything that Daylen remembered him to be, like a manifestation from a dream. He was wrapped in a hooded, green cloak and it was torn with random spots of patchwork from prior repairs. He bore a longsword at his hip and the sheath was scarred and beaten almost as much as the boots on his feet.

As Rahlen made his way forward, children surrounded him, pulling on his sword and tugging at the bow on his back. Despite his rugged appearance, he was kind and patient with the children, tussling their hair and engaging in their play. He reached into a pouch on his belt and pulled out a hand full of coins and odd trinkets from his travels and handed them out to any who were interested. The kids responded with excitement, jumping up and down before frolicking off to play. The adults gave him a nod and shook his outstretched hand, their respect and admiration written on their faces. When Rahlen had made his way to Bolinda's home, he stopped and gave a heavy sigh, in recognition that he had made it home, at last.

"Rahlen Dimere," Bolinda said.

He extended his hand and she used it to pull him forward and smothered him in a long embrace. He kissed her forehead.

"It has been a long time," Rahlen said.

Bolinda looked up at him and he stared a moment into her eyes, saying nothing, but everything that needed to be conveyed in regard to his appreciation and contentment was written on his face.

Nilderon bowed to his old friend.

Bolinda released Rahlen from her embrace and allowed him to properly greet his old, wizard friend. It was then that Rahlen brought his attention to Daylen. There was a sparkle in his eye at the moment of realization of who it was that stood before him.

"Good day to you Rahlen; I am Daylen."

Rahlen looked misty eyed, and while he said nothing more than hello, there was nothing else needed to convey his pride.

"I have been waiting for you," Daylen said.

"And I for you. All of your life, in fact."

"I'm not sure if the time is right," Daylen began, "but-"

He was silenced with Rahlen's reassuring words. "Of course it is. The fact that you found Twilight tells me all I need to know."

Bolinda placed a hand on Rahlen and Daylen's shoulder. "Perhaps we should go inside, there is much to discuss. I will have the guards bring some food and some wine. It is cause for celebration."

After a delicious meal and pleasant conversation, Bolinda took a moment to brief Rahlen on what Daylen had been told about Twilight, the history of FéLorën, and about Zantigar.

Rahlen listened attentively, packing a long wooden pipe, his feet up on a tipped, wooden chair. Lighting the pipe, he took a drag. "There is little need to delay." He blew a thick stream of smoke, and the fragrance of herbs filled the air. Addressing Daylen, he said, "Until you are at Zantigar's side, each day that passes is a day you are not living at your full potential."

"How do I find Zantigar?" Daylen asked.

Rahlen motioned to Nilderon, who was the one who discovered the wizard's whereabouts.

Nilderon leaned forward in his seat, resting his arms in his lap. "Listen carefully," he advised. "Zantigar lives amongst a rough, mountainous region known as the Cragel Mountains. There is a small tribe of people native to the region, known simply as the Cragels, who will be able to guide you to a mystical place known as Whispering Falls. Once you pass through the cave beneath it, it is said that you will find him. Or, perhaps, he will have already found you."

There was concern in Daylen's response, "Does he know that I am coming?"

Nilderon shook his head. "Unfortunately, he is unaware of your quest, and he is unaware that we know of his hiding place. There is no way to know if he will help you. Zantigar has been insistent on secrecy and a consequence of this is the uncertainty of how he will receive you."

Bolinda poured herself her third glass of wine. "He might not take well to having his privacy disturbed, but if he is a believer in the way of FéLorën, then I have no doubt that he will accept you."

Daylen looked to Rahlen for guidance. "This journey could be for nothing?"

Rahlen met Daylen's gaze. "It is important that you have no expectations."

Rahlen appeared sympathetic to Daylen's position. "If you question your pursuit then there is nothing more to discuss. Only you can decide if you are ready. If you are, Fate will sort out the rest."

"I don't question if I should go… I'm just unsure if I can do this alone," Daylen said.

"You will not be alone," Rahlen advised. "I am going with you as far as Whispering Falls."

Daylen was shocked and by the look that Bolinda and Nilderon gave, he knew he was not alone. "You will sacrifice your time, and risk your life for me? Why?"

Rahlen shook his head. "It's not for you, it's for the cause. My fortitude stems from doing that which gives my life purpose and as I see it, our paths are aligned. Your success is our success."

Daylen believed in Rahlen far more than he believed in himself. There was comfort in knowing he had the ranger's guidance. "I will go."

"Let Fate shine upon you both." Nilderon raised his glass of wine. "And let Zantigar accept you with his good graces."

Bolinda remained silent, twirling the glass in her hand.

Rahlen blew a circle of smoke and leaned forward toward the table. "Show us what is in store for us, Nilderon."

Nilderon outstretched a map on the table. His finger trailed along the borders of Vixus, then slid south over Juniper River, covering a vast distance of plains and forests before stopping on the Cragel mountain range. "This is your destination, Daylen. Before reaching the Cragel Mountains, you will pass through the town of Juniper and the city of River Ale. These stops may provide brief sanctuary as you brave the treacherous realm of the Wanton Lands."

Rahlen disagreed. "I've found sanctuary more often in the wild than in any city, but we will need supplies and can use these locations to our advantage."

Daylen studied the map; the distance was far enough that Daylen could not fathom the time it would take. "And if I make it to Zantigar and succeed in convincing him to help me?"

Rahlen remained silent and Nilderon deferred to Bolinda for a reply.

Bolinda had been silent, observing the conversation from a distance. She scooted her chair forward and placed her hands over the map. "You learn all that you can. Win the heart of the Legionnaire in the way that only an apprentice can. Tell Zantigar of Twilight, convince him to return to the world he once fought for to rekindle the dying light of our cause."

Rahlen tapped his pipe against the side of his boot, allowing the ashes to drift to the floor. "Fate permitting, you return to Twilight with Zantigar, and we start a revolution."

~CHAPTER 13~

Twilight was shrouded in dark rain clouds. Rain fell softly, the threat of a storm brewing. Daylen walked beside Rahlen, his mind full of all he had learned and what was to come.

Rahlen lowered a ladder to the forest floor. "We won't make it to Whispering Falls without assistance."

Back on the ground of Lonely Wood, Rahlen led Daylen to a single cottage, not unlike Lobire's, where an elven woman stood. She tended a small, but flourishing garden, a wooden basket dangling from her wrist. Distracted by the woman's chore, Daylen failed to notice a large Woodsmen approaching from the door of the cottage.

The Woodsmen called out to Rahlen and Daylen took notice. His nerves tightened. This Woodsmen had a similar physique to the Woodsmen that Daylen saw on the edge of Lonely Wood, except this Woodsmen was well groomed and his skin was darker, his body chiseled with muscles from year of labor and adventure. One of his hands rested on a large utility belt around his waist. A shovel rested over his shoulder. "Great to see you, old friend!" The Woodsmen said to Rahlen.

"Likewise," Rahlen replied.

Hogar dropped his shovel to the ground and gave Rahlen a sturdy handshake. "So, you have returned to the serenity of Twilight, I see."

"Something always brings me back, my friend. There is no other place like it that I know of."

"And it has been your lifelong mission to find it," Hogar said.

Rahlen looked amused. "Perhaps."

"Good luck finding it without me," Hogar said. "Only then…"

"True enough, old friend," Rahlen replied. He motioned to Daylen. "Hogar, I would like for you to meet Daylen."

Hogar, tall as he was, kneeled to Daylen's level. "Hello, young man."

Daylen nodded.

"Daylen is Donovan Sylver's son," Rahlen informed Hogar.

Hogar stood. "Well, you don't say. I have heard a lot about you, Daylen. Pleased to make your acquaintance."

"How do you know of me?" Daylen said.

"Hogar and I have been on many adventures together," Rahlen advised. "Including a trip to Brunhylde to visit your mother. He is the closest thing I have to a brother and there is no one I trust more."

"Truer words have not been spoken," Hogar said. "And I am grateful you are home, brother."

Rahlen cut straight to the matter at hand. "I am looking for someone who might be able to assist me on an important quest. It requires someone I trust. A brother."

Hogar's face grew grim. He turned to the elven woman, who returned a worried glance. "Why don't you come inside, where we can talk more comfortably."

Daylen followed Rahlen and Hogar inside the cottage. The elven woman disappeared into the back of the house. He took a nearby empty seat and turned his attention to the lifelong friends.

"This quest is for Daylen," Rahlen said. "He needs protection through the Wanton Lands, as far as the Cragel Mountains."

Hogar was silent a moment. "Cragel Mountains, eh?" Hogar scratched at the stubble on his broad chin. "It is a long and dangerous road."

"It won't be easy," Rahlen said. "Which is why I could use your help."

The elven woman appeared in the hallway, a sadness in her eyes. A baby cried from the back room. Daylen could sense hesitation in Hogar, hanging upon the will of Hogar, who appeared stuck between the loyalty of two opposing forces.

"I am married now," Hogar said. He turned to face the elven woman. "My wife, Trishka."

Trishka nodded at Hogar's guests.

Rahlen nodded. "Good day to you, Trishka." Rahlen appeared to realize the error in his assumptions. "I… I am sorry, I should not have just showed up like this."

Hogar shook his head. "A lot has changed since you last came through Twilight. I am a farmer now."

Rahlen rose from his seat and Daylen followed Rahlen's lead.

"I want to go with you, Rahlen," Hogar said, sensing Rahlen's discomfort. "You saved my life on more than one occasion."

Rahlen waved his hand in defiance. "And you have saved mine, you have no obligation to me. Your duty is to your home and your wife. I should not have intruded." He turned to address Trishka. "I appreciate your time, and it was a pleasure to meet you." He nudged for Daylen to follow and bid farewell to his friend.

Rahlen led Daylen out of the cottage and walked toward the rope ladder.

"Wait!" Hogar's voice called out from behind them.

Daylen turned and saw Hogar approach. He carried a double-bladed axe in his hand. "My wife and I would not be fortunate to live in this peaceful place if not for what we had accomplished together. If taking the boy to Cragel Mountains is important to Twilight's cause, then I cannot sit here idle. I must fight for its survival."

"Your wife's opinion must be taken into consideration." Rahlen said.

"I have her blessing," Hogar said.

There was a long pause before Rahlen responded. "Then we are lucky to have you with us."

As they walked, Daylen glanced to the cottage and could see the elven woman's silhouette in the window. There was a baby in her arms. It left a sentimental impression, her presence in the window as they walked away. She had to be sad. It felt wrong to separate Hogar from her. The separation of family and the consequences it had on a child were troubling to him and it was something he understood all too well. He had to make sure the sacrifice they were making was worth it, which meant he would do everything in his power not to let his companions down. The future unclear, he turned to scale the wooden ladder into Twilight.

~CHAPTER 14~

Bolinda offered Daylen a bedroom above Twilight tavern, which he gratefully accepted. He unlaced his boots and sat at the edge of his bed. The day had been exhausting, and he appreciated the solitude the room afforded. The window provided a grand view of Twilight and the treetops. For a moment, he thought of his home in Brunhylde. It was a miracle he made it this far, he thought, and when his thoughts went to the future, he wondered how Zantigar would receive him.

A knock came at the door, and he was slow to rise. Moving across the room, he opened the door.

"Good evening," Rahlen said. "How are your accommodations?"

"Wonderful; I will make sure to thank Bolinda before we leave." Daylen stepped aside to allow Rahlen to enter.

"Anything I can do?" Rahlen asked.

"I don't know what to say," Daylen said. His focus was fixed on the sacrifice Rahlen and Hogar had made to help him. "I appreciate everything you are doing."

"We, of Twilight, have been waiting a long time for another wizard. It is worth the effort, to me, to all of us. Although, I don't get the impression you feel the same. What is troubling you?"

"I am doubtful of our success. The consequences of failure, the stakes, it is a matter of life and death."

"You are in good hands," Rahlen said.

"I know." Daylen lowered his gaze to the floor. "But I don't want to let you down."

"Stay alive, and you will have returned the favor. What is important is the gifts that you will be able to share with others one day, once you have studied magic and the ways of FéLorën with Zantigar."

"He is a Legionnaire, isn't he?"

Rahlen looked amused by Daylen's curiosity. "If there was a title to give to one greater than a Legionnaire, he would have it."

Daylen forced a small smile.

Rahlen placed his hand on Daylen's shoulder. "I will do everything in my power to protect you. We- Hogar and I, we won't fail you." Rahlen proceeded toward the door. "Sleep well. Tomorrow, our quest begins."

"I feel as though I am at the edge of world," Daylen said.

Rahlen turned at the door. "That sounds like a perceptive awareness of the present moment. You are about to embark on a great quest. Years of wondering, waiting, have led to this point in time. Embrace this moment. Do not poison it with fears of tomorrow."

Daylen lowered his head. Memories of childhood returned to him. Memories of Rahlen visiting him. Maybe it was the look in Rahlen's eyes, or the safety of his presence, but for a moment, Daylen wondered if this feeling was what it felt like to have a father. "What if Zantigar does not accept me?"

Rahlen stepped away from the door and returned to Daylen's side. "Do you want to know a secret?"

Daylen raised his eyebrows in anticipation.

"Zantigar helps you, or Zantigar does not, it makes no difference."

Daylen looked skeptical. "How can you say that?"

"Because the pursuit is what matters. Nothing more. Whatever happens, is okay as it happens. It is as it was intended to transpire. That is not to say that everything happens for a reason, per se, maybe it does, maybe it doesn't. But things work out as they should, even when it feels like they don't. That is trust, trust in Nature to do not what is best for you, but what is best for all. Sometimes it works in your favor, and sometimes it does not."

"So, if Zantigar turns me away. I haven't failed?"

"No more than Zantigar has failed to see a good thing when it comes his way. A Legionnaire can make mistakes, too." Rahlen turned and reached for the door. "This is not a world of pass or fail, but of simply navigating one situation to another to the best of your ability. What will matter, at the end of the day, is the life you led, what you stood for, not what came of it."

Rahlen opened the door and was startled to see Bolinda standing in the hall.

She looked up at him with a mischievous glance. "I was eaves dropping."

"I can see that," Rahlen said with a smile. "Did you acquire what you were looking for?"

"Why yes, I actually came to speak with you," she confessed. "To both of you."

Rahlen opened the door fully, so she could enter.

Bolinda moved to the center of the room, nodded to Daylen and then turned to face Rahlen. "I am coming with you."

Rahlen looked surprised. "You want to join us on our quest?"

Bolinda nodded. "Yes, I need this." She turned to Daylen as if looking for his approval.

Daylen, shocked, looked to Rahlen. "Yes, please. I don't know what else to say, other than thank you."

Rahlen knew better than to resist her wishes. "I agree, it will be a pleasure to have you."

Bolinda, expecting the need to state her case, was pleased with the ease of their acceptance. She turned to Daylen. "Listen to Rahlen, Daylen. What he speaks is true. It is our effort that matters and nothing else."

Rahlen guided Bolinda toward the door. "We should leave Daylen to ensure he gets proper rest. Tomorrow is a big day; for all of us."

Bolinda nodded, bowed to Daylen and followed Rahlen out of the room, closing the door behind them, leaving Daylen with much to reflect upon as he crawled into bed. Sleep would not come easy, but when it overtook him, it was deep.

*   *   *

During the night, Daylen had a dream. He stood on a cliff, one side of a wide chasm. A strange figure stared at him from the other side. The figure looked familiar, from a distant dream. It occurred to him the stranger was the same figure he saw in Lonely Wood when he blacked out. He shouted toward the stranger, longing to understand who he was. The divide was too far for him to jump across. His footing escaped him and he began to fall down the cliff. Tumbling to his death, he woke moments before smashing against the rocks below.

Rahlen stood over him. "Daylen, wake up. It is time."

PART II

THE QUEST

G.
G.

"Blind is the wave that believes it is separate from other waves, that does not recognize itself as the ocean; aware only of the chaotic surface and oblivious to the calm depths below."

- Erramond the Wise, 13 B.F.

~CHAPTER 1~

North, past the kingdom of Vixus, Mullen Empire sprawled across the land of Valice. For generations, Mullen rivaled with its southern neighbor, Vixus, competing for territory and debating over difficult trade policies. Military growth drove the peace between the two kingdoms, but it would take a single event to tip the tides of power and rock the balance that kept them at a safe distance.

There was nothing more threatening to the fragile state of peace than that of the Desert Portal. It stood between the two empires, beckoning to be conquered. The Desert Portal, in all its mystery, was believed to be the key to enormous power, with unimaginable wealth and resources within. This potential led to a series of escalating skirmishes that all but ended the peace that existed since The Final War. Declaration of war between Mullen and Vixus never came to fruition, so the lives lost on both sides were omitted from historical record. However, the aftermath of such feuding caused the desert sands to be covered in the blood of many soldiers on both sides, so that the desert became known as the Redlands, and the path which led to the portal was named the Trail of Lost Souls. The Redlands remained unclaimed and the Desert Portal, itself, was possessed by no empire.

The Trail of Lost Souls was treacherous. It was home to many wild beasts, scorching heat, and violent sandstorms. Nevertheless, there were a brave few who made it to the gates of the Desert Portal. After entering, they never returned to tell their tale. The Desert Portal remained a mystery, its secrets tempting the greatest heroes. Mullen's army had suffered catastrophic losses as a result of the battles with Vixus, and valiant knights in their attempt to explore the portal. This forced Mullen to rely heavily on Mullen Academy for new recruits and new spells replace the losses they incurred.

At the heart of Mullen Academy, in its upper echelon, lived a sorceress named Muranda. She had spent the last twenty years of her life in service, trained by the greatest Legionnaires of her kingdom. The power of the empire rested in her spell book and her thin, frail hands. She had convinced King Mullen III that if anyone had the strength to conquer the Desert Portal, it was she.

However, power was not what she longed for. Even though she had reached the status of Legionnaire, there was no spell in her book that could cure the pain that plagued her heart. She longed for Sir Robyn, a just and skillful Mullen Lord, who had promised to marry her upon his return from the Desert Portal. While others desired fame and wealth, his decision to brave his way through the gates of the portal had been a failed attempt to prove his love for her. Proof that Muranda never needed. His mad obsession with the portal jeopardized their love, something he swore would never end. Tear stricken, she waited in her tower for his return. There was no solace for her grief as the months turned to years.

From her window, Muranda watched over her land with an empty, dying heart. Believing the worst fate had fallen on Sir Robyn. She longed to enter the portal, prepared to sacrifice her life if not just to be reunited with her one true love. After years of sorrow, there was nothing worth living for, and no greater motivator than love, to take a chance and cross to the other side of the Desert Portal gate.

Tonight, the moon shined bright, the rain fell like soft whispers, and a cool breeze chilled her. Tonight, like every night, she cried.

"Tonight…"

The voice startled Muranda. She looked around her empty room. "Is there anybody there?"

The wind rose, animating the curtains with ghost-like life, and chilled her skin through her thin night garment. Muranda rushed to the window and closed the shutters. She took a seat at her desk and stared at her reflection in a large oval mirror. Flowing red hair framed her soft, pale face and her dull, faded green eyes were filled with sorrow and longing.

Through the mirror she saw shadow shift behind her.

"Tonight…"

Muranda jumped from her seat, positive to have heard the voice, certain of a presence within the room. "Who is there?" She commanded in a brave voice.

"Show yourself, or I shall make you suffer." Her eyes were no longer sorrowful, but glaring with anger. She appeared alone.

"Tonight…" The voice whispered against her ear. She could feel breath against her bare neck.

She turned to find nothing. An overwhelming sensation of grief struck her, and she feared she was losing her mind. It was as if the presence she felt had found a way to penetrate her psyche, feed on her sadness and weaken her mind.

Fearful, she moved to her bed. She grabbed a portrait of Sir Robyn at her nightstand and brought it close to her breast, burying her face in her pillow.

"Muranda?" the voice whispered from the shadows.

In the voice, she felt longing, desperation as if in search of a lost soul. "Robyn?" Her voice was weak, escaping like a gentle, hopeful breath.

"Muranda, where are you?"

She rose from her bed, expecting to see Sir Robyn's ghost, saw a dark, undiscernible shape floating above her bed. She sighed, unafraid, and fell back into bed, her red hair flowing across the crumpled sheets. Her chest heaved as she clutched the portrait tight against her. "Hello, Death," Muranda caught herself saying. "I am ready to join my love."

The Dark One appeared from the shadows and raised his silver cane above her body. He spoke as he lowered the onyx stone at the cane's tip upon her forehead. His voice was the voice of many. "Robyn is not in here, with us. You will never see him again!"

Muranda's face contorted in horror as she realized her death was not going to bring her the peace she sought. Her impulse was to rise and strike Death in the face, but it was too late. Her body twitched in spasms as the onyx stone pulled at her soul. Her eyes rolled back and blood poured from her mouth, drowning her screams. She moaned in pain, as her soul was stripped from her body, imprisoned within the onyx stone.

* * *

King Mullen III awoke the following morning to the news of his prized wizard's death. Muranda's spell book had disappeared, which was a tremendous loss to the kingdom. The state of Muranda's lifeless body, colorless eyes, and face frozen in an expression of terror made it evident that she had suffered death at the hands of the Dark One. It was clear that the Dark One was as powerful as the myths suggested. The king called for a meeting with his trusted advisors. It was determined that there was only one thing to be done; to call upon the High Council of FéLorën.

~CHAPTER 2~

There was absolute darkness and the emptiness of utter silence. Blind to all material objects, the lone figure sat receptive, finding no separation between himself and the darkness. Aware of silence, Beauty was the silence.

His name being spoken disrupted his concentration. Beauty strained his eyes, unable to see. He reached out his hand into the darkness, but the candle was not where he had left it. Blind, he spoke, "Popi, Popi is that you?

"Vamillion will be here soon," Popi said.

"Oh, Popi, it is you!" It has been so long."

"Days," Popi reminded.

Beauty squinted his eyes in a helpless attempt to see through the darkness. "I would not know of days, Popi, not from within here, within the dark."

Beauty saw a spark and then a candle was lit, revealing Popi's thin, long face and dark, elven skin. His eyes were the brilliant color of emeralds.

"We don't have much timc. Vamillion is on her way."

"What is it, Popi? Tell me."

"As if I need to? You, of all people, know the outcome of all things. You… inside that beautiful mind of yours."

Beauty's prophecies always unfolded in waves, triggered by specific words or thoughts. He felt it had always been Popi's intention to bring forth the visions. Beauty knew that today would be no different. Although he feared what Popi would cause him to see, he cherished Popi's visits, as his days were spent alone.

"Tell me what you know of shadow prophecy," Popi said.

"Shadow prophecy?" He questioned, curious.

The candlelight revealed a disturbing smile on Popi's slender face.

"Popi… Are you up to no good?"

Popi ignored Beauty's question. "What you see is always truth. Every prediction you have made has been correct. Your mind has proven to be a very powerful weapon. Could it be that you have visions of the future? Or does the future bend to your visions? Who is the puppeteer?"

"I am no god, Popi, if that is what you are implying." Beauty was humored at the thought. "I see the future like pictures in a book, clear as I see you now."

Popi shook his head. "It does not really matter how it happens, Beauty. All Vamillion understands is that whenever you predict something it happens. Do you see the power of persuasion at your command? You can convince Vamillion to do whatever you want her to do. This is the basis for shadow prophecy... making one believe that what you say is going to happen, so that the true events of the future can unravel."

Beauty sat a moment in silence. The clarity of Popi's words sunk in, slowly. He saw waves of disturbing events unfold in his mind. He shook his head in defiance of what he saw, overwhelmed by the catastrophic events the future held. He mumbled something incoherent and felt a sense of déjà vu. His one, good eye widened. "The book of time is unraveling. It is spawned by shadow prophecy."

Popi watched with a devious smile. "So you understand? How knowledge, once discovered, can never be unlearned."

"Yes..." Beauty spoke as if he was half inside a dream, mesmerized and terrified by visions only he could see. He knew what he must do. He would tell false fortune to Vamillion, and like his puppet, she would carry out the inevitable future. Although he remained her prisoner, he was now the master. Instead of a spectator, he was now a pawn in the game of life.

Beauty heard the lock to his chamber unlatching. Popi blew out the candle and drowned Beauty in a world of darkness. His eyes could not adjust and he panicked at the realization that his friend had left him, disappearing as he often did, without a trace, as if he were never there at all.

"Beauty?" Vamillion's voice shattered the stillness. Her chilling voice sent shivers down his spine. He waited, watching from the shadows, as the light from the world above poured onto the dungeon floor.

"Beauty?" Vamillion called again. "Do not play games. Light a candle so that I may see you."

Beauty did as he was told, he reached his hand into the darkness and found the candle that once was not there. Or was it? He thought. He lit the candle.

"Ah, there you are, my child. I heard you speaking to someone. Talking to your imaginary friend again?"

Beauty remained silent.

"Today is an important day for me and I would like for you to cooperate as much as possible."

Every day was important to Vamillion, Beauty thought. Her urgent demands had led to violence upon him in the past and he knew better than to upset her. "What is it, mother?"

"What do you think I want?" She snapped. "You think I have time for games? I want the future. Tomorrow I am leaving for Mullen."

Beauty knew about Mullen, and what was to transpire. He could not hold back a smile.

Vamillion continued, not aware of Beauty's mischievous glare. "I have been called upon to attend a meeting with the High Council of FéLorën. What they wish to discuss can have a tremendous effect on the land of Valice."

Beauty closed his one good eye and thought of the meeting. The event, like a stone, fell into the river of time. Frame by frame, like the rippling of waves, the future ran through his mind. The future, only possible if he did as Popi suggested. He would give Vamillion a shadow prophecy, nothing short of a bold face lie. "I see the meeting. There is confusion and mistrust."

"Explain what you see!" Vamillion's excitement was mixed with impatience.

Regardless of the consequence, Beauty knew what he must say, he could envision his next words, like a shadow enslaved to that which casts it. "Fear Mullen, for their army is growing. Soon, they will wage war with us."

Vamillion shuddered. She raised her slender hands to her mouth. "This cannot be… How? And yet… how could I have been so blind as not to see?" She looked away, her mind racing, trying to put the pieces together. Trying to make sense of Mullen's intentions, she spoke, "Perhaps that is precisely the point. It is madness, and it is exactly why it would work. We would never suspect such a move…" She turned quickly to face Beauty. "If not for you."

"It is true," Beauty lied.

"You must tell me when. Tell me all that you know."

Beauty lowered his eyes from Vamillion's stare, fearful that she would be able to read through his lies. Yet he moved his gaze back to her when he spoke again, for the words he now said were true. "Never; as you will strike first. I see death. So much death." Beauty knew that Vamillion would never give up the element of surprise. She would strike first; she would start a war.

Vamillion appeared to struggle with processing all she heard. There was much to plan, much to discuss before her trip to see the High Council in Mullen. These details would be worked out with Beauty before the night was through. The madness she feared in Mullen was now her own. "If war is what Mullen wants, then war is what they will have!"

~CHAPTER 3~

The High Council of FéLorën comprised of a select few wizards, known as Elders, who were the keepers of the ancient ways of FéLorën. They represented the supreme authority of the land, having been formed to keep the peace after The Final War. The war in which the races united to defeat the army of Omnias, and the world of Heldon reclaimed its original name of FéLorën.

As wise, powerful beings, the Elders were selected to shape the new world, and were once the most respected people in the world. Now, after generations, they were reduced to mere figureheads representing a philosophy that was becoming lost. However, their status did come with power, and they were requested by kings, chieftains and leaders alike in times of desperation, when ancient wisdom was sought. The High Council was called upon as a final measure to resolve issues that modern practices and modern views could not.

On the continent of Valice, there were twelve Elders. It had been many years since their assistance was needed. However, King Mullen III requested the audience of the High Council, and as tradition allowed, all kingdoms were invited to participate. It was a call to action that reminded the world that the teachings of the Elders, the ways of FéLorën, still held a place in society. As such, all the powerful clans across the continent of Valice sent representatives to Mullen Castle.

The Dwarves of Red Mountain sent their chief advisor, Brey. He was an old dwarven warrior adorned in ceremonial armor and a striking horned helmet, fashioned with jewels from their mining caves. The Braxton Dwarves from Thunder Mountain sent their noble gnomes in honor of their kingdom. Elven nations, such as Fey Zynx, sent their two top diplomats. Various wood elf tribes made a showing, as well, dressed in natural clothing of their forests with matching organic jewelry, and tattooed skin. The elves of Xyntharia sent their enchanting elven priestess, Xynara, and several elven clerics. The Xyntharians' flamboyant dress and brilliant glimmering decorations made a striking impression.

An orc chieftain, from one of the more civilized orc populations, commander Turtleskin, made his appearance. His entourage of orc warriors and servants in tow. His ceremonial chains and mix-matched armor of leather and steel was in stark contrast to the other cultures around him.

Many human tribes came to Mullen. The MacNeil Clan was represented by King MacNeil, himself, which was an honorable gesture. There was a priest from Ederin, a wizard from Fairland, and Vamillion, the High Priestess of Vixus.

Over two hundred figures of royalty and influence found themselves in King Mullen III's Great Hall, sitting amongst each other at large oval tables. Flags and banners of each tribe colored the hall and golden chandeliers hung from the high ceiling. Shiny goblets covered the polished surfaces of the tables. At the head of the center oval table was King Mullen III, and as the host of the evening, the seats before him were reserved for the twelve members of the High Council of FéLorën.

King Mullen bowed graciously to his guests and all visiting delegates returned a bow to King Mullen and then to the twelve elders, before taking their seats. "Thank you all," King Mullen said, sitting, "for attending this banquet in honor of the High Council of FéLorën. As I look out before me, I see the likes of many glorious empires. Kings, queens, wizards and clerics, priests and warrior chieftains… Let me welcome you, with deep, heartfelt enthusiasm, to the kingdom of Mullen, and to these proceedings. Seeing you all here, now, makes me realize what an extraordinary land the continent of Valice truly is. For those who reside on continents beyond our seas, and to those few kingdoms on Valice that could not have representation with us this evening, let me quickly send a prayer and a reminder that the spirit of your kingdoms are present and hope the light finds you well. In the words of the Elders, 'diversity defines the one,' and this gathering is proof of how brilliant and beautiful our unity is. I am saddened to think how long it has been since our last gathering. Yet, I am overjoyed to see there is still an underlying peace amongst us all, and tonight, we honor our connection by coming together."

King Mullen III raised his goblet. The guests followed, raising theirs.

One of the Elders was a stock, old, dwarf named Galeck. "On behalf of the High Elders of FéLorën, let me express our gratitude for your decision to call forth these proceedings within your kingdom, and for your hospitality."

King Mullen III nodded. "I think I speak for all of us within this room, when I say that it is an honor to be of service to you."

Xyvandia, an elven Elder on the High Council, stood. In contrast to the warm smiles of those who surrounded him, his face was stern and grave. All in attendance gave the elf their full attention. "And us, ever in service to all of you. If only such meetings were to be held in more pleasant circumstances. As it is, it is unrest which brings us together this evening. There is a troublesome issue that concerns us all. An entity, of which its origins we do not know, has been taking the lives of wizards far and wide in a brutal, violent manner. The very mention of this entity strikes fear in all wizardborn. Its influence and power is opposed by us all. It goes by many names to many cultures, but I believe it is universally accepted and understood to be known, quite simply, as the Dark One. The legends and myths around this figure have traveled far and wide, to all corners of the world.

"No one has ever seen this presence and lived. There has been speculation as to whether this entity even exists, but the murders are real, and they continue. Let us take a moment to reflect upon this grave concern that is haunting the minds of my fellow council members, and the primary reason King Mullen III has called for council."

Outbursts of opinions filled the Great Hall. A mere scoundrel, was the opinion of one vocal guest, whose perspective was met with boos. Death, Himself, was exclaimed by another, to enormous agreement from many. Some referred to the Dark One as the spirit of Erramond the Wise, who had returned to the land to punish those who had failed to live by the teachings of FéLorën. Most agreed that the Dark One was not of this world and it was suggested that it was a presence that emerged from the portals, from a dimension beyond their own.

Through the loud conversations and opinions no one could hear the heartfelt voice of a seemingly common man within the audience. He tried to gain the attention of those around him, but to no avail. He pressed his way through the crowd and stood upon one of the oval tables, kicking the goblets to the ground in a loud clatter.

"By the gods!" King Mullen III shouted. The hall was silenced, and all eyes fixed on the guest standing above them.

His face was cluttered with deep scars. One of his eyes scanned the audience, daring someone to contest him, the other was buried beneath a thick scar, the wound visible beyond the edges of his dark eye patch. "My name is Derek Bon. I am a bounty hunter from the town of Adon, found in the land of Fairland. I am a Mageslayer, specifically, and I have seen the Dark One."

His proclamation silenced the hall at once. Having the undivided attention of the many in attendance, he continued, "I was hunting a rogue wizard through the Redlands. My quest brought me to the Trail of Lost Souls, as I edged, ever nearer, toward my bounty." Derek's voice was mixed with bold, wild passion and troubling fear.

Derek continued. "Far beyond a sandy dune, I heard the faint sound of someone's voice. I crept low to the ground as I made my way up the sand, careful not to make my presence known. Until I spotted the rogue wizard I was searching for, lying on his back, in pain. He was speaking in a whimper, like a loon, as if talking to someone, but there was no one there. I assumed that he had gone mad from the heat of the desert. I was just about to make my way to him when I saw it. A black apparition, complete darkness, like a void of emptiness against the horizon. A tear in the very fabric of reality from which a shape shifted and swayed like the heat waves from the tops of the rolling dunes. A mirage, I thought, a simple trick of the mind, but it changed shape with such complexity, molding into various unrecognizable forms, that it was beyond what my simple mind could fathom."

Derek stepped from table to table until he was above the Elders, where King Mullen III resided. Guards began to advance from their position on the walls, but King Mullen III waved his hand in command for them to halt.

Derek crouched to his knee and looked to the elders. "A feeling came over me. I was stricken with terror. Absolute terror. This entity, it was the reflection of pure evil. The words the Dark One spoke I could not make out from my position, but it seemed as though the voice was the voice of many voices speaking in unison, like demons from the hells below. A silver cane emerged from the shadowy blackness and rested on the wizard's forehead. After that-" Derek shook his head, as if unwilling to believe what his own eyes had witnessed. "After that, I saw the wizard's essence being ripped from his body and enter the silver cane. I sat in fear, I could not move. Yet, my presence had been detected. After the Dark One placed the silver cane back into the deep void of its being, it turned and looked directly at me. From the black probed two red, beady eyes which shined like fire from the underworld. My heart stopped for a moment and I felt as if I were drowning in my own fears. I must have blinked, my eyes teared up. Rubbing my eyes for but a moment, all at once, the figure was gone."

There was a silence that filled the Great Hall. It lasted a moment, and then came the sound of two hundred guests erupting into gossip. Derek Bon jumped down from the table and rushed toward the nearest exit. He was swarmed by spectators who demanded to know more. He slipped through the crowd when the guests were startled by the loud banging on the table from King Mullen III, who exclaimed he needed order.

As soldiers filed out in search of Derek Bon, a human Elder on the council stood to address the guests. "The words of Derek Bon may or may not be true. The fact remains, no one knows who or what the Dark One is. No wizard is safe until we understand what is going on. We, the Elders, cannot find anything within the text of FéLorën to explain this phenomenon, or instruct us on how to banish it. Is there anyone among us who can confirm the words of Derek Bon? Is there anyone who has a clue as to the explanation of this mysterious entity? Is there one amongst you that can shed light upon our predicament?"

Vamillion had watched in silence, amused by the amount of time the guests debated and theorized as to the Dark One's identity. They were fools, all of them, she thought. They did not know that the Dark One was a powerful god, and since she began to worship the entity, it was if her life was blessed with purpose and power. She felt the Dark One gave her Beauty, the child prince of King Averath, that the Dark One guided her in the creation of the School of Necromancy and led to her dominance and rule of Vixus in the shadow of Queen Abigail.

Not one of the guests in council, nor the Elders themselves, could pinpoint what she had come to understand, and it gave her the edge required to assume dominance over the other kingdoms of the world.

King Mullen III stood and addressed his guests after a long debate, grabbing the audience's attention with his stern voice. "It appears we have yet to understand and learn of our mysterious threat. Based off our discussions, each kingdom will donate resources and minds to the threat of the Dark One, and the High Council of FéLorën has agreed to act as liaison over these matters. What one kingdom learns shall be shared with all kingdoms, so that we might face this threat, together. In unity is strength."

The crowd repeated. "In unity, strength."

King Mullen III bowed. "Now, with the council's presence, and with such prestigious representatives of the many rulers of Valice, I would like to take a moment to address a concern that is personal to my people, so we might find a common understanding and resolution.

"My kingdom is in dire need of expansion. Aware that land is precious to us all, I have set my sights on a region that none occupy. It is the Redlands that I have set my sights. Expansion would better the lives of my people, who are struggling to live off land that is running out of resources and room for our growing population. We have become too dependent on trade and this has cost my kingdom a fortune, the burden of which rests heavy on my people. By moving into the Redlands, we can begin to mine and reap the rewards of minerals and spices that would aid our trade and lessen our deficit."

The representatives of Valice that were present grew silent, for they knew of the controversies surrounding the Redlands, and the violent struggle that has taken place between the Mullen and Valice.

King Mullen III turned to High Priestess Vamillion, directly. "Priestess of Vixus, please speak to your Queen, so that we may come to an arrangement that is beneficial to us all. Certainly, there is something in our vast kingdom, a service that can be afforded by one of our many tradesmen that will compensate you for granting us the Redlands. We are prepared to provide a thirty percent investment in the mining of the Redlands for ten ages. Ten percent beyond that, for the rest of time. Vixus would reap the rewards, without the labor."

Vamillion remained silent, listening with grave concern spawned from a deeper understanding. Based on Beauty's prophecy, she assumed this was Mullen's first move to attempt to claim the Desert Portal, to close in on Vixus. She did not believe King Mullen III's intentions were true.

"An increase in military production is required," King Mullen III continued. "A stronger military presence would protect the workers. Sacrificing my soldiers to cleanse the Trail of Lost Souls is a price I am willing to pay to civilize a section of Valice that has been long overrun with wild beasts and exiles. It is an effort that I see will benefit us all."

High Elder Xyvandia said, "It appears King Mullen III has honorable intention in his expansion and for the growth of his military forces. You have done a great service by asking permission from us, and considering our opinion. You have our blessing to proceed with negotiations with Valice. Fate permitting, you will sign an agreement that is mutually beneficial. Be sure that the final agreement is delivered to the High Council for our records."

King Mullen III bowed his head to the Elder and then turned to Vamillion.

"I am certain that we can come to a pleasant arrangement," Vamillion said.

"Splendid!" King Mullen III roared, raising his glass.

Vamillion silently scoffed. How frivolous the discussion had been. The High Council's blessing was meaningless. They were trapped in the past, in a time of peace, when times were changing faster than they could understand. Beauty had foreseen Mullen's advancement, but this could not be conveyed to the Council. The knowledge was her burden to bear. The Council was oblivious to the power of the Dark One. To protect her people, she would take matters into her own hands. For now, she would play along.

The evening continued with song and drink over trades and arrangements between kingdoms. Vamillion entertained all of Mullen's suggestions, thinking it best to not let on that she was aware of his plans to invade. Over the next couple days, she helped King Mullen III draft a proposal that she felt Queen Abigail would agree to. It was a generous offer for Valice, Vamillion believing the generosity from Mullen was due to the fact that they had no intention of honoring the arrangement. Vamillion was not going to be blinded by kindness.

*　　　　*　　　　*

When Vamillion returned to Valice, she held private council with Queen Abigail. She explained Mullen's intent to advance, but failed to mention the generous offerings, or an explanation of what Vamillion believed to be an excuse to advance in neutral territory. She didn't even bother to show her the proposal that was written. Instead, she informed the Queen as to King Mullen III's true intention, explaining that Mullen received the blessing of the High Council to advance into the Redlands.

Queen Abigail was rightfully troubled by the news. "This goes against the treaty we had worked so hard to maintain over the years. How are we supposed to maintain peace and harmony under these conditions?"

Vamillion responded, "The High Council is blind to our concerns. They are also powerless to stop Mullen Empire's true intent; to claim the Desert Portal and remove us from the land! Beauty has prophesized as much. There is nothing left of peace and harmony and I question if it ever existed. It has been an illusion, a meaningless treaty, signed by a meaningless council. A new age is upon us and the Dark One is proof of this. It is empowering to realize the lies and deceit of FéLorën, that there is no such thing as union amongst empires, lest we allow ourselves to be destroyed in the process."

"Be careful what you say," Queen Abigail pleaded. "By the gods, I beg you. It is treasonous to the High Council to speak as you do."

"FéLorën is gone, don't you see? Did the gods not make us in their image? And what are we but violent, selfish, and deceitful worms. The world is suffering from an unrecognizable disease. The teachings of FéLorën only hide the truth of our cold existence behind a veil of lies.

"The Dark One, now that is a god worth worshipping. He has allowed me to see past the political nonsense that binds the weaker kingdoms to false philosophies and dying gods. To rise above our pathetic state of existence requires power, don't you see? Power is not gained from sitting around waiting for handouts or preaching shallow words of harmony. Look to the harsh lessons of the wilderness, look to the ravishing patterns of history… it's about crushing your opposition, taking what you want by whatever means necessary. To survive, for our people to survive, we must act."

Vamillion caught her reflection in the window, noticed the passion in her eyes. She felt as if she were waking from a dream, and it was the threat of Mullen invading which brought clarity to her mind. Beauty's prophecy had revealed Mullen's true intentions and she realized she could no longer wait to make her move. There was much that needed to be planned, and quickly. She caught Queen Abigail staring at her through the reflection of the window. "You think I have lost my mind? Truth is, I am awake, at last. If evil is what this land is really driven by, then I will own it, so it is mine to control. Once controlled, only then can evil be vanquished."

Vamillion looked deeper at her reflection. "Power is what protects us. What greater love is there than that which provides protection? Power; is love." She lowered her gaze. "We have no allies in this world, we have ourselves. Tomorrow, you will gather The Knights of Brownstone, inform them that Mullen is preparing to go to war with our people. Tell them we will not wait to receive them."

"If it must be done," Queen Abigail said.

"Weak rulers die, Abigail. Just as King Averath died." Vamillion reminded. "Beauty predicted it. We shall do what must be done."

Queen Abigail nodded in understanding.

"We will build our forces and strike before they have any idea what has hit them. When our forces are ready, you will stand before the people and you will tell them that we shall protect them, that we shall not fail them. In time, you will be remembered in history as a hero to your people."

~CHAPTER 4~

Beauty thought of the years ahead with dread and unrest. The visions shown to him, triggered by conversations with Popi, led him into a panic. He knew he would not know peace until he could speak to Popi again. As if answering Beauty's prayers, Popi was beside him, dressed as a jester and face painted as a clown. Beauty frowned.

"Why so sad, friend?"

"The future…" Beauty whispered as he looked to the ground.

"Is glorious," Popi suggested. "Vamillion did just as you asked her to do. She has prepared for war with Mullen and the High Council of FéLorën will be exposed as a powerless institution, once the world catches wind that their wishes have been undermined." Popi walked on his toes, balancing on the cracks in the floor with his arms outstretched.

"What is glorious about any of this?"

"It is not your fault, Beauty. Remember you are just reading history, just playing your part."

"Not anymore." Beauty felt like an instrument of a grander design, disliking his role in history. Before shadow prophecy, he had been an outsider, a casual observer. There was pleasure in his separation from the world. As if it somehow made him not a part of all the wickedness his visions revealed. It was the only thing that made his prison tolerable. "It is my fault, the war to come. I sent Vamillion to the High Council with a suspicious mind. I could have stopped her."

"But not the war," Popi reminded. "Your prophecy already ensured it. Who knows what would have happened had you not warned Vamillion. You have protected your people. In any case, what would happen if you destroyed the delicate web of time and changed history as you wished? Perhaps, the world as you know it would come to an end." Popi smiled. "Your part, the future, it has to happen!"

"Why, Popi?"

Popi performed a cartwheel, landing to his feet beside Beauty's dresser. "Why? Why anything? It is not for us to know. Just be glad for your part in the play."

"Play? Is that what all of this is? The future will be more frightening than you know. You are just a clown and do not know everything. There is something wrong with the world and not even you are safe, Popi."

Popi's eyes widened, and he placed his hand to his chest. "Me? I am just a dream, Beauty, a figment of your imagination. Remember? Don't start getting confused."

Beauty turned away. "You are real to me, and that is what matters. You alone listen to me. Hear me now, when I tell you the Dark One is poisoning the world."

Popi's eyes gleamed with excitement. "The Dark One is playing a part, just as you play yours." Popi seemed to feel Beauty's inner turmoil. "I know what you must do."

Beauty raised his head, hopeful of Popi's words.

"Remain silent. If you refuse to say anything more to Vamillion than you will no longer feel responsible for anything. Your conscious will be cleared. Besides, you know more than anybody that there is nothing more you can do."

Popi had a calm, collective mindset and had always had a way of speaking to Beauty that put him at ease. Beauty rose to his feet. "But I don't know how it is all going to end."

"We will figure out the ending together," Popi said, leaning against the dresser. "We both know you are helplessly lost without me."

In that moment, Beauty was frightened of Popi's clown-like face, the smile beneath the exaggerated, painted smile. It mocked his tormented mind. "No, Popi, the future is mine, alone, to bear. There is nothing you can do."

Popi jumped onto Beauty's dresser, his short legs dangling inches above the ground. The bells at the end of his pointed shoes jingled. "I am here for you. After all, you created me. I will always look after you."

"I am glad for that. One day, Vamillion will change, right Popi? Good has to prevail."

"Good? Bad? It's not really relevant. Do as I suggested; and speak no more of the future to Vamillion. She has all that she needs to know."

Popi's words caused a glimpse of the future to unravel in Beauty's mind, but it was hazy. It was just as Popi suggested. He realized he would do as Popi said and remain silent, no matter how furious it made Vamillion. Assuming it was destiny's plan, he vowed never to tell another prophecy to Vamillion, no matter what his visions predicted. This thought put his mind at ease and removed any fear of responsibility for the future. "How am I supposed to remain silent?

Before Popi could answer, Beauty heard the door to his chamber open. Without notice, Popi was gone, no longer dangling from the dresser.

Vamillion entered with a smile on her face. "I have a present for you, Beauty." She placed a large mirror on Beauty's desk.

Beauty raised his hand to the glass and marveled at the reflection that mimicked his every move. He had never seen a mirror before. When he raised his hand to stroke the mirror's smooth surface, he saw the hand in the mirror's reflection do the same. "This is… me?"

Beauty ran a finger across his facial scars. With caution, he touched his artificial right eye.

"I did a good job, didn't I?" Vamillion said. "You can hardly tell the eye is fake."

Beauty disagreed. The artificial eye rested behind scars, within an open socket, a pupil and iris painted in the center, staring with a haunting, lifeless look.

"I am sorry for all the pain you have endured, Beauty. Try to understand that all of it was for a good cause, a greater cause than you or I can claim. I love you, my son." She placed her thin hands on Beauty's shoulders and gave him a delicate kiss on the top of his head. She lifted a blade toward Beauty's head. "Would you like a haircut?"

"If it pleases you," Beauty said.

Vamillion began to cut his hair, slicing through the tangles. "Beauty, my darling…"

Beauty was afraid of what she might ask of him. He promised himself, and Popi, that he would not speak another word of prophecy and was already starting to dread the consequences of that decision. "Yes, mother?"

"Tell me more about our future." Vamillion ran her hand across Beauty's head, as if petting a precious animal. "Mullen has received permission to grow his army and mommy needs to know what happens next."

Beauty closed his eye. "I can't say."

There was a stark moment of silence. "Can't or won't?" Vamillion raised the blade to Beauty's head and began to trim his hair, but her sudden movements reflected her growing anger as she tugged his hair tight, cutting with vigorous motion.

Beauty stared at his reflection in the mirror, at his artificial eye, a sign of the cruelty in Vamillion's heart, her lack of compassion at the cost of her desire for prophecy. He swallowed his fear. "I cannot tell you, Mother."

A sharp sensation of pain struck his face. In the mirror's reflection, a fresh gash was on his cheek. He watched the blood rise to the surface and then drip down his face.

"This is not the time to play games," Vamillion warned. "I will ask you one more time and if you fail to answer..." She placed the blade against Beauty's ear. "It will be very unfortunate."

Beauty twitched at the feel of the cold steel. "Mother, please. There is nothing I can tell you right now. There is nothing I can do about that."

"You know something. For reasons I don't know, you are refusing to talk to me." Vamillion applied pressure to the blade against his ear. "What did your imaginary friend tell you? What is your mind telling you?"

"I am telling you the truth," Beauty lied.

Vamillion shook Beauty in his seat. It startled Beauty, who began to shut down. This seemed to quell her aggression. Her voice softened, as if attempting a new tactic to get to his mind. "The future of this kingdom lies in your head. Do you want to see us crumble to ashes?"

Beauty fell into shock and mumbled to himself. "Popi, Popi, where are you?"

"Popi is not real!" Vamillion screamed. She raised the blade in the air, threatening to slash him, but he did not flinch. She slapped him across the face, stinging the open wound on his cheek. She took a deep breath. "Patience has its place. And time, time is on my side... We will discuss these things at a later date. "She placed her thin hands on his head, her delicate fingers running through his hair. "You need rest, your mind needs rest. Your future, our future, depends on it."

Beauty rocked back and forth in his chair, waiting for Vamillion to leave. After several long moments of silence Beauty heard the chamber door close. The comfort of isolation and silence followed. When he opened his eye, he was greeted by the twisted reflection of himself staring back at him through the mirror. He could now not only feel, but see his suffering. The slice of the razor on his cheek would leave another scar on his face. Disgusted by his reflection, he slammed his fist into the mirror, sending a spider web of cracks across its surface. He marveled at the new reflection, a carnival of faces that stared from every angle of the distorted mirror. He searched for Popi through the myriad of reflected faces, but he was nowhere to be found.

~CHAPTER 5~

An eagle called out from above. Daylen lifted his head upwards to witness Ayrowen's graceful flight through the storm clouds. Wings outstretched, she glided above her companions, calling out in excitement for what lay ahead.

"The river is not far from here," Rahlen said. He came to a halt and surveyed their position. "This is as good a place as any."

"Agreed." Hogar dropped a sack of food he was carrying to the ground and searched his belongings for camping supplies.

Bolinda walked up to Daylen, bearing a warm smile. "How are you holding up?"

"Good," Daylen said, and he meant it. He was filled with a strange sense of optimism; eager to accomplish his quest.

This seemed to please Bolinda. "You have kept up well; for a wizard."

Daylen caught that she was teasing him. "We don't have to stop now."

"No, this spot is perfect, Daylen," Rahlen said. "The river is not far. We want it close, but not too close. It attracts all sorts of creatures. Give Hogar a hand with the campsite and make your bed against the rock formations over there. A good night's rest will be important."

"Where are you going?" Daylen asked.

"I am heading to the river's edge to fill up our waterskins. Fate permitting, I'll find us some dinner."

"Not without my help, you won't," Bolinda remarked.

"Perfect," Rahlen responded. "Fate has offered her angel. Hogar, can the two of you manage the camp?"

Hogar had gathered a pile of rocks. "Don't worry about us, Rahlen. Just make sure to bring back something we can cook." Hogar gave Daylen a wink.

Bolinda tousled Daylen's hair. "Rahlen and I will be back before sundown."

Rahlen had already started off, disappearing into the trees. Bolinda hurried off to catch up with him. High overhead, Ayrowen followed her master above the field. Daylen assisted Hogar with the campsite and when it was completed, he found a comfortable resting place beside the fire pit. The sounds of crickets and frogs made for a peaceful, reflective moment as the afternoon sky began to darken.

Hogar made his resting place close to Daylen and used a small boulder as a stone seat. He pulled out a piece of wood and proceeded to carve into it with a small knife. Daylen noticed that a wing and the chest of an eagle had already been formed out of the chunk of wood. Due to the level of detail, it must have been something that Hogar had been working on for many nights.

Hogar saw Daylen looking with interest at the project in his sturdy hands. "I am making a sculpture of Ayrowen." He held the sculpture out for Daylen to see.

"It must take a lot of patience."

"Patience, yes, and many years of practice." Hogar reached into his belongings and pulled out a finished carving, a symbol that rested comfortably in the palm of his large hands. "Here; take it."

Daylen grabbed the carving and turned it within his thin fingers. It was incredibly ornate. He was immediately taken at how the hands of such a large man could manufacture such a treasure. Complex patterns covered its surface and the shape reminded him of an elongated star, multi-sided like a gem, but it was only wood, smoothed until it almost shined. "It is beautiful," he remarked. "What is it?"

"It is a special talisman, possessing more than meets the eye. It is blessed and it will protect the one who carries it. I call it Ophelia, after the goddess. I did not desire to try and create her in human form, so I made her into this abstract piece. I guess you can say it's a seed."

"Who is Ophelia?" Daylen said.

"She was the daughter of Felicia, who is sister to Glaven. Ophelia, always curious, ventured deep into the underworld and was devoured by the hellhounds, as the story goes, but they did not know who she was. When the hounds ate her heart they grew wings. Realizing what they had done, fearful of Glaven's wrath, they took Ophelia's dismembered body and buried it in the soil above the underworld. From her remains grew a tree, the branches swirling into the heavens and the roots swirling into the hells below; the tree receiving its nourishment from both worlds. The tree united the realms, and reminded the people that the light and the dark were unequivocally connected. As the tree required nourishment from both, so too does all life. That is, if it is to be lived in harmony, if it is to be valued, like the tree of Ophelia. Thus is the story of old. In modern times, her story is a reminder of duality. Where there is light, there must be dark, and the balance should be kept in our lives."

"Where there is good, there must be evil?" Daylen suggested.

Hogar nodded. "Yes, you got it. Not only does one require the other, but one should accept both necessary aspects of life.

"I don't understand why evil is necessary," Daylen said. He studied the carving in his fingers. "It sure is beautiful." Daylen attempted to hand the figure back to Hogar, but Hogar raised his hand.

"You keep it."

Daylen shook his head. "No, I can't take this from you."

"You are not taking it from me. I am giving it to you. It is the least I can do."

"I don't understand."

"You are the son of Donovan, you are wizardborn. There is a lot to hope for in you. You can use the talisman's guidance."

Daylen resisted. "Not sure it's wise to put hope in me."

Hogar insisted. "Please."

Daylen was not comfortable with people putting faith in him, when he had so little faith in himself. He looked at the carving again. Perhaps, it was only fitting that he leave his fate to the gods, although he had never put much faith into them. Deep down, he believed in little, and when he was honest with himself, he was more afraid then he had ever been in his life. He was certain the worst was yet to come. He took the carving from Hogar's hand. "You knew my father?"

"Just the legends," Hogar said.

A legend. Daylen was realizing that Donovan had a profound impact on many. As much as Daylen wanted to know everything about his father, it would not compare to being able to see him face to face. Talking with Hogar as the afternoon progressed, he learned that Donovan was a great diplomat and trusted friend to King Averath. Donovan was responsible for the alliance of Vixus and Mullen and was said to have introduced King Averath to his first wife, Liana. The union was no small feat, bringing two empires together as one, through the love of two individuals. Their marriage was regarded as the golden era of Vixus.

Donovan was a knight who chose diplomacy over war, his intellect over his brawn, and chose a life of compassion. However, learning much from Hogar, he did not receive an answer to the question that troubled him most; who killed his father and why?

*　　　*　　　*

Rahlen and Bolinda moved quick through the trees, Bolinda leading the way through the shrubbery. He was impressed, as always, in her quick footed determination and tracking ability. She had not lost her touch in the years since governing Twilight. The strong curves of her legs, the solid strength of her arms, were signs that she had remained disciplined, giving her an admirable edge. This edge was reflected in her piercing eyes, that Rahlen saw each time their eyes met. A lesser man would be apt to mistake her beauty as weakness, or as a prize to be obtained, an object to own.

Bolinda stopped and placed her hands to her waist. With a giant sigh of relief she said, "Oh, I have missed this terribly, Rahlen."

Rahlen stopped beside her. He thought of how the trees around her seemed to exist only to frame her, the sun's sole purpose was to light the ground before her. He observed their surroundings, content to experience the moment with his old friend.

"I envy your position in life, you know that?"

Rahlen was amused by her statement, but she was not being sarcastic. She breathed heavy, sweat glistening on her skin, the weight of the world was resting on her brow. She must have felt the burden often, and it only now seemed to reveal her true age. Lines on her forehead, the corner of her mouth, lines that did not exist when Rahlen had adventured with her, years ago. "Whatever are you getting at?"

"The open land, the smell of the air… this is where I was meant to be."

Rahlen nodded, but he disagreed. "You are too valuable for the ranger life. Your leadership… your kindness… you have people who depend on you now, and rightfully so. Twilight is much bigger than all this, much bigger than me, and it needs you."

"Needs me, does it?"

"Yes," Rahlen insisted. "It needs your heart."

Bolinda smiled, but it faded quickly. "Oh, you don't understand how hard it can be. You just ride the tide, wherever the wind takes you." She turned to him, tilting her head.

"You over simplify my duty to the cause, and the hardships I endure, the sacrifices I make," he replied. "All of which adds up to someone you should hardly envy."

Rahlen's eyes bore a constant distance, something intangible to describe, that distanced himself from others. A quality brought by time, times of hardship, of pain and sorrow. Regret and love once felt and love lost. His stern, unwavering sobriety, the seriousness he placed on his role in the world, seemed to humor her in this moment. Her lips curved in a smile of both admiration for him and for his frustrating stupidity. She turned to him, resolute, putting her hand in his. When she noticed his eyes on her lips she leaned forward and kissed him.

When she pulled away, she laughed, appearing to adore his bewildered expression.

"What?" he said.

"Nothing," she lied.

"You kissed me."

"And?"

Rahlen shook his head, smiling all the while. "I don't object, to the contrary, I mean- it is the reason I am smiling; it's just…"

"We cannot forget that love is above all else. Without it, what do we labor for? Don't shake your head at me, Rahlen, I'm being serious. Why do you carry yourself all over the forsaken land? Why do I commit myself to Twilight? And why do we take this young wizard on this quest?"

"Duty."

"Love, Rahlen. We do it for love. Even you, as much as you hide behind your obsessive goals, your sense of duty; you understand this, I know you do. You callous imbecile."

Rahlen chuckled. It was the first time he laughed in as long as he could remember, but it figured. The last time he laughed was probably in her presence, many years ago. "I do, thank you. Thank you for being an ever present reminder."

"Reminder that you are an imbecile?" She flirted.

"That's the heart I'm talking about, the heart that Twilight needs."

"Yea, right," she said and turned away abruptly. Her mind appeared to be racing with thoughts of the quest, Twilight and duty. "I know." There was a sadness in her voice; disappointment and longing.

"Quite the anomaly you are. You are equally skilled with your heart as you are with your sword," he said, failing to make her smile.

"I'm the best," she said. "Don't forget it."

"Better than I?" He challenged.

"I always found you to be better with your hands."

Rahlen blushed. He moved his hands to her hips. "Always the incorrigible one..."

Bolinda pulled away and her expression was not the expected outcome he intended, as he saw concern distort her face. She looked side to side, suspiciously. Rahlen, knowing the alarming look well, instinctively grabbed the hilt of his sword and his senses returned to the surrounding landscape. It was then that he recognized a foul odor.

"Do you smell that?" Bolinda asked, after a silent moment of surveillance.

The stench was invasive and strong. "How could I not? To the river; quickly!"

Bolinda put a hand to Rahlen's chest to stop him. "Just me, just like our old adventuring days. Cover me and I will investigate."

Rahlen nodded, grabbing the bow from his back. "Quiet –"

"As a mouse," she finished and blew him a kiss.

She sprinted through the shrubbery toward the river. Rahlen followed behind at a safe distance, removing an arrow from his quiver. Surveying the horizon, he looked for the unseen threat, wishing to discredit his growing fears. The smell, it was a smell he had not encountered in many years. It can't be, he thought.

When Rahlen made his way toward Bolinda, he could see she was standing over something beside the river. She knelt over it a moment, then stood again.

Rahlen shifted his focus to the horizon, his eyes darting for signs, warnings in the thickets. Birds fluttered by.

"A body," Bolinda called out when it appeared the area was clear of any threat.

"Is it human?" Rahlen said. Rahlen continued closer, his focus still centered on the horizon, searching for ambush points.

Holding her nose, she said, "I think it's a human, Rahlen. But the body is… pulverized."

Rahlen kept his bow outstretched, but jogged up to Bolinda until he was standing over the body at her feet.

"This kind of violence is awfully familiar, Rahlen." There was a faint trembling in the back of her voice. She suppressed her fears well. "Back when Twilight was being built I got a name for myself by defending the town from the likes of those barbaric enough to wreak this kind of havoc."

"That smell. I doubted before, but now that I am closer…"

"The tracks, Rahlen. They are all around us."

Rahlen had hoped, prayed that his intuition was wrong. But he could not ignore the tracks below him, the depressions of narrow feet, with four elongated crooked toes. "It is more than rotten flesh that fills the air, I'm afraid." He shuddered and peered across the river and into the forest beyond.

"Goblins," Bolinda whispered. "I hate the smell of goblins."

~CHAPTER 6~

After filling their waterskins at the river, Rahlen and Bolinda followed the goblin tracks long enough to determine their route into the Wanton Lands and then made their way back to camp. The goblin presence that fowled the air had also chased off the animals. They shared their discovery with Hogar and Daylen when they returned.

Night had descended upon the campsite and Daylen huddled close to the fire, his eyes peering into the surrounding darkness. His mind raced with images of goblins.

"There looks to be about four or five of them," Rahlen said.

"That is hardly something for us to fear," Hogar said. He gave Daylen an assuring nod.

"This is true, Hogar," Bolinda said, "but it is important for Daylen to know that goblins, while easy prey, are vicious creatures. They have but one purpose and that it is to feed, their food of choice has always been the flesh of unlucky travelers. They cannot be reasoned with; only their thirst for blood compels them."

"Goblins rarely travel alone," Rahlen added. "While there appear to be four or five of them, bigger numbers are bound to be nearby. How many, it is hard to say, but their tracks traveled in the direction we are heading, into the Wanton Lands."

The firelight conjured shadows on the faces of Daylen's companions. The spooky illusion combined with the stories of goblins caused unrest. The thought of goblins stayed with him well through the night and although he needed his sleep, he could not bring himself to relax. The wilderness was home to many unfamiliar sounds and each one of them spurred his fears. Daylen gave up on getting any sleep and rose from his bedding.

It was Bolinda's turn to watch the camp, so she was gone, circling the campsite. Rahlen was asleep, but Hogar was silently carving away on his sculpture of Ayrowen by the fire. He too, seemed to have trouble sleeping.

Daylen took a seat beside Hogar. He was much more comfortable at his side. Daylen was growing fond of him, due in part to the time they spent together waiting for Rahlen and Bolinda to return, sharing stories.

After a long moment of silence Hogar said, "Do you have any hobbies?"

Daylen brought his knees to his chest and wrapped his arms around his legs to keep warm. "I read, sometimes."

Hogar nodded in approval. "You have had an education. That's good."

Daylen was aware that he was one of the only children of Brunhylde who could read. Most the children in his hometown didn't quite understand the purpose it served. And perhaps, with the limited future the peasants had, they may have been right. It was his mother who had taught him, which was extraordinary, since the peasant women of Brunhylde were forbidden from learning how to read. Daylen knew his father had something to do with her education. If he had not taken his time with his mother for granted, he would have asked her of all the things that his father may have taught her. "Do you have parents, Hogar?"

Hogar lowered his eyes. He was silent for a moment and had stopped carving. Daylen thought that he had brought up some tough memories for Hogar, which hung heavy on his mind.

"You don't have to answer, if you don't want to," Daylen said.

"We all have parents, right? Mine are dead now, though."

"I am sorry," Daylen said. "I didn't mean to bring up painful memories."

"My parents were simple farmers. They kept to themselves, living away from the civilized world. Mountain people, they were. My father taught me how to hunt, how to live off the land, and how to fight. My father was a skilled swordsman and axe wielder. He had learned from his father and his father before him. I am from a long line of warriors, a legacy of killers to be more exact." Hogar spoke in a dissatisfied tone. "I have traced my lineage to a time before The Final War."

Daylen ignored Hogar's distaste for his past. "You are lucky to know your bloodline," Daylen said, "To be a part of history. I wish I had a father to teach me how to be a warrior."

"I want to show you something." Hogar reached into the bag at his side and pulled out another wooden carving. It was a circular piece, with a tree at its center, rich in detail. The roots of the tree led down to a single seed and like snakes, wrapped around it.

"You made this?" Daylen said. "This is just as beautiful as the carving you gave me."

"My father made this one," Hogar said. "How to fight was not the only thing he taught me. However, what this object represents could not be farther from beauty. If you were to flash this symbol anywhere in the world to those who study history, it would offend them."

Daylen was confused. "Why?"

"Because of what it represents." Hogar held the carving up to the night sky. "Looks harmless, doesn't it?"

Daylen narrowed his eyes in suspicion. "If it represents something so bad, then why do you keep it? Why did your father make it?"

"It is a reminder for me. This carving is a seal of my ancestry. My ancestors performed violent, horrific acts upon the world. They attempted genocide. No matter how dark the past is, for my people, I must remember where I am from. With that knowledge, I hold the power to change my life and rise above their hatred. Many people of my kind are lost, without direction. They fail to accept what they are and where they are from. They drink to forget. My father is no exception. He didn't understand that it is in the recognition of one's past that one can understand themselves, all he could have been. Instead, there was only rage and self-loathing, until the day he died."

Daylen stared at Hogar, studying the distant look in his eyes.

Hogar continued. "For me, the carving also serves as a reminder that evil is real, that it is among us, but more importantly, it is within us. You, Daylen, are capable of horrendous atrocities. However, evil can be faced and evil can be conquered… whether by sword, pen, or in the shape of a simple piece of wood."

"Your ancestors were from Omnias, weren't they?" Daylen had heard of the atrocities that led to The Final War.

Hogar nodded. "The Dark Knights of Omnias, they were called. Unparalleled in their skill, without equal in their hatred for mankind. There is no denying the horrific nature of my ancestors, but they were bred that way; taught to hate. They were brainwashed by a kingdom and a religion that did not value people, including themselves. They had no love in their heart and the priests corrupted their weak minds into seeing the world as a threat that had to be extinguished. My father told me when he gave me this carving that to wipe all memory of the Dark Knights would be to risk repeating history. It is important to understand that what happened to my ancestors could happen to anybody. It was what my father could never understand, why he was so eaten up inside. The knowledge of my past, and the knowledge of what happened to my father has helped me to move on and to forgive."

Daylen was engrossed in Hogar's words. Recognizing one's own path, where one is from, was crucial to Hogar's peace, regardless of whatever horrors the past revealed. Daylen did not know who he was, where he was from. It was in that moment that his desire to know more about his father was not just a childish wish, but imperative to unlocking his own identity.

Bolinda returned from surveying their surroundings. "You two still awake?" Her eyes caught site of the carving in Hogar's hand. "The Dark Knights of Omnias," she stated. "It's rare to see one of those trinkets. Is that an original?"

"No," Hogar said.

"It still shocks me how a kingdom could participate in so much violence," Bolinda commented. "I often think that if it weren't for their hatred, then the kingdoms never would have united. In a way, it seemed necessary. Why is it that people must endure so much suffering before they are able to awaken to the possibility of something greater?"

"People are weak. It takes the threat of annihilation to get them to change," Hogar suggested.

"My mother was always skeptical of FéLorën, as a force that could persuade humanity to evolve to a more peaceful existence," Bolinda said. "It is something her and I did not see eye to eye on. What do you think, Daylen? You think there is hope for people to change?"

Daylen contemplated this question for a moment. Ultimately, he was uncertain of what was possible, but uncertainty left room for possibility. "I'm not sure about others, but my mother taught me that change was possible for me. I was always raised to believe that I was capable of amounting to anything I desired. I would like to think that I am not so different from anyone. So, yes, it is possible, so long as it is what people truly desire."

"You sound like your father," Hogar said.

"So what of you, Daylen? What do you 'truly desire'?" Bolinda questioned.

"I suppose that I just want to be happy."

Hogar nodded. "Something that I imagine everyone wants. Is it enough, to simply want happiness? Does the pursuit of one's happiness guarantee a life of virtue? What if you derived happiness from the pain and suffering of others? Are you still entitled to pursue happiness?"

"I haven't thought about that," Daylen said. "I would like to believe that true happiness is a universal thing, accomplished only from being good and doing good deeds in the world."

"Happiness doesn't cut it for me," Bolinda remarked. "It's not deep enough. Happiness, on its own, is such a limited experience. What if you got your wish, and you knew only happiness, don't you think you would be unable to relate to the world? How would you grow, how would you build character? Would you be remembered over time? For me, I welcome sadness as much as happiness. Pain, as much as pleasure. Give me the challenges of life, give me the full spectrum of emotion and experience and I will show you a person that is not necessarily happy, but has peace of mind. Accepting what life throws at you, the good and the bad, allows you to take on adversity with courage and accomplish great feats. Someone like that, is someone who will be remembered."

"And that is why Bolinda is a leader amongst those of Twilight," Hogar said. "Admirable, my lady."

"Yes, you have given me much to think about," Daylen said.

Daylen's mind was no longer occupied with thoughts of goblins, or of any challenge in particular. Instead, he saw his problems as an opportunity and found wisdom and clarity in that approach. Sleep came, eventually, and it was the most restful night he had experienced since his quest began. It was a good thing, too, for there was much ground to cover in the days ahead.

Rahlen was relentless in pushing his companions as far as possible through each moment of daylight. Before long, and three days sooner than expected, Daylen found himself traveling deep into the Wanton Lands. As the days passed, the physical exhaustion of travel through the forests tested his strength.

The wilderness was like a monster, unto itself; like a large, living organism. Every plant, every beast, every sound, formed a part of the monstrous life of the Wanton Lands. Traversing over fallen trees, large boulders, and through thorn-ridden bushes and strangling vines took a physical toll on his body. The bugs, snakes, and foreign creatures without names, slithered from the dark recesses of the forest crevices, challenging his ability to maintain peace of mind.

Day by day, Rahlen led them to and from the river. It was their life source, and their guide through the Wanton Lands, but the river was also home to many wild beasts that sought the same nourishment that they did. Rahlen and Bolinda whispered of more goblin tracks, yet they had managed to steer their party clear of any confrontations.

Rahlen had remained solemn, obsessed with reaching their goal before the winter weather became severe. Bolinda was close to his side, matching his determination. They led Daylen further into the unknown, while Hogar provided what security he could, walking at his side. On multiple occasions, Hogar carried Daylen on his back, when Daylen's legs became too weak to continue. Daylen tried his best to manage on his own and refused assistance when it wasn't necessary. He pushed himself with each daily venture, attempting to hold his own and keep up with his seasoned travelling companions.

Meanwhile, the winds grew stronger. Daylen crossed his arms around his chest in an attempt to stay warm, concentrating on each forward step, his destination too far to conceive, the burden too heavy to realize. Warm, inviting nights were a thing of the past, along with the friendly banter that had occurred between them on such occasions. Another cold, restless night, and the morning sun beckoned them onward. As usual, the day began with a quick trip to the river.

Daylen collapsed at the river's edge. He cupped chilled water in his thin hands and brought nature's rare blessing to his lips. Rahlen stood behind him, glancing up down the waterway. Ayrowen had been on Rahlen's arm, her talons gripped into his protective, leather sleeve, but she flew from her perch at once, disappearing over the trees.

Hogar moved to Rahlen's side and pointed a ways down, to an empty canoe banked on the opposite side of the river.

"What do you make of it?" Bolinda said.

Rahlen studied the condition of the canoe, the weathered wood, the way the water had marked the side of the boat. "It banked sometime this morning. The owner cannot be far off." He looked to Hogar, who was eager to investigate. "Take Bolinda with you."

Hogar and Bolinda disappeared into the wilderness, advancing in the direction of the abandoned canoe, but avoiding the clearing along the river's edge.

Rahlen put his finger to his lips, motioning for Daylen to be silent. He handed Daylen a waterskin to fill and then removed his bow from over his shoulder. He focused his attention through the trees on the other side of the river, searching for signs of the canoe's owner. As Daylen leaned over and filled the waterskin, the heard only the sound of the river's slow current.

Without warning, a man sprang from the trees, charging from behind. Rahlen turned, and managed to yell for Daylen to run, before a club came down on his head and his body collapsed to the ground.

Daylen ran, uncertain of Rahlen's condition. He looked in horror toward the attacker, a large burly man, dressed in furs and rags and staring at him with wide, crazed eyes. The club he wielded over his head was dripping with Rahlen's blood. The woodsman let out a bellowing cry and Daylen took to the trees as fast as he could move.

He jumped over hedges and dodged tree limbs, moving deep into the forest without a moment to gather where he was headed. He could hear the woodsman behind him, and the distance between them narrowed. A moment later, the club was at his back, just grazing his skin, but the force threw him face first into the forest floor, knocking the wind from him.

From above, he could hear the woodsman howl. He turned onto his back and caught murderous glare of the woodsman. He was face to face with the violent, unmerciful aggression of man. He envisioned his death, quick and absolute and wondered how moments earlier, the future was wide open to him. He closed his eyes, then the woodsman's howl came to an abrupt stop. Daylen opened his eyes to see a sword protruding from the woodsman's stomach, blood gurgling from his mouth. His body fell forward, sliding off the blade. It was then that Daylen saw Bolinda standing behind the woodsman, the sword tight in her hand. Before the woodsman dropped to the ground, Hogar lunged into view and swung his axe into the woodsman's chest. The woodsman folded over and collapsed, lifeless to the ground.

Daylen felt the blood of his attacker on his face and let out a sigh. Bolinda extended her hand, helping Daylen to his feet. He watched Hogar dislodge the axe from his fallen foe and Daylen could think of nothing more than of Rahlen's wellbeing. "Rahlen," he managed to gasp, catching his breath.

Hogar ran back to the river's edge, while Bolinda stayed with Daylen to protect him. "Are you okay, Daylen?"

Daylen shook his head, he was numb, uncertain of his condition. "Rahlen… Something has happened to Rahlen."

"Look at me! Are you okay?" She forced him to focus.

Daylen nodded rapidly. "Yes, I am fine."

Bolinda nodded and grabbed his hand to lead him back to where Rahlen was left behind. "Stay close to me."

Daylen wanted to run, but he realized his legs were wounded when they did not respond well to his command. Bolinda extended her arm for support. By the time they made it back to the river's edge, Rahlen's body was propped against a tree. For a moment, a crushing fear consumed Daylen. However, Rahlen turned his head, and despite his wound, he forced a painful smile. His face was covered in blood from a gash on his head.

Bolinda knelt beside him. She checked his pulse, the focus of his weary eyes, and the wound on his head, which Hogar had wrapped with the sleeve of his shirt. "Where is Hogar?"

Rahlen raised his arm and pointed into the forest.

Bolinda walked to Rahlen's bow and picked it up off the ground. "Are you capable?"

Rahlen nodded, grabbing the bow.

Bolinda placed her hand on Daylen's shoulder. "Stay with Rahlen. I'm going after Hogar."

Daylen obeyed her command. He took a seat beside Rahlen and unsheathed Sylver from his side. He held his blade tight, his hand trembling. It had all transpired so quickly, and he was powerless to stop it. Danger had come without warning, and he had run.

Rahlen turned his weary head toward Daylen and placed his hand on Daylen's arm. Without words, Rahlen's gesture confirmed that he felt relief in knowing that Daylen was okay, despite the worn expression on his face and the pain he must have felt. This reminded Daylen of his own pain, increasing exponentially as the adrenaline died down. He was forced to wait at Rahlen's side, wondering if Hogar and Bolinda would return.

*   *   *

Bolinda came across a body lying on the forest floor. It was a Woodsman, no doubt another owner of the abandoned canoe across the river. This unfortunate man had an axe-sized wound in his body, which had taken his life. The Woodsman's equipment and the skeletal trophies on his belt, confirmed the Woodsman was a goblin hunter. His treasures were of goblin decor; bone necklaces and bracelets, hunting knives and even a goblin skull. She assessed that this was a particularly savage group of Woodsmen who would not be willing to negotiate peacefully. Based on the remains, and the lethal axe wound, it appeared Hogar won this particular battle.

She surveyed the scene, her mind playing out the skirmish as she looked to the tracks on the forest floor. Hogar was nowhere in sight, but he had travelled deeper into the Wanton Lands, away from the river. She was startled, when she caught sight of a boy standing by a tree. It was a child Woodsman, standing so still, that she almost did not see him camouflaged amongst the trees. He was disheveled and dirty, with long mangled hair that covered his face. He was dressed in torn rags and at his side he held a blowpipe in one hand and darts in the other.

Like a wild animal of the forest, the boy did not speak, and while he was small, he had the potential to be dangerous. However, Bolinda knew that the boy could also be protected, saved, and become an active citizen of a town like Twilight, if the boy was willing.

Bolinda, to appear less threatening, lowered herself to her knees and smiled at the child. "I'm not going to hurt you," she said. "Are you alone?"

The boy did not move, but looked to the dead body on the ground and he tightened his grip around the weapon in his hand. Bolinda feared that the fallen Woodsman could be his father, in which case friendly relations could prove quite difficult to accomplish. Yet, diplomacy was worth the effort, if it meant the life of one so young could be spared.

"It's okay, child…" she reached into a pouch on her belt and pulled out some food. "You must be hungry."

The boy's eyes widened, yet his distrustful instincts prohibited him from moving forward. She continued to encourage the boy to come to her and just as the boy moved his leg forward the sound of someone advancing caused the child to retreat several feet back.

Bolinda stood and withdrew her sword, only to realize, Hogar had returned. He had a hostage, a woman, who was unkempt and as savage looking as the men who attacked them. A dart flew through the air and penetrated Bolinda's shoulder. Hogar whipped in the direction from which the dart came and saw the child, who shot a second dart from his blowgun that buried into her thigh, sending her to the ground.

The woman broke free from Hogar's grasp and ran to the child.

"Hogar, don't!" Bolinda screamed, as she saw him raise his axe.

The woman ran to her child and grabbed him, preventing him from shooting another dart. They held each other, shaking. Their faces shared a sense of both fear and anger.

Bolinda rose to her feet, grimacing as she placed her hand on the dart in her thigh. "Let them go." Her heart was touched by the position the mother and child found themselves in. Having been a bastard child herself, an exiled vagabond, it crushed her spirit to see what the wild people of the Wanton Lands had succumbed to in order to survive. Under different circumstances, she could have been a friend to them, and offered salvation in Twilight.

Hogar eased his grip on his axe and lowered it to toward the ground. He did not have the stomach to hurt them.

The mother and child, seizing the opportunity from Hogar's hesitation, ran into the forest.

Hogar yanked the dart out of her shoulder and she cried out in response. Grabbing the dart in her thigh, she braced herself before pulling the dart from her leg.

"Are there others?" She managed to ask, between the pains.

"Not anymore," Hogar said. He looked in the direction the mother and child had fled.

"We should get back," Bolinda said.

Hogar offered her his back and she climbed up onto him, wrapping her arms around his neck and her legs around his waist. He picked up the darts from the ground and placed them in a pouch on his belt and then carried Bolinda back toward the river's edge.

~CHAPTER 7~

Beauty sat alone in his chamber, lost in the imaginary world of his mind. He waited for the prophecy to come, to plough through time like a destructive monster. There was the shriek of metal against metal as the bolts and locks were raised and the chamber door squealed as it opened. Vamillion entered the dark room. Her eyes seemed to have trouble adjusting, and she moved with slow, cautious steps.

When she finally saw Beauty in the darkness she said, "How are you feeling?" She lit the candle on his dresser. "Has your mind revealed what is to come?"

As Popi had demanded, he remained silent.

"Why do you make this difficult? Why would you treat your mother, the only person in this world who loves you, this way?"

Although Beauty wanted to say nothing, he was drawn to defend himself. "I told you long ago not to put your faith in the Dark One. I warned you and you didn't listen."

Vamillion struck Beauty across the face. The blow sent him to the floor. "You ungrateful bastard."

Beauty felt tears well up in his eye. Through the distorted lens of tears he saw Vamillion standing over him with a small black dagger. It was the same black dagger that was used to remove his eye years ago. It was no accident that she chose to appear with it. Its sharp, jagged edge still terrified him and reminded him of her cruelty.

"I will speak," Beauty cried. "I will tell you whatever you want to know, just put the dagger away."

"The Dark One asks of the Necromancer, Glazahn. When will he be able to aid the empire? When will he discover the spell that has been promised me?"

This was the prophecy that Beauty feared above all others. The spell that Glazahn would discover was seen in Beauty's mind the minute he had foreseen the coming war with Mullen. The consequences promised to be devastating and irreversible. "The timing is unclear, but I can tell you that it is not discovered underground, but in a forest."

"Glazahn? In a forest? I don't have time to work out these riddles. Mullen is preparing for war as we speak. We must act now; there must be something I can do."

Beauty wiped blood from his lower lip, still in pain from the wound that Vamillion inflicted. His eye trailed off into space. "I see diplomats in Xyntharia."

Vamillion relaxed her grip on the black dagger. "The Elves? Why?"

"I see Mullen troops, using Xyntharia River as a means to advance their forces."

Vamillion was doubtful of the outcome. "And why would they help us, they have never been ones to help humankind."

"They won't help us, not directly. They will refuse helping our cause, but in doing so, they will also prevent Mullen from using the river."

This news caught Vamillion's attention. "Tell me more…"

Beauty heard the jingle of a jester's bell in the darkness and was reminded of Popi's demand for silence. Vamillion appeared not to have heard a thing, but Beauty felt the presence of his friend close in the darkness and wondered if the ringing of bells was a warning only for his ears to hear. Fearful he had said too much, he shook his head. "I can't see any more at this time."

Vamillion slipped the black dagger into a purse on her belt. "This information is helpful. I will see to it that you are well fed tonight."

Vamillion left Beauty's chamber, but before the chamber door could come to a squeaky close, he was smacked in the face, the force of the blow sending him crashing against the wall. He did not have time to see the hand that struck him, but he heard the shrill voice of Popi upon impact.

"You little fly!"

"P-Po-" Before Beauty could respond, he was struck again, this time, with a clenched fist.

"P-Popi," Beauty cried. "Why are you-"

Popi's hand was over his mouth. There was a rage not unlike madness that filled Popi's wide eyes. "Shut your mouth, you dirty little worm! We had an agreement that you would speak no more!" he released his hand from Beauty's mouth with a violent shove, sending him back against the wall.

"I was scared, Popi. Vamillion was going to hurt me…"

"Like this?" Popi struck Beauty in the face again. "I thought you were my friend. Now, you are all alone, with no one to help you."

Beauty began to cry out, but Popi placed his hand back over Beauty's mouth. "I figured as much from you. You are weak, and disobedient, and not worthy of any friends!"

Beauty struggled, but could not get out of Popi's tight grasp.

"Now, I'm going to make sure this mistake never happens again." Popi forced Beauty to look him in the eye. "Do you know what I'm going to do, Beauty? Have you seen this in your precious prophecies?"

Beauty's eye was wide with terror, as the future events unraveled in his mind. He shook his head in a violent frenzy, forced to experience what was to come, prior to it coming. The horror of his visions, the atrocity of what Popi was capable of, the fear and confusion around what Popi had become, made him wonder if he had lost his mind, whether anything he believed, or even saw before him, was even real. Imaginary, like Vamillion always insisted.

As if a mirror to Beauty's deranged perspective, Popi bore a smile as mad as the look in his eyes, an unhinged evil. "Now that all this is coming together for you, lets carry on with destiny, shall we? Let's hush you up, once and for all!"

Beauty's muffled screams filled the darkness of his chamber, but there was no one to hear him cry, no one who would come to his rescue.

~CHAPTER 8~

Daylen saw the apparition and he knew at once he was dreaming. First seeing this figure after slipping into unconsciousness inside Lonely Wood, he was intrigued that this stranger continued haunting his dreams. He found himself chasing the specter through a labyrinth of stone. The faster he ran, the farther away the figure appeared, leading Daylen deeper into the twisting and turning maze.

Losing sight of the specter around a corner, Daylen called out to it. Being without solid form, a phantom, it still seemed real to him. He decided to call it by the only name that was fitting, and he called to it with all the desperation his voice could muster, "Ghost!"

Daylen got no response. As he rounded the corner, Ghost was nowhere to be found. The labyrinth continued in various directions, the paths too numerous to account for. Confused, he felt dizzy, and stared wide-eyed, as his vision rose above his body. He was beside himself, on the outside looking in, rising and rising until he could see his position within the large vast labyrinth, its hallways stretching out far across the horizon for what appeared to be eternity.

Panic seized him and he screamed. The sound of his own voice woke him from his restless sleep.

~CHAPTER 9~

When Daylen awoke, Rahlen and Hogar were already awake and packing the campsite. He was pleased to see Rahlen up and about, having feared the worst from the head injury. He was curious as to why he was not woken earlier. By the time Daylen had gathered his belongings, Rahlen and Hogar were both standing over Bolinda's body. She had not yet risen for the day, which was unusual. Daylen approached with curiosity.

It was clear Bolinda was in pain.

"I'm fine," Bolinda said, somewhat annoyed, in response to Rahlen's inquiry. "My muscles are killing me, give me a moment and I will rise."

Rahlen knelt beside her and placed his hand on her forehead. "You are ill."

Bolinda did not deny it. "I have felt better."

It was a casual response, one made of pride. Rahlen appeared to see through Bolinda's stubbornness. Truth was, Daylen had never seen her look so unlike herself and his companions could see this, as well.

"Let's get your shirt off," Rahlen requested.

Bolinda tried, but winced in pain when she tried to lift her arms up. The shoulder where the dart had penetrated was unable to assist. Hogar brought her shirt up over her head and shoulder, exposing the wound. Inflammation was expected, but unlike the night before, the location of where the dart had entered had turned black, and puss was escaping from where it had entered.

Bolinda, unable to see the wound, searched Rahlen's face for a sign as to her condition. Appearing to recognize the concern on Rahlen's face, she took a deep breath, which was painful to complete. "Don't give me that look," Bolinda said to Rahlen. "I don't need you getting all melodramatic on me."

"Rahlen, grab my pack," Hogar referred to a small leather pouch that was usually tied to his waist, which contained the darts that wounded Bolinda.

Rahlen went to retrieve the pack.

"I'm going to need to take a look at your upper thigh," Hogar demanded.

Bolinda tried to raise her bottom off the ground. Her struggle in carrying out this this menial task worried Daylen.

Taking out his knife, Hogar tore her pants at the seam on her thigh and pulled the fabric away from her wound.

"What is your pain level?" Hogar asked, looking at the black spot on her thigh.

Bolinda was looking at the wound herself, now able to witness with her own eyes the abnormal infection.

Rahlen returned with Hogar's pack and removed a dart from the pouch. He studied the dart carefully, looking for signs of what might have been laced at the dart's edge. Hogar grabbed the pouch from Rahlen and retrieved a pinch of herbs which he rubbed into the infected area of Bolinda's wounds.

Hogar looked to Daylen. "Can you get a fire going and boil some water? Once it is ready, pour these herbs in." He handed Daylen the herbs. "Quick now."

Daylen hustled to the fire pit and did as instructed.

Rahlen knelt beside Bolinda and shook his head. "I don't know what kind of poison it is. If it were just your leg, we would have more time, and could consider amputating it, but the exposure to your back…"

Bolinda nodded. Having seen enough of the black sore on her thigh, she started to stand. Rahlen tried to help but she hit his hand away. "I got this. I'm sore, but I'm not crippled."

She pulled her shirt back down. "Just so you know, nobody is taking my leg without losing their own." Bolinda added. "Is that understood?"

Rahlen forced a smile. "Understood."

"Rahlen," Hogar asked. "The closest town?"

"Juniper," Rahlen said. "Three days, two, if we pushed ourselves."

"Juniper," Bolinda said, with a sense of apprehension. It was a small town, but dangerous. Independently run by a gang of local warriors, it provided weapons, food, and lodgings for adventurers who braved through the Wanton Lands. It was a hostile, unpredictable environment, which was as unsafe as the surrounding Wanton Lands. The town was infamous, known for brawls and murders as much as its ale. However, as crude and barbaric as it was, it was certain to have a medicine doctor.

Rahlen surveyed their surroundings and pointed to the rocks in front of them. "From there, it would put our sight above the trees, give us a chance to spot a more accurate distance to town."

"I'll see if I can find a safe way up," Hogar said.

"Let me climb it," Daylen said. "I can get up there from here."

Rahlen looked uncertain. "You took quite a beating yesterday, you sure you're up for it?"

"I am a good climber, and it will save time."

"Let the boy give it a try," Bolinda said.

Rahlen assessed the danger. Hogar had already wandered off to find another way up the rocks. "Okay, I will stay down here with Bolinda. If for any reason the climb gets too rough you come back down immediately."

Daylen nodded. He handed Rahlen the herbs for the water and jogged up to the rock. He rubbed his hands together and began his climb. The first few feet were easy. The rough surface of the rock created ample footholds. He kept his body close to the rock's surface and used whatever crevice he could find. As he climbed, the slope of the rock steepened and the footholds became harder to navigate. The nearby trees grew close to the rock and at times, provided the necessary stability for him to advance up the formation. Loose gravel trickled down and his eyes followed their descent as they skipped their way to the forest floor. He could see Rahlen and Bolinda below and at that moment realized if he fell he would die.

He turned his gaze to the sky, the top of the rock formation was not far ahead. When he was within arm's reach of the top, he extended his arm. With loose footing, he stretched to grab the rock's ledge before his foot lost its grip. A chunk of the rock beneath his foot gave way and tumbled toward the surface below. His body dangled a moment, testing his strength. He struggled against the weight of his body and lifted himself up. His arms trembling from exertion, he extended until his torso rose above the cliff's ledge and he locked his elbows in place.

He opened his clenched eyes. The excitement of his triumphant ascent shattered in an instant, when he caught site of a bony, pale green creature standing above him with large, hungry eyes. The creature shrieked, revealing its sharp, bloodstained teeth between strands of drool.

"Goblin!" Daylen screamed at the top of his lungs.

Pinned against the rocks ledge, held up only by the strength of his arms, Daylen unlocked his elbows as the goblin lunged forward to grab him. Gravity took hold, pulling him down. He slammed his chest against the side of the rock, causing his hands to lose their grip on the rock's ledge. The goblin peered over the ledge, its green menacing face was the last thing he could make out before he lost sight and descended. He scraped along the rock's surface, flinging his arms wildly, attempting to grab the limbs of a nearby tree. His skin shredded as he turned and tumbled, unable to grab hold of anything. In a stroke of wild luck, his arm became lodged in the joints of two intersecting branches, which stopped his fall. He heard the crack of bone and a pop as his shoulder gave, dislocating from its socket. He hung, his body numb, the world still spinning before he passed out.

* * *

On the forest floor, Daylen's companions were experiencing their own set of problems. Hogar had traveled around the rock formation and hollered for aid, having run into opposition of his own. Rahlen was quick to rush to him, sword drawn, just as Daylen shouted, "Goblin!" from above, leaving Bolinda behind to watch Daylen become lodged in the tree.

She did not hesitate in coming to his rescue. The soreness in her muscles was ignored as she scaled up the tree with dexterity common only amongst those of eleven genes. She was close enough to reach Daylen when she caught sight of the goblin above, who driven by the craving for flesh, lunged from the rock's ledge and grabbed hold of an adjacent tree.

As the goblin scaled down the tree, it was a race to the ground below, as Bolinda freed Daylen's arm from the branch that supported his weight and then scurried down. The goblin's descent was fast, but no match for Bolinda, who arrived on the forest floor in time to place Daylen on the soft soil, withdraw Sylver from Daylen's scabbard, and plunge it into the goblin as it jumped upon her.

The blade pierced the goblin under the chin, the power of her thrust and the gravity of the goblin's descent drove the blade through its head, exploding it like a rotten pumpkin. Its body twitched on the ground before falling still at Daylen's side. He was still alive, breathing softly, although unconscious. His body was bruised and torn apart, his dislocated and broken arm flopping limp out of its socket. She did not envy the pain that waited him whenever he was to regain his consciousness.

* * *

At the other side of the rock, Rahlen caught up to Hogar where four goblins had encircled him, looking for an opening in his defensive maneuvers. Hogar swung his axe before him in wide arcs, shifting from side to side, front and back, keeping the aggressive goblins at bay just long enough for help to arrive.

Busy in their distraction with Hogar, the first goblin fell victim to Rahlen's blade with ease. He brought his sword down on the goblin between the neck and shoulder, the force of his assault, crushing the goblin to the ground as the sword slid through its pale, green body. Standing at Hogar's back, they both went on the offense, with a joint series of aggressive strikes they each felled a goblin, leaving just one goblin left behind. It stopped, abruptly, and turned to run.

Rahlen took chase, and Hogar was close behind, having to pull his axe from goblin remains. The creature led them all the way to the top of the rock formation, where it stopped with no more room to run, having come to the same ledge that Daylen had fallen from.

The goblin, aware that it was pinned, turned to its assailants, bearing its jagged teeth, hissing and growling in an attempt to strike fear. Hogar swung his axe overhead for momentum, then brought it crashing down upon the goblin, which tried to block the blow with its forearm. The axe split through the goblin's defenses. Its screams were silenced as it fell, lifeless, from the ledge.

From the top of the ledge, Rahlen could see Daylen's limp body below, and Bolinda at the boy's side, attending to his wounds. He let out a heavy sigh of relief and looked out across the expansive Wanton Lands. The town was at least three days away, twice that if Daylen was unable to walk.

"We don't have time," Hogar assessed, staring across the horizon.

"Not if we don't split up," Rahlen informed.

Hogar said nothing, his silent expression communicated a grave concern.

"I will take Bolinda to Juniper. So long as Bolinda has the strength, we can be there in two days' time. Watch after Daylen, tend to him, as long as it takes." He pointed to a hill in the distance. "Bolinda and I will wait for you there."

Hogar lowered his axe and leaned on it as a crutch. "There is great risk, Rahlen."

Rahlen shook his head. "There is no one in this world I trust more. No one else I would rather have at Daylen's side." The look in Rahlen's eyes matched the conviction in his voice.

Hogar placed his hand on Rahlen's shoulder, he knew there was no other option. "I will not let you down, brother."

"I know," Rahlen replied.

They stood a moment longer, side by side, staring into the horizon beyond the vast forest of the Wanton Land, the winter winds blowing fierce against their faces. Below them, the miles of terrain between them and their destination spread like an unpredictable adversary.

~CHAPTER 10~

Daylen felt the pain of his body before he opened his eyes. Reality came into view as did the awareness of his physical condition and he moaned. He sat up, his head pounding.

Hogar heard his cry, and was at his side in a moment's time. He placed his hand on Daylen's arm. "How are you feeling?"

"Okay," he lied. His whole body was in pain, his arm, especially, but it was no longer out of its socket and rested in a sling. Hogar must have taken care of it while he was unconscious. He would survive and he could not bring himself to complain, not when he knew that Bolinda ran the risk of dying.

Daylen tried to stand, but before he could find out if it was possible, Hogar forced him down in place. "Not so fast," he warned.

"Bolinda…" Daylen whispered with concern, in a dry voice.

"She is with Rahlen," Hogar said. "They have gone ahead, without us."

Daylen leaned back. He would be lying to himself if he didn't feel relief in this fact.

Hogar lifted Daylen up with gentle care and placed him on a stretcher made from the materials the forest provided. It must have taken quite some time to make and this led Daylen to wonder just how long he had been out. He thought of asking, but his body told him to lay down and remain silent.

"We will make up for lost time, if you allow me to pull you," Hogar said.

As Hogar began to pull him on the stretcher he stared up at the sky and watched the canopy pass above him. It was not long before his eyelids grew heavy and closed.

*　　　　*　　　　*

Rahlen trudged through the wilderness with obsessive determination, while Bolinda rested her body, strapped to his back, arms clutched tight from over his shoulders. Sweat poured from his head and his breath was heavy, his body teetering from exhaustion. It started to rain and his steps began to slow in the mud. His footing faltered and knelt to the ground in need of rest.

They had covered a lot of ground the previous day, but this was when Bolinda still had the strength in her legs to keep up with Rahlen's pace. By the time today's sun lit the sky, Bolinda was having trouble keeping up, and by midday, her leg no longer functioned as directed. She dragged it along, while the pain in her chest made breathing difficult. When the exertion of travel stole her breath, and dizziness overcame her, Rahlen picked her up and carried her over his shoulder. By early afternoon, after a break and an attempt to eat, he made a sling for her to rest in on his back.

If he could carry on at the speed he was at, he figured he could be in Juniper by morning. The question was whether Bolinda would live long enough to see the sunrise. He found shelter from the rain in a dense section of trees. When seated, he removed the sling and placed Bolinda gently on the ground. He was face to face with her. He stared at her. Her features were sunken, the dark circles under her eyes pronounced against the pale tone of her skin.

Her almond-shaped, elven eyes were distant, her radiant glow and lively spirit were no longer present. Death was consuming her, and she looked older and fragile. Her mouth had darkened, her lips thinned and creased in a resting frown. When she spoke, it defied all the physical trappings of her being.

"Hello, you." She brought her hand up to touch his cheek softly, her head hung, as if too weak to hold up. "Are you ashamed of me?"

"You inspire me."

Bolinda shook her head, as if Rahlen misunderstood her meaning. "We should have had a child together. It would have been a beautiful child."

Rahlen's expression saddened. He didn't want to focus on the past. Didn't want to focus on what could have been; not now. She was hardly recognizable. "I'm going to take a look at the wound, okay?"

Bolinda leaned forward in consent. He pulled her shirt up and over her head. He stared at the black mass below her shoulder blade, which had spread through her veins, black lines that traveled across her back and over her shoulder, inching close to her heart. Her breath was weak and erratic, her chest sunken, her skin covered in sweat. She wheezed and her neck pulled in tight with each struggled breath.

Rahlen placed his hand gently on her skin. The day before he had marked the size of the black infection and based on its progress now, knowing how fast it was traveling through her blood, there was not much time.

He must have stared at her in silence for quite a while, for when he returned from his thoughts she was focused on his gaze, as if interpreting his thoughts and aware of his fear.

"I can't feel my leg. My chest is numb, and I cannot even tell if I'm breathing, if I am alive or dead. Leave me, Rahlen." There was a cold look in her eyes. "Daylen is back there; somewhere. He needs you."

Rahlen shook his head. "We can't stop, we must continue."

Bolinda grabbed hold of his shirt and squeezed. "Not yet."

Rahlen stood quietly, attempting to process her condition, her request and his own thoughts and feelings. He gave a heavy sigh and leaned back against a tree. He thought of Bolinda's love… her devotion. He thought about their love, and how it had changed when he refused to raise a family with her, how they grew apart over time. How different his life would have been. He thought of the emptiness and loneliness that had come from the choices he had made... the kind of sorrow that can only come from hindsight. It was in these moments of weakness that doubt would find its way into his heart, like a poison all his own. It was in these moments that he reflected upon his decisions... to take to the road, to take on the burden of protecting Daylen and to partaking on this quest.

As if she could read his thought and pondered life choices of her own, she said, "Do you remember, Rahlen, when Donovan entrusted Twilight to me?"

Rahlen nodded.

"Do you remember what he said to me?"

Rahlen stared at her, hanging on her words, waiting since he could not recollect.

"I remember," she said. "I remember everything. I remember when you saved me from the wild. I was young, full of angst, bitter. You saved me from the wild and then you introduced me to Donovan, who gave me a home in what would become Twilight."

Rahlen smiled at the thought of Bolinda in her youth. He brushed sweat soaked strands of hair out of her face and admired the angelic, elven traits in her face. "You were wild, alright. Wild and free. Beautiful; inside and out. Your anger was misplaced, but the passion you harnessed and the lifestyle you chose led you to me; to us, to 'the way.' You should credit yourself for everything."

"The anger I held for my mother, for the kingdom which exiled me... I believed all the lies. I hated my half elven blood. I was ashamed and believed I was less of a person for it. I explained everything to Donovan, years later, when he asked me to look after Twilight and to govern it. Do you remember? I thanked him for the opportunity. I told him about all of the awful self-loathing and how unworthy I felt. Donovan told me my perspective was not truth, but a poison. A poison, Rahlen. Do you see the irony? Donovan said if my poisonous thoughts didn't take my life, it would take my will to live and that it wouldn't make much difference after that. He believed in me. You both did. You saw me not as I was, but what I was capable of. Your belief in me… it saved my life. It is why I stayed in Twilight, it is why I accepted my duty to protect it. It is why I never left. I was indebted to you, and to Donovan, because you believed in me. We all sacrificed in our duty, in the decisions we made to serve our way of life, to preserve it and to defend it."

Bolinda placed her hand on Rahlen's. "Your path is the saddest of all… I wanted to give you so much, wanted to end your loneliness. You have Daylen, now. You have a child who depends on you. I believe in you; Rahlen." She closed her eyes a moment, struggling through a bout of pain before focusing on Rahlen again. "It is my turn… to return the favor… to believe in you."

Rahlen nodded in understanding, felt her hand tighten around his saying, "You just worry about what you need to do, right now. I'm going to get up. Going to strap you to my back and we are going to travel all through the night. Are you ready for that?"

Bolinda closed her eyes, preparing herself, mentally, for the journey ahead. "For Daylen…" she whispered.

"For all of us," Rahlen said. He scooted next to where she lay, placed his arm around her and for a moment he held her tight. "Up on three," he said, grabbing her wrists. He gave her a smile of encouragement and paused to admire the smile she returned, despite her pain. "One, two…"

~CHAPTER 11~

It took four days before Daylen was able to stand on his own two feet. He could hobble for a period of time, the majority of pain centered in his upper body. He carried a walking stick as a crutch beneath his good arm, relieving Hogar from having to pull him on the stretcher for a short while and then he would lay back on the stretcher again after Hogar received some needed rest. Neither spoke about why they pushed themselves so hard. They had plenty of time to reach the meeting place, but longing to reconnect, a feeling of incompleteness without Rahlen and Bolinda at their side, provided the motivation to travel as quickly as possible.

It happened to be the middle of the day when they arrived at the designated meeting place. Daylen insisted on walking into camp, and with the aid of his walking stick, hobbled along with Hogar at his side. The campsite turned out to be well built and well hidden, with an overhang constructed with interlocking trees, branches, leaves and mud, blocking the rain and camouflaging the camp. A couple of garments were hanging to dry to the side, a fire pit was in the middle of the encampment. Freshly cooked rabbit hung above the fire pit, the smell of food filling the air, caused Daylen's stomach to growl and his mouth to water.

Fastened to a nearby tree were two horses. They neighed and shifted as if startled by their presence, which in turn startled Daylen. He turned to Hogar with excitement, "Horses!"

Hogar smiled, setting his axe down beside the stretcher and looked around for signs of his companions.

Daylen, fascinated by the horses, walked up to them slowly. They shifted nervously, but relaxed with Daylen's calm approach. He placed his hand on the side of a horse and rubbed it gently. The horse, neighed again, and Daylen smiled. "That a boy…"

"Girl," a familiar voice called out. "She's a good girl." From the bushes, Rahlen emerged and walked toward Daylen with his arms outstretched.

Daylen rushed to him and embraced him in a hug. "Rahlen! I've missed you guys."

Rahlen gave Daylen a warm embrace and a pat on the back, before tousling his hair and stepping back to look at him. They stared at each other a moment in quiet appreciation. Rahlen looked different to Daylen. Time in the Wanton Land had changed him. He looked wild, like a native of the region, having adapted to his environment. His face was painted with mud and green pigment, which camouflaged him like a hunter. If not for his joy in seeing his companions, he was quite an intimidating sight to behold. Rahlen inspected Daylen closely, carefully looking over his wounds. He inspected the bandage on Daylen's head, the bandage on his leg and his arm was in the sling. Turning to Hogar he said, "You did good."

"Thank you," Hogar replied. "Glad you noticed."

"I was hoping, praying, that you would both make it." Rahlen extended his arms for an embrace. "So glad to see you again, my friend."

Hogar pulled away. "You doubted me?"

"Not for a moment," Rahlen responded.

"Where did you get the horses?" Hogar asked.

"They are beautiful, aren't they? Unfortunately, I had an encounter with some adventurers on my way to Juniper... There is much to discuss about that, but these horses, well, they are the silver lining to all that transpired."

"Where is Bolinda?" Daylen asked.

"Follow me," Rahlen said. "She is in the forest a ways, just outside of camp. I will take you to her."

Rahlen led Daylen and Hogar out of camp. On their way, he began to explain what had transpired. "I came across a couple natives outside of Juniper. They were riding those horses you saw at camp. They were all bloody, having just escaped from some altercation. They saw me and sought to take my belongings."

"And failed, I assume," Hogar said.

"And I gained a couple fine horses for our travels for my troubles," Rahlen added. "But before the altercation, I was able to get news of Juniper, the reason they were all banged up. Juniper was raided, just two days before, by a goblin army."

Daylen's eyes widened, as he hobbled alongside his companions with the aid of his walking stick. "Did you just say a goblin army?"

"Thousands of them," Rahlen confirmed. "The town is in ruin, laid to waste. The majority of the citizens, the ones who survived the assault, fled to River Ale. Others, like the ruffians I encountered, are roaming the land, homeless, surviving by the only means that they can, by robbing and stealing from other hopeless wanderers who are in a similar position. The camp I have made is safe, for now, but we should not stay long, provided Daylen is up for it, of course."

Daylen hobbled alongside his companions, following Rahlen into the thickets of the forest, his mind focused on Rahlen's words. He was baffled by the details of what had transpired. "Help me understand something. If Juniper is destroyed, then how is it you were able to get medicine for Bolinda?"

Rahlen stopped abruptly, having led his companions into a small clearing. A large oak tree stood before them, like a monument. The tall grass swayed to the current of the winter wind, and a serene quiet compelled their silence. Below the oak tree was a neat pile of rocks.

Rahlen walked to the stones and stood before it, his head bowed.

"I don't understand…" Daylen said. He felt weary and his legs shook beneath him. He took a seat by the grave and placed his hand on the rocks.

Hogar placed a comforting hand on Rahlen's shoulder. His dry voice cracked as he spoke. "She gave her life for a higher cause. She died an honorable death and as she always wanted, she will be remembered, through us."

"Always." Daylen closed his eyes. Anxiety took hold of him and he began to shake. "It is all my fault. The pain, the suffering… Bolinda's death." He raised his head toward Rahlen, with tear-filled eyes. "She died for me; how is that right?"

Rahlen broke his silence. "The only way to make sense of all this is to rise and to continue forward. Use your anger and your frustration as a means to finish your quest."

Daylen shook his head, unable to feel anything beyond regret. All he could think was to end the madness, prevent future heartache from occurring by finding a place to hide. "We should stop this, before someone else dies."

"Our next course of action must be planned carefully," Rahlen instructed. "You are in need of medical attention, Daylen, and there is not only a goblin army to avoid, but a scattered variety of disenchanted, homeless ruffians about, who are looking to take advantage of the helpless for the sake of survival."

"Whatever we decide, we can't stay here long," Hogar suggested. "Juniper may be gone, but further southeast, down the road from Juniper, lies River Ale. On horseback, the roads will be less treacherous than traveling by foot, and we can make good time."

"It does seem to be our only choice. However, traveling into River Ale is like entering the heart of the beast," Rahlen said with concern. "Juniper was hostile enough, while it stood. River Ale is three times its size and three times as dangerous. Daylen could find a healer, and we could look for new weapons to help us on our quest."

Hogar turned to address Daylen. "You must be hungry, Daylen. Let's return to camp. After a meal and a night's sleep we should be on our way."

Back at the camp, Daylen ate a good meal for the first time in days. The walk to Bolinda's grave and back was enough to weaken him, considerably, and he feared, by the pain in his side and weakness of his arm, that his wounds suffered from the harsh conditions of travel.

Very little conversation took place the remainder of the day. A solemn silence possessed each of the weary travelers. Thoughts of their loss, and of the road ahead, gave little room for optimism. Daylen watched his companions with admiration as they walked with him. He appreciated all they had done, all they had sacrificed to get him as far as they had. He sat by a warm fire and stared at the trinket that Hogar had given him many nights ago, the wood carving of a seed, which Hogar instructed was a symbol of hope, a symbol for the goddess Ophelia. Was it nothing more than a piece of wood? He wondered. As the darkness consumed the camp, and the firelight dimmed with the passage of time, Daylen pondered if returning to Twilight was the best course of action.

He was wrestling his thoughts, alone in the dark, when from the quiet evening he heard a whimper. It was faint and distant, somewhere just outside the camp... ghost-like, a sound of sadness and longing that haunted his mind. He could hear it only for a moment, then again. He rose to his feet and with his crutch, walked into the dark of night without making a sound.

After a few feet, he came to a shadow, a person hunched beside a tree. He was alarmed by the sight, and thought that he may be sleeping, as his thoughts went to Ghost, the strange figure who haunted his dreams. It was not until he grew closer that he realized it was Rahlen, wiping tears from his eyes, staring into the darkness.

Daylen was turning to leave, when Rahlen saw him. Once recognized, Daylen stepped forward and cautiously sat down beside him.

Daylen studied Rahlen's face. The seasoned, harsh lines in his companion's skin, and his sad eyes spoke of immeasurable hardships. Captivated, he looked up with Rahlen to the starry sky. They silently shared in the beauty of the moment. A profound contrast was felt between the beauty before them and the loss in their hearts.

~CHAPTER 12~

Daylen sat behind Rahlen as the horse carried them into Juniper. Hogar rode beside them, and in unison, the horses slowed their advance to a gentle trot as they passed through what was left of the Juniper gates. The town within was demolished, leveled by catastrophic destruction. No building stood, nor did any man or woman, except the three travelers staring at the debris.

Daylen stayed in the saddle while his companions hopped off their horses. He stared at the violent destruction beneath the hooves of his horse. Men, women and children with their skulls cracked open, empty of brains, their stomachs torn apart, were scattered across the roads. Slayed goblins lay thrown amidst the carnage, dismembered or slaughtered. The stench of decomposing flesh permeated the air, forming a devastating shroud of death.

The path of destruction carved through town from west to east. The town walls toppled from the sheer weight of the goblin army. Buildings lay blasted to smithereens, leveled from goblin pyrotechnics. The citizens of the town had been grossly outnumbered. The sight of the dead women and children confirmed the sudden and unmerciful nature of the attack.

It was no surprise that most of the casualties lying about were goblins, since they were nothing but mindless, hungry savages. One step removed from untamed animals. Their weapons were primarily their own claws and teeth, and were no match for those equipped with shields and armor. However, what they lacked in brains and technology they more than made up for in numbers and their knowledge of explosives. The town of Juniper was no match against the combined strength of a goblin army.

Not all the citizens had been slaughtered. Based on the tracks from town, most had fled southeast, toward River Ale, while the goblins spent the next couple days feasting on the dead before heading northeast.

Rahlen was hoping a quick trip through town would identify useful supplies, such as some food for the days ahead, but the town was wasted save for a few salvageable arrows. "We have little time," he said. "The goblins are regrouping. They will be heading for River Ale next. If we are quick, we can avoid them."

Rahlen jumped back on his horse and Hogar followed his lead, mounting his horse, as well. "Let's ride!"

They followed the signs that led south to the town of River Ale, leaving the remains of Juniper behind them. Daylen could see, from his seat behind Rahlen, the destructive path of the goblin army. Their tracks leveling the forest, creating a road of desolation that traveled far and wide up and over the hills.

Pushing their horses to move as fast as possible, stopping for nothing beyond food and sleep, they wasted no time in reaching their destination, their horses kicking up dust as they raced. The trail was vacant, void of travelers. A strange calm was observed across the land, a quiet that comes after a devastating event. Along with a fear of what was to come.

Daylen noticed massive billows of smoke rising through the air high over the trees. They entered a large valley, where River Ale sprawled like an impressive, massive fortress. The homes, shops, and facilities were surrounded by massive walls of stone. The smoke, visible from the trail, was smoke of chimneys and commerce, signs of a thriving, independent community that had flourished with its use of coal and innovative manufacturing industry. As an independent town, it was controlled by its inhabitants and required its own defenses. It had its own military, constructing its own weapons and armor. Claiming to be a town of the people, for the people and free of empirical rule, it was controlled by the strong arm of a tyrannical gang, the Blackcoats. Its leaders fought their way to the top with their sharp wit and unhinged tyranny.

The locals consisted of people who had run from their pasts, carried secrets, or who were greedy for political power. River Ale provided an opportunity for those not born to aristocracy to rule, provided they had a cold heart and tough skin. Whatever brought a person to River Ale, all reasons were suspect, but none of the locals were as dangerous as the outfit that made up The Blackcoats gang.

Being independent from conventional law required the development of a complex government organization. There was racial and class equality which was rare within a kingdom and unique, progressive innovations in technology and social sciences. However, day to day life was harsh and cruel. The laws were crude in their simplicity and punishments severe, in contrast to the progressive advancements of the townsfolk. This dichotomy represented cultures of the past, as well as the future.

Daylen stared in wonderment as their horses trotted closer, their bodies dwarfed by the massive walls. The ominous presence of the town grew as they came to its giant iron gate. From behind the walls, a bustling city could be heard. On either side of the iron gates stood orc guards. High upon the walls, men shouted incoherently to the visitors below, and raised their spears into the air.

Daylen found himself intimidated by all the intensity and commotion. He clutched to Rahlen and attempted to hide behind him when the orc guards advanced.

The orcs were alarming in appearance. Stocky, tall, and muscular, they growled, tusks protruding upward from their lower jaw, their noses like snouts. They bore a look of disdain, unaware or unconcerned with hospitality. They stared at the visitors, scrutinizing every inch of them and their belongings. One of the orcs reached up and grabbed Daylen. He pulled him from the horse with an aggressive tug after Daylen resisted. He felt the mighty grasp of the orc and could sense they could easily crush him.

"Careful!" Rahlen barked as he dismounted. "The boy is wounded."

Hogar followed his companion's lead and dismounted. He stepped away, hand on the hilt of his axe, as he watched another orc grab Rahlen's sword from his saddle. He shifted nervously, anticipating an altercation, and began to question their decision to visit.

The iron gates opened, and a tall, thin man walked toward them. He had long, greasy hair pulled back carelessly and tied in a sloppy knot. His long mustache curled at each end. Whatever he carried on his person was hidden underneath a long, black buttoned overcoat that fell below the knee. Behind him, marched two additional orcs, followed by four men in similar black overcoats which were opened and pinned back behind the hilt of the swords at their waist, exposing crude, mismatched armor.

The man with the mustache stopped abruptly in front of the visitors. He carefully eyed the travelers up and down and then parted his lips in a crooked grin. "The name is Gramel."

Rahlen took initiative to speak on behalf of his companions. "I am Rahlen." He waved his hand. "This is Hogar, and this young fellow who your orc is holding against his will is Daylen."

The guards closed in around them. Daylen was trembling beneath the grip of the orc, who grasped his arm uncomfortably. Gramel nodded and then motioned for the orc to release Daylen. "Where are you from and to where are you headed?"

"We are from Vixus, just a small outpost town at its border. Our destination is further south. We hope to make a quiet home outside of empirical rule."

"Surely, you are aware of the goblin infestation in the Wanton Lands?" Gramel motioned to the orc that had taken Rahlen's sword.

"We just passed through the remains of Juniper," Rahlen said.

The orc approached Gramel and extended the sword to him, which he took. "We could use a few healthy fighters. You seem to be a man who knows how to handle steel." He unsheathed Rahlen's sword. He ran his gloved hand over the flat of the blade. "A fine instrument you carry." He turned the blade over and raised the hilt to his eyes. "Beautiful craftsmanship... superior design. It is hardly the apparatus of a common Vixus peasant, or soldier, for that matter. What business do you have in River Ale? Just plan on passing through?"

Rahlen nodded. "This young man needs to see a cleric. We have coin, and aim to purchase commodities from your shops, support your local businesses, and to fill our stomachs."

"I see," Gramel extended Rahlen's sword, as if to offer it back to him. When Rahlen extended his hand to retrieve it, Gramel quickly pulled it away. "I was quite hoping you were looking to stay awhile."

"Unfortunately," Rahlen replied, "we are pressed for time." His arm still extended for his sword.

Gramel rested the sword over his shoulder. His crooked smile disappeared and he looked to the crowd of soldiers and guards which had gathered quietly outside the gates. "If you wish to stay and help us defend the town, then I will be inclined to let you in. You can get the items you need, at a fair price, and help your young companion get the healing he requires. After all, what good would a wounded soldier do us?"

To this question, the guards chuckled.

"I wasn't expecting the city of River Ale, which prides itself on liberty and freedom from oppression, would place conditions upon entry through its gates," Rahlen said.

"These are trying times," Gramel said. "My people are on edge and anticipate a horrific showdown with a goblin army, the likes of which have not been seen for many years. It is my job to keep them safe. Safety comes with the loss of liberties that you may be accustomed to."

Rahlen looked to Hogar, whose unease was evident. He gripped his battle axe with sweaty, itchy palms, his eyes darting anxiously through the crowd that had closed in. The offer was not ideal, and the company even less, but it seemed they had little choice in negotiations. Receiving a confirming nod from Hogar, Rahlen accepted the terms of their entry.

Daylen peered past the city gate, and observed the swarm of citizens, the streets overcrowded with patrons of River Ale and the displaced townsfolk of

Juniper. They stood eager, swords and pikes and spears in hand, restless for battle, hoping for the opportunity to spill goblin blood.

"Show us the way," Rahlen said.

Gramel's face lit with enthusiasm and his crooked smile reappeared. "Welcome to River Ale."

~CHAPTER 13~

Gramel led Rahlen, Hogar and Daylen through the iron gates and into the bustling streets of River Ale. The crowds gathered shoulder to shoulder, a frenzy of anticipation and fear with the news of the goblin invasion.

Gramel explained the particulars of River Ale, as the orc guards shoved citizens out of the way, creating a path for Gramel to lead his visitors. A citizen protested Gramel's advance, and yelled profanities. An orc guard was quick to silence him with a swift crack to the skull, and then a second orc guard kicked him repeatedly on the ground until the protester no longer moved.

Gramel stepped over the body. "Watch your step," he warned. "You can never be too careful here in River Ale. I won't lie to you, you are in the biggest hell hole east of Valice. Our numbers grow daily, but there are a few among us who insist on testing my authority. For every coin made, someone is looking to take it, and for every ally gained, another is trying to kill me. You know you are in hell when the only Valicians you can trust are orcs. They are brutish, inclined to resort to violence to settle their quarrels, but they are as loyal as dogs when you have broken them, and reliable. As you can see, they can make quite an impression."

Daylen stared at the cobblestone path and the body of the fallen citizen at his feet. He could not determine if the was still breathing. He noticed the crowds were much more inclined to stay out of Gramel's way when they saw the swift and cruel treatment of one who hindered his advance through town. The road opened and they entered a quad, a stage was lined with men who had been lynched. People shoving each other in excitement, or anger, reacting impulsively to their environment.

"Things have gotten particularly unruly since opening the gates to the citizens of Juniper," Gramel continued. "I do apologize for their wild tendencies. I am starting to question whether it was the right move to make, offering them refuge. However, if the size of the goblin army is as big as they say, then I am not afforded the luxury to be selective in the help I receive."

Gramel paused and pointed to the men hanging, lifeless, on display in the center of the quad. "Those who held positions of leadership in Juniper were fools to assume they had any sort of power here. The leader of Juniper wished to express his point of view which, unfortunately, differed from mine. Those hanging beside him were those loyal to him. I realized, long ago, a town cannot have too many chiefs."

"Of course, there were others who sought to cause trouble, but my people are incredibly faithful, if not to me, then to River Ale. They beat to death those who caused disruption. You see, I have successfully ran things here by staying out of people's affairs, only stepping in when absolutely necessary. You would be surprised at what a group of people are capable of when left to their own devices. A robbery takes place, and the citizens impose justice as they see fit. A murder, a rape, whatever the offense, the people will see that justice is done. There is no need to hire constables, to impose any government laws, when the people are the eyes and ears of the streets, each with sword in hand; judge and executioner as required. I would wager we have less crime than most cities because of it."

Gramel looked back toward Rahlen, who stared from behind his camouflaged face. "Hell, for all I know you are a bunch of murderers and rapists. I am not one to dive into anyone's personal affairs, there must be some reason why you guys left Vixus, am I right? That is the beauty of River Ale, you see. All are forgiven when you walk through these gates. All deserve a second chance, I am a firm believer in that. Yet, if you make the wrong choices while on these streets, well, I don't believe in third chances."

Past the quad they continued down several winding streets. Daylen felt the anticipation of battle stirring in the people he passed. There was a bloodthirsty hunger in the people of River Ale, of the likes Daylen had never seen. Trouble was bound to occur, he could feel it, and he was uncertain as to whether he was more afraid of goblins than his current company.

"Ah," Gramel sighed, coming to a halt, before a large two story structure. It was a tavern occupying the bottom floor and the levels above served as an Inn. "We are here."

In front of the tavern was a group of drunks, spouting about the end of the world and death to all. There had always been a mysterious link between goblins and bad omens. Goblins were mindless, yet mysterious creatures, which would appear only in traumatic times – as if something dark and evil drew them from their caves, beckoning them to surface to ravage the land. It had been twenty years since the last goblin invasion. It struck north, during a rebellion within McMullen's empire, and was not considered to be a coincidence. As if the madness of war and the rise of hate and unrest drew the goblins out like sharks to blood.

A group of orcs ignored the drunken ravings of those proclaiming the end of the world, as they boarded the tavern windows. They were being instructed by warriors in black overcoats, not unlike the one Gramel wore, which signified their allegiance to the Blackcoats. They cracked their whips at the orcs, who worked without protest. Tobacco smoke poured from the tavern's entrance when the door swung open. As Gramel led Daylen and his companions inside, a pack of battle dwarves made their way out. The dwarves were drunk, hollering into the sky at no one in particular, arms around each other in comradery as much as to hold each other up.

Inside, the tavern was surprisingly quiet, save for a few remaining patrons. As the door closed behind them, Daylen found himself enveloped by a thick haze of smoke and the potent stench of beer. A stage where musicians once played was cluttered with broken mugs and upturned tables. The entrance was guarded by rough looking characters in black overcoats and the remaining patrons occupied the back corner of the bar and whispered mysteriously to one another.

"There are many taverns and inns in River Ale, this one here just so happens to be the safest," Gramel said. It is protected by people I can trust, which means you can rest at ease. Let me introduce you to Pavo, the bartender of this establishment."

Pavo stood behind the bar, wiping its already pristine surface, staring at the guests Gramel had brought through the door. He was a particularly ugly fellow, with an oversized nose, big ears and a large forehead. His skin was blistered and covered with boils and scars that he attempted to hide behind a scraggly long beard that grew in uneven patches.

Gramel led his guests to the bar. "I have recruited some fighters," he said to Pavo. "I want to set them up with a room, somewhere they can be protected and looked after."

"Can I get you fellows something to drink?" Pavo said in a hoarse voice.

Rahlen, speaking on behalf of his companions, declined the offer.

"You will have to excuse the state of things around here," Pavo explained. "You will find that we are not quite prepared to provide services to the general public just yet, but always welcome to provide service to friends of Gramel."

"Pavo is the new owner of this establishment," Gramel said. "The previous owner had to be removed. There was a disagreement, a misunderstanding, if you will, and we could no longer be business partners."

"Which room?" Pavo asked Gramel.

"Eleven," Gramel said.

Pavo handed Gramel a set of keys on a sturdy metal ring. Gramel led his guests upstairs. The mysterious patrons at the back of the bar eyed the visitors suspiciously as they passed. Upstairs was a long hallway of rooms stretched out across the length of the building, blocked by three gates.

"Gate one is key one," Gramel explained, shifting the keys across the metal ring until finding the key marked with a number one. He placed the key in the lock. "Now, these gates are old and rusty. If you find the gate won't open, don't be afraid to get rough with it, it will give with a little insistence."

Gramel had to wiggle the key to get it to turn and then shove his body against the gate. Once open, he led his guests down the hall.

Daylen found himself on edge and still held Rahlen's cloak. A quick look at Rahlen and Hogar's confirmed they felt uneasy, as well. The dark hall and security were all negative signs of what was to come.

"These gates are designed for the guests' safety," Gramel continued. He led them over the second gate, which was lying on the floor. It looked as though it had been beaten to the ground. "Watch your step, watch your step. As you can see, you don't need to worry about key number two."

Past the second gate a door to one of the rooms was ajar, a dim candlelight shone through and Daylen could hear whispering from within. As he passed the room he saw four or five men standing over a table. The room cluttered with boxes and the bedroom appeared to be used as storage space. Someone appeared at the door and the door slammed shut, startling Daylen. He averted his gaze, focusing down the hall.

"Are there other guests who will be staying here tonight?" Rahlen asked.

Gramel approached the third gate and placed key number three into its lock. "As Pavo said, the Inn is not open to the public as of yet. Some of these rooms are for my personal use and you may notice people occupying the rooms for a short time. I have many projects. It is not easy to run a town. It requires a lot of offices where business can be conducted. Do not attempt to interfere with the goings on around here. Mind your own business and there won't be any trouble. Pavo can assist you with drinks and food, but that is all. If it is entertainment you seek, whether it is girls or boys, or both, they can be found in plenty of the other establishments in town. If you need any recommendations, I am happy to oblige."

"That won't be necessary," Rahlen said. "We plan on keeping to ourselves."

"Wise," Gramel said. "I recommend you stay put and let me or Pavo assist you with your needs as they arise."

They made their way to the end of the hall and past the fourth gate, where only two rooms remained opposite each other; rooms eleven and twelve. Standing in front of room eleven, Gramel handed Rahlen the set of keys. "Is there anything I can get you?"

"We need to see a cleric straight away," Rahlen informed. "Our companion is in great pain."

Gramel nodded, "Of course. I'll see what I can do about that. Wizardborn are a rare commodity in these parts, and require protection. Allow me time to make preparations."

"Today, I hope," Rahlen said.

"Meet me in front of the Mystic Eye, tonight, at midnight," Gramel replied. "It is in the Southern part of town, four blocks off the main road. I will have Pavo draw up a map for you."

"And weapons?" Hogar asked.

"I will make sure a variety of weapons are brought to your room and you can make your selections."

"And food," Daylen added.

"Consider it done," Gramel said. "I will see that your requests are satisfied and will see you tonight."

Rahlen opened the door to room eleven and led his companions inside. A small rectangular window, with bars, positioned high on the wall, just inches below the ceiling, provided the only natural lighting. The room was bare, save for a writing desk with a lantern and piles of crude bedding made of hay and worn sheets.

"This looks like a prison," Daylen commented.

"At least it keeps the locals away," Hogar said, attempting to see the positive side of their arrangement.

Rahlen was concerned. "This room leaves us no way of escape, save for the way we came in."

"This whole situation is alarming," Hogar stated. "Why board us here, where no one else is staying? This is not an Inn, it's a guild. Gramel led us straight to his lair… why?"

Rahlen threw down his belongings. "To keep us close. I don't believe he trusts us as much as we don't trust him."

"What have we done to cause mistrust?" Daylen said.

"Because we travel with a wizardborn," Hogar suggested.

"Do you think he knows?" Daylen questioned.

"Yes," Rahlen said.

"I don't like the situation we have found ourselves in, one bit," Hogar assessed.

"We have no choice," Rahlen commanded. "We will do as we are told and bide our time. Once we purchase our weapons and heal Daylen's wounds we will make leave. Until then, we keep low and watch our backs."

Hogar paced a moment before plopping down on one of the beds. He leaned back, still holding his axe.

Rahlen motioned for Daylen to sit on a bed and then helped him to remove his boots. Daylen leaned back and closed his eyes. Despite the makeshift beds, it was a blessing to lie down. With help, his pain would end soon. "Does it hurt?

"What's that?" Rahlen asked.

"A cleric," Daylen said. "Getting healed with magic… is it painful?"

"You won't feel a thing, I promise," Rahlen assured. "You should feel numb and warm and then you will fall into a deep sleep. Next thing you know, your pains are gone."

Comforted, Daylen asked, "Have you been healed before?"

"I have," Rahlen said. "Took an arrow in the stomach that would have taken my life had not a cleric been near."

"A wound I got was infected, and my leg started to decay." Hogar interjected and pointed to his calf. "I would have lost my leg if not for a healer."

Daylen's trepidation had been soothed and provided the ease required for a few hours of rest. A knock came at the door, awaking Daylen from his sleep. He looked to Rahlen and Hogar, who both jumped to their feet, startled.

Hogar hid behind the door, his axe in hand. Rahlen stepped forward, his grip on the hilt of his sword. Once Hogar nodded, Rahlen opened the door. His hand eased off his weapon when he saw Pavo standing in the hall with a tray of food. Behind him were three orcs, who held in their hands a stack of various weapons. Hogar stepped away, lowering his axe to his side and Rahlen invited them to enter.

Pavo moved to the writing desk where he set the plate of food. Daylen grabbed an apple from a bowl of fruit, taking a satisfying bite. He grabbed a hunk of bread and shoved it in his mouth. He hardly chewed as he wolfed it down.

The orcs spread their weapons on the bedding. They were old and used, but sufficient for fighting goblins. Hogar was drawn to a two-handed sword and picked it up, testing its weight in his hands. Rahlen inspected the collection of arrows and satisfied with their craftsmanship, placed them into his quiver. There was a shortbow amongst the weapons. He tossed it to Daylen. "Ever shoot one of these?"

Daylen dropped the apple to the ground and caught the shortbow in his hand. "I have shot a bow before, at home. I've never killed anything with one, though."

"Well," Rahlen acknowledged, "your chance is fast approaching. After you see the cleric tonight we can test your skill."

"I wouldn't say I'm excited about that," Daylen commented.

"Check this out," Hogar said with enthusiasm. He grabbed a steel bar with handles, to which a long black chain was fastened. At the end of the chain was a metal ball with spikes. "A morning star." He twirled it over his head before slamming it into the bedding beside him. The impact shredded the sheet and blew through the haystack beneath it, sending strands of hay through the air.

Pavo headed toward the door. "You find what you need?"

Hogar met him. "Yes. What do we owe you?"

Pavo shook his head. "You will work payment out with Gramel."

The orcs picked up the unclaimed weapons and walked out into the hall. Pavo followed. Upon leaving, he handed Hogar a scroll wrapped in a leather string. "Directions, to the Mystic Eye," then nodding, he closed the door behind them. "Good evening, gentlemen."

The dim light through the small, barred window had diminished, signaling the coming of night. Rahlen took the directions to the Mystic Eye from Hogar and moved to the writing desk. He lit the lantern and pulled out a pipe, packing it with leaf. Taking a seat at the table, he unwound the scroll and studied the map.

Daylen sat on his bedding, his hands were shaking. The night ahead, the threat of a goblin invasion, it was taking a bigger toll on him than he realized. "I don't think I have ever been more afraid."

Rahlen puffed on his pipe, sending a white cloud of smoke toward the ceiling. "Your focus is placed on an uncertain future instead of the present. Which tells me there is a future you wish to be a part of that you fear losing."

Rahlen cleared his throat and tapped the ashes of his pipe on the table. "Which begs the question, what future do you long for? In the wilderness, you questioned whether to turn back. Do your thoughts drift to the comfort of your home? Or do you long for something greater?"

Daylen looked to Hogar, who was leaning forward, interested in his response. He turned to Rahlen, as if expecting him to provide the answer. It took him a moment to focus not on the desires of others, but on his own. A truth struck him. "Yes, I want to be home, but where is home? It is unclear to me. It is nowhere I have been, not anymore, but perhaps it is somewhere I am headed. Until that day, this little square room will have to do. If we get through this, then Zantigar's home will do, provided he allows it."

Rahlen's expression turned to fatherly pride. It was in recognizing this feeling that Daylen realized he was where he belonged, no matter how terrifying the road ahead.

Daylen smiled, but looked down at his hands. "I can't stop shaking."

Rahlen placed his hand on Daylen's shoulder. "Be mindful of your thoughts, as they are one of the few things you alone can decide. That, and your pursuits. It is what defines you, and as such, they are the only matters which require your attention."

Rahlen shifted to sit beside him and picked up the short bow at his side. He placed it on his lap and ran his hand across its wooden surface. "You see that knot of wood in the wall across the way?"

Daylen nodded.

"Take this bow and this arrow and focus on that knot. Shoot the arrow at its center. Be mindful of your pursuit; to hit the center of the knot. Recognize that you control the bow in your hand, the pull of the string. You, alone, take aim. You control the rhythm of your breath, and the timing of the arrow's release." Rahlen handed Daylen an arrow and encouraged him to rise and take aim.

Daylen attempted to draw the bow, but the wounds were too painful. Recognizing Daylen's discomfort, Rahlen moved behind him and sturdied Daylen's hand. "I will draw the bow for you, all you must do is aim. Aim and breathe."

Daylen nodded, raising the bow toward the knot. Rahlen supported Daylen's frame and drew back the bow.

"When you release the arrow, the arrow is no longer in your control; it is in the hands of Fate. The wind, the obstacles that may or may not get in the way, these are unknown influences. You hit the target, you don't hit the target, it is of little concern. However, while that arrow is with you, you are responsible for providing the best opportunity for the desired outcome, and it is only this which should concern you."

Daylen breathed deep, the bow swaying slightly in his hand.

Rahlen advised, "When you are ready, give the command and I will release the arrow."

Daylen focused on the knot and after a moment of concentration he exclaimed, "Now!"

Rahlen released the arrow. It zipped through the air burying into the wooden wall. The arrow hit above the knot, and far from its center. Daylen lowered the bow.

Rahlen stepped in front of him and placed his hand under Daylen's chin. "Raise your head, young one. Did you do your best?"

"I didn't hit the knot," Daylen replied.

"I did not ask if you did."

"I did my best, but I didn't hit the knot."

"In time and with practice, you will," Rahlen informed, "or you will not. But, I trust you will always do your best."

"I assume there was a lesson in all this?"

"You brought your mind to focus on that which you control." Rahlen grabbed Daylen's hand and raised it toward his eyes. "Now look, as a result of your focus, you are no longer shaking."

MYSTIC
EYE
THE MYSTIC EYE

~CHAPTER 14~

The Mystic Eye resided far against the southern walls of River Ale, just as Gramel had described. The midnight hour did not prohibit citizens from occupying the major streets and could not quell the restlessness in anticipation of the battle ahead. But here in the southern most section of town, between the maze of backend streets and damp alleys, there was stillness and solitude. Rahlen tucked the map into a pocket in his cloak and pointed to the sign above.

The sign had the name of the shop carved in unrefined letters and the image of an eye, with rays of light coming from behind it. The symbol was ancient, discovered by Erramond the Wise when he uncovered the ancient text of FéLorën. The symbol was carved into the cover of the book. Over the last couple hundred years, the symbol became associated with wizardry and magic. To the common people of River Ale, the symbol only marked the entrance to an apothecary. For others, it was a secret code that designated a safe haven for rogue wizards. For fewer still, it was a sign that showed an allegiance to the way of FéLorën, the way of peace that united a world.

The question on Rahlen's mind was for whom was the symbol meant. If the owner of this shop was one of them, a follower of the ways of FéLorën, then he was oddly located in the most violent of regions.

Daylen saw the symbol and whispered, "I saw this symbol in Twilight."

"Yes," Rahlen said. "It is a familiar symbol to those of our cause, but we must be cautious."

Hogar nudged Rahlen and motioned to the alley. Gramel appeared from its shadows. He was cloaked in his familiar black overcoat, buttoned to the top, concealing the garments and equipment he carried beneath. His hair was pulled back beneath a weathered top hat. Beside him was an elf in a black over coat with long, blonde hair. His face was scarred from a serious burn. Daylen recognized this elf as one of the few patrons of the bar beneath their room when they first arrived in town. Even farther in the alley was a figure who was too dark to see, intentionally shrouded as to not be noticed.

Gramel pulled out a pocket watch, fastened to a gold chain. The movement alarmed Hogar, who raised his axe. Rahlen remained steadfast with his hand rested on the hilt of the sword.

"I do appreciate punctuality," Gramel said, shoving the watch back into his pocket.

"That man, in the shadows," Rahlen said. "I want him out where I can see him."

"Don't get excited," Gramel stated. "He is my associate, as is the elf." He motioned for the figure in the shadows to move forward. "Come, so I can make a formal introduction."

The figure advanced into the light of the street. He wore a black cloak and his face was hidden in the shadows of his hood. His hands were stuffed into the cuffs of his sleeves where they could not be seen.

"I don't care who your associates are," Rahlen said. "I want to know why they are here, and why you felt it necessary to bring them with you tonight. I want that man's hands where I can see them."

The hooded figure revealed his hands. His palms had an intricate symbol branded into them.

Upon noticing the markings, Rahlen narrowed his eyes. "A wizard? Why did you find it necessary to bring a wizard?"

Hogar shifted his feet nervously, his hand tightening on his axe. Daylen shifted behind Rahlen, sensing the growing tension.

A crimson dagger dropped from the sleeve of the wizard and into his branded palm.

"Put the dagger away," Rahlen warned.

"Rahlen, please," Gramel began. "This is my security. I have been accommodating. I have offered you room and board, food and weapons. I have trusted you, despite the dangerous situation on our hands. However, I know not who you are, or your intentions. I have a cleric inside these doors who is very important to me. How am I to know that you are not a Mageslayer, sent to kill the only cleric in town? Now, you have taken precautions, just as I have. Let's stop this nonsense and get down to the business at hand. You have a companion in need of assistance and you mentioned that you have coin to pay for his healing."

Rahlen motioned to Hogar, who stepped forward with a coin purse and tossed it toward Gramel's outstretched hands.

Gramel caught the bag and handed it to the elf at this side, who opened the pouch and fumbled through its contents. Gramel waited until the elf gave an assuring nod.

"This is how this is going to work," Gramel said. "We are going to inspect the boy over, make sure he carries no weapons. Then, the boy enters alone."

"What assurance do we have that he is going to be safe?" Rahlen asked.

Gramel smiled. "You have my word… and I am a man of my word."

"As am I," Rahlen replied. "So let it be clear when I say that you will die, along with all your friends, if anything happens to him in there."

Gramel was un-phased by Rahlen's threat. "Bring the boy forward."

Rahlen stepped aside and motioned for Daylen to approach. Daylen handed Rahlen his short sword, Sylver. Rahlen placed the sword at his side.

The wizard slid his crimson dagger back into his cloak and approached, looking Daylen over carefully, before patting him down. Daylen's eyes caught the reflection of the wizard's eyes beneath the shadows of his hood. "A wizardborn," the wizard hissed.

"Wizardborn, you say?" Gramel moved forward.

"The eyes, the frail, gentle hands. I'm sure of it," the wizard said.

"Just passing through town, are we? Looking for a home south of River Ale… with a wizardborn?" Gramel laughed out loud, a greedy look in his eye. "The extra risk, and my silence, is going to cost you. Fifty gold bits."

"Check with your elf, that pouch is filled with one hundred gold bits," Rahlen informed.

The elf exchanged glances with Gramel and nodded in confirmation.

"Well, then. I'm keeping the change."

"As we expected," Rahlen replied, "in hopes that this stays between us."

Gramel crept toward Rahlen and his voice dropped to that of a whisper. "I am willing to return your one hundred gold bits and offer you an additional four hundred if you are willing to part ways with the boy. You will be free to leave, tonight. Consider your obligation to defend River Ale absolved."

"That is out of the q-," Rahlen said.

"Ah-ah-ah," Gramel interrupted. "Don't be so quick to answer. I will only offer this once. Consider for a moment this peaceful trade, a simple parting of ways."

"No," Rahlen said.

Gramel laughed, looking to his companions before returning his gaze to Rahlen. "Okay, no hard feelings."

"Go, Daylen," Rahlen said, never taking his eyes off the Blackcoats before him.

Daylen looked to Rahlen and then to Hogar, who nodded and urged him toward the Mystic Eye. "Everything will be okay," Hogar assured him.

"Go on," Rahlen insisted. "We will be waiting right here for you."

Daylen stepped toward the door to the Mystic Eye and hesitated before extending his hand for the door knob. His companions and the Blackcoats waited, in a tense standoff. He turned the knob cautiously, the door giving with a gentle shove. A bell dinged overhead, alerting his presence to whoever waited inside. He looked back to his companions and shut the door behind him.

The Mystic Eye was, on the surface, both a quaint apothecary and an antique store of various collectibles. Dimly lit, it smelled of old books and stale, dusty air. Bookshelves cluttered the room, creating narrow passages to walk between. Daylen shifted between the large leather-bound books, jars filled with curious oddities, antique apparatuses, and jewelry both modern and ancient.

The ceiling was covered in astrological images. Constellations, celestial signs and charts, and a display of the cycle of seasons was painted on the ceiling's wood surface. On the wall were mounted, stuffed birds as if frozen in flight. There was an owl, the soft candlelight reflecting in its large eyes; an eagle with its wings outstretched, claws extended. A raven loomed in the shadows as if perched in observation, casting a look of judgement upon any who entered the shop.

As Daylen made his way through the narrow, twisting passages of bookshelves, he came to a long counter at the back of the shop. Behind the counter were rows of shelving stacked with jars of medicine and potions. Each bottle labeled in fancy lettering, the names of which were foreign. No one was behind the counter. The lanterns were unlit; creating a shroud of darkness, save for a passage that was illuminated with warm glow, drawing his attention.

Daylen crossed over the counter and through the passage door, which led to a steep flight of stairs. The smell of incense, and the attraction of light below, beckoned him onward. He descended quietly and turning the corner, found himself in a basement that looked not unlike a dungeon. Cold and wet, except for the direct heat of torches lining the cobblestone wall, he moved to the center of the room where a table sat. Behind it, a man stood. , He was not dressed like a wizard, or as Daylen imagined a cleric to be, but as a common peasant in a worn tunic and patched pants. The man was clean shaven and bald, his face narrow with defined features accentuating his large, welcoming eyes. It was clear he had been waiting for Daylen to arrive.

The cleric raised his hand slowly. When he spoke, his soft voice was soothing and inviting. "You must be Daylen. Please, have a seat on the table."

Daylen looked at the table before him; it was crude and made of stone. There were hinges on the edges where chains and cuffs had once been.

The cleric, as if understanding Daylen's reservation, spoke in a hypnotic voice. "Do not be afraid. I have done my best to remove the remnants of this chamber's past. It used to be a holding cell and a room for torture. Yet, this purpose it no longer serves. It is a place of healing now, a place of refuge."

Daylen stepped closer and placed his hands on the cold, stone tabletop.

The cleric continued. "As a rogue wizard, I am forced to lead a life hidden among the dark recesses of an evil past, in order to live unseen. My goal is to provide the service of healing to all, regardless of who they are or who they once were. I cannot help my surroundings, but I can help you. And I intend to. Lie down on the table, and let me take a look at your wounds."

In an uncanny way, the cleric reminded him of Ghost, the figure from his dreams. Like Ghost, there was something that drew him in, attracted him, and allowed him to give in to the cleric's command. He struggled to lift himself up onto the table. Once settled, he stretched out across its surface. The cleric studied a large book, the pages discolored with age. He stopped on a page of interest and read the writings carefully. After reading a passage from the book, the cleric placed his hands inches above Daylen's body. Closing his eyes, he hovered his hand over every inch of him, stopping momentarily over wounded areas, mumbling words in an unknown language.

Daylen felt the cleric's hands warm with unnatural heat. The warmth traveled through Daylen's body. His body temperature rose, until he lost all sensation. He was no longer conscious of his body and felt as if he floated in suspended animation. Bodiless, he floated into the recesses of his mind. He closed his eyes. In the void of nothingness a bright, yellow symbol flashed. It was the same phenomenon that he experienced in Lonely Wood, but the symbol was different. The symbol faded, but the yellow light was slow to dissipate. Behind the light was a figure of a man. He knew at once, without question, that he stood before Ghost. This time, the figure seemed more substantial, less ethereal.

Daylen was suddenly pulled from his trance. He became aware of his body, aware of the table beneath him. The cleric was standing over him, hands at his side, and a warm smile on his face.

"How are you feeling?" The cleric asked.

Daylen leaned forward. He felt no pain, only a slight lightheadedness. He put his arms out in front of him. His broken bones had healed and his bruises and cuts had closed. Scars now remained; his skin having healed in moments. "I feel... wonderful. How did you…?"

"We are similar, you and I," The cleric said.

"Well, truth be told, I am a wizard," Daylen said.

The cleric had a peculiar, knowing look in his eye. "You are much more than that, my young friend." He moved to a counter, where he wiped his hands with a warm, wet towel. "As a rogue, much like yourself, I have been forced to live a sheltered life, in hiding."

"With your skills you can do anything, go anywhere," Daylen said.

"My place is here. It isn't much, but it's mine. A place I can call home."

"I am still in search of my home," Daylen remarked.

"River Ale can be a home to you. You can be my apprentice. I can teach you all that I know and pass on my legacy."

Daylen tried to imagine a life in River Ale, wondering if this could be his salvation, his purpose. As miraculous as the cleric was and as kind and masterful his skill, it was not Daylen's place to stay with him. He may not have known where he belonged, but it was clear where he did not. If he had not been obliged to his mother and his companions, he may have considered the offer. Had he been truly alone and had he nothing to lose, he would have embraced the opportunity. In that moment, with his health never being better, his mind never clearer, he smiled at his realization. Despite his prior feelings of loneliness, he saw that he was not alone and that he had much to lose by giving up on his quest.

Daylen finally spoke, "I am sorry, but I cannot stay."

The cleric nodded. "I understand. I envy your journey. To be young again, to discover my calling for the first time. You will bring great things to many, one day."

Daylen hopped off the table and headed toward the stairs. He stopped abruptly and turned back to the cleric. "How did you know?"

'Know what?" The cleric asked.

"That this was your home?"

"Perhaps, it is because I am needed here. It isn't much, I know, but serving these townspeople gives my life purpose. I discovered some time ago, that it is not riches or power that provides happiness, but a life in service to others."

Daylen smiled. He was anxious to get back to his companions and to continue on the path that would give his life meaning. "Thank you," he said, and made his leave.

~CHAPTER 15~

"Vamillion, darling," Queen Abigail said, catching her breath. "I am not sure why you insist on living at the top of Moon Tower, there are so many wretched stairs."

"Thank you for coming," Vamillion replied.

"You hide up here, you conspire, you plan. Meanwhile I am left to deal with the duties of running this land."

"Are you displeased with your position?"

"Of course not. How about you? Your place in this tower does leave much to be desired." Queen Abigail looked at the clutter around her with a look of distaste. "How can you stand working in this space?"

Queen Abigail paused to review her surroundings. The room was crowded with Vamillion's academic devotion to both spiritualism and science, to which she valued with equal measure. Books were scattered on the table, chairs and floor. Tools of mysticism were dispersed across the room. Markings of sacred text and images decorated the walls and the various appliances of modern technology were positioned wherever there was a space for them.

A telescope was positioned at the window. It drew Queen Abigail's attention. "You don't need to answer that, my love." Queen Abigail continued, leaning over to stare through the eye piece. The telescope was focused on a constellation. "I am just overwhelmed. Do you realize how much effort goes into convincing the people of Vixus that your plans and schemes are in their best interest? That war is necessary for lasting peace?"

"The people are in my best interest, my Queen. They always have been."

"I know, but are they aware of what's in their best interest?" Queen Abigail pulled away from the telescope. "It has been so long since I have been in your study. I have been curious as to the goings on here."

"Devotion, my Queen," Vamillion responded. "I have little time for other luxuries."

Queen Abigail thumbed through a series of books cluttered on the desk. She quickly lost interest. "You know, there are servants who can assist with this sort of mess."

"Everything is precisely where it need be."

Queen Abigail moved away from the desk, placing her hands into the warm fuzzy pockets of her bearskin robe, and turned to face Vamillion. "You have news for me?"

"King Averath's son," Vamillion said, "has finally prophesized again."

"At last, I was starting to think the boy's brain had turned to mush from all these… instruments you use on him."

Vamillion directed Queen Abigail's attention to the table, where a map was unraveled. "We need to send a diplomatic convoy to Xyntharia."

Queen Abigail placed her hand to her chest. "The elves?" She spoke with an air of disgust. "Why?"

Vamillion explained Beauty's predictions and Queen Abigail became aware of Mullen's desire to use Xyntharia River as a means to sneak an army toward Vixus.

"And they will help us?" Queen Abigail asked in surprise.

"Not intentionally. They will decline an alliance, but hearing news of Mullen using their river as passage will cause them to take matters into their own hands."

"Well," Queen Abigail said. "We should listen to the boy. What choice do we have? He has never been wrong before."

"I am glad we are on the same page. I will send delegates to Xyntharia at once." She pointed to a dark snakelike design on the map that represented the Xyntharia River. "Mullen will be focusing his army south along Xyntharia River in what they believe will be a sneak attack, only to be stopped by a mighty elven army. We can position our troops to the north, and move upon the citizens that are expanding into the Redlands. They will be greatly outnumbered and vulnerable. Expecting to surprise us, Mullen will come into a surprise of their own!"

"The knowledge you have obtained from your devotion has made you a dangerous woman, Vamillion," Queen Abigail said. "You do Vixus a service which cannot be repaid."

"Then I have your approval to send my diplomat into Xyntharia?"

"Of course, who are you sending?"

Vamillion retrieved a scroll from her desk drawer. It was diplomatic negotiations written for the eyes of the Xyntharian nobles. "I am sending Diamus of Cassalire, Your Majesty." She pointed to the bottom of the scroll. "I will need you to sign here, and stamp your seal over here. It is proposing an alliance, which they will refuse. It is just formality; a means to notify them of Mullen's intentions."

"A formality, yes." Queen Abigail signed the alliance proposal. "But it is an important mission. Can Diamus be trusted?"

"With my life," Vamillion assured. "I have him under my control, Your Highness. I have managed to charm the most brilliant wizard I have ever met. Imagine how he can be used to serve our cause."

"He is not from Vixus, and not even a Valician, for that matter. His power is impressive, his mastery of the dark arts, but it is all the more reason to distrust him."

"Diamus has sworn his loyalty to me. We have Beauty's prophecy as reassurance."

Queen Abigail narrowed her eyes in suspicion. "You are in love with this one, aren't you?"

"Have you forgotten that I am a priestess?" Vamillion reminded. "My love is to the gods."

"Yes," Queen Abigail said. She had grown suspicious of her advisor's loyalty. She had seen what Vamillion had done to King Averath with her own eyes. How long before her time would come? "But we are human and we all have our needs. I must leave now. A royal hunting expedition returns soon, consisting of some men with great influence over the people that need speaking to. Tonight, an extravagant feast is being held in the main hall. I ask that you attend, and bring Diamus with you."

"Thank you, it is an honor."

"Very well, then. I will show myself out."

"Please, allow me," Vamillion opened her study door. "I have business of my own to attend to downstairs and will walk you out."

* * *

Vamillion waited until Queen Abigail left the Moon Tower before opening the trap door on the ground level. She grabbed a torch off the wall and entered the darkness below, taking careful steps in her descent with the help of the firelight. "Beauty? Beauty where are you?"

She received no reply, but she heard him scurry to the corner of the room, where the firelight did not penetrate. "Beauty? You will answer me."

Vamillion waited in silence, but still got no response. "You will speak to me, one way, or another." She extended the torch in front of her and moved toward the corner of the room. When the light illuminated Beauty's face, she screamed.

Beauty was shaking in fear. His lips were sewn shut with leather strips; dried blood from the crude surgical procedure covered his face. He cowered from the light and from Vamillion's expected wrath, whatever it turned out to be.

Angered by what she saw, she moved toward him slowly and extended her hand to his lips. She ran her fingers gently over the stitches, and he flinched, pulling back in pain. She spent the afternoon removing the stitches, struggling through Beauty's muffled tantrum. He moaned in pain as the leather was pulled out through each incision. He wanted to make words but couldn't. When the last stitch was removed and his mouth opened to cry out, she noticed his tongue had been cut off by a crude, sharp instrument. She stepped back in disgust, horrified by what he had done to himself. There was no clerical spell which could re-generate that which had been amputated, and as a result, there was no way that Beauty could ever speak again.

~CHAPTER 16~

Daylen gave an enthusiastic smile when he exited the Mystic Eye and met his companions on the street. Rahlen was smoking his pipe and Hogar was carving the wooden sculpture of Ayrowen. The morning light was creeping over the horizon and was a surprising indication of just how long he had been under the healing spell of the cleric.

Gramel came forward, a smile on his face as wide as Daylen's. The blonde elf and the cloaked wizard stood in the distance. "Ah, you see? I am a man of my word."

Rahlen ignored Gramel. He approached Daylen and gave him a quick look before giving Daylen a hug.

Hogar rose from his seat. He put his carving away and said, "It's good to see you are not hobbling, little man."

"I will see you all back at the Inn, later, boys," Gramel said. "It has been a pleasure." He waved to his companions, and they left through the alleyway in haste.

"Can we get out of here, now?" Hogar asked. "I have spent too much time with unpleasant company."

Rahlen pulled Daylen aside. "We are going to look for a way out of here, Daylen. We are not sticking around for the goblin army to arrive." He removed Sylver from his belt and handed the short sword to Daylen.

Daylen clutched the sword, inspecting it briefly. "Lead the way."

Rahlen was quick to navigate them into the streets. The southern roads were not as crowded as the center of town, but as the sun began to light the sky, people started making their way outdoors. Rahlen stuck to the least busy streets to avoid attention and guide his companions to the far edge of town. They came to a large wall. Every two hundred feet was a parapet between which guards marched. With expectations of the goblin invasion, the walls were also filled with locals.

They walked along the edge of River Ale, studying the fortifications and looking for any opportunity to escape undetected. Daylen was looking up at some commotion on the walls, when Rahlen grabbed him and pulled him close, motioning for Hogar to lean in. "We are being followed by Blackcoats."

"If only we could have avoided dealing with them," Hogar said. "If only we could have avoided this whole town."

"What do they want?" Daylen whispered.

"They either don't want us to escape, or they look to bring us harm. They are armed and flanking us."

"Things have gotten strange ever since Gramel discovered we travel with a wizardborn," Hogar shared.

"Whatever the case," Rahlen said, "we should head back to our room, in hopes that they are just keeping an eye on us. We shouldn't do anything suspicious or give them reason to detain us."

"The Inn is their guild!" Hogar reminded. "You aim to take us back to the lion's den?"

"Yes," Rahlen said, leading them toward the center of town.

Daylen recognized the blonde elf with the burned face from outside The Mystic Eye. He was trailing behind and to the right, weaving between those who passed by. His sword was unsheathed, and he did not hide a glare focused in Daylen's direction. Their eyes met and Daylen looked away.

Rahlen led Hogar and Daylen into the crowded streets. The inn was getting close. They cut between warriors, ruffians and peasants in an attempt to avoid a confrontation. The Blackcoats following them appeared determined to cut them off before reaching their destination.

A hand grabbed Daylen's arm. Rahlen, still holding Daylen's hand, pulled him hard, loosening him from the grip of the Blackcoat. With a mad dash, they pushed through the crowd and swung the doors to the tavern open.

Inside, a few patrons were having their breakfast ale, and turned toward the entrance startled by their abrupt arrival. However, two ruffians in black overcoats stood by the stairs that led to the bedrooms. When they withdrew their swords, it was clear they had been expecting their arrival.

"Stay with me!" Rahlen called out, as he let go of Daylen and unsheathed his sword.

Daylen did as he was told, standing behind Rahlen, he withdrew Sylver from his side. He had no time to process the reason for the assault.

The two Blackcoats advanced from the stairs and stopped several feet in front of them. There was a moment of hesitation, as the attackers assessed their strategy.

"Are you sure you want to do this?" Rahlen asked. "You can put your swords away and save yourselves."

Hogar twirled his axe in several intimidating practice swings, before positioning it over his head. He crouched low to the ground, waiting for the two predators to make their move. The patrons at the bar began to form a circle around them. Just then, the tavern door burst open, and the blonde elf entered. As he charged forward the two Blackcoats made their move.

Rahlen and Hogar took positions to defend the assault. Rahlen faced the two unknown Blackcoats and Hogar faced the blonde elf. They moved together, their backs against Daylen in order to protect him. Daylen clutched Sylver tight in his sweaty hands, uncertain if he was capable of defending himself.

The Blackcoats struck in unison, hoping to end the foray in one combined assault. Rahlen was quick to block the attack, catching both the enemies' swords against the hilt of his own. With a quick twist and thrust, one Blackcoat lost the grip of his sword and it flew to the ground, skidding into the crowd of gathered patrons.

Rahlen continued the defensive swing of his sword, for a counterattack that slit the unarmed ruffian's chest. As he bent forward in agony, Rahlen leaned into him just in time, using the victim's body as a shield, which caught the sword of the second attacker. As the Blackcoat pulled his sword from his ally's body, his defenses were lowered. Rahlen buried his sword into the Blackcoat's stomach, shoving the lifeless human shield against him, sending both Blackcoats to the ground.

Hogar was keeping the blonde elf at bay, warding off each of the elf's sword strikes with the flat steel of his axe. The elf was agile and quick, striking with such speed that it prevented Hogar from attacking. He parried, time and again, the clatter of steel on steel, his defenses slowing as the sharp edge of the elf's sword came nearer with each advance, forcing him off balance.

Rahlen grabbed Daylen and pulled him toward the staircase. "Let's move!"

Hogar caught the elf's sword in the edge of his axe and for a moment, he was able to stop the swings. Using the weight of his body, Hogar lunged forward with a mighty yell, and shoved the elf backward. The elf landed on a table, which tipped under his weight. Using the momentum of the table's fall, the elf somersaulted backward and to his feet before the table collapsed.

The maneuver allowed Hogar the chance to flee, following Rahlen and Daylen up the stairs and to the first locked gate. Rahlen fumbled through the keys in search of key number one. The blonde elf stood at the bottom of the stairs, but was not alone. The black-cloaked wizard had come to his aid and was standing beside him, his arms outstretched, pulling up the sleeves of his cloak.

By the time Rahlen found the key and unlocked the gate, the elf and the wizard were at the top of the stairs. The wizard's hands began to glow with a bright orange light, and he yelled, "Abazar!"

Rahlen swung the gate open as Hogar yelled, "To the floor!" shoving Daylen and Rahlen through the gate and face first to the ground as a streak of fire blazed from the wizard's branded palm, through the hall and over their heads. The heat of the fire searing their skin as the flames missed by inches and burst against the gate ahead. The wizard fell to one knee in a fit of coughs, winded and dizzy from his spell.

Rahlen, pinned under Daylen, kicked gate number one from the ground in an attempt to shut it between them and the attackers, but the elf threw himself into the gate's path, as it collided into his shoulder and bounced back against the wall. The elf swung his sword down in a blind rage. Hogar raised his axe sideways, blocking the repeated strikes, but losing his grip on his weapon with each blow.

Daylen could see Hogar's grip slipping. The elf swung his sword again. This time, the collision sent Hogar's axe to the ground, leaving Hogar hopeless. Daylen sensed Rahlen shifting beneath him, unable to get free. The elf raised his sword to deal a final deathly blow, when Daylen rose to his feet, lunged forward and drove Sylver into the elf's chest. The elf's eyes widened, his sword faltered overhead, and the hesitation was long enough to allow Rahlen, now free, to swing his sword from the ground, cutting through the elf's ankles. The elf collapsed just moments before Hogar acquired his axe and brought it down into the elf's head, crushing it into the floorboards.

Daylen, fueled with adrenaline, ran down the hall, jumping over the broken second gate. His heart pounded in his chest. Rahlen, now on his feet, followed him, with key number three in hand. Hogar turned his attention to the wizard, who was regaining his strength. Seizing what opportunity was left, Hogar ran to the wizard with his axe in hand, intending to take the adversary's life swiftly. As he raised his axe, he was met with surprise as the wizard sprung forward, the crimson-colored dagger dropping from the sleeve of his robe and into his hand. Hogar caught hold of the wizard's wrist and fell backward, pinned to the floor. The wizard was on top of him, trying to press the dagger into Hogar's face. Hogar clutched the wizard's wrist tightly and was able to hold the dagger's point away. The wizard's frail build was no match for Hogar's strength.

As he squeezed, Hogar crushed the wizard's frail wrist within his tight grip, and the dagger fell. He swung his fist into the wizard's face, but the wizard was determined to fight. He punched repeatedly, until the wizard lost his will and rolled onto the floor. Hogar grabbed the crimson dagger and drove it into the wizard's neck.

Rahlen opened gate number three and reached the room. Hogar picked up his axe and walked down the hall toward him with determination. Daylen opened the door to their room and was met with arms reaching for him, grabbing him by the neck. Gramel's voice was in his ear as he struggled to break free. "Easy, boy. I don't want to hurt you... but I will if I have to."

Before Gramel could turn toward the door, Rahlen hit him on top of the head, sending him to the ground. Daylen pulled away from his grasp and moved to Rahlen's side.

Gramel scurried toward the weapons and grabbed the morning star. Before he could even raise it, Rahlen chopped off Gramel's arm with the swing of his sword. Gramel fell to the ground, screaming. He writhed, rolling in his own blood. "What have you done? You are dead. All of you are-"

His voice was silenced as Rahlen brought his sword down again. Gramel's head rolled inches from his body. Daylen stepped away, speechless. He stared at Gramel's lifeless body curled on the blood-soaked floor.

Hogar appeared in the door, covered in the wizard's blood. He looked to the dead body on the floor and lowered his axe. "What now?"

There was commotion in the tavern below. Loud angry voices could be heard, slamming doors and the scurrying of anxious feet. He could hear arguments, but no one appeared when Rahlen peaked his head out of their room. The commotion grew and filled the streets. he sounds of hundreds of people yelling in unison, and the sound of charging horses could be heard through the narrow window.

"It's a mob out there," Hogar exclaimed. "The bastards are preparing to lynch us!"

Rahlen shook his head, as he focused on the noises outside. "No, no it's not us they are after." Horns blazed from outside in alarm, and the pounding, the chanting, grew to such a fevered pitch that it reverberated in their chests. "War is upon us. The goblin army is drawing near."

"Should we count ourselves lucky?" Hogar said.

Daylen felt panic take hold. "We need to leave! Now!"

"We need higher ground," Rahlen said. "Grab the short bow, Daylen, and follow me to the roof."

Locating the roof access, Rahlen led his companions to where they could assess the situation and gain knowledge of their surroundings. The roof top had just one exit to the street; an iron ladder that led down the side of the building to the alley. There was also access from the interior of the inn below, which they had used to access the roof.

Daylen followed Rahlen to the roof's edge and stared at the street below. The citizens were gathering into formations, rows and rows of makeshift soldiers. Blackcoats were dispersing weapons and armor from horse-drawn carriages and attempted to maintain order. They were shouting orders and cracking whips at those who failed to listen. Orcs provided muscle when required, but fortunately the majority were anxious to defend River Ale and fell in line.

Daylen watched the bloodthirsty citizens below. Observing the fragile state of order, he pondered whether the town of River Ale stood a chance against a goblin army. Having seen firsthand the destruction the goblins caused to Juniper, he doubted there was much hope. He wondered if the town should survive. The harsh governing law in place by the Blackcoats and the barbaric sense of justice made him question if their actions might have drawn the goblins from their caves. Perhaps, the emergence of the goblins was nothing more than a tide forged from the hands of the gods, meant to crush every last living man, woman and child who inhabited these walls.

Daylen also wondered if he had a chance of surviving. Did his life suffer the same fate as River Ale, and if not, was that not the judgement of the gods? Had some strange cosmic circumstance brought him here to perish? The sun made its way toward the center of the sky and Daylen waited with his companions as he reflected on their predicament.

Hogar knelt in prayer, waiting. Rahlen paced back and forth along the roofs ledge, his bow in his hands, his quiver stuffed with as many arrows as he could carry. After several trips back and forth he stopped in front of Daylen. "Once the goblins strike, we will have our chance to escape. I don't want you to be heroic, I want you focused on me and follow my lead. We will stay out of harm's way and focus on our exit. Do I make myself clear?"

Rahlen must have sensed Daylen's distraction. The boy was focused on the pounding of his anxious heart, his thoughts somewhere else. Rahlen gripped Daylen's arm, gaining his attention. Rahlen had that familiar somber look in his eyes. When he had Daylen's undivided attention he said, "Your father was working on bringing peace to Mullen and Vixus."

Daylen's troubled heart sank at the mention of his father's name. He wondered if this had anything to do with the likelihood that they would not live another day and required some sort of confession. He listened intently to what Rahlen had to say.

"Crooked politics were at work, in Vixus," Rahlen began. "Deception that I did not fully understand. I know your father was a good friend to King Averath. They knew each other when Averath was just a prince. Averath's father, King Argimele, entrusted Donovan with his son's life. When Donovan became a knight, he was asked by King Argimele to be a sparring partner to his son, to push him and to guide him. You see, Donovan was trusted beyond all others. He was wise in the teachings of FéLorën, which earned him great respect in those days. His character was something to aspire to, something that King Argimele was hoping would rub off on his son. And for all intents and purposes, it did. Averath became a magnificent leader, but was also an intellectual, and lived with compassion. It is said that it is this trait that Queen Liana admired most in her king."

Daylen was eager to get to what troubled him most. "Then why was he killed?"

Rahlen shook his head. "Politics are dangerous. It's the only arena where friends can be enemies and enemies can be friends. There was evil at work, deep within Vixus government; things outside of King Averath's control. Someone didn't want peace between Mullen and Vixus, and sought to destroy King Averath's relationship with your father. As long as your father was alive, peace would exist between the two kingdoms and King Averath could not be misguided. This is why he was killed.

"Your father was framed. His credibility was stripped, so that King Averath would no longer trust your father's advice. You see, contrary to modern times, Vixus used to be something special, a kingdom to be proud of. Your father had a big role in making it what it was. He loved Vixus and what it stood for."

Daylen tried to imagine a time when he had positive feelings about Vixus. Having only experienced his kingdom after his father's death, he couldn't fathom the thought.

Rahlen's voice turned grave. "There is a priestess in Vixus council. Her name is Vamillion. Your father told me that she was responsible for sowing the seeds of hate into the kingdom. She had spoiled the mind of King Averath and turned the law against your father, once she secured her position as the king's advisor. If there is any one person responsible for what happened, it is her. It is feared that she is now the true ruler of Vixus."

At last, Daylen had a name, a person responsible for his father's death. What was this feeling? He was troubled before, but now, his heart was filled with rage, a desire for revenge. He didn't want to partake in the fate of the people of River Ale, but here he was amongst them. He didn't want this to be the end, not after hearing about the priestess responsible for his father's death. His life had just begun, and he was trapped in a sea of viciousness. His hands were already bloodied by the sword, having fought and killed for survival. He would be forced to fight again. If he lived through this moment, it felt as though the fighting would ever end. Daylen wondered if survival was only possible with bloodshed.

The sound of a deep, resounding drum sounded in the distance like a slow, determined heart. Hogar rose to his feet, looking to Rahlen and then walked toward the edge of the roof. The drumming was not in the streets below, but out past the walls, through the trees and from the eastern horizon.

River Ale was eerily silent. The voices of its patrons hushed as all ears were focused on the steady, growing beat. The drumming became louder, and the beat faster as additional drums began sounding off, mimicking the rising rhythm of Daylen's own heart. He looked to Rahlen with fear.

"Goblin war drums," Rahlen said. "The time is near."

As it became clear what was to come the citizens of River Ale erupted with commotion. The first wave of goblins could be seen moving across the horizon toward River Ale. The rapid beat of the drums were joined by the sound of thousands of hollering goblins, their voices drowning the commotion in the streets. A feverish pitch rose with the pounding of thousands of goblin feet as they tore across the valley.

~CHAPTER 17~

The ground shook and the buildings trembled. Rahlen placed a firm hand on Daylen's shoulder as the stampede vibrated through his body. He watched as trees toppled like toothpicks under the goblin charge, revealing a row of battering rams. The goblins pressed on, intent on crushing whatever obstacle stood in their way.

The warriors cried out, pumped with courage, as the battering rams crashed into the walls of River Ale with a resounding crescendo. The swarm of goblins followed, smashing against the walls like violent waves of the sea. The gate gave way and the streets filled with goblins. Screams and cries accompanied the bloodshed, as the goblin horde clashed with the protectors of River Ale with the clatter of steel.

Daylen felt an arrow fly from Rahlen's bow. It plummeted into the sea of green flesh and buried into an unlucky goblin's face. Rahlen grabbed another arrow from his quiver and placed it on his bow. With a steady arm, he pulled back the bowstring and released his grip, sending another arrow into the air, its destination forcing a second goblin to the ground. Daylen raised the short bow in his hand, grabbed an arrow and focused his sights on the streets below.

Before Daylen could release his shot, a loud explosion shook the rooftop and a bright flash of fire and light rose from the street. A wooden building, hit by the explosion, crumbled to the ground. Pieces of large debris crushed goblins and people below. Clouds of black smoke rose to the sky, along with the screams of those hit by the bomb's blast.

The sudden devastation shocked Daylen to his core. He focused on the scene below and caught sight of goblins with explosives strapped to their backs, throwing themselves into an adjacent building in a suicidal act of carnage. The building blew to pieces, the combustion blazing in another climatic crash, causing Daylen's ears to ring. Rahlen was yelling something at him, but he could not hear his words. Moments later, a building across the street suffered a similar fate, and the loud crack of the explosion further intensified the high-pitched screaming in his ear. He tried to focus on his surroundings as he heard a series of repetitive explosions pounding in the distance. The eastern wall came tumbling down. Moments later, the western wall followed suit, allowing the goblin horde to invade from all directions.

The streets were covered in smoke as the clashing swords and shields rang. Daylen turned to his companions at the roof's edge, near the ladder to the alley. Rahlen was shooting arrows into the alley below, while Hogar made sure goblins that climbed the ladder never reached the top. Daylen ran to their side. In the distance, the sound of another explosion rang out.

Hogar swung his two-handed sword with wild, repetitive motions, hacking all that made its way to the roof. The climbing goblins were helpless, trapped on the ladder's steps and unable to defend themselves. The only threat was the onset of fatigue as he fought back the goblins, now climbing the ladder in packs, one on top of the other. Rahlen continued to release arrows into the swarm of ascending goblins. Hogar jabbed his sword through a goblin chest, the sword buried too far into its victim to be pulled out in time for the next rushing goblin. He shoved the goblin with his sword still stuck in its body, the force causing it, and those that we near the top, to fall to the alley below.

Hogar grabbed the morning star at his feet. A few goblins reached the roof. He swirled the morning star and sent it crashing against the nearest skull. Rahlen threw his bow to the ground and unsheathed a sword in each hand, preparing to meet the assault. Daylen held Sylver out before him.

Hogar swung the morning star in wide arcs over his head, creating a safe distance between himself and the goblins circling him. Despite their efforts, Daylen could see they were outnumbered. It was only a matter of time before they were drowned in a sea of green, to be shredded and devoured by claws and teeth.

Daylen stepped back to the ledge, as Rahlen and Hogar gave what appeared to be a valiant last stand, sending goblins to their death one after the other, the bodies piling up around them as new goblins took the place of those before them. Daylen peered over the edge, contemplating jumping to this death rather than being eaten alive. It was at that moment that he noticed a goblin bomber running for the tavern, the fuse on its back blazing. He raised his short bow and fired to the street below, the arrow flying inches past its target and snapping upon impact with the street below. With sweaty, nervous hands he brought another arrow to his bow, realizing that he would not have another opportunity should he miss again. He led the goblin enough to match its frantic pace and let the arrow fly. The arrow buried in the goblin's shoulder, whipping the goblin around. The goblin faltered back, disorientated long enough for the fuse to reach its end and detonate, blowing the goblin into tiny fragments. The explosion grazed the front of the building. A rush of flames reached for the sky as smoke, rich with the odor of those burning below filled the air. The roof caved forward as the fire ate through the building's frame.

Daylen slid toward the fire with the collapsing roof. His companions were close behind, the roof giving out from beneath them. Hogar and Rahlen slid down with the goblins following. They fell through a wall of flames. When the roof descended low enough, Daylen tumbled to the ground. Rahlen and Hogar jumped down beside him.

Their chance to escape appeared through a collapsed wall. The street was temporarily cleared of enemies from the blast. There was no time to pause as Daylen followed Rahlen and Hogar into the street. The goblins from the roof toppled to the tavern floor, rising to their feet to pursue them.

Rahlen grabbed Daylen's hand and led him into the chaos of battle with Hogar at their side. The ringing in Daylen's ears had quieted enough to hear Rahlen urge them to move quickly, their window of opportunity shrinking. Hogar lost the morning star in the fall, but grabbed the axe strapped to his back and swung it before him. Daylen held onto Sylver and running over massacred remains was led into the smoke-filled alleys.

Rahlen flung Daylen against the wall of a building, as a goblin chariot, adorned with skulls and spikes, trampled through the street. The chariot was set ablaze. The driver, littered with arrows, dropped lifeless beneath the chariot wheels. The chariot collided into a nearby building, its crude frame crumbling to pieces. Its path of destruction left a clear trail through River Ale, but the streets were filled with shooting flames and burning bodies. Those who still stood were engaged in violent combat.

The opening through the crushed city wall was a beacon of hope. Beyond the wall's crumbled frame was the Wanton Lands, where they held a slim chance for survival. As they made their way over the wall's remains, they encountered several goblins. Rahlen let go of Daylen and unsheathed his swords. He charged with Hogar into the advancing goblins, attempting to protect Daylen from their assault. One goblin flung himself into Daylen, sending them both to the ground. Pinned beneath the goblin, Daylen struggled to keep the Goblin's claws and teeth from digging into his flesh.

Freeing his arm, he drove Sylver into the goblin's stomach, spilling its guts upon him. He stared up at the goblin, watching its monstrous, hungry eyes roll back into its head. He felt the insanity of the battle consume him, feeling as though he was becoming as monstrous as the creatures he was fighting. He saw

Rahlen kill his victims with quick, lethal strikes of his swords, sending sprays of blood through the air. He rushed to Daylen and helped him to his feet, pulling him into the Wanton Lands.

Hogar brought his axe into the side of a goblin's head. A second goblin lunged for his leg and bit into his calf. He hollered as the goblin's razor-sharp teeth buried into his muscle. With the vigorous jerking of its head, it took a chunk of Hogar's flesh into its mouth. Hogar swung his axe down before the goblin could take another bite and dealt a fatal blow.

Hogar turned to his companions and struggled to catch up to them, hobbling as he swung his axe into another goblin. Another jumped on Hogar's back and buried its teeth into his shoulder. Hogar hollered, flinging the goblin over his back and to the ground below him, splitting the goblin in two with his axe.

Ahead, Rahlen and Daylen came upon a large company of goblins, proving that escape into the Wanton Lands would not be easy. "We are trapped," Rahlen said, winded.

"Like hell we are," Hogar said, now standing at his side. His leg and shoulder bleeding profusely. Rahlen looked at Hogar, as if in honor of a silent oath to one another. Like countless times before, they stood side by side with sword and axe, greeting a hellish hardship with heroism and the conviction to overcome adversity. They nodded to one another and ran forward.

Daylen followed. In the seconds before the collision, Daylen braced himself, contemplating if this was how it would all end. Hogar punched a goblin in the face, the blow causing the goblin's legs to kick out from under it and sent it crashing to the ground. Hogar's axe lopped the head off of another. Rahlen made use of both swords simultaneously, blocking a goblin attack with one while slaying another. They maneuvered and struck as if they were of the same mind, the way that only two seasoned warriors who had fought side by side for many years could do. Rahlen and Hogar defied the odds of survival, but the goblins had circled them, and their advance was relentless.

Daylen joined in, slicing the chest of a goblin open with Sylver before plunging his sword through another. A goblin swung a club into Rahlen's back, sending him to one knee. Before the goblin could strike again, Hogar was there with his axe, and chopped the goblin down. The attack turned to defense, as Rahlen and Hogar struggled to keep the goblins at bay. Daylen ran forward, providing a much-needed assist, slicing open a goblin that threatened Hogar's exposed body, just as Hogar was focused on defending Rahlen.

Daylen's surprise assault allowed Rahlen and Hogar to move back on the offensive. A goblin claw slid into Rahlen's forearm before it died at his sword. He trudged forward, swinging his blades in a fury, dropping goblins in a rage of bloodshed. Hogar buried his axe in one of the creatures, losing grip of his axe. He had no time to retrieve it and was forced into hand-to-hand combat as they surrounded him, clawing and biting at his exposed skin.

Daylen stabbed at the goblins that surrounded Hogar. Beneath a pile of goblins, Hogar continued to punch his way through them, one at a time, sending them reeling back before plunging on him again, cutting him and biting him and pulling him to the ground. Daylen killed those that he could, but soon drew the attention of four goblins and was forced to fight them off.

Rahlen managed to slay those that were in his way and ran to Daylen's defense. One after the other the goblins fell to Sylver and to Rahlen's swords, until Daylen was free. By the time they made it to Hogar, the swarm of goblins were devouring his flesh as he relentlessly continued bashing their skulls with his bare hands, his body torn to shreds.

By the time the last goblin was slain, Hogar no longer moved beneath the pile of goblin bodies. Rahlen threw the lifeless goblins off of Hogar, calling out to him. Daylen stepped back, shaking his head, as Hogar came into view beneath the carnage. His face was unrecognizable. His body was a mangled mess, his skin torn back to the bone. Rahlen called out for Hogar but heard no reply. Rahlen tried to pick him up, but his limbs dangled at his side, his head wobbled loose on his thrashed neck. Rahlen brought Hogar's lifeless body to him and squeezed it tight as he strained to hold back his anguish. He rose to his feet, covered in blood.

Daylen fell to his knees. Out in the trees, goblins could be heard scurrying, another wave approaching. Behind them, in River Ale, a series of explosions were set off, only a few structures remaining. The sound of battle raged over the crackling of fire. Smoke billowed into the sky, blocking the sun's rays. Daylen shook his head. Rahlen stood over him. He accepted Rahlen's outstretched hand and was helped to his feet. Rahlen looked him over for any vital wounds beneath the goblin slime, blood and sweat. Finding none, Rahlen gripped Daylen's hand tight. When Daylen looked into Rahlen's eyes he knew what must be done. Together, they ran into the Wanton Lands, leaving Hogar's lifeless body behind. In front of them lay a narrow path to salvation.

~CHAPTER 18~

The Tower of Illusions loomed over the west wing of Vixus Academy. Dwelling within, young ambitious magicians practiced their trade. A spiral staircase ascended nine stories; each floor housing classes for advancement in wizard training. Upon the ninth floor, the legendary Masters of illusion dabbled with their magic, their discoveries offering the most critical breakthroughs in the art of illusions for the kingdom of Vixus.

On the first floor, at the bottom of the spiral stairwell, stood a statue of Erramond the Wise, the most famous of all Illusionists and founder of the Way of FéLorën. Those wizards with the title of Initiate, Seeker, and Scholar, walked past the statue, going about their business and their education without giving it a second glance. Vamillion stood at the statue's base, waiting for the crowd of students to disperse.

As the last students shuffled into class, Vamillion slid a key into a concealed hole in the wall behind the statue. The wall slid open just far enough to enter, revealing a secret passage. She traveled down a steep flight of narrow stairs, far below ground and far from the eyes of the schooling wizards above. She walked the cold stone steps, the damp air and spider webs welcomed her to the secret world below the Academy. At the end of the stairs, she came to a thick iron door. Forged into the metal was a skull.

Using her key, she unlocked the door and entered the hidden chambers of Necromancy. Lanterns lit an expansive hallway lined with metal doors. The doors had narrow, barred viewing slots, confining the horrors within. Vamillion focused on the dark shadows beyond the iron bars, attracted by the curious sounds. The rooms were inhabited by wizards deformed by their own dark spells and with prisoners who were used as guinea pigs for the Necromancer's to practice their craft. The cries and moans from these victims of Necromancy filled Vamillion's mind with unholy images of what these helpless, imprisoned souls endured. As she passed, deformed hands clawed and grasped through the iron bars.

A Necromancer exited a nearby room, slamming the door behind him in order to suffocate tormented screams within. Vamillion recognized the wizard.

'Vamillion, My Liege," the Necromancer said, bowing repeatedly as she approached.

Vamillion motioned for him to rise. "Rasatharian, how are your studies coming along?"

"Progressing, Master." Rasatharian's slender, sunken face heightened his grim appearance. "We have lost another Initiate to our studies. This makes four in the last three weeks." He lowered his head. "Too many souls have been sacrificed to their art, and not enough students remain to fill the classrooms."

Vamillion motioned for Rasatharian to follow her as she made her way down the hall. "How long have you been below ground?"

"I am a third year Magi, Master."

"Three years?" She asked.

"Yes, Master, since the beginning. I watched with my own eyes as the gate to the school of Necromancy first opened. I have seen young wizards come and go, the majority consumed by madness or contorted into one form of abnormality or another."

"It is the price one pays, in search of new discoveries. The work of pioneers is never easy, nor without danger. It is a noble privilege," Vamillion reminded.

Rasatharian nodded. "I do not believe I have ever properly conveyed my gratitude for all you have done for me and for my kind. My life is indebted to you. Always."

"It is not your loyalty that worries me, but the souls above ground. They take their lives for granted and do not see the blessings I have bestowed upon them. You, on the other hand, have proven to be a most reliable and dutiful servant and a successful student. You are well on your way to becoming our schools first Master. It is because of your courage that our studies will advance our kingdom into a new era. Tell me, is there any who have been here as long as you?"

"There is only one who is still alive. His name is Ty-Ular. Unfortunately, he has gone mad. He resides behind one of these iron doors, My Liege."

Vamillion stopped and turned to face Rasatharian. "Congratulations on your success. I am appointing you Chancellor of the school of Necromancy."

Rasatharian was stunned. "My Liege, you are too kind, and I am undeserving of such a position."

"Are you suggesting I have made a mistake?"

Rasatharian stumbled for the words. "Of course not, My Liege."

"Your loyalty and perseverance make you the most experienced personnel on staff. How could I appoint another?"

Rasatharian fell to his knees and kissed Vamillion's hand with his thin lips.

"Rise; and listen to me." She waited until he rose. "It will be your duty to inform me as to the goings on and the progress of this institution. I will be readily available for any concerns you may have and to receive the knowledge of any key advancements."

"As you command, My Liege."

Vamillion placed a silver key into Rastharian's frail, pale hand. "This is a key to the door of Necromancy. It is also the key to the Moon Tower, where my personal study resides. You are free to roam the world above."

"Your Majesty... I-I..."

"You were the first to greet this magnificent hall and I would be proud to have you be the first Necromancer from Vixus Academy to walk upon the land of our holy empire. Today, you are making history. Of course, you must tell no one of your craft, and be discreet in your travels. You have a huge responsibility – to me and to this kingdom. Do not disappoint me."

Rasatharian bowed. "I can't find the words to convey my gratitude."

Vamillion motioned for Rasatharian to continue walking with her. "What good will you be to me if you can't find the words? Be proud, you earned it. And your opinions will be invaluable to me."

Rasatharian nodded. "I have several concerns, if I may be so bold as to inform you. The lack of help from the outside world and the secrecy surrounding our work is crippling our progress and imposing a serious danger to our students. We need the support of other wizards. If we could work closely with the clerics from the Holy Academy, we could heal the many Necromancers that get ill. A Necromancer's spell power is typically greater than his understanding, and as a result, we are victim to our own craft."

Vamillion acknowledged his concerns. "I am fully aware of the negative aspects of our secrecy. Now that King Averath is dead, I am making headway with Queen Abigale. One day, I assure you, Necromancers will walk the land proudly displaying their craft for the world to see. You must be patient. The Queen is doing much to sway public opinion and it is but a matter of time."

They came to a steel door and Rasatharian slowed his pace. He bowed to Vamillion. "Understood, My Liege. If my services are no longer acquired, I have reached my destination."

"Put your work aside for now, Rasatharian. As my Chancellor, it is imperative that you learn of the inner workings of this Academy. Follow me."

"As you wish, Master."

She led him to a stairwell, to a lower level that Rasatharian had never seen. The hall was decorated in royal colors, carpeted and lined with fine chandeliers and paintings. At the end of the hallway was an elaborately decorated wooden door with finely crafted hinges.

*　　　　*　　　　*

"What are you, Glazahn?" Diamus circled his apprentice slowly.

Glazahn clutched a bronze staff in front of him, his head bowed in concentrated prayer. "I am the center of the universe."

"And your destiny?" Diamus questioned.

"To control myself; to control the universe," Glazahn responded.

The door opened, interrupting Diamus' teachings. He turned to greet his visitors. "Ah, High Priestess…"

Vamillion and Rasatharian entered the room.

"To your center," Diamus spoke to Glazahn.

Like a soldier in training, Glazahn stood tall, tightening his posture like a statue.

"Diamus, let me introduce you to the Chancellor of the Necromancy Academy, Rasatharian."

Rasatharian bowed.

"Rasatharian, this is Diamus, Senior Administrator, and presiding Headmaster of the Academy in my absence."

"We have met before," Diamus said. "Congratulations, Rasatharian, on your new title."

"I am pleased that you have met, I would like for you two to work together closely," Vamillion informed Diamus. "If there is anything that Rasatharian can do for you, Diamus, just ask of it."

"I am at your service, Diamus," Rasatharian said.

"There is much for us to discuss to get you up to speed," Diamus informed. "For now, it is best for you to acquaint yourself with the students of this academy in your new role. Show that they are of service to you and at your command. I expect strict discipline for their own safety. We cannot afford to continue losing Necromancers to their art, and I am relying on you, Chancellor, to see to their safety."

"Consider it done, Legionnaire," Rasatharian said.

"Let me introduce you to Glazahn, a young and bright wizard of the dark arts. He is an apprentice of mine, working directly under my leadership. He is respectful to the laws of the school and as such, will show you the upmost respect."

"A pleasure," Rasatharian said, addressing Glazahn.

"Chancellor," Glazahn bowed. "The pleasure is mine."

"Well, well, well, Diamus…" Vamillion said, giving Glazahn a once over. "There is quite a change in your young apprentice. He is no longer the bumbling child I first met. You are doing magnificently."

"He is a good apprentice," Diamus said, "dutiful and loyal. You will be glad to hear that he is no longer a Seeker. He is an Initiate and ready for the next stage of training."

"He has learned his first spell?" Vamillion asked with excitement.

Diamus handed Vamillion a piece of parchment with foreign symbols on it. If she was a Necromancer, the symbols would speak to her as if they were her native language. However, as priestess, she was a Holy Cleric and the symbol was meaningless to her. "Tell me what it says. Is it strong? Is it everything the Dark One promised?"

"Instead of telling you, why don't I show you?" Diamus said.

Vamillion took a step back, skeptical. Rasatharian looked on, nervous and apprehensive.

Diamus laughed. "There is nothing to fear, except fear itself. Please, indulge me."

"Very well," Vamillion said.

Diamus took the parchment from Vamillion's hand and began to read the symbols out loud in a foreign language. As he spoke, a moan filled the room. Shivers ran up Vamillion's skin and she saw Rasatharian also felt the uneasy chill in the air. Diamus began to chant, the moans growing louder, screams and cries filling the room. By the time Diamus finished the spell, the voices were maddening.

Vamillion braced herself against a table, struggling to hold her composure. Rasatharian, affected more deeply, cowered on the floor in the fetal position and shook with terror, having succumbed to the voices. When the spell ended his fear disappeared. As if exiting from a trance, he looked around embarrassed, and quickly rose to his feet.

Diamus was weak from the incantation. He slumped in his chair to rest.

"This spell came from Glazahn?" Rasatharian said, impressed. "It is most intriguing."

"My spell power made it stronger," Diamus said, "but it is his mind which brought it to fruition."

"It is an impressive start, but this is not the spell the Dark One had promised us," said Vamillion.

"Patience," Diamus said. "The spell reflects a strong talent for conjurations. I am excited to continue his training." With weak, shaking hands, he picked up the parchment that had fallen to the ground. There was something he was holding back from saying and Vamillion recognized his hesitation.

"Something troubles you…" Vamillion's eyes narrowed with suspicion.

"There is one concern that should not be ignored," Diamus said.

"Tell me," Vamillion said.

Diamus looked to Glazahn, "Tell the High Priestess."

"After learning the spell, I grew weak," Glazahn informed. "Casting the spell must have been too much for my mind and body to handle. I - I was overcome with nausea and a deathlike illness. I stumbled to the floor and fell into a deep sleep."

"He is modest, this one. He slipped into a coma for two days," Diamus clarified. "I was uncertain if he would ever wake from it."

The concern in Vamillion's face relaxed after a moment of reflection. "Glazahn, you will give us a great gift one day, of this fact, I am certain. Worry not about such phases, it is only a sign of just how powerful your magic will be. I need you to leave us, now. Diamus, Rasatharian and I need to speak with you in private."

Glazahn nodded and looked to Diamus for permission, before leaving the room. As the door shut behind him Diamus rose to his feet, the strength coming back to him. "I worry for the boy's life."

"He will give us the spell the Dark One promised us, Diamus. That is all that matters. Once he bestows us with that gift, it will be of little importance whether he lives or dies. Such is the nature of our world. We must push him, we must get our hands on that spell. Time is of the essence. Which is why I am here; and why I have brought Rasatharian with me today. I need your help with a diplomatic issue."

"I am not even a citizen of your kingdom," Diamus reminded. "And Rasatharian is a Necromancer, who must remain secret."

"This mission is secret from even the deepest political puppets of this kingdom. Truth is, you are the only person I can trust, and you will have Rasatharian for assistance."

Diamus was eager for adventure as he had been cooped up in the dungeons of the Necromancer Academy for far too long. The fresh air would do him and his apprentice some good. "Where will I be heading?"

"To Xyntharia to deliver a message to the elven lords." Vamillion produced a scroll of the alliance request, which was signed by the Queen, and handed it to Diamus. She also laid out a map of Xyntharia on Diamus' table. Over the course of the evening, she discussed the logistics to their travel. Rasatharian was then excused with orders to prepare for the journey and to tie up loose ends with the students.

After Rasatharian's departure, Diamus' eyes lightened with intrigue. "The city of Xyntharia!" Diamus said with excitement. "Magnificent. I have read books of its splendor and gazed at paintings of its marvelous halls. To think I shall set foot inside..."

Vamillion moved close to Diamus, her eyes brightened to mirror his. "I knew you would be perfect for this."

He studied the devious curve of her smile, marveled at the sinister secrets locked behind her eyes, as she inched closer to him, as if drawn to his mesmerized glare. It was obvious to him she was eager to be close and to feel his touch. He was mesmerized, knowing he would be unable to resist her desires.

She placed her thin hand to his chest. "Thank you, for all your assistance and your loyalty." Her eyes lingered on his and her gaze softened, inviting passage to her soul, a dangerous but intriguing world of exotic mystery.

Diamus stared into her seductive eyes, felt her playful fingers at his chest, her lips moved close to his. Was she prepared to release the monster inside of him? He wondered and searched her soul for an answer.

Waiting for her to draw nearer still, he stared at the curve of her lips with anticipation. She stopped, inches from his mouth, and looked into his eyes again. He could feel her soft breath against his face. He brought his hand to her cheek, felt her soft skin and ran his hand through her hair to the back of her head. She leaned forward and bit his neck, the sharp sting of pain awakening his senses. With her long black hair between his fingers, he squeezed his hand into a fist, pulling back her hair and forcing her lips to his. He kissed her passionately, her hands untying his robe. His mouth moved down her neck and lingered at its base, kissing the contours of her skin. He was drunk on the feel of her flesh on his lips. She arched her head back and sighed, pushing her pelvis against his. His hands pulled at the strings on her corset, until it was loose and he tugged it down to her hips. She slid her hand between his legs and felt his lust for her.

Diamus grabbed the fabric of her thin chemise in his hands and tore it down the middle, exposing her soft, pale breasts and blush-colored nipples. She pushed away, standing before him, her bare chest on display, she was a goddess, and her forbidden body was to be his. He reached out to grab her, but she denied him the pleasure. She slid around the table and opened the door to his bedroom chamber. Her seductive walk beckoned him to follow as she stopped before the corner of the four-poster bed and removed her clothes behind its sheer curtain. He stood in the door and watched. She stepped away from the curtain, her naked body exposed to him as she lit the candles at his bedside, and then crawled onto the bed. The candlelight accentuated the curves of her body, the flickering glow illuminating her skin.

Diamus let his robe fall to his feet, closing the door behind him as he joined her. He kissed her legs as they opened for him, his mouth traveling the length of her body as he made his way on top of her. She was wet and inviting and he took her, her nails running down his back. His thrusts were met with pain equal to the pleasure of penetration, as she dug her nails into him until he bled.

She brought her finger to her mouth, the taste of his blood fueling her desire. Her desire excited him. Beneath her beauty and soft skin, she was a monster of darkness, like he, and her passions rivaled his own. He brought her hand to his face and tasted the blood from her fingers. She shoved her fingers into his mouth, his tongue dancing between them before she pulled her hand away and slapped him hard in the face, the rings on her finger splitting open his cheek. He leaned back, but she rose forward in hunger, licking the blood that dripped from his face. He shoved her back to the bed and reached in the bedside table, procuring a small blade.

He ran the edge over his heart. Piercing his skin, he bled down his chest. He pulled her head to him, and she sucked at the wound, pulling away with blood filling her mouth. The pale skin of her face covered in the gore of his mutilation, running down her neck and collecting at the curves of her heaving breasts.

She offered him her arm and he took it in his grasp. He ran his hand down the smooth underside of her forearm and kissed it gently before putting the blade to her flesh. He made a small incision where his lips had been. She gasped at the sensation, her body arched, the pain mixed with the pleasure of feeling him still inside her. She climaxed, unable to control the moans that escaped her lips, as he sucked on the blood that poured from her arm.

With sudden strength, she flipped Diamus over onto his back and straddled him. She leaned over and grabbed the candle beside the bed and brought it to her lips. She gave a devious smile, and blowing softly, extinguished the flame. She rocked back and forth on top of him, her hips gyrating with increased intensity and tipping the candle, poured hot wax onto his chest. Searing to the touch, the wax hardened against his inflamed skin. Her thrusts timed with the consecutive contact of dripping wax. Seeing Diamus close his eyes in ecstasy, reaching his climax, she reached hers for a second time, throwing the candle to the floor, pinning his arms to the bed. In satisfying release, he let out a primal cry. Struggling for breath she collapsed on top of him, her body and his as one. She heaved in sighs against his body.

She rolled off of him and stared at the ceiling. Diamus looked at her in admiration and lust. As his strength returned, his mind lingered on his mission. "What you ask of me, what you desire… it is dangerous," he spoke. "This quest to Xyntharia, it is trickery… and a treaty will offend them. If they mistrust my intention, if they suspect foul play, they will imprison me, or worse."

Vamillion turned to face Diamus, her head resting on the arm he placed around her. "You need not worry. Beauty has prophesized everything. There is no way we can fail."

Diamus removed his arm from around her and shifted uncomfortably. "How can I trust this Beauty person, whom you hide away from the world? What you say about him… disturbs me. How do I know he even exists?"

Beauty is most certainly real, but he is a tortured soul, fragile, and must be kept safe from the world and from himself. Imagine a child, sheltered from the world, but his mind seeing so much. He has to be contained, and he has to be parented with strict authority. I never wanted to hurt him… but he left me no choice. All I have done, I have done for him, he does not understand the sacrifice that is required."

"Children are defiant by nature. He believes you are his mother, does he not? It is his nature to crave independence."

"I suppose he already has it," Vamillion remarked. "What he did to himself, it is unthinkable. He cut his own tongue out to defy me. And if that wasn't enough, he sewed his mouth shut. He is perverse and tormented. Remarkable, and full of so many secrets."

Diamus smiled at the thought and placed his hand on her skin. "We all have a shadow we must face, a darkness to embrace."

Vamillion sighed. "Without the magic to heal him, he is lost to me. It is only a matter of time before I will be forced to bury him. He is useless to me, now."

"I want to meet him," Diamus said.

Vamillion pulled away. "No, I'm afraid not."

"I did not ask," Diamus clarified. "I must meet the one who is deciding my fate. It is the only way I will help you."

Vamillion eyed Diamus carefully, as if weighing her options. "Have you not listened to my words? He is disturbed and fragile. I am afraid of how he'll react."

Diamus was not concerned by what Beauty might or might not do. "You said yourself, he is of no use to you, now. What harm can there be?"

Vamillion lowered her eyes, submitting to Diamus' request. He was the only man who had challenged her will and won. Diamus knew that Vamillion needed him more than she had ever let on, and her giving into him set a precedent that changed their relationship and exposed vulnerability that Vamillion never wanted to reveal. For a moment, there was a look on Vamillion's face that made Diamus wonder if the power he held over her would one day lead her to kill him. She smiled suddenly, her face changing and her voice extinguished such dark thoughts. "You will be the first person ever to see him."

"Where did Beauty come from, anyway?"

Vamillion took a moment to respond, as if weighing how much information to give him. "He is the son of Averath," she admitted.

"*King* Averath?" Diamus questioned.

Vamillion confirmed his assessment with a sly smile.

"Then that would make him…"

"The king," Vamillion finished. She rolled out of bed. "Come, let us bathe. I want to enjoy the little time we still have before you have to leave. I will take you to Beauty before your departure."

~CHAPTER 19~

Diamus followed Vamillion to the Moon Tower. The first floor was a cold, empty room of cobblestone with a winding, ascending stairwell and torch lit walls. Instead of taking the stairs to her study, she led Diamus beneath the stairs, to a wooden trapdoor. She unlocked the latch and swung the trapdoor open, a warm glow rising from the depths, lighting a series of stone steps to the dungeon below.

It was not often that Beauty lit the dungeon in firelight, preferring the dark to the awareness of his surroundings, but Vamillion had no reason to suspect anything unusual stepping down into the dungeon. When she caught sight of the chamber, her eyes widened in awe.

"Oh my…" Diamus whispered behind her. He turned in a circle to absorb his surroundings. The walls were decorated in a detailed mural. Every square inch of the cell was covered with bright, fragmented images, detailed scenes seemingly out of context. Portraits were painted beside foreign symbols, castles floating above brilliant landscapes, battles painted in the sky, troops painted in excruciating detail. Despite his talent, it appeared that nothing, within all of Beauty's imaginative depictions made logical sense. It was as if the images were abstractions of Beauty's mind, a visual collage of unconscious thought.

"It's like a dream… a dream on display," Vamillion whispered, mesmerized.

Beauty was placing the finishing touches to his masterpiece. Standing on a wooden chair, he reached to the top corner of the wall, applying the final strokes of paint to a floating eye, bright rays of light shining from behind it. Aware of his guests, he turned to greet Vamillion and Diamus. His scarred face, the lifeless stare of his fake eye and the fresh wound from his mouth created a striking, twisted display of the torture he had endured.

Diamus paid little attention to the boy's appearance but was drawn to his artistic talent. Being surrounded by such vivid imagery was an exhilarating experience. "Not a dream, but far from it." Diamus placed his hand to his chin in contemplation. He recognized seemingly random landscapes and his eyes gazed upon a remarkable landmark. A windmill on a rolling green hill, but not just any windmill. It was painted in fine detail, including the dilapidated ladder that ran up the outer wall, with the broken third rung, leading to a bronze bell at the top. "I know this place.... Most fascinating. I can hardly believe it. It is in Cassalire, my homeland, on the continent of Oryahn. How is this possible? It's as if he has painted the inner most private memory of my childhood. We have never even met, yet he knows the private details of my life experience. He knew I would be here. Knew I would enter his chamber and see this painting and be touched by what he has created. He is not mute, Vamillion, he is speaking to us."

"Beauty? What have you painted for us?" Vamillion asked, knowing he had no means to respond.

"Why else would he paint it?" Diamus interjected. "What other purpose does it serve, but to tell us of his extraordinary ability? Through his art, he speaks and connects to us. These images are worth more than words can describe or express. I have never felt such emotion as this, never felt the hand of destiny before in all its majesty. It's touch, like that of a gentle god. Comforting, to feel so small in the cosmos."

Beauty stepped down from the ladder. The look in his eye and the nod of his head affirmed Diamus' words. He reached out to Diamus and grabbed his hand.

Diamus was moved by Beauty's fragile touch. "He must feel this all the time, the connection to time, the embrace of destiny. He is a miracle. We are in the presence of greatness, something much greater than you or I, Vamillion." Diamus began to analyze all the images, his mind was reeling, wondering what significance they had. Who were the other images painted for? What purpose did they serve? And how would the interpretations shape their future?"

Vamillion looked at the paintings and saw chaos on display, years of interpretation possible. "There is too much."

Diamus spun around to take in the full scope of the art. "Over here," Diamus pointed. "There is a story being told. The paintings are like a narrative."

Vamillion looked. "Prophecy," she concluded.

"But of course!" Diamus exclaimed. He returned his focus on Beauty. He looked past the scars and saw the intriguing qualities of Beauty's soul. Diamus raised his hand to Beauty's face. Beauty flinched, as if by instinct, like a tortured animal. Diamus was careful with his touch, frightened by what the animal in Beauty might do. Despite Beauty's obvious nervousness and distrust, he stayed perfectly still, seemingly as interested in Diamus as Diamus was in him.

"It's as though he can see straight into my soul, seeing all that I hold secret. To him, there are no secrets. What an incredible power." He placed his hand on Beauty's cheek. "What kind of monster lies within you? What power do you hide from even yourself?"

Beauty reached out and traced the wrinkles on Diamus' face, outlining the contours of his natural frown as Diamus' hand traced the contours of Beauty's scars.

"Can you hear me?" Diamus said.

Beauty nodded.

"You say that Mullen wishes to attack us? I must go to Xyntharia and speak to the elves?

Beauty nodded.

"Will I be safe?" He was quick to request. Yet he filled with terror in an instant. "Wait – please. Don't answer that. I – I do not want to know." Diamus shivered, a cold chill running through him. "I trust you, Beauty. How can I not? You haven't even heard of Xyntharia beyond your visions. You don't even know what Xyntharia is. The gods, they speak through you, don't they?"

Beauty did not confirm the answer to his question.

"Share more with us, will you? Explain your paintings to me."

Beauty moved to his desk. He shoved paints to the floor to clear space and placed a piece of paper down. He grabbed a quill, dipped it in ink and began to write. Diamus moved beside Beauty and looked over his shoulder, reading the two simple words he placed on the page: "*I cannot.*"

"He has been refusing me for weeks," Vamillion said. "He is a liar!"

Diamus silenced Vamillion with a wave of his hand. There was a fear in Beauty's eye. A raw terror. "Beauty, please, write something to us, something we can use."

Beauty set the quill on the table to confirm he would say no more.

"He expects us to interpret the paintings instead of just writing words. It is unacceptable." Vamillion said. "His defiance will cost him, dearly."

Diamus studied Beauty's face closely. In Beauty's expression, there was a desire to abide, but it was as if he was prohibited to explain. Prohibited by whom? He wondered. "We should speak above, in private. I have seen enough for now, and I have what I need to trust in my mission."

*　　　　*　　　　*

Beauty stood in the silence of his cell, the trapdoor slamming shut, leaving him alone to face the future alone. His body began to shake.

Popi's voice filled the room like a phantom. "Very good, Beauty. Very good. You told them nothing."

Beauty closed his eye and cried.

*   *   *

Diamus took a seat opposite Vamillion's desk and glanced at her books and papers. After gathering his thoughts, he spoke. "Does anyone else have access to Beauty's chamber?"

Vamillion was startled by the question. "Of course not. No one knows he exists except the Queen and I, and only I have the key to his room."

Diamus nodded, deep in thought. "He is conflicted, dealing with an intense struggle in his soul. He may very well be insane, but his mind still runs, his prophecy still unfolds. As long as that continues, he should not be executed. Just think, he may know what lies beyond the portal."

"I know," Vamillion said. "Why do you think I have put up with his defiance? You think it has been easy? I have spilled my blood for him, toiled endlessly for hours over his secrets. I have bent over backwards for him, all the days of my life, trying to understand what is locked away in his mind. I have done everything in my power, without killing him, to understand his world. No potions, no magic I know can reveal the truth. I am forced to hang on the boy's every word."

"You are not alone in this. I am here to assist in any way that I can."

Vamillion slumped in her chair, resting her head on her table. "Do you understand the incredible pressure of relying on another like this? The empire rests on a fragile balance. I am afraid. I am a slave to Beauty. The Dark One, he promises unlimited power as long as the boy succeeds in helping me. My faith in this is the only thing that grounds me. Meanwhile, my clerical powers have dwindled. A price I pay for turning my back on the old gods, I imagine. Another sacrifice I made. Every spell I cast brings crippling pain, pain stronger than ever. I cannot see my future beyond what Beauty predicts. I can't think beyond what Beauty allows me to think." She leaned back in her chair, her emotions weighing her face into a frown. "I have lost my way." She looked to Diamus with a vulnerability she had never revealed, as if looking to him for guidance. "It didn't use to be this way. I need pain to feel connected to anything or anyone."

From across the table, Diamus took her hand in his. "We will do this together. With Beauty and the Dark One to guide us, we cannot lose. We have only to trust. Find yourself and prepare for what is to come. If not, all you have accomplished will slip through your fingers. Be strong, my love."

Vamillion wiped a solitary tear from her cheek, regained her composure, and shut out any further emotion. She would punish herself for her momentary weakness, through the act of carefully selected self-mutilation. It would align her to the present moment and release her from her anxieties, from that which she could not control. It would strengthen her will and devotion to her pursuits. She would succeed no matter the cost. If not for herself, then for her kingdom, the people that depended on her. "Kiss me," she said, leaning toward Diamus.

~CHAPTER 20~

"Daylen… Daylen, wake up."

Daylen opened his eyes. Rahlen was standing above him.

Rahlen placed his hand on Daylen's shoulder. "You were crying."

Daylen rolled over on his side and mumbled. He had dreamt that Ghost was drowning and that there was nothing he could do to save him. He could only watch as Ghost sank deeper and deeper into a violent sea, until he was no longer in view. The loss he felt was unbearable, as if he lost a part of himself. "A dream… a terrible dream."

"A dream, nothing more." Rahlen extended his hand and helped Daylen to his feet.

There was a void in his heart, where his companions once resided and guilt that propelled him to his feet. He winced in pain as he stood. He had grown quite accustomed to pain. Pain was a reminder he was still alive. Pain was like a loyal companion. It was there with him, in his ribs, his shoulders, and his pounding head. Despite his discomfort, he considered himself lucky. There was no more River Ale, thousand dead. Then, he realized there was no longer a cleric to heal him should he suffer the fate of another major wound.

He rubbed his eyes and wiped dried blood off his face. Although the intense experience of the last two days could drive one insane, madness would not come for him, although at times, he wished it did. No matter how hard he tried he could not break away from reality, the painful reality of existence. The drive to survive. Over and over he could hear the screams of battle in his mind and explosions.

Rahlen appeared weary, but sober. Perhaps, when Daylen had seen as much battle as Rahlen, he would grow used to this life. He looked to the ground beneath him for his belongings. All that was left was his father's sword, Sylver, and the wood carving of Ayrowen in his pocket, which Hogar never had the chance to finish. He grabbed Sylver and sheathed it at his waist side.

Rahlen placed his arm over Daylen's shoulder and pointed towards the tall mountain range in the distance. "No more than two days from here lies the Cragel Mountains. It is there, with the help of the Cragel people, that we will reach the final leg of our quest." He squeezed Daylen tightly. "We are almost there."

Daylen found it hard to imagine his quest would end or what it ultimately meant. He felt less prepared than ever to greet Zantigar, which was the opposite of his expectation when he first set out on his adventure. "I cannot believe it is almost over."

"Nothing will be more gratifying than finishing the quest that took the lives of our friends. Their sacrifice will not be in vain," Rahlen said.

It seemed unfair to Daylen that others had died for him. They gave their lives so he could have his own. Each death killed a part of himself. He had since fallen into deeper confusion, frustration and anger. He had thought this quest would help him make sense of the world, but all it had done was expose more chaos questions. What he now knew was that he lived in a world he did not care for.

Rahlen sensed Daylen's turmoil and stepped away. He had a way of seeing into Daylen, placing himself into Daylen's experience. "You have displayed courage that before, in Brunhylde, you never would have imagined possible. You have grown in more ways than you realize. Our fallen friends, they live inside you now, in both of us. Their spirits are a part of us, their voices inside us. Recognize this connection. Recognize their love. Bolinda would want you to understand this. Let Hogar's strength and determination push you forward and Bolinda's heart ease your troubled mind. They would be so proud of you. I am proud of you."

Daylen looked to the sky. The clouds had parted, but the rain continued to fall. He tried to understand the force behind each passing moment. "I know now why this is called the Wanton Lands. I know what makes the wolves hungry, what fuels goblin rage, and what causes the plants to grow thorns. I just wonder what we are all fighting for. What right do I have to exist in spite of another? And who I am to complain about what does not unfold in my favor?"

Daylen looked to his frail hands. The rain fell on him, dropping into his open palms. "The world is a cruel place. It is time I accepted that, whether I like it or not." He looked to the Cragel Mountains, the goal in the far off distance, and started walking.

The Santian River cut through the Wanton Land, dividing the forest from the Cragel Mountains. By the time Daylen and Rahlen made it to the river, the daylight had been drowned in dark storm clouds and then snuffed out by the ensuing night. The air chilled from the plunging temperature.

They crossed over a wooden bridge into mist and fog that swallowed the rocky terrain beneath their feet. From the depths of the mist, the Cragel Mountains loomed overhead, its jagged peaks penetrating the passing storm clouds. Rahlen's cloak whipped violently in the wind, serving as a marker for Daylen who trailed behind just far enough away that the fog threatened to swallow him into oblivion.

The land was no longer consumed with wild plant life. The natural overgrowth was replaced by large boulders and steep rock formations. Daylen struggled to keep up, his feet slipping on the hard stone. His strength was tested as he clung to steep ledges. He balanced himself on small footholds as the downpour of rain impeded their ascent.

A bolt of lightning ripped through the night sky, lighting the next step before a resounding roar of thunder filled the sky. Rahlen had made it to a safe plateau and leaned over to help Daylen. The flat expanse of rock served as a trail, spiraling further up the mountain. The next flash of lightning revealed a massive crack in the mountainside, which led to a cave, a deep, dark expanse that provided shelter. Rahlen hollered over the crashing rain, pointing out the dry safe haven. Acknowledging their destination and eager for reprieve from the storm, Daylen ran toward the dark passageway.

The large, expansive entrance and wide passage appeared like the descent into a dragon's throat. Rahlen pulled on Daylen's tunic. "Not much farther."

Daylen stopped abruptly, his eyes unable to pierce the blackness of the cave. "I can't see anything."

A roar suddenly shook the cave walls. A resounding boom rang in the distance, deep within the dark. Boom. Daylen and Rahlen looked at each other. Boom. The ground shook beneath them with each crescendo. Boom. Rahlen withdrew his sword. Boom. The sound grew near. Boom. Louder. Boom. Stones and pebbles fell around them. Boom. Boom… boom, boom.

Daylen's face was white, as a giant emerged, a massive beast of a man too tall to stand within the cave. A deafening roar escaped his throat, with vile breath that soured the air.

'Outside!" Rahlen exclaimed. He pulled Daylen into the pouring rain. The giant followed, with a club made of the trunk of a massive redwood, the strength of which could topple a castle wall.

The giant met them on the mountain path. It brought its foot down to crush Rahlen, but he maneuvered between the giant's legs and swung his sword into its calf as he passed beneath. The giant's tough, weathered skin was hardened like a reptilian creature. The blade, unable to penetrate, only angered the giant more. With rage, it screamed. Daylen ran past the giant's legs. The giant, slow to maneuver, brought his club crashing down into the mountainside, the rock beneath it splintering into an explosion of stone shrapnel, the mountain path collapsing under the force of his strike. The velocity of the crashing club blew Daylen forward onto his face. The fall saved him from the projectile stone that came whizzing overhead. Rahlen helped Daylen to his feet and together they scurried up the mountain. The giant was close behind, his stomping feet booming behind them, the ground shaking beneath their feet and throwing them off balance.

It became clear they had no chance of outrunning the giant. There was no choice but to confront the beast. Within three sweeping strides, the giant was overhead. Rahlen stopped suddenly and turned to face the predator. "Run Daylen, run for your life and don't look back!"

Rahlen stood tall, planted in front of the giant. He looked up at the massive figure before him as it raised its club overhead. A shriek rang through the air. It was Ayrowen, swooping down toward the giant, her lethal talons raised and targeting the giant's eyes. He screamed as Ayrowen's razor sharp claws split its eye. Rahlen then cried out as he plunged his sword into the giant's leg with all his might, sending the monster to one knee. The club came down next, intent on crushing Rahlen beneath its massive weight. Rahlen jumped aside just in time, rolling with the gust of wind generated from the giant's blow.

Ayrowen had swooped down with another attack, this time, her talons plunged into the giant's wounded eye and with her tight grip, ripped the eye from its socket. The eye still clutched in her talons as she arched back toward the sky. The giant let out a billowing cry, raising its arms into the air in protest.

Daylen stopped running, his fear of leaving his companion behind stronger than Rahlen's command for him to run. He was not going to let another tragedy strike. He ran back down the mountain pass, Sylver unsheathed. Before he lunged toward the giant, a spear, thrown from high on the mountain ledge, buried into the giant's neck. In turn, Rahlen jumped and with the weight of his body, drove his sword into the giant's chest, plunging the blade to the hilt. Holding onto the sword, his feet could not touch the ground.

On the ledge above, four warriors appeared, descending with pikes and nets. Daylen plunged Sylver into the giant's leg. The hard, reptile-like skin could not withstand the blades sharp edge. The giant's eyes widened; his club raised overhead. The giant's movement blowing Daylen to the ground. Rahlen attempted to pull his sword from the giant's chest, but it would not give. Losing his grip, he dropped to the mountain path. He had only a moment to breathe before the club swung into his side, his body wrapping around the club like a fabric doll, the swing of the club sending his body soaring into the mountainside, where his body molded, limp and broken against the sharp contour of rocks.

Leaning up from the ground, Daylen screamed. He did not notice the advancing warriors as they struck in unison with pike and net, the series of piercing wounds and the weight of the nets sending the giant crashing to the ground, where it remained pinned and helpless in the confines of the netting. The warriors repeatedly pierced the giant's skin until its struggle seized, and it breathed its last breath in a gurgling whimper.

Daylen's senses returned. He heard Ayrowen call from above. He ran and collapsed at Rahlen's mangled body. Rahlen's head was split open from contact with the rocks. Miraculously, his chest still rose as he struggled to breathe. He opened his mouth to speak. He raised his hand and grabbed Daylen's arm. "Don't be… afraid."

Daylen clutched Rahlen's body. "Don't leave me, Rahlen."

Rahlen's head fell back, his breath, no longer escaping his lips. His last words repeated in Daylen's mind, echoing into a deathly silence. Rahlen's grip on Daylen's arm loosened and his hand fell limp to the ground. Daylen clutched Rahlen's body and shook back and forth, tears running down his face. From behind, Daylen made out a soft angelic voice.

"Are you okay, young one?"

Daylen turned and looked through his tears toward a woman standing above him. Articles of tattered, mismatched armor covered her feminine frame. From under a dented, silver helmet, thick red locks draped down on each side of her pale, freckled face. Her eyes were bold, like those of a weathered warrior. Her features hardened by light scars.

At her side was a broadsword and in her hand was an oblong shield, beaten and deformed from prior battles.

Daylen found it difficult to speak. He composed himself the best he could. "I am Daylen."

The woman stepped down to Daylen's side. "And your friend? What was his name?"

Daylen looked down at the body in his arms. It took him a moment to respond, as he struggled to process what he saw before him. "Rahlen."

"I am sorry for your loss," the woman said. "My name is Echo. If there is anything I can do…"

Daylen looked up and stared into her eyes. He lowered Rahlen's body to the ground and stood. He tried to find meaning in the sorrow he experienced. He was left wondering why he still lived. It did not matter, nothing mattered. He felt there was no future in having no one to live for. "He was my friend."

"He was brave," Echo said. "I witnessed his heroism. My companions and I have been hunting this giant for quite some time, and your encounter led us to his cave. His name was Berege, Berege of Backmountain. He was a long way from home, a reckless giant. Lost and hungry, most likely exiled from his tribe, he thought to feed on the simple people of Cragel. Your friend helped bring the end to his reign of terror."

"I appreciate what you are trying to do," Daylen said. "To make his death mean something. I wish it helped."

Where are you from, young one?"

Daylen was not sure how to answer. He thought of where he belonged and was uncertain. He followed the feeling of his heart, until he thought of the one place that he would like to settle down. "Twilight."

Echo looked at the lifeless body at her feet. "Rahlen of Twilight." She bent to one knee in prayer. "We are forever grateful for his courage and his sacrifice." Echo rose and turned to face the three warriors who were standing at a respectful distance. "Come on, boys."

The three mountain men walked to Echo's side. "This is my brother, Northwind. The other two are like brothers, but not by blood. They are courageous, just as I am sure Rahlen of Twilight was. This is Horizon, and Canyon Breeze. We are protectors of Cragel. Our ancestors guarded dragons that used to roam these mountains many, many years ago. Our fathers and their fathers tell tales of the preservation of the dying breed, of fending off Dragonslayers. They were the famous Dragonriders from days of old, in a time before history."

Northwind removed his helmet, revealing his chiseled, stern features, a sturdy rock of a man. "Now, we hunt giants, orcs, anything that tries to destroy the people of Cragel. As my sister has said, we will assist you in any way that we can."

"I would like to bury Rahlen," Daylen said.

"Consider it done," Echo said.

The Giantslayers helped Daylen bury Rahlen's body and soon after, he found himself in their company. Four strange reptilian beasts of dragon descent were at the campsite that Echo led him to. They stood on their hind legs, no taller than Daylen, with long necks and reptilian faces. Equipped with a harness and saddle, the beasts were used to scale up mountains in ways that no horse ever could.

Noticing Daylen's fascination with the peculiar beasts, Echo said, "They are Cragons. Go ahead and touch, they are gentle and domesticated."

Daylen placed his hand on the Cragon's head. It closed its eyes, pleased by his touch, its tongue slithering past its teeth. When he walked away, the Cragon followed him to where he sat.

"He likes you." Northwind handed Daylen some dried meat. "Feed him, and you will have a new best friend."

Once situated around a fire, sheltered from the rain, Echo explained their plans. "My companions and I are looking for another giant. It goes by the name Grumb. We are too close to catching him to turn back now."

Daylen wrapped the blanket Echo gave him tight around his body. He had a full stomach and the warmth of the fire. He was grateful for Echo's generosity and hospitality.

Echo had taken off her helmet and armor with a great sigh of relief, glad to be able to relax. She brushed her long red locks with her hands and stretched her legs out by the blazing firelight. "We would be willing to have your company, if you are looking for work."

"I appreciate the offer, more than you know," Daylen said. "And you have saved my life. But I must leave first thing in the morning. Rahlen died trying to get me to my destination. I cannot change my plans; I cannot ignore the mission my friend died for."

"I would argue if I felt it would do any good," Echo said. 'I can see in your eyes and can hear in the conviction of your voice that there is no swaying you. I was a warrior child once. I have traveled a long road to get where I am today, and I have let nothing stand in my way. Who would I be to stop you? Your journey is a sacred one."

"How do you know?" Daylen said.

"We are all on a sacred journey," she replied. "You heading to Cragel?"

Daylen nodded.

"The mountain pass is dangerous. Promise me you will be safe, and I will pray that tomorrow brings fortune your way."

Daylen stretched out and closed his eyes. He listened to the crackle of the fire and was fortunate to be in the company of the Giantslayers this night. Despite being in their company, he never felt more alone. Numbness took hold, shock of all that had transpired left him dumbfounded. He could still hear

Rahlen's last words and thought back on the lessons that he had taught. He remembered the trust and hope that Rahlen had placed on him. He would press onward as Rahlen would have wanted, he would live his life for those who had died for him, in their memory. He would do right by those who had found worth in him, even if he did not see it. Rahlen had been right, he thought. He was not who he once was. The Wanton Land had changed him. And those who traveled with him had become a part of him. The memory of their lives would stay with him, like seeds of hope.

Daylen lowered his head to the ground and closed his eyes. Before he fell asleep, Echo and her companions sang in soft, haunting harmony. They sang of days of old, ancestors and dragons and of fire and ice and the air and the sea. They sang of travels to far off places, encounters with foreign faces and the lessons learned from a life lived by sword and shield.

Daylen dreamt of adventure, of traveling with Rahlen, Bolinda and Hogar. He did not want to wake. In the morning, Daylen parted from the company of the Giantslayers. He exited quietly, before they awoke. He moved up the Cragel mountain range. He was alone again, just as he was in the beginning. The brisk morning air offered the fresh scent of a land cleansed by rain and it was a fitting start to the next phase of his quest.

Something advanced from behind him. He looked back and saw Echo. She was dressed in her armor again and riding a Cragon. In her hand she held the reins to a second Cragon, baring no rider. As she approached, her lips parted in a smile that warmed him in a way that only the beauty of a valiant woman could.

"I brought you a gift. I could not bear the thought of you traveling alone all the way to Cragel, not after your assistance, and of your sacrifice. Cragel Village is high up the mountain, where the elevation prohibits vegetation from growing, with freezing winds and snow. The air is hard to breathe. You will need help, so I have brought you a Cragon. This one, I believe, took a liking to you last night. Take him."

"I cannot," Daylen began to say, but he was interrupted by her stubborn voice.

"You will die without its help, Daylen." She held out the reins. "Take the Cragon."

Daylen grabbed the reins. The Cragon shuffled its feet with excitement and raised its head for Daylen's touch, its tongue slithering. Daylen smiled. "I don't know what to say."

"You're welcome." Echo turned her Cragon to face down the mountain pass. "May there be a road."

"Thank you," Daylen said. Before he could say a farewell, she whipped the reins of her Cragon and sped down the mountain. He looked at his gift. The Cragon sneezed and tilted its head side to side, waiting for his command. Attached to the saddle was the blanket he used the night before. He untied it and wrapped it around his body.

Ayrowen called out from above, she circled the Cragon with distrust, or perhaps envy, keeping a fair distance from Daylen's new companion. The Cragon was nervous of Ayrowen. Daylen placed his hand on the Cragon's long neck. "Easy fella'," he said beneath his breath. The Cragon jerked at his touch, but remained obedient, lowering his head and back for Daylen to climb aboard. Once stable, the Cragon rose on his hind legs. Daylen gave a soft nudge and the Cragon took off down the trail, running with gallant strides. Daylen clutched tight to the reins, surprised at his speed, as the wind blew in through his hair, bringing a smile to his face.

The Cragel Mountains loomed higher than he could have imagined, the path winding ever higher into the gray clouds and then above, where the bright light of the sun shone unobstructed. Over a day's travel, he had traversed over a vast snow-filled landscape. Unique, natural stone wonders marked the path before him.

What would have otherwise taken days, was achieved in hours. As the sun began to set, he entered Cragel Village. He noticed many caves dug into the side of the mountains on either side of the trail. Thick, stone pillars marked the entrance to the village. There was no gate or wall separating the village from the outside world. No one resisted or protested his arrival. Instead, the natives of Cragel exited their caves, one at a time, and greeted him with a bow and a casual smile.

They were dressed in animal furs. The majority of people were over six feet tall and had large, wide upper bodies with massive shoulders. Their unique build afforded them large lungs, allowing them to sustain a vigorous work life at this high altitude. The village, itself, was built directly into the mountains. There were no wooden structures for shops or homes. Wagons moved past, carrying meats and vegetation from the lower valleys.

Darkness was descending and even with the warmth of the thick blanket Echo had provided, he was reaching a dangerously low temperature. Not interested in dabbling in village affairs, he looked quickly for a native who could assist him with shelter. A native happened to be pulling a wooden carriage into the village.

"Do you know where I can find an Inn?"

The native stared at Daylen, looking him up and down. When he spoke, it was in a language that Daylen did not understand.

"Shelter, a place to sleep for the night?"

The native stared at Daylen and studied his expression. He waved for Daylen to follow.

Daylen was led to a cave, where he was greeted by a warm fire and other natives. Even though they could not speak to each other, they were friendly. Daylen was treated as an honored guest. He showed the locals his Cragon and Sylver and they shared with him beads and bracelets. As the night progressed, he was invited to other caves and to the common areas of the village. There were children playing and men and women cooking and weaving clothes. Others were crafting tools, instruments, pots and utensils. As natives came and went, he realized the native who led him to the caves had a family that was larger than he was accustomed to. In fact, Daylen could not make out the man's wife, or his children, or his brothers or sisters. A woman the man clearly loved seemed to be his wife, but when the embraced another with equal intimacy, he reconsidered this thought. The children treated all adults as parents, listening to the guidance of the elders in equal measure. The small children played together, living out their imaginations in creative play. Young adults worked with the more experienced adults, learning how to craft tools.

Cragel Village was a community like none Daylen had experienced. The community shared all. There were no possessions and no ownership of any kind, of one another or of the tools they used. There was happiness on their faces, a harmony between them. In the evening, the dinner that was prepared was magnificent. The lack of communication through words did not hinder his connection with them. In fact, the simplicity of communication through actions only heightened the relationship between them. Daylen's visit turned into an extended stay, a much-needed break from his quest. A reprieve, from the harsh and cruel experiences of his journey. In the warm care of the Cragel people, he stayed in their company for another night. A festival was held. He was offered a ceremonial tea which was bitter to taste, and warm in his stomach. Before long, he no longer felt the burden of the weight he carried. He was no longer aware of who he was, he was something more than he had previously believed, something greater than his physical form. He felt a strong connection to his surroundings.

Daylen watched, mesmerized, as the natives danced, sang, and acted out dramas, the stories unlike any stories Daylen had ever witnessed. Natives played the roles of abstract things, such as rain, time, and death, as if these were actual people. As these characters, they enacted tales of the creation of life and the birth of stars and of the mountains.

The children approached Daylen in curiosity and tugged at his clothes and the sword at his side. They seemed to laugh at him, his strange clothing and belongings. The adults were quick to send the children scurrying on their way, to be caught up in the next distraction. Daylen envied their laughter, exploration, and innocence. He noticed a girl his age continuously looking at him. Her soft, inviting eyes and boldness struck him. He tried to avoid her stare, but she was persistent. Communicating only with their eyes, he had never felt any one look at him in such a way. When he finally acknowledged her, she came to him. She did not speak, but her eyes expressed her interest. She kissed him. He pulled away and she laughed, grabbing him in her arms and touching her forehead to his.

They stared into each other's eyes. He laughed and then he was overcome with sadness. Tears fell down his face and she seemed fascinated by this reaction. Her expression confirmed that she understood his pain and his joy, that she knew there was little separation between them. That joy and pain were linked, one emotion could not exist without the other. Without words, this shared knowledge opened up their souls and ability to trust one another. He found his hand comfortably placed within hers. They sat together, enjoying the attentive sweetness between them. Reflecting on his time with the Cragel's, he did not feel alone. He felt a part of a community, a family, where the feelings of others and awareness of their experience took precedence over individual need.

Stories turned to music, where rhythmic drumming fueled his spirit and took him to far off spaces. The villagers danced around a blazing fire, their silhouettes cast upon the mountains, swaying to the hypnotic beats. The night passed like a dream. When sleep finally came, it was in a seamless blend with his waking reality, so that it wasn't clear just when, exactly, he fell asleep. He had the warmth of affection, the girl's soft arms wrapped around him. There was the feeling that something had been forgotten, a calling which he had ignored. He knew that in the morning, he should leave, but in this moment, he was right where he needed to be.

*   *   *

Ghost rose from a deep blue sea. Like a magician, he levitated inches above the water. He had no face, no recognizable features of any kind, just a shell of a body. Daylen knew who it was. He could hear Ghost speaking to him in a voice that resonated in Daylen's own mind.

"I am waiting," Ghost said.

Daylen's heart pounded. "Waiting for what?

Daylen awoke to find the man who first led him to the village standing over him.

It took Daylen a minute to understand what was happening. He remembered that the day before began with a struggled conversation to explain to the Cragel people that he was looking for Whispering Falls. Drawing with sticks in the dirt, he described where he needed to go and it was made clear they would lead him to his destination.

Daylen rubbed his eyes. He followed the man to a table where other natives were eating. The food was presented in large serving bowls, and shared. The girl who had struck a chord in his heart was sitting at the table. She smiled at him. He took a seat beside her. After eating, she rustled his unkempt hair with amusement before jumping up to leave.

"Wait…" Daylen called out, not knowing her name, not knowing if anyone had a name in the village. She turned and acknowledged him. He raised his hand up. "Goodbye," he said.

She smiled playfully. She raised her hand, mimicking his gesture of farewell, then turned and left. Daylen shook his head. He cleaned his plate of every last crumb, savoring the nourishment the meal provided. Afterwards, as promised, the man led Daylen out of the village.

Their path descended steep along the opposite side of the Cragel Mountain. Much of their descent was by ladder or narrow stone step. The trail ran beside a flowing mountain stream. Their path intersected the stream multiple times by wooden bridge, fallen log or rope. They veered into mountain crevices just large enough to squeeze through and up and over boulders and through dark catacombs. When they reached the light after exiting a long narrow cavern, they were greeted by crystal clear water cascading from the mountain. The impact of water on the rocks generated an impressive wall of sound and sprayed a light mist into the air, the light refracting into rainbows. Bright green wildlife grew through the cracks in the mountain. The natural splendor drew hundreds of butterflies. Daylen turned to his guide, expecting to catch him sharing in the experience, but the man was solemn, as if plagued by a disturbance.

The man pointed to the waterfall. It was clear that he would go no further. Something in the region concerned him. There was fear in the man's eyes. He put his hands together and bowed to Daylen and made his leave, back in the direction from which they had come.

"Thank you, for everything," Daylen called and watched as his guide disappeared around the bend.

Daylen moved forward with caution. Unsure what to be looking out for, he made his descent. Despite the beauty of his surroundings, a nervous tension gripped his stomach as he knew his final destination was nearing. God, angel, or demon… something spooked his guide, and as Daylen approached the cascade of Whispering Falls, he braced himself for whatever greeted him on the other side.

PART III

ZANTIGAR

Do not question what you see, but why you see it. Reality, as you perceive it, exists within you. Perception is creation, in action. It encompasses all, including the perceiver. Once this has been realized, the world is seen as it is, a reflection. So, look, and ask; who am I? The answer is limited only by the level of your awareness.

-excerpt from "Modern FéLorën Co-Creator Handbook" 296 A.F.

~CHAPTER 1~

Vamillion watched from the top of the Moon Tower as Diamus of Cassalire left for Xyntharia. She waited, as the royal red and blue colors of Vixus banners disappeared over the horizon. When the caravan could no longer be seen she turned to her desk, its surface cluttered with Beauty's sketches and paintings. She had spent days in her tower, obsessing over Beauty's artwork. Interpreting their meaning proved to be a challenge, as each artistic expression were fragments of visions, pieces to multiple stories illustrated out of sequence. Her eyes were drawn to several familiar characters. She recognized her own figure and the figure of a shadow-like presence with red eyes. She assumed this dark shape was a depiction of the Dark One, yet she was not sure.

There was also the image of a wizard that she did not recognize. He was old, his wild hair as white as the canvas, rising like flames from his head. The wizard was painted with such realism, that she believed this figure was an integral player in the future. The wrinkles of his skin made him ancient in appearance, his eyes were like those of a madman, fierce and bold. His face was frail in contrast to his eyes, his cheeks sunken, and his nose long and slender. Vamillion was at a loss as to the wizard's meaning. In frustration, she flung the painting to the floor and rested her head on her desk.

Filled with a desperate rage, afraid of the unknown, she screamed.

*　　　　*　　　　*

From under the stone floor of the Moon Tower's foundation, Beauty could hear Vamillion's scream. He stared into his shattered mirror, his face painted like a clown. His skin was powdered pale white. An exaggerated smile painted over his lips, rising across his cheeks. Eye shadow darkened the contours of his eye. He looked into the mirror and raised a brush of black paint to his artificial, ivory eye, filling it until it looked like nothing more than an empty socket. He marveled at the reflection before him. Amused, he sat in silence, and waited for time to run its course.

~CHAPTER 2~

Daylen climbed down a short ledge and slid to the foot of the waterfall. Mist clouded his vision as he approached the cave. He could hear voices from beyond its entrance and this alarmed him. He tried to make out the words. There was crying beyond the waterfall and a voice that expressed deep sadness. Faint laughter rose above the sad cries and then there was a low, bellowing scream, as if someone had fallen into an endless hole.

Daylen jumped into the lake, submerging his lower body in the cold, ice water. He waded toward the distant sounds. He dove, headfirst, resurfacing beyond the waterfall and at the entrance to the cave. He looked behind him. The voices now seemed to emanate on the other side of the waterfall, the side he had just come from. "Whispering Falls," Daylen whispered, understanding how it got its name.

Turning to face the darkness, his composure was shattered by a snickering voice. "Yes, Wizardborn. Welcome to Whispering Falls."

Daylen felt an unsettling weight in his stomach as he tried to peer through the veil of darkness. The roar of the waterfall was echoing into the recesses of cave the before him. "Zantigar?"

"Come forward, you must enter the dark if you wish to see the light."

Daylen hesitated, untrusting. "I... I cannot see you."

"There is no need to see, my friend, when you can feel." The voice instructed. "And you, young wizard, have grown to feel so much. So much heartache, so much pain. So much… fear."

Daylen reached out in front of him, searching for obstacles in his way. He moved to the side with slow steps, until his hand touched the surface of the cave wall. It was cold, wet, and rough to the touch, but it helped him find his bearing. Cautious, he continued forward. After several steps, when the dark consumed him completely and the crashing sound of the waterfall sank into the distance, a face emerged. It loomed, floating bodiless in the shadows.

The stranger's green eyes studied Daylen closely. His face was pale and wrinkled, the hair on his head was dark, thick and curly. Rising from the locks of hair were two small bone stubs; broken horns that protruded from his forehead. His blistered, cracked lips parted into a slender smile, revealing sharp, jagged teeth. "I am Nasavine."

Daylen stumbled backward, alarmed. "Are you a demon?"

"I mean you no harm." Nasavine stepped forward. Much to Daylen's relief, there was a body connected to Nasavine's eerie face. Yet, his body revealed another surprising characteristic. His legs were those of a goat and with hooved feet. He was dressed like a gypsy, with a fine, embroidered vest and was adorned in sparkling jewelry.

"I want to congratulate you," Nasavine said with a peculiar grin.

"What for?" Daylen said in suspicion.

Nasavine chuckled in amusement. "Why, you have completed your quest!"

Daylen was shocked by Nasavine's prophetic insight. He had already referred to Daylen as Wizardborn and now seemed to be aware of his travels. He wondered what else Nasavine knew. "I have accomplished nothing," he said.

"How can you say such a thing?" Nasavine hissed. "You have come such a long way."

"State your business," Daylen demanded. "What are you looking for?"

"For you, of course. To welcome you to an enchanted realm. I know the great lengths you have traveled, and I know the sacrifices you have made at the costs of others. Trust in me, as a friend, and I shall reward you, kindly."

"I am not sure what you can do for me, nor why you even would," Daylen said.

Nasavine pulled a silver trinket from his vest pocket. It was an amulet attached to a thin chain. "This is Dumaji. It is an ancient relic forged by the gods." There was a twinkle in his eye as he spoke. "Infused within this amulet is life energy of divine nature. It has the power to protect you and to guide you to your destination with ease, and comfort."

"Protect me? From what?" Daylen slid his hand to the hilt of his sword.

"I thought you would never ask. It can protect you from that which haunts you and confines you from living the life you were meant to live. I offer you the very thing that can strip you of the force that threatens your very existence."

"What is this you speak of?"

"Fear," Nasavine hissed. His eyes widening to emphasize the word. "This amulet can wipe fear from your mind. After all, fear is the Dark One's key to stealing your soul." Nasavine's tongue slithered between his jagged teeth as he spoke, and his eyes widened.

"The Dark One? Who is that?"

Nasavine hunched over in excitement and snickered. "You have not heard? Surely, in all your travels you have heard of the Dark One. You are a wizard, are you not?"

Daylen's grip on the hilt of his sword tightened. "I am no wizard."

Nasavine's face grew solemn, his eyebrows scrunched at the bridge of his nose. "You cannot lie to me. I know who you are… as do all of us."

Daylen looked side to side. "Who else is here?"

"What is that? You cannot see them? You do not *feel* them?" Nasavine's eyes shifted. "How unfortunate... just as unfortunate as your connection to the Dark One. Fear is in you. It is a part of you. As long as you fear, he will find you." Nasavine stepped back, his body concealed once again in darkness, his face floating in shadow. "We only wish to protect you, Wizardborn. Wear the amulet tight around your neck if you wish to survive. Without it, there is no certainty, and the road ahead will be long, and arduous!" Nasavine frowned, as his face slid into the shadows. His voice echoed in the cavern before fading away.

Daylen lunged forward, reaching out to grab Nasavine, but to no avail. "How do I know you are not a demon?"

There was no answer. The Dumaji rested on the ground before him. He looked at the markings on the amulet. Surrounded in darkness, he felt the unnerving crawl of fear on his skin. He wondered what waited for him on the other side, wondered if his fear was warranted. Nasavine was right to suspect fear in him, so perhaps he was right about the amulet's protective qualities. He bent down and picked up the amulet. To be safe, he did as Nasavine suggested, and fastened the amulet around his neck. If nothing else, it was a sign of his willingness to cooperate with creatures in a realm he did not understand. He took a deep breath and continued through the dark cave.

After walking a short distance, he could see a penetrating light at the end of the cavern. It was a tunnel and stepping out he entered a snow filled landscape. Bare and tall birch trees spread as far as the eyes could see. With no unique landmark in sight, the trees created the illusion that any and all directions, save the way from which he came, were the same. No longer with a guide, and no longer in the company of his companions, Daylen felt vulnerable and lost to his surroundings. He walked forward in the only direction which felt like progress, until he was surrounded by the birch woodland and the way back to Whispering Falls disappeared. The sky darkened by storm clouds, and he moved forward aimlessly, without a sense of direction.

Something flashed between the trees, registering as a blur, but he could feel the breeze as it passed, swooping close to his body. He looked through the trees in search of what had appeared. Before him, an eagle arched above the trees, floating long enough to be noticed, and then dived ahead.

"Ayrowen!" Daylen shouted with excitement. "Oh, my trusted friend, I was lost without you!" Daylen ran in the direction of her flight, sure-footed and with newfound inspiration. Struggling to keep up, the trees whipped past as he dodged across the forest landscape. Suddenly, a lone cottage stood before him. It was a rickety old cottage, weather beaten and dilapidated. From the thin layer of frost covering the windows, Daylen could make out a light. From the top of a pebble stone chimney, thick gray smoke rose, absorbing into the storm clouds above.

Ayrowen landed on the roof. She turned her head to the side, her dark eyes staring straight at Daylen. Daylen smiled, thankful for her guidance. When he drew close to the cottage door, Ayrowen took to the sky, disappearing above the trees.

A metal ring was fixed to the center of the door, rusted over from years of neglect. Moss covered most of its surface, along with the wooden slats of the door. Daylen clutched the ring and knocked. He waited, nervously, uncertain of what awaited him. The winter winds picked up, and whistled through the limbs of the surrounding trees, lifting dead leaves like spirits into the air. He knocked again, this time in greater force.

Only the wind responded.

Daylen could still see light through the window, but there was too much frost to see the interior. Perhaps, a fire was lit to warm the resident's return. He crossed his arms tightly around his chest, in a feeble attempt to get warm and checked his surroundings. Around him was a woodland labyrinth. To turn back and lose himself in the woods, with no direction or purpose... the thought convinced him he had no choice but to act. Before he could question his decision, he grabbed the doorknob and turned the handle.

The door swung open with little resistance. He was anxious to feel the warmth of the fire and to sit in a comfortable chair. He decided he would wait here for as long as it took for the resident to return. Yet, he was greeted with darkness. The warmth of a fire was nothing more than an illusion. If not a form of magic, then perhaps it was a figment of his own imagination.

Facing the entryway of a dark room, he noticed a silhouette, a shadowed figure. "Hello?"

An old, raspy voice responded. "It is rude to enter a stranger's home, uninvited."

Daylen's eyes struggled to adjust to the darkness of the cottage interior. As if granting a silent wish, the cottage was illuminated in light. Candles on the walls lit in an instant and the fireplace erupted in strong, healthy flames. An old man sat alone on a soft, padded chair.

Daylen was startled by the figure before him. He did not know what to expect, but he had little doubt that he stood before the one he had traveled so far to meet. "Zantigar?"

"Sometimes," the old man responded. His body was thin and his face sunken.

Daylen stared at the old man before him. Below wild, white brows, Zantigar's penetrating stare captivated his attention. His eyes were faded and colorless. Before Daylen found the words to speak, Zantigar rose from his chair and moved toward him slowly, as if frail with age. Daylen's mind raced with thoughts and questions as he attempted to understand the mere existence of the two-hundred-year-old man standing before him.

Zantigar raised a thick eyebrow. "Were you looking for me?"

Daylen nodded.

"Well," Zantigar said. "You seem to have some understanding, however shallow it may be, as to who I am… but I am at a loss as to who you are."

"I am Daylen."

"Of course, you are," Zantigar said, with a hint of sarcasm.

Zantigar raised his voice. "Who are you?"

Daylen took a couple steps backward, realizing that he had angered the old wizard, but unsure how. "I-I don't understand."

"You would think, despite your obvious confusion that you could at least inform me as to who you are," Zantigar said. His anger growing as he neared.

Moving backwards toward the door, Daylen shifted, stumbling over objects on the floor. Zantigar continued to speak, lowering his voice. "I knew a man named Gron. Many claimed to know him. All who knew him recognized his odd taste in clothes, the funny limp to his walk. However, they all had quite different opinions of him. This is because Gron was a man like all men, who placed himself in many different roles."

Zantigar held Daylen's gaze under his intense, colorless eyes. "Gron wore many different masks, you see. He would change from day to day, sometimes moment by moment. How then could any person know who he was, who he truly was?"

Zantigar did not wait for Daylen to answer. "The story of Gron is a tragedy, really. For, like most minds, he was victim to a world of labels, blind to the ever-changing reality that he himself could not describe with any real accuracy just who, exactly, he was. Why, I ask, would so many different people, with so many different opinions as to the nature of this man, all call him by the same name? As if by some magical quality, the very pronunciation of his name convinced themselves that they knew who he was?"

Daylen did not know how to answer.

Zantigar turned away, un-interested in an answer. "Could there ever be a more powerful form of illusion in the world? An illusion that has tricked so many people, including the one who conjured it? And to think, it didn't even take a spell!"

Zantigar faced Daylen, raising a commanding finger his direction. "May this be a lesson to you. This lesson is free, and no other one will be. There is no magic more powerful than non-magic."

Daylen stood, perplexed.

"Reality," Zantigar alluded, raising his hands in the air as if to summon the answer to the mysterious, "is the greatest trickster of all. The fact is, no name would ever truly describe Gron. The joke, ultimately, was on him, alone. Such a limited man… how sad."

Zantigar stopped before Daylen, who waited by the door, unable to speak.

"I ask you yet again. Who are you?"

Daylen pondered this otherwise trivial question as if the answer were a complicated riddle. "Well," he said, clearing his throat with a nervous cough. "If what you say is true, then I would have to say this is a trick question. A question with no answer."

Zantigar shook his head in pity, a slight sign of amusement on his face. "I ask you who you are and you wonder if it is a trick question? You are more lost than you look. And let me say that does not bode well for you."

Daylen was taken back by Zantigar's accusation. "I - I was never good at..."

"Who are you?" Zantigar interrupted.

Daylen backed himself into the doorframe.

"Who are you?" Zantigar's voice rose with impatience. "How can you know where you are if you don't know who you are?"

Daylen braced himself at the open door, the cold of the winter wind against his back. "I am afraid I do not understand."

"Goodbye, now," Zantigar said, waving his hand in Daylen's direction as if to shoo him away.

Daylen tried to defend himself. "Help me underst-"

"Goodbye to you!" Zantigar yelled, his patience stretched.

"Wait! I beg you. If your question is to determine *where* I am, than I am here; with you."

"You could never be farther from the truth. For you, lost one, are outside!" Zantigar shoved Daylen. Daylen tried to keep his footing, but his feet slipped on the frosted ground sending him stumbling into the snow.

Daylen heard the cottage door slam shut. Humiliated, he screamed, "That is why I am here! To find out who I am!"

There came no reply. He was surrounded by emptiness, silence and the cold. Connected to nothing, having lost those who cared for him only to fail, he buried his face in the snow, feeling its chilling sting on his face.

He felt Dumaji against his skin, the amulet that Nasavine had given him. The artifact that was to rid him of his fears, had grown warm around his neck. It glowed and radiated with a mystical aura. As if the amulet sensed his fear of failure, it became warmer until it burned.

"*You are worthless and weak.*"

Daylen wondered who had spoken. "Was it me?" He thought. "Did I think out loud? Were the words spoken at all?" Daylen convinced himself that there was no worse place to be, no worse time than now. However, he would sooner die than give up. There is nothing more to lose, he thought. "Nothing," he whispered.

He stood and faced the cabin. "Who am I?" he whispered. He walked to the door and knocked. There was no response, but this did not surprise him. This time, he wasn't going to require Zantigar's approval to feel a sense of self-worth. He turned the knob and flung open the door. The cottage was illuminated in the glow of candlelight. Zantigar was not in the entryway, and this gave Daylen an opportunity to study the room that he did not have before.

The cottage was in complete disarray. The floor was cluttered with dirty dishes, books and knick-knacks covered in dust. In the empty spaces, between the shelves, desk, and stacks of books, were large blocks of wax candles, melted down after months of use. For a moment, Daylen was lost in the shapes of wax. In the melted molds he saw dripping caverns, melting faces, animals and castles. He could have remained lost in the wax designs for a lifetime if Zantigar's voice had not shattered his trance-like state.

"Who is there?"

The question was simple. A question that any person would ask another if one happened to walk into another's home. Yet, he did not see it as an easy question or as a polite, hospitable introduction to conversation. The question was a test, a puzzle far more complex. Zantigar was sitting in his padded chair, but it had been relocated to the back of the room, facing a fireplace. Zantigar's eyes were transfixed on the flames.

"I am a wizard."

Zantigar's attention turned from the fire, the flames reflecting in his eyes. "You? A wizard?" He turned back to the fire. "What do you know of being a wizard?"

Daylen closed his eyes, attempting to come up with an answer that would satisfy the old wizard, he was at a loss for words, his mind on more than just this trivial question. He longed for the conversation to move on to other important matters.

Zantigar gave a heavy sigh and stood to face him. "Can you cast fire from the palms of your hand?"

Zantigar took a step forward.

"No," Daylen said.

"Can you bring rain on an otherwise sunny day?" Zantigar took another step closer.

Daylen shook his head.

"Can you bring a castle to the ground, with the wave of your hand or cause a mountain to slide into the ocean?" Zantigar's voice raised, as did his hand, and his eyes were wide with a look of madness.

"Not yet," Daylen said.

"Not yet," Zantigar mocked in a disappointed tone. "It makes no difference, because none of these things define what it is to be a wizard. Just because you are wizardborn it does not make you a wizard. Would it be any different to suggest that I am a knight by simply wearing a knight's armor? Your perception is weak, to the point of blindness. Your mind is clumsy, and your manner is pathetic. Leave this place. Let me be in peace. I am tired and I am old, and I am sick to death of what this world has left to offer. You are a product of our world's decline and nothing more than the symptom of a disease which confines FéLorën to this disgraceful form of existence."

Daylen was not afraid, and the amulet still burned on his chest. He wondered, for a moment, if the amulet around his neck was responsible for his sudden courage. "I have traveled a long way and sacrificed all that I had to get here. I may not know who I am, or who you want me to be, but I know what I am not. I am not pathetic, and I am not weak."

Zantigar raised his thick eyebrow in response to Daylen's defiance. "How can this be true? When all you have shown me has proven otherwise? You think you are the only person in life who has sacrificed? There are plenty of people who have failed, why can't you accept your fate?"

Daylen shook his head in protest. "I am lost, I will admit that, but I have made the most of what I have been dealt in life, and I accept my fate, which at this moment, I leave entirely in your hands."

Daylen stepped forward. He realized if Zantigar wanted him gone then Zantigar would have to use magic to will it so, or he would have to strike him dead. But Zantigar did no such thing, and in some way, this meant he was accepted, at least in some small degree. It meant there was some hope, however faint. "I pray for the better world you speak of. I have sacrificed much, as did my companions, those I loved most, who gave the ultimate sacrifice for me to find you. They were from Twilight, a town that practices the way of FéLorën that you speak of. There was Bolinda Lynx, the Half-elf; who had a heart of pure gold, despite being abandoned by those who should have loved her unconditionally. Hogar the Woodsman; the strongest, bravest warrior I have ever met, and the most selfless and giving person I have ever known. Rahlen Dimere, the ranger and the closest thing I have ever had to a father, who believed in me and guided me to you. They died for me... and why? I ask myself that every day. I lie awake at night, unable to sleep because I can't wrap my head around what they saw in me, hoping that when at last I found you, you could help me understand. So, I could make something of my life and find my purpose. When sleep comes, it is with fevered nightmares. My only dream is to train with you; it is all I have left. Without it… there is nothing."

Zantigar's face had changed, his features calmed, and his voice grew soft and sincere. When he repeated his familiar, loaded question, it was presented this time with genuine curiosity. "Who are you?"

Daylen rolled his eyes. "I am nothing," Daylen said, never being more certain of anything before in his life.

"You have not spoken truer words," Zantigar said not with disdain but with admiration.

"Right," Daylen responded, expecting to be put down. "Are you forcing me to leave, because I don't know if-"

"How?" Zantigar asked, before Daylen could finish.

Daylen wondered what Zantigar's question implied. "What do you mean, 'how'?"

"How could you leave, when you have stripped yourself of all that is unreal?"

Daylen was taken by Zantigar's statement. "Unreal? Another riddle?"

"No riddle, I have not the time or the patience for such trivial games. You say you are nothing. It seems to me that that which is 'nothing' would be unable to 'leave' anything. So, I ask you how that is possible."

"Wait, you don't want me to leave?"

Zantigar waved his hand and shook his head. "Please, stop speaking, for your own sake." He mumbled under his breath awhile, shifting toward the fireplace, no doubt cursing at Daylen's way. He waved his hand toward the interior. "Come and sit by the fire. You would be amazed at what the flames can teach you. The Season of Wither is knocking and will be longer than expected this year. If you wish to see tomorrow, you best find comfort here, where it is warm. If, of course, you will accept me."

Daylen's heart softened with relief. "Accept you? A smile spread across his face at the absurdity. He shook his head in disbelief. Moments ago, he had prepared for failure. To accept what life had in store just as Rahlen had advised him to do. Now, the tables had turned and Zantigar's fury had disappeared. A bright road of hope spread out before him. Somehow, by means unknown to him, he had won Zantigar's acceptance.

~CHAPTER 3~

Daylen walked along a desolate beach. The air was cold, but the sun was bright. He was struck by the wonder of his surroundings. In the distance, he could see a shape. Daylen approached with curiosity. He saw Ghost stretched out in the sand, washed in from the sea.

He ran toward the stranger, eager to help and to meet him face to face. Ghost lay on his stomach, his face pressed into the sand. Fearing he was dead; Daylen placed his hand on Ghost's back. Ghost raised his head and turned to Daylen. Daylen jumped back, startled to see that where a face should be was only darkness, a void within the outline of his head. Ghost raised a hand toward Daylen as if begging for help, but Daylen, intimidated by the vast void of an endless, empty eternity, was afraid to help.

Daylen shook his head trying to erase this nightmare from his mind. Ghost started to sink in the sand. Realizing that the land was threatening to swallow Ghost whole, Daylen overcame his initial fears and reach out to assist, only to realize that Ghost was an apparition, fitting of the name he was given.

Daylen called out, "What can I do?"

Ghost continued to sink.

"Tell me! What can I do?"

Ghosts body disappeared under the sand leaving only his outstretched hand above ground. Daylen continued his futile efforts to grab hold of Ghosts hand, until the fingers disappeared beneath. A tremendous sense of loss consumed him. He was left alone, standing on the desolate shore. The totality of this awareness bringing him to the verge of tears.

*　　　　*　　　　*

"Wake up!"

Zantigar's voice shocked Daylen from the sandy shore and returned him to his body. He opened his eyes. The mysterious necklace which Nasavine had given him was burning hot against his chest. His panic at losing Ghost vanished when he remembered that he was in Zantigar's care. With this realization came solace and relief. "I was dreaming."

Zantigar was standing over him. "Were you?"

The tone of Zantigar's question disturbed him. The honest inquiry had terrifying implications. Daylen rolled out of bed and rubbed his head. "I am awake now."

"That remains to be seen," Zantigar said. "You must pardon me, but I have forgotten your name."

Daylen sighed, not wanting to go over this again. "I am Nobody. Nothing, remember?"

"Nonsense, I am looking for your mortal name, or should I just make one up for you?"

"Daylen," he said with hesitation. "I was thrown out of your cottage for calling myself that yesterday."

"A cottage, is that what you think this place is? Interesting."

Daylen's confusion was growing with each exchange.

"Another time." Zantigar picked up a blanket that Daylen had kicked onto the floor during the night. As he folded the blanket he mumbled, "Of course your name is Daylen. Of course, you are someone, even nothing is something. If you forgot that, you would disappear completely!"

"You confuse me," Daylen said.

"Yes, well, you didn't need to tell me that. I can see that for myself."

Daylen gave Zantigar a serious look, demanding a moment of reflection. "If I may ask, who are you? You know, in a deeper sense? How would you answer the question you had posed to me yesterday?"

"Well, considering my home is the universe and I am a product of my home that must make me the universe. However, I am nothing, which makes the universe nothing. Therefore, I am everything."

Daylen was just as lost as before, only now he wondered if he should have bothered asking the question. "Look, I need your help."

Zantigar placed the neatly folded blanket on the edge of the sofa, and he rubbed his hand across its soft surface. "Actually, you don't. Yet, it's understandable. Confusing wants with needs is a common mistake. There is nothing I can help you with at the moment, except tea. Would you like some?"

Daylen shook his head. "No, I don't want tea. I want answers."

"Ah, but is that what you need?" Zantigar asked. "Perhaps you can give me some assistance."

"What could I possibly help you with?"

Zantigar pointed across the room. "The dishes. Look at this place, it's a disaster."

"You can't be serious. I need your help, for real, and you want me to help you with this meaningless stuff, instead? This is your mess, not mine."

Zantigar shook his head. "I wish you wouldn't speak; you really haven't earned the right. Yet, it is clear you need external motivation. A clean house is clean mind. If that is not a sufficient reason, then realize that you will earn your stay in this…." Zantigar paused a moment, as if looking for the right word, and then with a smile he said, "Cottage."

"I understand," Daylen said, able to understand his gratitude, more than his growing anxiety. He grabbed at the amulet around his neck. It still burned and his skin had grown agitated. He assumed it was the magic of the amulet warding off fear, or demons, so he did not take it off. He rubbed the irritated skin beneath his collarbone.

Zantigar narrowed his eyes. "What are you doing there? What is this?" He grabbed Dumaji and yanked it from Daylen's neck.

"Hey! That is mine, what are you doing?" Daylen reached for the amulet, but Zantigar was too quick, jerking his hand away so that the necklace was out of reach.

"Answer me!" Zantigar commanded.

Daylen gave up trying to get the amulet back, feeling childish. "It was given to me by someone named Nasavine… although he was more like a creature than a man. He said it would ease my journey and drive away my fears. I think it was working. So, can I have it back, please?"

"No."

Daylen chuckled, now it was Zantigar that was asking childish. "Really?"

"You want my help? I am helping." Zantigar threw the amulet to the floor, breaking it in half.

Daylen jumped forward in alarm. Then, seeing the broken amulet on the ground he leaned back in awe. A black, steaming liquid spilled from the center of the amulet and melted like acid through the floorboards. With the steam came the stench of something rotten and fowl.

"Daylen's eyes widened. "What the?"

"That amulet could never help you." Zantigar said, with a calm certainty in his voice.

Daylen confused by the sight of the broken amulet, felt a sudden rush of relief, and was grateful for Zantigar's help. "How did you know?"

"By the very nature of its purpose. One's path should never be easy, and fear should never be discarded, but confronted. Pushing away your fears turn dreams into nightmares, until your nightmares no longer stay contained in your dreams. Is there anything else this Nasavine gave you? And do you always accept gifts from strangers?"

Daylen shook his head, wondering if the amulet played a role in his nightmare about Ghost the night before.

Zantigar grabbed a broom from against the wall. "One of many deceptive outcomes from belief in needs. Your need to destroy fear, your need for salvation. Mere tools for corruption." He swept the amulet into a neat pile.

"I know Nasavine. He is a little nuisance, a bothersome imp who has been hanging around for far too long, at that. He thinks I do not notice him, but I do. He is someone's little minion. That is what imps are, you know, little troublesome creatures that latch to someone, because they can't think for themselves, doing devious deeds for their master. I have been meaning to have my way with that little bug. He has managed to wiggle his way into my world, and it is about time for me to do something about it."

Daylen stared at the remains of the amulet on the floor, shocked it could be responsible for so much deception. His trust had been misplaced, and he was prone to make dangerous calls in times of desperation. In times of need. He realized that his lack of insight could be the death of him. "Zantigar, teach me how to be a wizard."

Zantigar had been mumbling ways in which to rid himself of the imp when Daylen's request distracted him. "What's that, now? A teacher? A teacher is not what you are missing. You are missing yourself."

"Please; no riddles," said Daylen.

"Riddles? I speak exactly as is necessary, as specific as is required to say exactly as I mean," replied Zantigar.

Daylen realized conversation with Zantigar would take some getting used to. "How can I be missing myself?"

Zantigar smiled. "Excellent question." He motioned for Daylen to stand. And guided him toward the dirty dishes. "Start here."

Daylen nodded and grabbed a dish with reluctance. "Why won't you teach me?"

Zantigar reached into a cabinet and grabbed a box of matches. "A teacher tells you how to do something… how to wield a sword or how to ride a horse.

They bestow information onto the student, who in turn puts the information into practice."

Zantigar struck a match and brought it to a candle next to the dishes. "You don't need a teacher. What is required of you is not to obtain additional information. Quite the opposite. You need only to look within, to look to the place void of information."

Daylen was perplexed. With rag in hand, he scrubbed vigorously on the plate before him. "What lies between information?"

"Nothing," Zantigar stated. Once the candle was lit, he brought the match to his lips and blew it out.

"Like me," Daylen whispered. "I am nothing," he recalled.

"Perhaps you are not missing yourself, after all." Zantigar said.

Daylen stopped scrubbing and stood a moment in silence. For a short time, there were no thoughts and in that space between thoughts was stillness. In the stillness was a void that made him think about his dream of Ghost, the figure with a nothingness where a face should be.

~CHAPTER 4~

When Daylen finished the dishes, he went to Zantigar who sat in silent contemplation by the fireplace, his eyes closed. Taking a seat beside him, Daylen remained silent as to not break the wizard's concentration.

Without any indication that he was aware of Daylen's presence, Zantigar spoke, his eyes still closed. "You see yourself as the combination of your life experiences and acquired knowledge."

Daylen pondered this realization a moment before responding. "Yes, I suppose that I do." He was already prepared for the flaws of this assessment to be pointed out to him.

Zantigar gave a heavy sigh. "What a burden it is to carry so much. Tell me about your journey," Zantigar said. "What did you experience on your way here?"

"What would you like to know?"

"Tell me all that is required so that I may understand who you see yourself to be."

Daylen erred on the side of caution, and he explained everything from the beginning, starting with his mother Claudia and the wooden box she left for him. Perhaps, it was exactly what Zantigar wanted to hear, because he listened intently and wished not to skip any detail. Daylen described the struggles, the encounters and the deaths. He was stopped often and questioned about his feelings at specific moments. When Daylen finished, he felt like a weight had been lifted off his shoulders, as if the reenactment somehow healed wounds he did not know existed, giving clarity to his struggle.

Zantigar was quiet for some time before speaking. "I look at you and see a confused young man who is trying to cling to a familiar world, an unreal world. An imaginary world. This world is made up of your past, that can easily define those you have lived with, but in no way resembles you. Who are you?"

Daylen remained silent.

Zantigar leaned forward and grabbed Daylen's blade, Sylver. Pulling the sword from Daylen's belt, he placed the steel close to Daylen, allowing him to see his own reflection. Daylen noticed the world SYLVER engraved across the blade, directly over his reflected face. "Are you Sylver? No, it is but a name, abstract, bearing only what you reflect on it. Are you your past endeavors? No, you have been living as a ranger, following Rahlen's lead. Rahlen did you an incredible service, no doubt, but perhaps not in the way you imagine. He saw you for all you can be."

Daylen turned away from his reflection.

"At this point you should not worry yourself with what you have been but think of what you can be; as Rahlen did." Zantigar handed Sylver back to Daylen. "Your power lies not in following other people's footsteps, but in creating your own. No two people's destinies are alike, no two paths are the same."

"Where does my path lie?" Daylen said.

"Before you now, always." Zantigar leaned back in his chair. "You are trying too hard to accomplish something that requires nothing from you at this point, other than to let go."

"I feel like such a blind fool. How come it is so hard to let go?"

"You want to be a wizard. I am suggesting you already are one. Therefore, there is nothing I can teach you. If I taught you to be like me, I would be doing you a great injustice, for you would know nothing of yourself."

"Then why am I here?"

"To open your eyes to what is already here and open your mind to that which you already know. If you are unable to realize the true meaning of your journey, then there is nothing I can do for you."

"You have heard my tale, learned of my struggles. What am I failing to see? Daylen asked.

"Fear," Zantigar said. "Fear has dominated your life. It has consumed every aspect of your experience. Why? Because you see yourself as separate from the world you inhabit. Being alone, lacking what you desire. Desire that you interpret as what you need. With this mindset, how could you not be afraid?"

Daylen felt a chill to the room and rubbed his arms with his hands to get warm.

Zantigar noticed Daylen's discomfort and leaned forward to grab firewood from the floor. "A fine example of what I speak of can be found in analyzing that which transpired in Lonely Wood."

Daylen stretched out on the floor as Zantigar filled the fireplace, anticipating the warmth of roaring fire. He longed to understand what had happened to him in Lonely Wood, to hear of Zantigar's interpretation of what transpired. The roots to his magic were connected to that frightful experience. The eerie landscape that had heightened his fears and his will to survive, led him to cast the only spell that he had ever conjured, and with mysterious effect.

"There is nothing tied more closely to your blood than the land itself. You were born from the land and from the land you receive your magic. In a moment of life and death, your mind overpowered your state of being. You wished to survive at all costs and by instinct, your body knew what it had to do. You know now, what you are capable of. You need to understand your relationship to the external world, in order to control your power."

Zantigar placed his hand on the pile of wood in the fireplace. He closed his eyes in concentration. With the command of a solitary word, "Abazar," fire sprang from his hand lighting the fireplace.

Daylen watched in amazement, attentive to Zantigar's control over the magic he conjured.

Zantigar moved his hand away and the flames at his fingertips were extinguished. "When you first came to my door, you said you did not ask to be a wizard and it was not what you wanted to be. It is the sacrifices you must make, that causes you to feel this way… and rightfully so.

"Lonely Wood was not the threat, nor was the wolf which attacked you. Those were manifestations of your fears. To be a wizard you need to understand that the woods are a part of you. What you perceive and your experiences are nothing more than a reflection of what you think, feel, and believe. The danger is you, not your surroundings."

Daylen wanted to understand the practical implications of this. The power that Zantigar suggested was close to inconceivable. "If what you are saying is true, then I conjured the wolf?"

Zantigar nodded in agreement. "Precisely. You do not live in the world; the world lives in you. The wilderness of Lonely Wood *was* you. Having insisted for years that you live in a world apart from you, you were engulfed by it. You have held the false belief that you are a victim to nature, when in fact, you *are* nature, and you have feared yourself. It blinds you from the truth. Truth is the only thing with the power to destroy fear."

Daylen shook his head. "I'm having trouble believing."

"Remember the power that sprang from your hands. Remember the wolf. In that experience lies proof of the mind's power."

The memory of the wolf flashed in Daylen's mind. He was reminded of its ferocious face as it attacked him, remembered in horror the feeling of it sinking its teeth into his flesh. It was hazy from there, but the feeling that overcame him was real. The change that overcame the wolf was a miracle. The change that overcame him, a miracle. "I was the wolf," he whispered.

"If Lonely Wood was just a reflection of your mind, and the wolf a physical representation of your fear, then who was your true enemy?"

The answer shocked Daylen to his core. "Myself."

Zantigar poked the wood in the fireplace with a stick, stoking the fire. "What I am asking you to do is to rise from your self-victimization, your own helplessness, and empower yourself with positive, perceptive existence."

"It seems impossible, it doesn't seem real."

"Is that so? What is reality but what your mind's eye perceives and your interpretation of it? You are a magician, after all. It is time you start putting some faith in the actions you once deemed impossible. The Woodsman you met on the edge of Lonely Wood fueled your mind with the fear of wolves, and low and behold, a wolf attacked you. Do you find this to be a coincidence?"

It was hard for Daylen to grasp or to believe any coincidence was more than a lucky chain of events. However, he came to Zantigar to be awoken. He came for wisdom, for insight, and to know of his talents. To learn from a Legionnaire, to obtain the key to his existence, and to unlock his power, this was the purpose of all of this. But this new reality Zantigar posed was full of paradoxes. "What of those who travelled beside me? I shared my experience with Rahlen and Hogar and Bolinda. I did not create their reality."

"You are correct, it was not their reality." Zantigar said.

This confirmation raised doubt in Daylen. "What if you walked through Lonely Wood with me, where would you be?"

"I would be in the same place, physically, but my mind would view the world from a different perspective, a different dimension, if you will. Lonely Wood would be no 'lonely wood' at all. It would have been my enchanted garden, a moment of opportunity, unchained by the invisible force of fear that had tightened its grip on you."

Daylen was intrigued. This was the reason for why he felt so alone, so lost in the world around him. Was this his own creation? This thought seemed possible. His loneliness was a reflection of his perception. He realized that his perception was misguided, by a civilization which called the woodland Lonely Wood to begin with, and by the people that fueled the myth of its dangers.

"Prepare to meet the most powerful entity in the world, Daylen… yourself. If you need proof as to how powerful your mind is, look no further than this very room." Zantigar's eyes widened, and the room darkened. The flames in the fireplace dwindled to a smolder, as if commanded to do so. "Do you believe in me? Do you believe I am alive, even after all these years?"

Daylen was disturbed by Zantigar's questions. Daylen did not believe that Zantigar existed only in his mind, but the possibility that life led to this very meeting, as an outcome of Daylen's awareness, did not seem outside the realm of possibility. Zantigar was real, as real as the ground he walked on, that was the great miracle that defied all previous narratives of what he deemed possible. "Yes," Daylen said. "I believe in you."

~CHAPTER 5~

Daylen wiped sweat off his forehead, hot from exertion. Steam rose as the cold, winter air met his skin. He took a deep breath and swung an axe down on a block of wood, splintering it into pieces. His back was sore, and his arms trembled as he raised the wood pieces from the forest floor and placed them in a nearby pile. His fatigue gave rise to frustration. He wondered why Zantigar had not shown him any spells yet and could not imagine how he could ever create one for himself. He lowered the axe to the forest floor and looked at his calloused hands in confusion, the very hands that had somehow shined and subdued the aggression of the wolf in Lonely Wood. Taking a deep breath, he closed his eyes, as if to find the answer within himself.

"In need of a break?" Zantigar's voice startled him.

"No, it's not that. I am just… discouraged. I've been thinking about our talk yesterday and my reality has not changed. I do not see things as you do."

"Think less," Zantigar brought a cup of tea to his lips. "It is not about any reality I may want for you. You should be concerned only with the reality that you want for yourself. Don't be too hard on yourself with all that thinking. And don't confuse being lost with having uncertainty. Uncertainty can be useful. It kept you from the Academy, did it not?"

Daylen nodded. "In a roundabout way, yes."

"Then you are in better shape than I was at your age. I was a product of the Academy; I was a slave to the system and did not see my self-worth until much later in life. Because of this difference, you could become a far greater wizard than I."

Daylen laughed in disbelief. The thought was preposterous to him.

"It is true. Why would you laugh? I made too many mistakes in my younger years. I have seen and experienced too much evil and partaken in too much evil, myself. But you, you have the opportunity I did not. You have the chance to create a powerful world for yourself." There was optimism in Zantigar that he seldom revealed. "I must admit, I am eager to see your progress unfold."

Daylen had not been able to fathom how he could ever be as great as Zantigar. For a moment, Zantigar's words caused the mental barriers of doubt to disappear, allowing Daylen to see a future of limitless possibility, if even for just a short while. Frustration brushed the hope from his mind. "Then show me the way! Something, so I can make some sort of progress."

"Show you what? That tree, that cloud, the brush on the forest floor? Look inward, Daylen. Probe into the inner you, the wizard within. The true you is locked in a drawer of your mind. Tucked away for so long that it is hard to recognize with all the dust that has collected. All you have to do is become him. It is truly that simple."

Daylen turned away. "You make it sound so easy."

Zantigar sipped his tea. "Come, that's enough wood for now. There is tea inside for you, and there is something that I can show you, after all, that may help you."

Daylen followed Zantigar into the cottage. He grabbed a cup of tea from the counter and met Zantigar by a bookshelf. Zantigar ran his index finger along the spines of books until he found one of his liking. "Ah, this one here."

Daylen tried to read the book's cover, but Zantigar had opened it too quickly. A cloud of dust took to the air as Zantigar flipped through the pages, stopping on an intricate illustration. Daylen leaned closer. "What is that?"

Zantigar swung the book from view and snapped, "It is what you see! Stop wondering what you see and contemplate *how* you see it."

Daylen raised his eyes in apology.

Zantigar cleared his throat and brought the illustration back into view, his finger still holding his place in the book. On the page was a shield, an ancient crest. Within the shield was a winged lion, its mouth open in a roar, exposing its sharp teeth and its eyes were narrowed aggressively.

"What do you see when you stare at this picture?" Zantigar said.

Daylen tried to see the winged lion for more than it was, to see what it represented. "A monster, I suppose."

"And why?" Zantigar beckoned.

Daylen's first reaction was to say it was because Zantigar showed it to him. It was as simple as that, but his gut told him to look deeper. "I see it because I am afraid?"

Zantigar responded with a question of his own. "Are you? Be honest with yourself, there is no wrong answer."

"Well, I'm not afraid of this image, of course. It is just a picture in a book." Daylen relaxed, contemplating why he described the image the way he did in the first place. "Yes. I suppose I am fearful. Not of the image, itself, but in the larger picture of things, yes." He looked to Zantigar in revelation. "So, if I was not afraid, I would not see the lion?"

"You said you saw a monster, not a lion," Zantigar reminded.

"Well, yea, I mean, it is one."

"I see," Zantigar said.

Daylen became suspicious. "I thought you said there were no wrong answers."

'I did."

"Then what?" Daylen questioned. "What do you see?"

"Light."

Daylen raised his eyebrow at Zantigar's response.

"Van la lien." Zantigar chanted the three foreign words, and the room went black. The candles were extinguished with a single command. Since evening was approaching, no light penetrated through the frost covered windows, rendering the room in complete darkness.

Startled, Daylen tried to focus, but could not make out anything.

"What do you see?" Zantigar said from the dark.

"I can't see anything."

"The monster in the book, is it still here?" Zantigar inquired.

"Of course," Daylen replied.

"Then how is it you see nothing?"

Daylen was tricked into answering the obvious. "Because… the light is out?"

"Because your perception has changed," Zantigar informed, his tone harsh with frustration. "Ent la lien," he recited, and the room illuminated as it was before, the flames of the candles returned unison.

Daylen's eyes struggled to adjust to the light. "How did you-" His eyes focused and Zantigar was standing before him, just as he was before. The book, however, was nowhere in sight.

"Do you understand the lesson?" Zantigar said.

"I think so," Daylen responded, feeling he had been tricked. "It wasn't the best magic trick in the world. I mean, the light was out when you hid the book."

"I'm not trying to dazzle you with parlor tricks for your amusement, Daylen. You thought the book was still in my hands, did you not?"

"Yes." Daylen realized he had made a critical assumption. The winged lion was still present, because he had no reason to believe it wasn't. "In the dark, my belief that the monster was still here made it so."

"Right. I, on the other hand, saw light reflecting colors before my eyes, nothing more."

"And in the light, I saw what I interpreted to be a monster," Daylen remarked.

"You saw an illusion. An illusion, created by the mind. A mind, coupled with eyes that cannot be trusted to see the truth. When seeing the image for what it truly is, the illusion and the fear are destroyed. It is as true for the image in this book as it is for the images you see in life. It's all light. When it comes to my perception, I fear the real thing in as much as I fear the image of it."

"Like magic," Daylen stated.

"Not *like* magic, it *is* magic. But don't confuse magic for spells. They are two entirely different things. Spells are but a fragment of what constitutes magic, a mere tool. A wizard can manipulate magic around all living things by using the tools of his trade. Do you see the difference?"

Daylen reflected back on his quest to find Zantigar. It seemed Rahlen, Hogar and Bolinda all had a magic quality about them, despite not being wizards. He was convinced that his companions embodied the magic that Zantigar spoke of, because of their artistry in perceiving the magic around them. It was proven by their lack of fear, even when confronting their own death.

Zantigar's face turned grim. "What is devastating to the land is when a wizard cast spells without understanding magic, the sacred energy that unites us. This has destroyed balance in the world and has led to the world's demise. No academy will teach the truth of magic, despite its importance. They only share the tools of the trade with minds ill equipped to handle such power. It is because of this that wizards have been unable to live in harmony with FéLorën. They have forgotten. It is the cause of great suffering, for wizards and people alike. This ignorance is detrimental in times of war."

Daylen lowered his head in thought. He realized that seeing the world with eyes of fear was not the perception of a wizard that can bring positive change. His mother had warned him that wizards of the Academy were robbed of their self-value, they were nothing more than soulless pawns to be led by ruthless kings. Daylen now understood it was because they were not taught the value of their work, the value of their own lives, and the value of others. This made them willing to destroy. Academy wizards have allowed their minds to be controlled. And for what? "Power," he remarked aloud. He thought of his mother and her hatred for the Academy. "What power is there in slavery?"

"Indeed." Zantigar leaned over and picked up the book of the winged lion from the floor.

Daylen was surprised to see this and smiled. "I thought you had made the book disappear."

"Even in the light, your mind's eye deceived you. Your eyes are not to be trusted in their present state. They are too trusting of the world's common illusions."

Zantigar opened the book to the winged lion again. "This crest was created by an ancient kingdom, long before your time, and mine. It is a symbol that was used to strike fear into the kingdoms' enemies. The point is, the symbol did not strike fear in the kingdom that wielded it, because they had created it. As the creators of it, it was a part of them."

Daylen recognized the connection. "If I am the creator of my world, then I won't fear it."

Zantigar waved his finger at Daylen with an inquisitive look in his eye. "The Woodsman you met outside Lonely Wood was aware of the illusion of the land. That was why he was able to hunt in Lonely Wood without becoming a victim to it. He was probably known in his tribe for his lack of fear."

Daylen nodded, understanding Zantigar's teachings, but wondered how to put it all into practice. He wanted to use this awareness as well as he had learned to use his father's sword. Becoming a true wizard was not quite what he had expected. It would take time and it would take discipline.

~CHAPTER 6~

As the week's past at Zantigar's cottage, the days fell into a steady routine for Daylen. He chopped wood for the fireplace, cleaned the house regularly, and was introduced to long periods of silence. Silence was never a stranger to Daylen, even before his time with Zantigar. Having spent much of his youth alone, the silence was a part of him, like an unnoticed shadow. With Zantigar, the silence became an active, conscious presence, if not a goal to obtain. Zantigar barked obsessively at any unnecessary noise Daylen made while performing routine activities. As a result, he avoided clatter while doing dishes and approached his chores with mindful care.

When Daylen wasn't going about his chores, he was forced to sit in silence and focus on the emptiness of his mind. At first, these exercises took place in the evening, for a short period of time. It was easily sustained, but against his will. The exercises increased, as did his tolerance, until morning and evening were consumed in meditation. What first was met with resistance, Daylen began to appreciate. His journey, up into this point, was filled with so much chaos and suffering, that the silence became a luxury to be grateful for. This appreciation was often distracted by his desire to learn spells, but he learned quickly, after failed attempts to rush things with Zantigar, that his impatience only prolonged matters. Despite a growing urge to leave the cottage and experience the world around him, it took faith in Zantigar to maintain his will and obedience.

Zantigar also meditated often, or otherwise spent his time in his room, out of site. He left Daylen to himself more often than not and Daylen knew it best to give Zantigar his space and his privacy. While Zantigar could be thoughtful and kind in his relations, he was also prone to rage that Daylen learned to avoid setting off. It was in moments of anger that Zantigar would conjure magic that caused Daylen to question the stability of his living situation, even his future.

One morning, during a day of silent reflection, Zantigar interrupted him, requesting Daylen to join him at the table. A book waited for them. He recognized the book immediately. It was none other than the book with the image of the winged lion.

Zantigar took a seat, motioning for Daylen to do the same, and placed his hand on the book. "This book has a greater purpose than to make you aware of your fears. It is a book of history. It will teach you much about your world and much about yourself. As wise men often say, how can one know where they are going, if they have no idea where they have been?"

Daylen had been fascinated with history since his conversations with Hogar. The experience in the Wanton Land felt like a lifetime ago, in part due to the drastic change to his environment and current living experience.

"This is the closest, most accurate history I could come by, for much of history that is written is flawed or misguided. Never trust history taught in a castle, Daylen." Zantigar raised his finger to stress his point. "It is used to control, not to inform. History taught by the empire is written by the victors of war, bent to the lens of how they want you to perceive it, not as it truly is. History from the point of view of any kingdom is an inherent conflict of interest and will never represent the truth as seen from the point of view of the people, the communities who suffered and changed as a result of the kingdoms' decisions."

Zantigar held up the book so Daylen could see. "This book was written by Erramond the Wise, after years of travel around the world, when the world was still known as Heldon. He understood that it was wrong to believe that a kingdom's perspective was the same as that of its people. The truth is what benefits the kingdom is often at the expense of the people."

Daylen was intrigued by the mere mention of Erramond. There had been no wizard who compared to his wisdom and might. Erramond was credited as the savior of the old world of Heldon and for whom, without, there would be no world of FéLorën. "I have heard of him. He is the creator of FéLorën."

Zantigar shook his head. "A common mistake. Erramond did not create FéLorën. He had come across the original texts on his quest for knowledge. He shared his findings with the world, showing people a way of life that had existed long before their time."

Zantigar's eyes became distant, as if taken back to another time. "He saved humanity and enlightened us to what was possible, to what is eternal. He brought balance to the world, and in the process, made peace with ourselves possible."

"What is FéLorën, exactly?"

"In the ancient language, FéLorën literally means One Land. However, it is more appropriately translated as Unified Land. The ancient text describes that once all races worked as one, there was no division, no separate kingdoms. All were equal in the eyes of each other. People viewed the world as it truly is; one collective, connected experience.

"Yet, time distorted the teachings. Peoples' hearts became shadowed with corruption. Erramond called it the manifestation of the "Grand Illusion."

"Illusion?" Daylen asked. "How so?"

"The illusion that we are separate from the world. Individuals, born into this world and not a part of it. There are many theories as to why this happened, but whatever the particulars may be, it was fear that drove the madness."

Daylen thought of his own fear. Fear consumed him throughout his journey, the same fear that caused him to see the monster in the very book in Zantigar's hands.

Zantigar brought his gaze to Daylen. "The old world of FéLorën was forever lost, buried and forgotten, as people born of hate and self-interest brought an end to the collective peace. War followed. Devastating destruction buried all reminiscence of FéLorën. The balance once held tipped to darkness. The victors of these wars wrote their conquests in the pages of their history books, solidifying their dominance. They made themselves out to be supreme and just in their delusions. The gods themselves changed and took new names. This became the world that I knew, the world of Heldon, which was all that was known for thousands of years."

Daylen shifted to a spot beside the fireplace and threw some wood in. He then scraped flint and steel until the sparks took flame.

Zantigar moved his chair close to the fire and continued. "FéLorën was an obsolete, forgotten way. It was not until the dawn of The Final War that Erramond found the ancient text, just in time to awaken the races of the land, unify, and defeat the darkness from completing its goal… the destruction of all humanoid life. The darkness of which I speak of was, of course, the Dark Knights of Omnias. A ruthless empire of god-like power. It took the unification of all kingdoms to prevent the extinction they sought. Upon the defeat of the Dark Knights, FéLorën reclaimed its influence and became the common name of the world again."

Daylen was beginning to understand the present state of his world, but at this moment, he was left with many questions, and felt his world ultimately resembled the description of Heldon, more so than that of FéLorën. There was something wrong with the world he lived in, despite the conclusion of The Final War. Before Daylen could ask his questions, Zantigar continued his history lesson, explaining to Daylen a mysterious outcome of The Final War, the portals.

"The dust of The Final War had hardly settled when people discovered the emergence of five portals across the land. Strange doorways to unknown realms, unlocked, or activated, if you will, by the outcome of the war. At first they were sought to be a reward from the gods. Time would suggest otherwise. For all who entered a portal, never returned." Zantigar stared a moment in silence, letting Daylen absorb the significance.

"You mean nobody has returned from the portal? No one knows what is beyond?"

"Erramond the Wise was the first to enter," Zantigar continued. "Famously, the Bolderahn Empire, the Dwarves of the Bolderahn Mountains, who were pivotal in defeating the Dark Knights of Omnias, all but went extinct. The king of Bolderahn, convinced that the portals were home to treasures far too great for any Dwarf to ignore, led his army through a portal gate. One by one, in line, they entered, swallowed up by the portal, never to be seen again. Thousands, never to return. Only a select few of the men remained. The empire was all but lost and the race of dwarves forever diminished to a small, fragile population."

"Unbelievable," Daylen remarked.

"You would think it would have swayed any further investigation, but the portals captured the imagination of every kingdom, and each culture had their own beliefs as to the purpose of them. Erramond became a god to the land beyond the portals. One would only hope that there is life beyond; that those who painfully have left us are in a better world, with Erramond as their king.

"The allure of these gateways is still undeniable, the mystery of what they contain too great for many to ignore. Obsession turned to possession and battles were raged over control of the portals, even though none understood them. Over the years it became clear that whatever the intention was of these portals, there was enough suffering and bloodshed over them, and enough disappearances within them, that they were ultimately considered a curse, by peasants and kings alike."

"Is this what you believe, Zantigar?"

"No. Perhaps, they are a curse for the un-evolved minds, which I assure you, most are. What I find to be certain is that the portals are not evil. For one, evil exists in the hearts and minds of those that will it to be, it does not exist beyond that. The ancient text found by Erramond described, in detail, the existence of these portals. If not in name, then in theory. The text stated the world was not contained in a sphere, but traveled forever, with mighty mountains and vast waters for all eternity. In fact, when Omnias was defeated in The Final War, it was believed by many that the world would unravel, as it was described in the ancient texts. In retrospect, it is hard to believe that the spherical world would unfold and span across time and space forever, but I believe the portals signify the escape from our spherical entrapment and that they could possibly be gateways to never ending lands in some form or another."

Zantigar lowered his head, his voice becoming grave. "But more important than portals and their purpose, I believe that FéLorën has not returned. It was a lie, a dream, mere propaganda spread by the newly appointed High Council of FéLorën if not simply to give their existence meaning and provide them with power. It is something I know now but did not know at the time. Of course, we all know that corruption is the shadow of power.

"The portals may be open, but it is just the beginning. The struggle for unity continues. Kingdoms may have united in the fight against Omnias, but true unity runs deeper, it must exist on the personal level, amongst all people of the land, all as brother to sister, as equals, connected, as one. Instead, we held on to our kingdoms and insisted on separation. How can anyone believe that FéLorën is here and now? The portals represent the limitation in our perception of the world and of ourselves, and a reminder of the advances in thought and practice that still need to occur."

Daylen understood. "A collective transformation."

"Yes," Zantigar said. "The portals are only entered by those who have no connection left to this world, nothing left to lose. The suicidal, the old, these are the travelers who passed the threshold of the unknown with sure steps."

Zantigar took a deep breath and closed his eyes. "I feel the world's pain and my frustration stems from the lack of compassion between the races and kingdoms of this world. I can choose my actions, but I cannot choose for the world, for the rest of the miserable souls that wander this land." Zantigar opened his eyes. "There is little hope for them, but there is hope for you. To know your place, to know your purpose, to find peace in the way. The way of FéLorën."

Daylen began to feel an urgency to mend the broken world. Zantigar's description of the life of those in ancient times reminded him of his own experience. "There is hope for others, too, Zantigar. The people of Cragel Village, for example. They live in the unity you speak of."

"Insignificant and not good enough," Zantigar replied, "as hard as I tried to awaken them."

"There is beauty to be experienced there," Daylen argued. "Something significant is manifesting."

"An exercise in futility. And look at the rest of the world; this is not the FéLorën of old, not even close. If Erramond the Wise were here today, he would be heartbroken at what humanity has done with the gift he shared with us.

"We are fighting again, like never before, as if The Final War against Omnias was fought for nothing! Most history books will say that Omnias was the evil as if everyone else was without fault. But this thinking is for simpletons. Who do you think spawned the army of Omnias?"

"The gods?" Daylen suggested, knowing next to nothing about The Final War, itself. The only thing he knew was that Hogar's ancestors were knights in the Omnias army.

"It was us. We created Omnias out of our hatred and misdirection. We gave rise to them. They were a symptom of a greater corruption. The Dark Knights of Omnias rose as a necessity, as a reaction to our terrible way of existence. It took the threat of world genocide to call the world into action. We should thank them for their purity of pursuit. We would not have united without it. This proves that the real success was ending the hatred in ourselves. Unity was achieved, in harmonious connection as FéLorën once was… or so we thought. In our short-lived alliance, the portals emerged. Imagine, one moment in time in which all were joined as one. It created such a powerful display of magic that worlds unknown to us opened up before our eyes. Now, imagine what could be done if we could sustain that peace and unity, remove the nation state and kingdoms from the map altogether, to truly be as FéLorën once was. Who knows what changes would come, what experiences could be shared!"

Daylen felt a rush of excitement. He marveled on how clear it all seemed, how people could physically alter the world they lived in by accepting a higher moral existence. Listening to Zantigar, he felt invigorated for the first time in his life, as if at last he could begin to see his life's purpose. "Then it is up to us to unite them!"

Zantigar looked toward Daylen with disbelief. "What bravery coming from one, who moments before, feared a winged lion in a book.

"There is nothing more worth fighting for than to restore peace. It makes sense to finish what Erramond started."

Zantigar forced a chuckle but was not amused. He was agitated and no good at hiding his anger. "You can, but not I."

"What are you saying? How can you give up?"

Zantigar's face contorted with rage. He snapped, "You know nothing!"

"But you can't just-" Daylen was shocked into silence by Zantigar's loud voice.

"Enough! Speak no more of such things to me. Quit this nonsense and focus on the present moment. Do you think of me as a fool? I have been around for hundreds of years! I have seen this world ripped apart from the inside. I have seen young men, your age and younger, sliced to pieces by the weapons forged by kings, out of greed, or for the simple sake of proving they could get away with it. Do not speak to me about stopping, about giving up, when you haven't even tried!"

Daylen was taken aback, shocked into silence by Zantigar's anger.

Zantigar continued with a raised voice. "This world is a hopeless mess, and its best you get that through your head before you suffer more than you can imagine. You think you've found your purpose? You think you know your way already? Then go! But don't think your delusions of grandeur are going to send me on a fool's errand. You have missed the point of this lesson, entirely. This world isn't worth saving!"

Daylen shook with anger. Upset by Zantigar's judgement, he could not stand to be beside him. He rose to his feet and stared at Zantigar a moment, wise enough to hold his tongue until he couldn't stand to feel the tension any longer. He stormed outside and felt the cold air on his skin. At last, there was a chance to do something important, no matter the outcome, instead of being a victim. He was tired of being helpless, tired of fearing the world around him. He stood in the brisk, winter air, and studied the labyrinth of birch trees surrounding the cabin. Frustrated at reaching his limitations, he still could envision a road from here. Unification was important. The portals, mysterious as they were, as scary as it seemed, must hold the answer; he could feel it.

He did not have the courage to enter a portal. There was a dark side of himself that played with the thought. Perhaps, his training would be complete the day he could stand before the portal and cross its gate into the unknown, unafraid. Not as a means to end life, but a means to begin it.

From the shadows of the birch wood forest, a familiar figure emerged, as if manifesting from the darkness, itself. He recognized the snickering laughter and stepped forward. "What are you doing here, Nasavine? What do you want from me?"

Nasavine rubbed his hands together. His snickering seized, but his smile remained. "I want nothing more than to set you free."

"There is nothing you have to offer, nothing I need from you."

Nasavine's smile faded, and concern befell him. "Where is Dumaji? Where is the gift I bestowed upon you?"

"I have destroyed it." Daylen exclaimed.

Nasavine shook his head. "Oh, you poor, helpless fool. Do you realize what you have done? You could have had everything you desired. The end of your journey was at hand. All you longed for, all you desired, was at arm's length away. Instead, you have chosen a long road of suffering and pain. Here my words and listen to them closely. In time, all you desire, will slip through your fingers. All your pursuits shall end in vain. All you have, will be lost."

As Nasavine's final words were spoken, he disappeared into the darkness between the birch trees.

~CHAPTER 7~

Daylen laid down for bed. When the surprise visit from Nasavine finally left his mind, he thought of the portals and what might exist beyond its gate. In a fragile state between wake and dream, Ghost appeared. Ghost's voice, as it called for Daylen, was the voice of Zantigar. When Ghost came close enough to be recognized, he had the face of Nasavine. Daylen shook himself from his dream state and opened his eyes, alarmed to hear Zantigar yelling from down the hall, as if arguing with someone. His eyes struggled to adjust to the dark of night. Zantigar screamed in agony. Daylen rose to his feet. All of a sudden, there was silence.

Daylen left his room and crept down the forbidden hall of the cottage. He did not let fear stop him. The fear was a challenge he accepted, as if in preparation of a future outside a portal. With arms outstretched in the dark, he followed the length of the wall, until he came to Zantigar's bedroom. He placed his ear to the door but could hear nothing. He reached for the doorknob, but before he could open it, the door flung open and Zantigar stood before him, with anger in his eyes.

"Never come to my room, do you understand? Never!"

Daylen nodded his head, his eyes wide. He could see past Zantigar into the room, just long enough to notice that the wizard was alone.

"There is no reason to ever walk down this hall, for any reason."

Daylen nodded.

"Promise me."

Daylen continued to nod.

"Say it!" Zantigar screamed.

Daylen flinched. "I promise."

Zantigar slammed the door, leaving Daylen bewildered and confused. He took a deep breath and went back to his room. His heart pounded in his chest. As he began to settle down, he could hear Zantigar yell again, arguing with someone who wasn't even there. Daylen hid his face in his pillow until he fell asleep.

~CHAPTER 8~

The morning brought a break in the clouds. Daylen prepared a bowl of porridge that had been simmering in a large cauldron. The taste was bland, but the warmth it offered was soothing. Zantigar entered the room and took a seat next to him. There was silence between them, with no mention of the night before. Daylen brought a spoonful of porridge to his lips, blowing it softly before consuming it. He looked to Zantigar's hands and was reminded of the strange marking on the old wizard's right palm. "What is that there on your hand?"

Zantigar placed his hand on the table, palm up, revealing an intricate brand on his skin. "It is a graduation mark from Hendor Academy."

Daylen eyed Zantigar carefully, observing Zantigar's shame in recalling the memory. "Hendor Academy is no different than Vixus Academy, right? A school for wizards?"

Zantigar nodded. "Hendor was a young, rising empire on the world of Heldon, prior to The Final War. I was a naïve boy. I made the mistake of trusting my own desires." Zantigar rose from the table and walked toward the window. "The Academy seemed to be the only road to follow. It was the only path I wanted to follow. To be a rogue wizard was to be a failure, an embarrassment. I was a fool to see it that way. The Academy was power, and power is what I wanted above all else. It was seductive, and I was married to my ambitions."

As a child, Daylen envied Glazahn for having the opportunity to enter Vixus Academy. Deep down, he wanted to be a part of greatness; to make a difference in the world. The Academy seemed the only way to achieve it. He wanted revenge for what the empire had done to his father but did not fully believe that academies was inherently wrong, despite his mother's warnings.

Zantigar continued. "I learned the spells of Legionnaires; I studied their work and continued their legacy. I was fascinated with it all. It was everything to me, but little did I know, it was just what the kingdom had taught me to feel and to think. They controlled me and my thoughts."

"How did they manage to do that?" Daylen asked.

"I was weak. A pawn for warlords to manipulate, a weapon. Nothing more."

Zantigar's words were starting to sound familiar to the way his mother spoke. Her feelings were the same toward knighthood and the servitude of Daylen's father. She saw no difference in being a knight or a wizard in the academy. Daylen looked up and noticed Zantigar staring at him with serious, penetrating eyes.

"Sad is the one who believes in the kingdom over their own divinity. History held the key to my awakening, it was just a shame it would come so late, when so much damage had been done. Erramond the Wise opened my eyes to the truth."

"Did you ever meet him, in person?"

"Once. Imagine my surprise when I noticed he bore no branding on his palm." Zantigar shook his head, the memory reminding him of his feelings at the time. "I was shocked to discover he was a rogue. Imagine that, your hero, the wizard you idolize above all else, a rogue. I could not fathom it, and at first I hated him for it. It rocked my belief to the core. I did not understand how he could be so worshipped, so beloved, when he was inherently treasonous to the kingdoms of Heldon. He was a Legionnaire by character, not by servitude. He was far better than any of us at the time."

"How did he get away with it?" Daylen asked.

"He was greater than all of us. Who dare slay Erramond the Wise? He was in servitude to the world, not to a specific kingdom. All kings cherished him because he shared his life with each of them, all kingdoms valuing his existence."

This point was fascinating to Daylen. To hear Zantigar speak, with such disdain for kingdoms, and yet Erramond must have appreciated them, or at least understood how to get along with them. Perhaps, it was the greatest magic achievement he had learned yet about Erramond the Wise.

"I would learn of his greatness," Zantigar continued. "In time, I would learn that there was more to being a wizard than my limited view. All I had to do was look, and I would see. That was it; that was all it took. I left on a quest of self-discovery that outshined any experience offered by the academy. Years in servitude to the system and it took just a brief suggestion from Erramond, and my world forever changed."

"What did you do?" Daylen asked.

"I wanted to know what Erramond knew. Wishing to be Erramond and not myself, meant my path was not yet true."

"When did you discover this?"

"I began a pilgrimage. I journeyed the world. It was this time of self-reflection and discovery that I understood what I was truly looking for. At last,

I was learning, I was seeing past the illusion the Academy created. There were years of conditioning I had experienced, a selfishness and desire that had corrupted my soul."

Daylen realized now why Zantigar was so insistent on Daylen finding his own path.

"The very first Academies were like prison camps, simply a place to contain the magic ones. Forced to serve at an early age, these poor wizards were told by kings that they were lower forms of life. Religion provided the guilt and created the loyalty required. Religion taught wizards they were evil; that through the Academy was salvation. Only in servitude, was their forgiveness. Only in slavery, freedom."

Daylen was angered. "How could wizards allow this to happen?" With such power at their fingertips, they should have been making the rules, not subjected to them."

"A wizard is only as powerful as they believe themselves to be. Guilt was a powerful tool. Imagine being told from birth that your very existence was bad. That their frail bodies were a punishment. Wizards may be powerful, but they are fallible. They craved acceptance, power, belonging, just as all people do."

Daylen was aware of his own frail limbs and had heard that a wizard's lifespan was compromised by the magic they wield. His own quest to find Zantigar was challenged by the physical barriers of his physique. He thought of the sickness that overtook him in Lonely Wood after casting magic. "It is spell casting that kills us, isn't it?"

"The more spells we cast, the more strain it puts on our bodies. In the end, it is the very power that keeps us alive which will ultimately destroy us."

Daylen narrowed his eyes. "What about you, Zantigar? You have lived for hundreds of years."

Zantigar's mind held a deep secret. "Indeed, I have."

Daylen knew better than to press Zantigar on the subject. Zantigar's tone was all that was required to stop him from prying, considering there was more he wanted to understand. He brought the conversation back to the topic at hand. "What was life like for wizards before the first Academies?"

"Worse, I am afraid." Zantigar moved to the fireplace and sparked a fire. The room was bathed in heat. "Our kind were hunted and killed. Burned at the stake or lynched. The academies created a great alternative to most. A worthwhile compromise that promised great power."

"We have come a long way toward acceptance since those days," Daylen realized, "but some things have not changed at all. You talk of Rogue Wizards, those who refuse to join an academy and must run forever. Like me. We must hide from service or be hung, just like in the old days."

"Of course," Zantigar said. "But it is better to be free and hated, then to be a slave and accepted." Zantigar extended his arms, his palm up so that the branding was clear. "Be proud you don't bare one of these."

Zantigar clenched his branded hand into a fist. "It doesn't matter what kingdom you are from; they are all the same. It is not for us to wonder why we are hated. The question is why do we love academies so much?"

Power was the clear answer to Daylen. He thought of his father. From the stories his mother told him, his father was not one in search of power. Although his father was not a wizard, he imagined the pain that Vixus had put him through and found little difference between his injustice and that of wizards. Anger brewed in Daylen's eyes. He thought of his childhood, of Glazahn, who had been his only companion. He had once envied him, but now he was saddened to realize that Glazahn was a pawn. "I doubt the ancient world of FéLorën had any academies. There must be something we can do to bring them down."

Zantigar took a seat at the table. "Who says we should do anything? Every wizard has his own choice to make."

"No, don't say that. Something must be done."

"If you don't know what to do young wizard, then there is nothing for you to do."

"I see," Daylen protested. "So I should just live here in the mountains like you?" There were many things Daylen admired about Zantigar, but there were plenty of things he had grown to despise. Their differences were painful for Daylen to accept. His apparent inability to make a difference in the world was a major point of contention. If Daylen had the knowledge and the strength of Zantigar, he would bring change to the world. "What are you hiding from, Zantigar?"

Zantigar gave Daylen a look of warning. "I never asked you to come here, and I certainly never asked you to do as I do. I have lived to see enough, and this is not my war. Let that be the end of it."

Daylen was no longer patient. "What next then? Death?"

The light of the fire danced upon Zantigar's wrinkled face. The shadows cast by the flames heightened his grim glare. "What do you know of death?"

Daylen believed he understood death well. He had lived a short time but had seen so many of those he loved die before his eyes. For all he knew, his mother was dead, too. If only Zantigar knew how many times Daylen had thought of ending it all with his own sword. Maybe he wouldn't have to. Maybe he could just walk through a portal gate and leave this world behind. Daylen did not want to sit with Zantigar any longer. He stood and moved to the door. "I need some fresh air."

Shoving the cottage door open, he stepped outside into the winter air. He kicked the stones at his feet. After a moment, Zantigar stood beside him.

"What am I doing here?" Daylen whispered. "I mean, there must be a purpose for it all, at the very least for those who sacrificed their life for me."

Zantigar put his old, frail hand on Daylen's shoulder. "I cannot answer that question for you. Do you hope to save the world? Perhaps, the world doesn't need saving. You want so much to be a hero, but perhaps the world doesn't need one."

"How can you say that when there is so much wrong with the world?" He shook his head in defiance. "You know I can't stay here and just wait for death."

"Are you feeling defeated because you realize you are bound to die? We all die, someday."

Daylen turned abruptly to stare Zantigar in the face. "Not you. You don't die. And you have not shared your secret."

There was softness in Zantigar's eyes, revealing a rare, subtle weakness. "Living as long as I have is no gift. I will be going soon enough."

Daylen studied the old wizard's withered face and his crooked shape. It seemed a high wind could blow his fail body away. "I see," Daylen said. He lowered his head toward the ground. If Zantigar was right, then he would be one more person Daylen would lose from his life. With sadness, Daylen said, "You are right. Foolish of me to think I can change anything."

Zantigar was about to speak, but paused, as if finding the silence to be best.

Daylen appreciated the silence. He did not need another's voice when he struggled to hear his own. "I have heard you, Zantigar. All I get out of it is misery. The world is such a bad place. It's funny how we still fight to continue to be a part of a world that does not accept us for who we are, a world that doesn't appear to want us."

"Be silent. Be silent and listen."

Daylen looked up to the sky. "I hear nothing."

As Daylen stood in silence, he heard Zantigar enter the cottage, leaving him alone. Daylen walked toward the trees. He walked without direction, without a destination. His mind raced with images of his fallen companions. In the darkness ahead, he imagined Nasavine. He could hear his slithering voice and sense his loathsome presence. He shook his head and cursed his own mind, hating his position and hating himself. Amidst the trees, only one thing mattered. He longed for happiness. He longed to feel excited about life, just as he had done when Rahlen came strolling into Twilight. It was easier to live for others, then for himself.

Daylen turned back and stared toward the low light from the cottage. He wanted to find his purpose. Until he did, he convinced himself he would not be free of his pain. The cottage door opened and Zantigar stood in the doorway.

"Come now, Daylen. Out of the cold. I believe it is time I speak to you of spells."

~CHAPTER 9~

Daylen followed Zantigar into the cottage. At the hallway Zantigar stopped and motioned for Daylen to wait where he stood. Daylen did not have to be told, he leaned against the wall and waited, as Zantigar made his way into his room, shutting the door behind him. After a moment, the door swung open and Zantigar was carrying a large leather-bound book. He passed Daylen at the end of the hall and motioned for him to sit at the table. Zantigar joined him, placing the book down on the table with a resounding thud. A cloud of dust rose from the book's binding.

Wide eyed, Daylen leaned forward for a closer look.

"This is my spellbook," Zantigar said.

"Spellbook?" Daylen reached for it, but hesitated. He was afraid to touch it. It was sealed with a gold clasp, jewels engraved on its cover. It must have cost a fortune to create the book, itself, and the contents of it were most likely invaluable.

"Go on, open it."

With Zantigar's permission, he unfastened the clasp and opened the cover. The binding was strong, but worn, and the pages were delicate and crisp to the touch. With so many pages, it must have contained volumes of spells from the last couple hundred years. The writing within, was of unfamiliar symbols and characters.

Zantigar was studying Daylen's expression with great interest and he leaned back when it became clear that Daylen was confused by the scribing. What once he apparently questioned, became clear. "You cannot read it."

Daylen shook his head. "It is just a bunch of scribbles."

"So it is."

Daylen looked to Zantigar for an explanation. "What does it mean?"

"Only a wizard who is of a chaos nature can understand this writing. Having gotten to know you quite well, I am not surprised at your inability to understand it. I did not suspect your magic to be aligned with mine."

"Then I am not a Chaos Wizard."

"You are better off for it. One day, you may find that you are a Nature Wizard, or maybe even a Necromancer. Who knows what you will be? But you will recognize the language as if it were your native tongue. I will never be able to read your spells, just as you are unable to read mine."

Daylen marveled at Zantigar's spellbook, nonetheless. "It is so big. There must be hundreds, maybe even a thousand. Did you create all these spells?"

"Heaven's no," Zantigar chuckled. One of the perks of being in an academy is that you gain access to every spell in your field of study. As you now know, there is an enormous amount of power at your fingertips when you work for an empire."

"So, all Chaos Wizards carry a book of this size?"

"No. They hardly carry more than a few pages at a time. If they are lucky, they get to hold on to one or two of their own conjuring, so long as it is not too powerful, or too useful to the empire."

Daylen narrowed his eyes. "How can an academy take away a spell that a wizard created from their own soul?"

"Like a woman losing her child, I would imagine," Zantigar said.

"So, this… how did you-?"

"I stole it," Zantigar interjected. "You are looking at the complete catalogue of Chaos spells created for Hendor Academy."

Daylen did not lift his eyes from the pages. It suddenly made sense. The size of the book, the jewels on the cover. No normal wizard would possess such a thing. "It must be worth a fortune."

"It is beyond price, Daylen. If anyone were to find out I have it, I would be hunted by every Mageslayer in the known world. They would not stop until I was found and paid the price with my life. A spellbook is a mighty weapon and one of this size does not only have the potential for catastrophic destruction, it accounts for hundreds of years of progress in the Chaos field of wizardry. Stealing it has set the academies back hundreds of years."

Daylen ran his fingers across the page before him. He realized what a rare treat it was to even see this spellbook, let alone to even know of its existence. "The spells within this book will never to be used by an academy again."

"And that, my friend, is precisely the point."

"Wow, I'm impressed Zantigar. The courage to steal it, the chance you took. It is the stuff of legends. I didn't know you had it in you."

"There is much you don't know about me," Zantigar protested.

"Well, yea, but I never figured you to be a hero among rogue, outlaw wizards."

"Perhaps that would be the case, if any rogue actual knew I had it. This is one accomplishment that stays with me, alone."

"And now me," Daylen acknowledged. "Why did you show me this?"

"Because I trust you, Daylen," Zantigar spoke, matter of fact. "It was also a sure way for me to know whether or not you were a Chaos Wizard."

Daylen closed the book and placed his finger on the cover. "You can do a lot of good with this, right?"

Zantigar gave a cynical look. "Chaos Wizards are not known for their spells of preservation and have not historically used their magic for good."

Daylen had concern in his eyes. Without being able to read the symbols, Daylen still understood that most of what resided beneath his finger was designed to destroy. "Your spells are evil?"

"Evil thrives in our choices, not inherent in objects, alone. As a Chaos Wizard, I have accepted my role in life as one who brings an end to things."

"How can you live with that?" Daylen asked. "It must be hard. I find it so hard to understand what place destruction has in FéLorën.

"Death is a part of life. You could say that death allows life. The seasons help us understand this. And it is something you come to terms with as a Chaos Wizard."

"How do you do that? How are we supposed to be okay with death?"

"By understanding that without death, birth doesn't exist. Without its opposite, there is no identification. In other words, all light casts its shadow, they are forever linked."

"It is hard to accept," Daylen admitted.

"You have not realized its importance. Chaos Wizard or not, you must learn to accept it. As a wizard, it is imperative. Look to the silence and to your meditations. It will become clear, in time."

Daylen removed his hand from the spellbook. "How many spells did you personally create?"

"Twelve," Zantigar sighed.

Daylen was surprised. "That is it? Twelve?"

Zantigar laughed. "That is quite a large number I'll have you know. In time, you will respect what I was able to accomplish. In fact, you will find all twelve in that book."

"One day, Daylen, you will have your own spellbook. It will be small, but it will belong to you, as it should. To be shared only with those worthy. It is your right."

Daylen was left wondering what his spellbook would contain and what class of wizard he was destined to become. He thought about the spell he had cast, by accident, inside Lonely Wood. It had been warm and soothing at first, and he felt connected to everything in a way that could not be described in words. However, the spell had also made him sick and confused. He was frightened at the memory of losing consciousness. It was scary to relive it.

That night, as Daylen's mind raced before sleep, he wondered what his spell power was capable of.

* * *

Daylen found himself in the company of the Cragel people. He was filled with joy to be united with the community again. He was participating in a game with a leather ball and wooden sticks. It was a game he was unsure how to play. He looked to the crowd that was watching and he was shocked to notice the faceless shape of Ghost, staring at him from the crowd. In this instant, he knew he was dreaming.

He felt an uncontrollable anger rise within him. "What are you doing here?" Daylen yelled, angered by this mysterious figure, which had haunted his dreams for so long.

Ghost did not respond. His silence only angered Daylen more.

"What do you want?"

Ghost's response occurred in Daylen's mind, alone. "To play."

"How? You aren't even real!"

"You need me."

"You are wrong," Daylen shouted. "I don't need anything that I don't already have."

The people of Cragel disappeared. The team and the game no longer existed. Only Ghost remained, and his words sank like a stone, deep in Daylen's heart.

"Without me, you will lose."

~CHAPTER 10~

Through dark, tainted eyes Diamus filtered the light of the morning sun, as he stared from his carriage at a mighty flowing river. His party of Vixus soldiers and the Knights of Brownstone on guard. At the front of the procession was the Grand Commander, Sir Lenoy Brundt. He stopped before the edge of Xyntharia River, the natural border which separated the Wanton Lands from the elven Forest of Xyntharia. The carriage came to a quick halt.

The guide of the Vixus cavalcade approached the royal carriage. A soldier opened the carriage door upon his arrival. The guide was a Half-elf named Geryld, a native mercenary hired to lead the troops through the kingdom of Xyntharia. Geryld was middle aged, with a chiseled, unshaven face and cold, beady eyes. He had long pointed ears, but the tip of his left ear had been cut off, and his face was riddled with scars. He wore a weather-beaten tunic and a thick, forest colored cloak. His knee-high boots were worn, and his disheveled appearance reflected the hardships he had endured. His stern expression was worn like a mask, as if to hide his disdain toward his employers; those who lived a life of luxury behind castle walls. Wise from the ways of the wild, he was not one to trust wizards, but for the price Diamus was willing to pay for his services, he was able to look past certain unpleasant characteristics, including the reason for their passage into Xyntharia.

Diamus gave Geryld a nod and decided to take this break in travel to stretch his legs and, beckoning for Glazahn to follow, stepped out from the carriage. Obediently, Glazahn followed.

Diamus stood in the brisk, morning light. "Good day to you, Geryld. What news do you have for us?"

Geryld spoke with a deep, native accent. "We have reached the border of Xyntharia. Before we proceed, I must explain the rules for entering the realm of the Elves." He waved to the front, grabbing Sir Brundt's attention. "It is imperative the knights are informed, as well."

When Sir Brundt made it to the carriage, Geryld continued. "The forest of Xyntharia houses two distinct Elven cultures. There are the High Elves, who rule over Xyntharia, and are located in the heart of Xyntharia Forest. These are the Elves you seek."

"It is," Diamus confirmed.

Geryld continued. "And there are the Elves that I warned you about, those that live on the outskirts of the Xyntharia kingdom."

"The Din Naqui," Sir Brundt explained.

"Correct, the Din Naqui," Geryld said in a tone that expressed both his hatred and his respect. "The Din Naqui are a primitive species, an ancient elven race that once lived in Xyntharia City with the High Elves, but were banished, forced to live on the outskirts of the city. They are an aggressive lot when provoked. They are also incredible hunters, spiritually rooted to the forest. As such, it imperative that visitors respect their home."

"There is no need to worry, Diamus," Sir Brundt assured. "This is why the Knights of Brownstone are here. The Din Naqui would be fools to challenge us."

Geryld sneered in Sir Brundt's direction. "The Din Naqui are not to be reckoned with."

"For the cost of your guidance, I expect to make it to the heart of Xyntharia unobserved," Diamus said. "Whatever we need to do to make this possible, just let me know."

"What you need to understand," Geryld said, "is you would have better luck hiding from the trees, themselves, than from the eyes of the Din Naqui."

"Are you saying that there is no way to travel unnoticed?" Diamus said.

"What I am saying to you is you have already been noticed. We must respect their laws."

"So long as they respect my steel," Sir Lenoy Brundt grunted, "we won't have any issues."

"Rule number one," Geryld said, ignoring Sir Brundt's empty threat, "swords are to stay sheathed through their realm. We must enter with peaceful intention. Number two: stick to the main trails. Do not, under any circumstance, proceed off the path. They don't take kindly to wandering and they don't like the forest land disrupted. And third, the Din Naqui do not have tolerance for, or trust, in foreign magic." Geryld turned his attention to Diamus and Glazahn. "As a result, you must stay in the carriage until we cross into Xyntharia City. Keep your spellbook hidden, and any staff you may possess. Keep the blinds shut, so they are unaware of your presence. If they approach our party, then leave the negotiations to me and keep your troops calm. They will treat any distrustful act as a hostile act. If they feel inclined to attack, it will be swift, and it will be without mercy."

"It would be an act of war," Sir Brundt exclaimed. "They have no business confronting us and any attempt to disrupt us will not be tolerated."

Diamus had similar feelings of frustration over the matter. "There is nothing I hate more than having to trust an elf, let alone submit to one."

Geryld was quick to reply, "My mother was a human from the town of Rubin. She was raped by a Din Naqui and impregnated with me. A year later, when my Din Naqui father heard of my existence, he returned to Rubin, found my mother, and killed her. This was the Din Naqui punishment bestowed upon a woman for raising a Half-elf. If the village of Rubin had not protected me, I would have died before my second year. I may have the blood of elves running through my veins, but I am un-phased by your detest for them. You can stop the petty threats and insults; they have no influence on me. You will trust in my guidance, or we will part ways."

Diamus had heard enough. "If following the law of the Din Naqui will expedite our travel, then we will do whatever must be done to make haste." Diamus pushed his index finger into Geryld's chest. "Just do the job you were hired to do, and get me to the High Elves in safety, or it will be your life."

Geryld met Diamus' glare with fierce, unwavering eyes. "It will be *all* of our lives."

Sir Lenoy Brundt nodded. "I will inform the troops." He turned and bowed to Diamus and to Glazahn before departing.

Diamus looked at Geryld. "You make it sound like the Din Naqui are invincible."

"They are masters of their domain. Passage is possible only if they permit it. Hopefully, the small size of this military procession will be enough to dissuade them from making an appearance."

Diamus stared across the river and into the morning fog that shrouded the forest of Xyntharia. He thought of Beauty's prophecy. If Beauty was as accurate a prophet as Vamillion suggested, then King Mullen III would be sending his troops down this very river in the near future and the High Elves would be there to stop them. Diamus realized he had to succeed, that the gods were on his side. The veil of uncertainty disappeared at once, under the protective assurance of Beauty's prophecy.

Sir Brundt returned to the carriage on horseback. "The knights have been informed and await orders to proceed. I will stay at the head of the procession with your command, Diamus."

"Proceed," Diamus said. And with those words he led Glazahn back into the carriage and they waited for the carriage to depart. A guard closed the carriage door, and the blinds were drawn. Glazahn remained obedient in his silence but clutched his thin spellbook in his hand with nervous tension. A command was shouted, and the carriage was off, its squeaky wheels turning across the uneven terrain.

Xyntharia Forest was thick and expansive, accounting for a region every bit as large as Vixus territory, all kept under the shade of massive, ancient trees. Between the breaks in the leaves, rays of sunlight beamed to the forest floor like divine light. The forest was oddly quiet and serene, and as the parade of Vixus knights made their way into its shaded realm, it was like stepping into another world. The forest's vast space and deep shadows created a feeling of mystery, causing the marching troops to move with cautious steps, their eyes and ears attuned to the depths of the forest.

Sir Lenoy Brundt led the rows of Vixus knights forward, trotting on his horse beside Geryld. Behind him, knights carried Vixus banners, the tips of the banners adorned small white flags. With nothing more that could be done to protect them, they were left to the mercy of the Din Naqui, who were nowhere in sight. No doubt they were aware of stomping caravan and the large wagon wheels of the shielded carriage turning.

The deeper they travelled into the forest, the more the outside world seemed to disappear, as if there was no realm beyond the forest. The wheels to the carriage creaked and growled over the dirt road, the noise of their procession echoing against the trees like an intrusive alarm. The carriage came to an abrupt stop, jolting Diamus and Glazahn. They stared at each with puzzled, concerned looks, unaware of the reason for stopping. From outside, voices could be heard. Diamus recognized Geryld shouting at Sir Brundt, and then shouted incomprehensible commands to his troops.

Glazahn opened the shade of the carriage and peered toward the commotion.

"Stop that at once!" Diamus whispered. "Do you want the Din Naqui to see you?"

Glazahn fell back against his seat, his chest heaving. "We need to know what is happening."

Voices were speaking in a foreign language, confirming Diamus' fears. "It is the Din Naqui. Remain seated and do not make a sound."

Diamus heard Sir Lenoy Brundt shout, "There is no need to check the carriage. Geryld, tell them not to approach the carriage or I will order my troops to engage!"

Geryld said, "You will do no such thing!" Then, began speaking in the language of the Din Naqui.

Glazahn appeared petrified, sunken in his seat. He closed his eyes and folded his hands in his lap, his lips moving in silent prayer. The carriage doors burst open, the light of the forest beyond, spilling into the cabin. The bright light burned Diamus' eyes. At the carriage door was Geryld and three elves of striking appearance. Their faces were covered in tattoos and pierced with bone, wood, and beaded jewelry. The almond shaped eyes of the Din Naqui widened in surprise as they caught sight of the two wizards within.

"Atah! Atah!" The Din Naqui yelled.

Geryld spoke above the Din Naqui, in a somber tone, waving his hand as if to beckon Diamus and Glazahn to step out of the carriage. "Step down, Diamus. Please." He shook his head and outstretched his arms. "You must do as they say."

Diamus started to protest but gave up when Glazahn forced his way toward the carriage. Diamus rose to his feet. A Din Naqui grabbed Glazahn and forced him to the forest floor and another grabbed Diamus' arm. "Do not touch me!" Diamus snapped, pulling his arm away.

Once outside of the carriage, Diamus surveyed the scene. The Din Naqui were all about. They stood at the front and rear. His eyes combed the forest and he realized there was an army of Din Naqui lying in wait. A vast number of them resided in the trees, camouflaged as if they were a part of the forest, their presence made aware only because it was as they wished. With bow and arrow, spear and pike, they waited.

Glazahn whispered under his breath. "We are surrounded."

~CHAPTER 11~

Geryld approached Diamus.

Before Geryld could speak, Diamus protested. "What do they want?"

"Please," Geryld said. "We are to be their prisoners. We are powerless to stop this arrest."

Diamus glared at Geryld. "Unacceptable. You will get us out of this mess, Half-elf, or by the gods you will realize there was more to fear in me than any elf."

Geryld addressed the Din Naqui in their native language. Diamus did not need a translator to realize the negotiations were not going well. After a series of harsh banter, Geryld turned to Diamus. "They are going to search the carriage."

"My spellbook is in the carriage. I am afraid I cannot allow it."

Geryld plead to the elves.

"That is enough, Geryld," Sir Brundt said, placing his hand on the hilt of his sword. "You have heard Master Diamus. The Din Naqui are not permitted to search the carriage. Any attempt to hinder us any longer will be construed as an act of war."

A Din Naqui saw Sir Brundt place his hand on the hilt of his sword and the elf responded by releasing his arrow. It wisped past Sir Brundt's head and buried itself in the side of the carriage with a resounding thud.

Sir Brundt fell into defensive formation without hesitation. "Defend the Legionnaire and his apprentice!"

Glazahn and Diamus leaped into the carriage, slamming the door behind them as they witnessed Sir Brundt raise his sword from his sheath and buried it into the nearest Din Naqui. The soldiers followed suit, unsheathing their swords and advancing on the nearest Din Naqui, circling the carriage to protect it. Arrows plummeted from the trees, finding their mark amongst the Vixus soldiers. They dropped to the ground, one by one, wounded or killed. Three arrows set to kill Diamus and Glazahn buried into the carriage door just as it closed.

Outside of the carriage, the sound of slaughter raged on, the carriage jolted side to side, the occasional thud as arrows collided against the exterior. Glazahn fumbled through his spellbook, unable to think, he decided to recite the only spell he created, since it was the only spell he knew by heart. As he chanted, he conjured the screams and moans of otherworldly spirits. Terrible cries rang from the depths of the forest, the haunting voices and shrill shrieks invaded the minds of both Din Naqui and Vixus knights alike. A primal fear consumed both parties, bringing the battle to a grinding halt.

As Glazahn uttered the last words of the incantation, he slid down to the floor of the carriage, exhausted and weary. Being a Necromancer, the spell did not have quite the same effect on Diamus as it did to others. A large enough hold on reality gave him the stability to retrieve his own spellbook and for his eyes to rest upon a spell powerful enough to tip the tide of battle.

Speaking in the foreign language of his dark art, Diamus chanted. The haunting moans of Glazahn's spell still moved through the air as Diamus' spell began. Outside of the carriage, screams of agony were followed by gasps, as the Din Naqui elves and Vixus knights slowly regained their wits. The ground began to rumble, and the carriage trembled, as the large wagon wheels struggled to balance on the trembling ground.

The carriage door burst open and Diamus fell to the forest floor, puking and coughing before unconsciousness took him. Glazahn, still weary from his own spell, remained on the floor of the carriage. Sir Brundt was in the doorway, Diamus on the ground at his feet. He extended his hand to Glazahn, while his other hand supported him against the carriage. The ground beneath him continued to shake with violent fervor. "We are experiencing a quake!" Sir Brundt exclaimed.

"It is no quake…" Glazahn managed to whisper through struggled breath.

Sir Brundt shook Glazahn, as if to wake him from a dream. Outside, the knights and elves struggled to make sense of what was occurring at the same time that they sought to defend themselves from one another.

Geryld was standing by Sir Lenoy Brundt's side, bewildered, along with everyone else. "We must run from here! Quick, while we have the chance! Follow me!"

Glazahn screamed, finally coming to his senses and rising. "I cannot leave my Master!"

The ground was still rumbling, and the forest floor ruptured in seemingly random locations. Sir Brundt picked Diamus up. "Leave it to me," he yelled over the chaos, and motioning to Geryld he said, "Now go!"

Geryld ran through the battlefield and into the trees. Glazahn and Sir Brundt in the rear with Diamus over his shoulders. The ground was ripped apart and the horror that Diamus had unleashed revealed itself. Skeletal arms reached out from beneath, breaking free from their place of burial. Across the battlefield, skeletal remains had risen and taken life, rushing to the nearest living entity with murderous intent. Whatever had once perished beneath their feet, whether elf, human, animal or monster, charged at both elves and knights, clawing through the flesh of the living.

A Din Naqui shaman was quick to unleash a spell of his own, to combat the undead army, adding to the chaos. After chanting the plants of the forest were animated, causing vines to wrap themselves around anything that moved that didn't have Elven blood. Tree limbs swung like giant clubs, knocking back knights and shattering skeletal attackers. Several Vixus knights, held captive by the tight grip of thorn covered vines were helpless to the attack of skeletons, which tore their bodies apart.

As Geryld led his companions from the battlefield, a vine from a tree overhead grabbed hold of Glazahn by the neck and yanked him from the ground. Geryld fell back to help Glazahn, and thanks to his Elven blood, the plant did not engage him. With a quick few strokes of his sword, the vine released its hold and dropped the apprentice to the ground.

Geryld helped Glazahn to his feet and led him to Sir Brundt who managed to escape to the edge of the battlefield. Four elven skeletons rose from the ground. Sir Brundt placed Diamus' unconscious body on the ground and withdrew his broadsword, eager to put his training into action. He swung his sword in a series of strikes, an unbroken cycle of advances. Upon contact, a skeleton shattered. He spun, following through with his strikes, and plunged his sword through the last second skeleton, dissecting its torso from its pelvis.

Geryld advanced, confronting the final two skeletons that stood in their way. With a wide swipe, he lopped the skull off a skeleton and watched it roll into the bushes. He lowered his guard but a moment, only to realize that the headless skeleton was still animated from the spell. The skeleton punched through Geryld's chest with uncanny strength and grabbed his heart. His body dangled from the headless skeleton's forearm as it reached up into the air.

Glazahn screamed at the sight. The skeleton retracted its arm, Geryld's heart still within its hand. Sir Brundt brought his broadsword down on the headless skeleton, the devastating strike toppling the skeleton into a pile of bones. Glazahn had no way to stop the fourth skeleton from lunging at him. Glazahn fell to the ground and the skeleton jumped on top of him, its hands wrapped tight around his neck, in an attempt to choke the life from him.

As the skeleton strangled the life from him, he had a vision. As death drew near, he saw symbols and foreign letters, which spoke to him in the unique language of Necromancy. He stared in horror, not from the experience of his life coming to an end, but because of the contents of his vision, and the awareness that came with deciphering the new spell. The bone hands of the skeleton squeezed harder still, and he felt the last breath of air escape his lips, his final thought being one of acceptance, welcome death's embrace over the hallucination induced by the realization of his latest spell.

Suddenly, the skeleton released its grip and toppled to the side as Sir Brundt shoved the skeleton off of Glazahn's body. The skeleton attempted to regain its footing, bracing itself for another charge, when it collapsed all at once, for no apparent reason. Glazahn gasped for air, shocked to still be alive. Sir Lenoy Brundt extended his arm to help Glazahn to his feet. "The skeletons are collapsing. It won't be long before the Din Naqui complete their massacre."

Glazahn grabbed Sir Lenoy Brundt's hand and rose to his feet. The Knight of the High Command then ran to Diamus' unconscious body and lifted him up and over his shoulder. He pointed into the distance. "Geryld was leading us in this direction, follow me!"

Glazahn was catching his breath, trying to make sense of the chaos he just experienced. He was numb from the hellish vision that was still fresh in his mind. He ran alongside his companions, putting the nightmare of the blood shed behind him, but unable to escape the nightmare of his mind. Beside himself, he pressed onward toward the heart of Xyntharia Forest, following Sir Brundt's lead one laborious step at a time.

~CHAPTER 12~

Diamus' eyes fluttered at the moment of consciousness, then opened. He was lying on a bed of fine silk sheets. On the ceiling, directly overhead, was an intricate, detailed painting of elven design. The air he breathed was filled with the pleasant aroma of wildflowers, suggesting a touch of magic in the air. He rose, alarmed.

Glazahn was seated beside Diamus' bed. He leaned forward as soon as he became aware of Diamus awakening. "Master…"

Diamus placed his hand on Glazahn's, grateful to see his apprentice. "Have we made it? Are we in the city of Xyntharia?

Glazahn smiled. "Yes." He motioned to the window beside him.

Diamus rose to his feet and peered out the window. His room was high in a tower of Castle Xyntharia, the city outstretched before him in all directions, in a vast circle. Complex roadways lead to the castle in its center. The tall buildings of Xyntharia rose higher than the trees of the forest, forged from minerals and diamonds. They sparkled in multicolor prisms against the sun's rays. Xyntharia city was an architectural phenomenon, a natural wonder of the known world, a display of artistic achievement as much as it was a functioning home for the high elves.

As much as Diamus hated to admit it, the elven people were of a superior mind. The air, itself, seemed light, almost intoxicating. In the distance, Diamus could make out the walls that surrounded the city. They were not just a barricade but served as a device that reflected waves of spell power that purified the air. Crystals redirected the magic, enhancing the spell across the entire city. The ongoing phenomenon could only be accomplished by a wizard of great skill and discipline, who was in constant meditation.

Diamus pondered in fascination. Glazahn moved beside him at the window, and they stared together at the city beneath them. Diamus looked at his apprentice and was shocked to find him staring into space with a grim expression, seeming to not only be unaffected by the splendor before him, but appalled. "My boy, you look as ill as I had felt the day before. What has become of you?"

Beads of sweat percolated on his forehead. His skin was pale, with dark circles under the eyes. "I have had a vision."

Diamus turned to his apprentice with intrigue. "Tell me, what is it?"

Glazahn stared into distant space. "I never imagined I would find myself standing in the beauty of an elven city. And yet, I am unmoved by its brilliance, the glorious colors have turned to black and the fragrance in the air spoils with each breath, all on account of what I have seen. I am left devastated, untrusting of my own mind, disbelieving I could ever conceive such… evil." He lowered his eyes in shame.

Diamus seemed unconcerned with Glazahn's wellbeing, only interested in confirming what he suspected. "It is a spell, isn't it?" Diamus asked. "You have discovered your purpose… why you are here… why you have been chosen."

Glazahn looked to his Master. Without speaking, his expression of horror confirmed it was true.

Diamus grabbed Glazahn by the arms, not to comfort him, but to snap him out of his disillusionment. "We have trained you because we knew you were destined for greatness, knew that you had a greater purpose to serve."

Glazahn shook his head. "This cannot be why I am here. You don't know what I have seen, you don't know the contents of my mind. I cannot serve such darkness. I cannot live with myself if what I have seen is to be my destiny."

"I am your Master," Diamus reminded, his eyes narrowing beneath the dark shadows on his face, as his voice raised. "The Dark One has granted you this spell so as to test our faith. You are a privileged individual, one who may possess the strength to control the empire if you so desire!"

Glazahn was distraught by Diamus' words and shook his head in disbelief. He did not want to believe what he was capable of and did not want to pretend that power was all he ever wanted… not at this cost, not with the loss of so many lives.

Glazahn's terrified expression only excited Diamus more. "Do not be surprised, apprentice. You should have known that your life had a purpose far greater than the average wizard. Why do you think Vamillion had such an interest in you? Do you think its mere luck that I am your Master? Together, you and I, we can rule this miserable land. Don't you see it? Vamillion is doing everything in her power to ensure that Necromancers are free to roam the land. When she has accomplished this task, there will be nothing to stop us from overthrowing her and claiming the thrown for ourselves!"

Glazahn looked out the window. "So much deceit; so much hate. It is not in me to do what you ask. I owe my life to Vamillion. Is this how I should repay her, by taking her life?"

"Don't be such a love-struck fool!" Diamus spat. "You have a far greater duty to help your kind; to raise the Necromancers to their rightful place. For far too long Necromancers have been persecuted or left to roam underground like rats. Do as you know is right. Wield the gift the gods have granted you. This spell, whatever sort of terror it is; it is a gift! An opportunity for Necromancers to not only walk upon the land, but to rule it!"

Glazahn was not fazed by his Master's grandiose plans.

"If you were to walk away from your calling, to ignore the voice of your own soul, you would live a life of utter loneliness, forever lost!"

Glazahn's face darkened, but there was a glimmer of light in his eye, as he heard these words to be true. There was no alternative but to embrace that which he knew he was. "Yes, I can see that now, Master. I see what you have been teaching me. I know what it is to accept all that I am." Glazahn took as seat beside his spellbook and looked side to side. "I need something to write with."

Diamus, as if one step ahead, was already holding a quill outstretched before him.

Glazahn took the quill in hand. "I will write the spell down and you shall see for yourself what it is I have discovered. Only then will you question if I am someone to admire."

There was a light rapping at the door. Diamus lunged toward Glazahn. "Not now, Glazahn. You must wait until we are alone. Better yet, until we are home, in Vixus, underground in the Academy of Necromancy."

The door opened. Diamus turned, alarmed. Glazahn stood.

Sir Brundt entered. His black armor had been polished to a brilliant shine and his face was clean, his short locks of black hair brushed back, his face freshly shaven, save for his long black mustache. "Glad to see you are well, Diamus."

Diamus bore a broad smile and approached the knight with outstretched arms. "Sir, you are a savior. I shall never be able to repay you for what you have done. You saved my life, you saved Glazahn. You have surely proven your might and your wisdom. I will make sure that Vamillion rewards you well for your service."

The Empress has been waiting," Brundt said. "Guards are waiting for us down the hall, when you are ready."

~CHAPTER 13~

The Empress of Xyntharia sat on a smooth, crystal throne raised upon marble steps. Beside the throne were six elven guards in armor, three to a side. Behind the Empress was a wizard cloaked in a light gray robe, his eyes concealed in the shadow of his hood. By the Empress' feet sat several naked, elven women on soft cushions. They did not show any care to their bodies being exposed. At first sight, to the uninformed, they appeared to be slave to their ruler, mindless objects for the Empress' amusement, but in fact, they represented the heads of Xyntharia government, the greatest minds of the empire.

The High Elves wore their military rank on their faces, tattooed to their cheek. The most common of soldiers bore a simple mark, and as they progressed up the ranks in service and status, the tattoo would be expanded upon, so that the most influential and powerful elves had elaborate, detailed markings that traveled down the length of their face.

The women beside the Empress adorned tattoos befitting of leadership, second only to the ruler of the realm. They were the brightest and the most cherished minds of the empire and yet they sprawled at the Empress' feet in playful, casual fashion, running their hands through each other's hair and grooming each other, seemingly paying no mind to their ruler sitting motionless in her seat.

It was common knowledge that women ruled Xyntharia. It was a woman's society and it always had been. The female was worshipped, both in body and mind. While nothing prohibited a man from holding high office, it was still rare for a male to hold a position of leadership. Quive, the cloaked wizard at the Empress' side, was one such exception to the norm. Women's superiority was not contested by the males. They believed their role was best served in military affairs and sporting activities. While both the men and the women shared a proficiency and adoration for the creative arts, an activity that was regarded in high esteem, and granted one the greatest respect, regardless of sex.

Elves, in general, placed artistic value on anything and everything, be it their architecture, their clothing, their craftsmanship, and their food. The world could not deny that elven made items, especially from Xyntharia, were always of the finest quality. Masters of aesthetic brilliance, it challenged the other races and nations to deny their ascendancy. It was a belief in their own superiority which had threatened humankind since the beginning of written history. Their boastful god complex instigated distasteful relations with all other races of the land. Forming an alliance with the Elves during The Final War was the final and most difficult obstacle in creating union and peace on the land. The sincerity of equality felt by the elves was still suspect, more so now than at the time of the world's unification.

When the visitors entered the great hall, the women averted their attention in unison, as if of one mind, giving the guests their undivided attention. Diamus, Glazahn and Sir Lenoy Brundt approached the elven spectacle while walking on a multi-colored carpet. The carpet led to the throne and behind the throne was an enormous, arched cathedral window. It served as a means to showcase the brilliant forest landscape beyond the confines of the hall and allowed the majestic light of the sun to fill the room. The carpet was infused with tiny mineral shards, which, like a multitude of prisms, reflected rainbows of light from the sun's rays.

"My name is Diamus of Cassalire. Let me thank you, Empress of Xyntharia, for offering such a bountiful meal this morning, for your medical assistance, and comfortable lodging."

Vi-Lir Zyraxyvarye, Empress of the elven dynasty of Xyntharia, parted her lips to speak, her voice had the tone of a musical note, which was pleasing to the ear and, by architectural design, echoed in the great hall. "Cassalire? From Northern Oryahn, quadrant three of what was once the capital of Omnias, many years ago?"

"That is correct, Your Highness," Diamus said with a bow. "I come on behalf of Vixus, as a messenger and a friend. I have taken my residence on the continent of Valice. I am indebted to Vixus Empire and I teach at their Academy."

Vi-Lir Zyraxyvarye narrowed her almond-shaped eyes, her thin mouth parted in a curious smile, revealing faint wrinkles, the only indication of age, on otherwise smooth features. "I can still remember the army of Omnias. Their black ships sailed to our land, mercilessly, like a plague, and almost succeeded in annihilating the races of the world from the planet."

"It is a part of history that we all regret, Your Majesty." Diamus stared at the elven ruler in deep concentration. She was a striking woman to behold, especially for being hundreds of years old, and having lived through The Final War. She had smooth, golden skin and a youthful appearance, despite her age.

Bald, her narrow face accentuated her large, elven eyes, which held an ancient wisdom. The tattoo on her face was intricate in detail, and she bore a tattoo crown around her head, accentuating her lifelong commitment to her sovereignty. She wore a fine, loose garment, her top open, so that her breasts were exposed. The rest of her thin frame leaving little to the imagination due to the see-through quality of her dress. She sat upright, her thin hands rested delicately on her throne, her legs parted slightly. Like the other women before her, she had no shame, all too aware that her beauty was just another aspect of her power, as was her mind.

Vi-Lir Zyraxyvarye studied her guests carefully, in silent judgement. "You have travelled far and have suffered greatly to the will of the forest. For this, I apologize, and hope our hospitality had cured what ailed you."

"Indeed." Diamus nodded graciously. "Your benevolence is unparalleled."

"Tell me, Diamus of Cassalire, what is the purpose for your visit?"

"Empress," Diamus began. "We come as your ally."

"Ally?" The Empress was quick to interrupt. "Such a relationship exists only in time of war, and in such times, is not so frivolously granted. Our world is at peace, sustained by the graces of the High Council of FéLorën. As such, we are family, brothers and sisters to one another. Now; how can the Elves of Xyntharia be of service to you?"

"Gracious Empress, I would not be standing before you today if I felt that there was not a dire situation, which is a mutual threat to us both. You have learned of what transpired at the last meeting of the High Council of FéLorën, no doubt. It has come to our attention that King Mullen III is preparing to wage war against us."

The women at the Empress' feet turned to face their leader, the first time they revealed a negative emotion. The Empress' expression remained unchanged, despite the alarming revelation. "I heard the council meeting was unfavorable, but I never would have imagined Mullen would be swayed to take such action. What need is there to break the peace that has lasted for hundreds of years?"

"The portal, Empress."

"You refer to the Desert Portal. This would be the same gateway that all who enter do not return from. Something I am sure I need not remind you of. Let Mullen have the gate, let him die trying to uncover its secrets if he so desires."

"With all due respect, Your Majesty, you fail to understand the significance the Desert Portal has on the human kingdoms. There is a god the humans have begun to fear. A new, rising god, that has promised that the future of wealth and power lies within the portals of Valice."

"The Dark One," the Empress presumed.

"Yes. If the Dark One can deliver what is promised, Mullen will have vast power, create a new order, a new age, which will threaten the continent of Valice, if not the world. We cannot allow Mullen to disrupt the balance on the land."

The Empress leaned toward her advisor. Quive whispered into her ear and she nodded after a moment, and then centered herself on her throne, directing her attention back to Diamus. "Tell me what you know of the Dark One."

"He is all powerful. He has forced servitude, by spreading his wrath upon our Legionnaires. In the shadow of the unknown, lies the power which will appease him. His teachings of what the darkness, and the unknown have to offer, has earned him his name. There is little else known about him. In that mystery lies his power. He insists it is what lies beyond the portal that will lead to his transformation and the kingdom that succeeds in obtaining the treasure within is promised power unequalled."

"You speak of this Dark One, as if you are in worship of him, yourself. Be careful of a life lived for power, as it is fleeting, and ever changing."

Quive leaned toward the Empress and she paused to listen to his whisperings. When he finished, she addressed her audience. "Stories of the Dark One have reached the ears of the High Elves. It seems his influence is not limited to humans."

"I know that you value your magic," Diamus said. "Look at what it has done for Xyntharia, look at how it has defined your entire culture. Imagine the power of one with the power to control the destiny of every wizard. It could change the face of the world. This god is one to fear, but his power is to be respected, less he destroys you."

"My advisor believes he has heard the voice of the Dark One. Resisting communication with this entity has brought him great fear. Your words confirm his suspicions."

"Your advisor should trust his instinct and should be careful," Diamus continued. "How long before he speaks to you, Empress? Will he want your servitude, or your death? Either is unacceptable. So, I implore you. Help us stop Mullen, so that we can stop the Dark One from growing in power. We do not know what the portal offers, but can we afford to find out?"

Vi-Lir Zyraxyvarye paused a moment and closed her eyes in reflection. After a moment, she opened her eyes. "I am sorry, Diamus of Cassalire. A war based on speculation is a war that cannot be supported. Furthermore, a war based on religious belief is unfathomable to us. Have the lives of men learned nothing from The Final War?" The Empress leaned back in her throne.

Diamus stepped forward. "To be clear, we in no way are requesting your contribution or support of war. On the contrary, we want peace. I, on behalf of the Queen of Vixus, are saddened by the chain of events which are unfolding. Mullen will be attempting to wage an attack against our empire. To keep their movements a surprise, they will be advancing along Xyntharia River."

"Is your intelligence accurate?"

"As certain as anything can be, Your Majesty. If you simply prevent their advance, then you will prevent war. We ask for your empathy, your servitude not to Vixus, but to the land of FéLorën, and we ask for the assistance that can only be provided by your wisdom, and your undeniable strength. It is a small price to pay for lasting peace." Diamus with a humble bow of his head, concluded, "Please, keep our request under consideration."

Vi-Lir Zyraxyvarye bowed her head and closed her eyes. She was slow to raise her head, as if in deep thought. She reflected on more than just Diamus' words, but by grander implications of her guests visit. Her eyes opened. "Thank you, Diamus of Cassalire, for this information. You have left me with much to ponder. If you are looking for a commitment, I am afraid I cannot afford you that luxury at this time. Unless you have other matters to discuss, I will consider our meeting adjourned. You will find rooms have been prepared for you and your companions. Feel free to take as much time as you need before your departure. Alert the chaperone and I will ensure an escort is waiting to ensure safe passage from Xyntharia Forest, so you can avoid the unpleasantries you experienced arriving."

~CHAPTER 14~

Glazahn rose from his bedding, unable to sleep, despite the comfortable accommodations provided by the Empress. He left his room and crossed the hall to where his master was stationed. He banged on the door, anxious to enter.

Diamus opened the door and stepped aside, allowing Glazahn entry. Glazahn moved to the center of the room, pacing, his mind racing with anxious thoughts. Sir Brundt was in the room and appeared worried due to a conversation that had been taking place before Glazahn interrupted.

Sir Brundt shook his head, looking to Diamus. "I fear that we have failed our mission. The Empress will not assist us, we will return to Vixus without an alliance, without even an empty promise of assistance."

Diamus placed a hand on Sir Brundt's broad shoulder. "You must have faith in what the future has in store for us. Our goal is accomplished, regardless of promises or alliances. We have placed the knowledge in their minds, like a seed. Give it time to grow."

Sir Brundt gave a reluctant nod. "As you say. I will see myself out."

"Please, and do not worry," Diamus said. "Your services have been immeasurable. Your Queen shall be pleased. You should consider our mission a success."

Sir Brundt had made his way into the hall, his mind at ease by Diamus' words. "Good night to you."

As Diamus closed the door, Glazahn still paced, unable to slow his mind. "I can't sleep, Master."

"Worry not, my apprentice. When we return to Vixus, we can begin our plans. With your help, we shall control the Desert Portal. Once Mullen is defeated, Vixus will be unstoppable. When the time is right, you and I will be controlling the kingdom, if not all of Valice!"

Glazahn took a seat. He put his head in his hands and after a moment he raised his head. "What do you mean by 'when we defeat Mullen'?

Diamus took a seat and slid his chair beside Glazahn. "There is a prophet. He has advised us of an imminent attack against us from Mullen's army. So, to protect our people, and to protect the school of Necromancy, Vamillion has a plan to attack Mullen before he can invade us."

"How can this occur if it has been prophesized that Mullen will be invading us?"

"The prophet has already confirmed that our preemptive strike will prevent Mullen from invading. Mullen's advance is only possible if we choose not to act. As Mullen sends his army south, across Xyntharia River, we will advance to the north. With the majority of his forces to the south, looking to take us off guard, those who enter the Devil's Crossing will be helpless to our advancement. Unbeknownst to them, as their northern advancing townsfolk are left with no choice but to surrender or be slaughtered, his forces traveling south will be stopped by the elves, and annihilated. All at once, the Mullen army will be stopped, their mighty army reduced to impotence. They will be at our mercy."

Glazahn lowered his head. "So, deceit, war, destruction; these are the only means by which to prosper?"

"The kingdom is relying on you, upon your spell. You will play a great part in our success. Your spell will save countless Vixus lives. To your people, you will be a hero and will change their opinion towards Necromancers forever. You, alone, may lead the way for our kind. One day, we will join the ranks of wizards in the light of the sun, far from the dungeons."

"How is it you know so much about my spell, before I have even had the chance to write it down?" Glazahn asked. "You have known about this, your prophet has told you as much, hasn't he? This is why I was chosen? To unleash the terror of my darkest fears?"

Diamus placed his hand on Glazahn's shoulder. "No; to save your people, to make Vixus great again."

"You don't understand, you don't know what my mind has seen, what my mind has created. It will be death to many when I unleash this spell upon the world."

Diamus tightened his grip. "You will do as instructed. You will live your life in service for the one who had mercy on your soul, if not for your own sake."

Glazahn thought of Vamillion, her mercy. He tried to pull away but could not escape Diamus' grip. "Is this what I have lived for? To bring death? How much destruction will it take to satisfy my Master's heart? How much sacrifice is required to pay off my debt to the kingdom?"

Diamus released Glazahn's hand. "There is no limit to the lengths you should go to protect our kind. Be glad that the priestess has not forsaken you. You have been blessed from her kindness, blessed with this opportunity, blessed to have received the spell you have learned. It is your right, your very salvation."

Glazahn believed it was Vamillion who held the keys to his salvation. Diamus spoke of betraying her, of taking her life in order to secure the throne. The clarity of his purpose manifested itself upon this realization, as a result of the madness from which there was no escape. He would not live to see Vamillion assassinated by the ones closest to her, the ones she had placed her trust in. He would not bear that guilt, too. Protecting her was the only redemption possible for what he was about to unleash on the world. He would find a way to protect her, no matter the cost.

He looked into his Master's eyes and knew in that moment that he would kill him. Not now, but one day soon, before Diamus could take away the only woman who ever showed him grace, he would bring an end to him. He smiled at the thought. The apprentice would slay the master, taking his title and taking his place beside the woman he loved. This dream was worth living for.

Diamus could see that Glazahn was coming to his senses, the color was returning to his face. "Do you see that for which you owe your service?"

Glazahn stared into Diamus' eyes, his voice strong in conviction. "Yes, Master. For the kingdom; for Necromancy."

~CHAPTER 15~

There was a part of Glazahn that wished he had died on the field of battle, wished that the skeleton had robbed his last breath. He wouldn't have to face the responsibility of what lied ahead. He stood before the doors of the Necromancy Academy, far below ground, waiting as the large iron doors slowly spread to grant him passage. He walked the hall as if he was walking to his own execution, as if the very act of writing down the spell he had envisioned would be the death of his spirit.

He entered his study, took a seat at his desk and with quill in hand transcribed the spell into his spellbook. All he once identified as being, whether an innocent youth, an enthusiastic student, or a dreamer; no longer existed.

He thought back to his home in Brunhylde, to the lone tree on the hill and a memory came to him. His friend, Daylen, pulled out a knife to carve his name into the tree. Glazahn heard a voice. He thought it was the voice of the tree, but he knew better, now. After spending time in the Academy of Necromancy, he recognized the sound of the dead when he heard it. The voice he heard that day, standing on the hill, the voice he heard every time he sat next to the tree, it was the voice of one who had been hung and buried on that hill, beneath the tree. He was deceived, fooled into thinking the tree had spoken. The dream of being connected to all things was shattered and the search for unity and peace, was over.

*   *   *

Diamus walked the spiral stairs of the Moon Tower. Reaching Vamillion's study, he opened the door and stepped inside. Beauty's paintings were thrown about, the room in disorder. Vamillion could not be seen, but voices could be heard from behind a large, velvet curtain, which hid the back section of the study from view. Up until now, he was unaware that there was even a room on the other side. He moved to the curtain and pulled back the veil. The dark room was softly lit with candles. Vamillion was enacting a ritual, the severity of her spiritual practice reaching new and terrible heights.

Naked, she lay face down on the ground, centered upon symbols and runes drawn on the stone floor. Candles circled her, as slaves went about final preparation to the ceremony. Each of them were also nude, but adorned the masks of forest animals. A servant wearing a rabbit mask pierced sharp, thick hooks into her back. They sunk into her skin next to old scars, revealing that this was not the first time she had partaken in this act. As the hooks pierced her flesh she gasped, blood swelling to the surface, pooling in the valley of her back. The hooks were attached to chains which were in turn fastened to the wall. Her hands and feet were shackled. Two slaves in deer masks, positioned on either side of her body, dragged the chains through a pulley apparatus. As they heaved, the chain tightened. The hooks tugged at her skin and pulled her body from the floor. The blood from her back dripped to the symbols beneath her. Her body rose like a drawbridge, the chains pulling her until her back was against the wall, forcing her arms outstretched and her legs spread. Her face was fixed in concentration, her mind focused on the pain, so that she was unaware of her audience.

Diamus slipped into the room, quietly. The slaves in animal heads turned to acknowledge his presence, but they said nothing. The sight of her body exposed, bound, caused his mind to reel and a chill ran down his spine. He wondered what lengths she was willing to go to satisfy her desires. He moved forward, until he stood before her vulnerable body. She opened her eyes. At first, she could not see anything. She was drunk on the experience, present in life only in the presence of pain. Raised and pierced, she was alive, and it was only in this state that she could feel the divine. Her eyes finally focused and fell on Diamus. His face was close to hers, his body close enough to touch. She smiled.

"You have returned to me," she whispered. She squirmed, trapped in her shackles. "What shall you do to me? Or have you come here merely to watch?"

He looked toward the slaves who held her up by chains. Their muscular bodies, forged from years of labor, remained still. Looking back to Vamillion, he met her smile with his own.

Vamillion tilted her head, inquisitively. "You wish to touch me," she stated.

He moved closer. He could feel the breath escape her lips, yet he refrained from touching.

Conscious of the hooks in her back, Vamillion winced from a wave of pain. She threw her head back, her soft neck exposed. Overcoming the agony, she smiled. "Or do you wish to kill me?"

Diamus grabbed her neck in his hand and squeezed, hard enough to constrict her breathing, but stopping short of making her pass out. He closed her eyes and parted her lips and he kissed her with passion, filling her mouth with his tongue. She bit him and he pulled away. He could taste the blood in his mouth, feel the sting from the gash on his tongue. He removed his hand from her neck, and she let out a gasp for air, her mouth covered in his blood.

The servants waited in patience, waiting for her command. He realized with a word, that she could command the slaves to kill him.

Diamus took several steps back, studying the amusement on her face. "You are insane."

"The Dark One, he is calling to me; drawing near," Vamillion whispered. "I feel his presence. This act, this feeling, it brings me close to the edge of the world... he will meet me here, as promised. Any moment now, he will reveal himself to me."

A thrashing came at Vamillion's chamber door, a series of pounding knocks. Spooked, Diamus turned toward the curtain expecting the Dark One to enter, a sense of dread overcoming him.

"Vamillion! Vamillion, My Liege, you must come at once!" Rasatharian's voice called from the other side of the door.

Vamillion looked to her servants. "Lower me; now."

The servants loosening the chains, lowering her to the floor.

Rasatharian screamed, "Something terrible has happened!"

"Rasatharian? What has he done?" Diamus looked to Vamillion, perplexed. "What have *you* done?"

Vamillion's shackles were released, and she rose from the floor. A servant held her robe open for her and she slid her arms into the sleeves, pulling the robe over her shoulders. The delicate fabric stung her back, as it soaked with blood. She tied the robe across her body while blood dripped down her legs. "Please, Diamus; get the door."

Diamus rushed to the door, closing the curtain behind him. Swinging it open, Rasatharian was hunched, out of breath, a petrified expression on his face.

"What is the meaning of this?" Diamus demanded.

Rasatharian pushed his way inside, not waiting for an invitation. "Oh, Diamus! I must speak to the High Priestess at once!" He looked side to side, frantic. "Where is she?"

Vamillion appeared from behind the curtain. She stumbled, weak, and braced herself against her desk. She was dizzy, just coming to from her ritual trance. Rasatharian fell to his knees at her feet. He cried out at the sight of her, trembling. "It is over!" He spoke through sporadic breath. "All of it, over. They are dead, My Liege; all of them… dead!"

BEHIND the VELVET CURTAIN

~CHAPTER 16~

Vamillion was disoriented, attempting to gather her wits as Rasatharian trembled at her feet and pulled at her robe. She looked to Diamus, attempting to figure out if any of what was taking place made sense to him.

Diamus kneeled beside Rasatharian and grabbed him with both hands. He turned Rasatharian to face him, to stare into his eyes. "Glazahn? Tell me, what has happened to Glazahn?"

Rasatharian shook his head. "I – I'm not sure. I… was returning to the Academy. Before unlocking the doors, there were screams. Wild, shouts of terror and desperation. I could hear Glazahn…"

"Is he alright?" Diamus said, with bated breath.

"He was yelling."

Diamus raised his voice in suspense, "What did he say?"

Rasatharian was still shaking his head, his arms trembling within Diamus' grasp. "He was raving, like a madman, yelling about the end of the world. Something about a god, the harbinger of death…"

Vamillion came to her senses. "The Dark One!"

Rasatharian nodded. "He must have seen him... a voice of many voices… a face of many masks. I dared not enter." He looked up to face Vamillion, ashamed, pitiful. "I could not enter."

"What else do you know?" Vamillion demanded.

Rasatharian turned away, as if the memory was more than he could bear. "I heard screams. The sounds of the Necromancers within… gurgling, gasping for breath, before falling silent, one at a time. I could hear them all, I could hear their agony, the torment and pain before the silence of death overtook them. My ear to the door, I listened." Tears fell down his cheeks.

"As the screams died down, one by one, the hall became still, the few remaining sounds, whimpers, faded into silence. And then a thud against the door, right against my ear! The voice of one trapped within was faint and weak." Rasatharian's eyes widened, "I called out, pleading for the wizard to speak to me. I struggled to hear, and could only make out his final words, 'Run… Run for your life. Dead… Everyone… Dead.'"

"How?" Diamus ordered.

Rasatharian shook his head. His voice shaking, afraid of what Diamus might do. "I do not know, My Liege."

Diamus averted his attention to Vamillion, for the first time, a look of desperation in his eyes. "Has the Dark One killed Glazahn?"

Vamillion shook her head. "The Dark One had nothing to do with this. It is Glazahn you should be questioning. What was the spell he discovered? What did he unleash?"

Diamus' was dumbfounded. He shook his head. "I… don't know. I instructed to him to go write it down. It was something big, something powerful. But the prophecy, the promise of power, I did not ever imagine this."

"We must assume the worst," Vamillion said.

Diamus closed his eyes. "He must be dead." Opening his eyes, he was fueled by anger, driven by deceit. "This is Beauty's fault. The prophecy is a lie! How will we know if anything is true, that Xyntharia will help us, that our kingdom will be able to stop Mullen's advancing army?"

"Fear not the prophecy! Nothing Beauty predicted has ever been discredited," Vamillion argued. "The spell has been written, but it has come at a great price. Perhaps, The Dark One has demanded this sacrifice and I say it is a small price to pay. What has transpired, while tragic, is only proof of the spell's power, and proof of the prophecy. We must get to the Academy and retrieve the spell at once."

"Have you not heard Rasatharian's words?" Diamus questioned. "The Academy is ruined! Who knows what hell has been unleashed."

Rasatharian nodded his head slowly in affirmation of Diamus' words and in horror of what must lie beyond the doors to the halls of Necromancy. "High Priestess, I beg of you, death awaits below."

Vamillion was struck with inspiration. "Beauty has the answer we are looking for." Vamillion opened a drawer to her desk and pulled out a drawing. She pointed to a depiction of a great hall, but not just any hall, it was the hall of the Necromancy Academy. It was unclear before, but clear in hindsight. In the hall were mounds of dark shapes lying on the floor. They were people. Necromancers. Dead, layered upon each other, in crudely depicted mounds. In the air above, in the milky haze of fog; a skull, a warning to all who enter.

"And these markings?" Diamus pointed to shapes in the fog that on first glance seemed like nothing more than waves of smoke.

Vamillion looked to where Diamus pointed. "Yes… it is more than it first appeared. It may be a language."

Rasatharian, inquisitive, rose to his feet. He peered over the drawing. "It appears… elven."

"No, not quite," Vamillion said. "They are symbols of magic. But they are written upside down, or something." She raised the drawing in front of her. "There are six symbols."

Diamus quickly wrote the symbols, flipped. His eyes lit up. "Yes, upside down, but also mirror imaged." He took the scribbles of the flipped words to a mirror. Looking into the reflection, he stood, silent.

Vamillion and Rasatharian both moved beside him to stare into the mirror. Diamus looked to Rasatharian and Rasatharian looked to him.

"What?" Vamillion barked.

Diamus lowered the drawing to his side, staring at his own reflection. Bewildered, he translated the six symbols of Necromancy that Beauty had coded into the drawing. "P, l, a, g, u… e." He whispered in trepidation, "It's a plague."

"A plague, unleashed in the halls of the Necromancy Academy?" Vamillion asked.

"Could it be anything else? It is spelled out, right before our very eyes," Diamus said. "If this is true, as long as the door between the underground and the above world is kept closed, we are safe. If you open those doors, the kingdom will be destroyed."

"How long must we wait?" Rasatharian inquired.

"Years," Vamillion said, distraught. "It could be years," she repeated. "Rats, fleas, various insects, they may carry the disease and live, allowing it to survive. This is not taking into account the specific strand of plague it may be, and ultimately, the nuances associated with the characteristics of this disease in spell form. Who knows, really, what attributes it carries."

Diamus shook his head. "No wonder Glazahn was afraid of his own spell. With Rasatharian's account, it seems the plague is powerful, killing everyone in a very short period of time." He paused a moment, the horror of it fading as he began to envision the benefits. "Do you understand what this spell could do for us? Just the knowledge of its existence, without even using it." He turned toward Vamillion. "Why, you could protect Vixus forever, the ultimate deterrent to those who oppose you, and the ultimate weapon to acquire whatever it is that Vixus needs. Land, resources… absolute control, which would lead Vixus to absolute peace."

Vamillion nodded. "Yes, this is everything the Dark One has promised. The question, now, is how do we get into the School of Necromancy, obtain the spell without getting sick or spreading the plague into our own streets?"

"Beauty must have the answer," Diamus reminded.

Vamillion scattered the paintings across her desk, pulled out the sketches and spread them on the floor. The three of them scoured the illustrations. Diamus pointed to a face which appeared often in Beauty's work. An old, frail wizard, with disheveled white hair and fiery green eyes.

"Zantigar Parkn," Diamus said.

Vamillion stopped shuffling through the art and looked up. "What was that?"

"This portrait. And that one and that one," Diamus pointed. "They are portraits of Zantigar."

"A Legionnaire, from long ago," Rasatharian added, rising to look at one such portrait. "He was a hero during The Final War, I have seen his image in countless books. It's him."

Vamillion narrowed her eyes. "I know who Zantigar is, but how? Why? Beauty only spoke of the future, not the past."

"The painting is so detailed, so real," Diamus commented.

"Without Beauty being able to speak, we are left to speculate and wonder," Vamillion surmised. "And like Glazahn's spell, we may not learn the truth of the paintings until it is too late."

"Perhaps, the key is with Zantigar," Diamus said.

"A dead wizard?" Rasatharian questioned, unconvinced by Diamus' suggestion.

"Yes," Vamillion responded. "Possibly. Yes, maybe. There can be answers to the future, from the past." She stood, stepping away from the drawings and paintings. "I must try to make contact with the Dark One."

"You are going back; behind the curtain?" Diamus asked, with concern in his voice.

"I must hear his voice, I know he could help us, if I could just draw him to me."

"The curtain?" Rasatharian asked.

"To do this, I must be alone," Vamillion said, never taking her eyes off Diamus.

Rasatharian rose from the floor. "What's behind the curtain?"

"Come, Rasatharian, you and I shall pay a visit to Beauty's chamber," Diamus commanded, still locking eyes with Vamillion. "There must be more to discover, more pictures, more clues."

Rasatharian followed Diamus to the door, bowing before they made their exit.

Vamillion waited until their echoing steps faded in the tower below, before carefully sliding her robe down her back. She winced, as the cloth irritated the open wounds as it fell to her ankles. Her skin exposed to the air, the wounds still fresh. She stepped over her robe and opened the curtain. The servants were kneeling, in wait of her command. She moved into the center of the circle on the floor and did not hesitate to lay, face first onto the ground, in the puddles of her own blood. "Rise," she commanded.

The servants rose, and without thought, picked up the hooks at their feet. The chains rattled as they dragged on the floor. She screamed, as the servants, sure of hand, plunged the hooks into her back.

The servants pulled the slack of the chains through the pulleys and, in return, pulled her skin until it raised her to the wall. Vamillion fought back the urge to cry out, harnessing the pain inside her. Focusing on controlling her breath, she exhaled slow, feeling the blood run cold down her legs. She breathed in. Her mind, quiet. She breathed out, the pain subsiding.

"Vamillion," The Dark One spoke. The voice comprised of many voices, announced his presence.

Vamillion opened her eyes. Disappointed, but not surprised, there was no one standing before her. The servants had returned to their kneeling position on either side of her. "I need your guidance."

"Yes," the Dark One assured.

"Glazahn is dead?"

"He has served his purpose."

Vamillion, starting to feel the pain return to her, focused a moment on her breathing. "How can I retrieve the spell?"

"You will die if you try."

Vamillion closed her eyes. "Zantigar, the painting. Why? What does a Legionnaire from the past have to do with the present?"

There was a long silence before the Dark One spoke. "Zantigar is alive."

All at once the pain came back, as Vamillion's focus was disrupted. The pain became hard to endure, and her limbs were beginning to numb. "Impossible."

"His power manages to repel me, for now. Breaking him will take time."

Vamillion remembered talking to Beauty, asking him who the old man was in his paintings and Beauty had written the words, "My savior."

"Zantigar could destroy everything for you," the Dark One said, as if reading Vamillion's mind.

When Beauty had told her that the old man in the drawings was his savior, she had not taken it literally until now. She thought the old man was an idol to pray to, a false hope to comfort Beauty in the dark. His existence, and knowing he was Zantigar, it changed everything. A chill overcame her at a sudden realization. "If Beauty prophesized that Zantigar would save him, then it will happen. Beauty has never been wrong."

"Leave Zantigar to me," the Dark One commanded. "Beauty's prophecy is no match for a god. It is I who gave him his power, and I, alone, who can take it away."

The Dark One's voice of many voices faded, and with the silence came unbearable pain. The Dark One's presence had left. Vamillion called out to her servants, and they rose, obediently, to lower her from the wall and remove her chains.

With the help of her slaves, she tended to her wounds, with the prepping and application of healing solvents. Her servants tending to her every need. She bathed quickly, anxious to get visit Beauty's chamber.

She ran down to the bottom of the Moon Tower and opened the trap door. It was quiet inside, but the torches were lit, lighting her way down the stone steps to where Diamus and Rasatharian were still waiting, their attention on the murals which covered Beauty's chamber. Beauty, himself, was asleep on his bed.

Diamus was startled by Vamillion's appearance. He raised his finger to his lips to warn her to be quiet. "Beauty just fell asleep, moments ago," he whispered.

"The séance was a success," Vamillion whispered. "The Dark One spoke to me."

"And?" Diamus said, eager.

"I'm afraid I have bad news for you," she began. "The Dark One has confirmed, Glazahn is dead. The spell is a deadly airborne sickness, which will kill any who enter the halls of the academy."

Rasatharian gasped, he did not want to believe all he had feared was true.

Diamus, composed, responded. "I was prepared for as much."

"The good news is that the Dark One will help us. My prayers and rituals have not been in vain. I think the sacrifice of souls has empowered him. It is as if, the more sacrifices of wizardborn, the stronger he becomes."

Diamus turned to the wall and pointed to another portrait. A middle aged, vibrant man, with chiseled features, thick black hair and a long, black moustache. Handsome, his appearance was reminiscent of one from an ancient statue.

Vamillion studied the portrait, the face looked familiar, yet she could not pinpoint from where. "Who is this man?"

"That, Priestess, is Sir Blake Brownstone."

"Yes… of course," Vamillion whispered.

"None other than the mighty knight, who tipped the tide of The Final War, the embodiment of the perfect knight," Diamus said.

"Our own kingdom honors his legacy," Vamillion reminded. "With the select few knights worthy of the title, known as none other than the Knights of Brownstone, who are led by Sir Lenoy Brundt. The greatest warrior of our age, just as Brownstone was once the greatest warrior of his age."

Rasatharian stared at the portrait. "Yes, but why are we looking at a portrait of Brownstone, himself? What is the significance?"

Vamillion turned to Diamus. "Is he still alive, too?"

"No," Diamus said, with an odd level of excitement in his voice. "He is not alive at all. And that may be precisely the point!"

"I don't understand," Vamillion said.

"I come from Northern Oryahn, the birthplace of Sir Blake Brownstone and the Dark Knights of Omnias. There are legends, myths, about what happened to Brownstone after The Final War. About his life after returning home."

"Tell me," Vamillion commanded.

"He shunned the world and the people on it. He retreated to escape from a world to which he felt he did not belong." Diamus shook his head, baffled by the mysteries surrounding the dangerous recluse. "What matters is that the Dark One has confirmed for you that any who enter the halls of the academy will be killed," Diamus reminded. "But how can you kill that which is already dead?" Diamus' eyes widened. "The only one who can help us is painted on Beauty's wall, just waiting there for us to find, showing us the way. Sir Blake Brownstone can retrieve the spell, *because* he is not alive. Because he roams the world, amongst the living… undead."

~CHAPTER 17~

Daylen woke and his heart was pounding. The scream from his dream woke him, abruptly. Zantigar suddenly screamed in agony from down the hall, as if his voice had invaded Daylen's dream. He was startled to awaken to the sound of Zantigar's frantic voice, but he had gotten used to Zantigar's bouts with insanity, talking to imaginary foes. This was not the first time Zantigar had yelled in aggravation. Yet, this time, it was different. There was urgency in his voice, a desperation.

Daylen struggled with what to do, knowing the hall was forbidden.

Zantigar screamed again and this sent Daylen to his feet. He heard a loud crash, followed by the sound of furniture being upturned and thrown across the room. The bustling about was reaching unfamiliar levels of madness.

Zantigar screamed again, but this time it was at the top of his lungs. Daylen brushed aside any concern and ran down the hall. His hesitancy at Zantigar's door was dispelled when Zantigar called out again. This time, the message was clear. "Help me!"

Daylen shoved his body against the door. The door was blocked by an upturned table and could only partly open. He managed to slip through the space allotted to him, climbing over the table and noticed Zantigar slumped over the side of his bed, unconscious or asleep. He was alone amongst a room in disarray.

Daylen moved to Zantigar's side and eased him onto his bed. His frail, skeletal body could be felt in Daylen's grasp. Despite all the power that Zantigar encompassed, he was hardly more than a corpse in Daylen's arms. It was difficult to believe that any form of magic could give this ancient wizard any life.

Zantigar's eyes fluttered open, his faded eyes revealed a soul that appeared weary of existence. Abnormal for Zantigar, he looked especially tired and disoriented. For the moment, he was unfazed by Daylen being in his room. On the contrary, he seemed pleased to see Daylen's face. His eyes were distant, and his chest heaved, as if it were difficult to breathe.

"Zantigar," Daylen said with concern. "Are you okay? Can you tell me what happened?"

With Zantigar's guard down, his energy weak, Daylen was able to see his mentor in a new light. In this vulnerable state, Daylen saw the wizard for who he was beneath the walls he built around himself in his more conscious state. The reality of Zantigar's age was showing through. He did not appear to be hundreds of years old, but as Daylen looked into Zantigar's decrepit eyes he knew he stared into the eyes of a wizard who stubbornly held on to the end of his life.

Zantigar raised his arm and placed his delicate, cold hand on Daylen's cheek. He managed to smile, and his eyes regained focus. Through a dry throat, his voice cracked, "Are you afraid?"

Daylen bowed his head. He knew what his answer should be, but it did not match his state of mind. Not until this moment, not until realizing that his mentor could be dead at any moment, did he realize the bond that he had formed with him. A bond that if broken would expose a gaping wound within him. He did not wish to be alone again, even though he knew that loneliness was a state of mind. "No, Zantigar," Daylen said, opening his eyes. "I am not afraid."

Zantigar appeared to recognize the fragile fragment of truth there was to Daylen's words. As if knowing the thoughts in Daylen's head, he responded. "Do not rely on me for strength."

Daylen nodded and placing a hand on Zantigar's heaving chest, tried to calm his panicked breath.

Zantigar's focus wavered. "When I am gone, what will be lacking Daylen? Search and discover, for this missing element is what is required to pass your true test. Focus your mind. Look not with your eyes. A mirror will not help you see your true reflection."

Daylen took a deep breath and closed his eyes. Fear of loneliness consumed him. He could not see that which was already within him, that which Zantigar wanted him to see. He began to tremble and did not want Zantigar to notice. He leaned back, away from Zantigar's grasp. "I am not ready."

Zantigar tried to rise. Daylen tried to convince him otherwise, but to no avail. The old wizard brushed Daylen's hands aside, and leaned up, bringing his legs across the bed until his feet met the floor. He paused before standing, wobbling a moment, then placed his hand on Daylen's shoulder for balance.

"Zantigar, please…"

Zantigar moved across the room. "Save your pity for another." He was looking for something beneath the upturned furniture and clutter on the ground.

"You can study until your head falls off, but you can only achieve something when you step up on that stage and perform."

Daylen stood up, wanting to help Zantigar find whatever it was he was searching for. He looked around the room. There was nothing out of the ordinary with the room, except for it being a complete disaster. His imagination and all the wild, ideas of what this room could have housed was dispelled by the ridiculous mess before him. "What is it you are doing?"

"This morning has helped me realize something of great importance." He grumbled and grimaced as he shifted through the mess on the floor. "We should get out and about. See the world. A change of scenery will do us some good."

Daylen leaned forward to assist, but Zantigar brushed him off.

"Ah, there it is." Rummaging beneath a few loose articles of clothing beneath bits of broken furniture he procured a magnificent staff made of brilliant, sparkling red rubies. Placing one end to the ground as a walking stick, he stood, taller and with more conviction. Zantigar's skin had returned to its original color, his frame, stronger, his eyes, lit with the fire that only a wizard of his power could exude.

Daylen was startled at how quickly Zantigar regained his strength. The staff sparkled at Zantigar's side. It was an extraordinary object of ostentatious wealth, but extravagant beauty.

"The first step is realizing what you need," Zantigar said, his voice, strong. "Of course, that is just the beginning. Do not long for certainty, be certain. Quit listening for the voice within and become the voice within."

Daylen was relieved to see his mentor back in full form, with only slight reservations about it. "That is quite the walking stick you have there."

Zantigar's face became solemn, and his frail hands clutched the staff until his knuckles turned white. "This is no mere walking stick, my boy. It is just as much a part of me as my mind, and just as dangerous, too. You must never touch it, do you understand?"

Daylen pondered if the staff was the sole reason why Daylen was never to go in Zantigar's room. It was precious to Zantigar, which was uncharacteristic of one who lived as a hermit, but it explained why it was locked away, unseen until now.

Zantigar continued. "I do not say these things because I don't trust you. I say it to protect you, dear boy. It is for your own safety."

"My safety?" Daylen asked, curious.

"Ever felt the sensation of heat so powerful that it melted your flesh instantly? The kind of flesh melting experience that makes pulling away impossible, because your skin is fastening itself to the very thing burning it, unable to break away until the skin has been pulverized, only bone left behind?"

"Is that what would happen to me, if I were to touch it?" Daylen asked.

"This staff has an intelligence all its own. It knows its master, as much as I know myself. Anyone else who dares attempt to possess it will suffer greatly."

"The staff," Daylen said, "it's a weapon?"

"I never leave home without it." Zantigar, clutching the staff, swung the door to his room open and stepped aside for Daylen to exit. "Let's go outside. Today is a good day for a walk."

"How long will we be gone?" Daylen asked.

Zantigar snapped, "Don't ask such trivial questions!"

"Okay," Daylen said, moving through the door into the hallway. "I just want to know what I need to pack."

"Pack as if you will never return."

Daylen stopped in the hall and turned back toward Zantigar, with a look of seriousness on his face.

"Did I not make myself clear?" Zantigar spoke, returning a serious glare. He had that crazed look in his eyes he was prone to get when he was worked up. "It is time to put your training to test. Your days as an Initiate are over, you are a Seeker, now. It is time for action; and the consequences of those actions will determine your future, if you are ever afforded one. Gather what you need. Quickly now, and meet me out front."

~CHAPTER 18~

The thought of being on the open trails, to partake in a new adventure, it was something Daylen could hardly believe. Stepping into the brisk, morning air, he was reminded of the quest to find Zantigar, and could remember the anticipation. He was older now; wiser, it seemed. This time, a Legionnaire was at his side. He could not help to think that everything he had trained for, all he had sacrificed, was leading up to this moment. The decision to depart was abrupt and the destination unknown. This notion caused him to feel an element of trepidation. Regardless, he felt alive, as if he stood at the edge of time, anxious to know what was in store for him.

The sun shone through the woodland trees. The snow from the Season of Wane was melting. The coldest time of the year had passed, but the chill in the air was a reminder that the Season of Bloom did not create a drastic change in this region of the land. As the wind picked up, brushing against Daylen's skin, he faced his mentor.

Zantigar stood against the current of the weather, his robe fluttering. He bore no signs of fatigue. Even though his body was thin and old, strength radiated from his eyes. He appeared driven, unaffected by the elements. His ruby staff sparkled in the sun's light and was an equally striking sight to behold.

Daylen believed that he was now, in some way, a part of Zantigar's legacy, which had already spanned for hundreds of years, maybe to continue for hundreds more. When Daylen felt happiness, sadness was quick to hit him in the gut. The last time he felt this good, he was with Bolinda, Hogar and Rahlen. The thought of them was bittersweet. It was all the more reason that he would take this day for granted. So long as he continued, so long as he tried, he was honoring all that his friends had sacrificed. He felt their presence with him now.

Zantigar led him into the birch woods. Although the snow was melting, the many white trees camouflaged against the horizon were still perceived to be a labyrinth to get lost in, if not for Zantigar's guidance. Daylen checked the sky, wondering if Ayrowen was still with him and watching over him. The thought of the open road made Ayrowen at his side a comforting thought. However, the sky was empty.

Passing between the birch trees with sure steps, Daylen did not even question where they were going, intentionally allowing the destination to present itself, as a surprise. "It was earlier than this morning that I was standing over your feeble body," Daylen said to Zantigar. "I thought you might die."

Zantigar reflected a moment. "Yes, fear is still your companion, and I am still waiting for you to end that friendship."

"I understand that; but what I mean is, you stand before me now with more life than I have ever seen in you. When do you plan on telling me how you do it? How have you lived for so many years?"

Zantigar stopped. "It is a mystery to you, I understand that. As such, it can obsess you. Don't let it. The fact is, I am here for you now. The means for all this to be true is not nearly as important, or as interesting, as the fact that it is so. I am here because you need me to be. Leave it at that."

Having gotten ahead of Zantigar, Daylen stopped and waiting for him to catch up to him. "How can that be true? I did not want Rahlen to die, or Hogar, or Bolinda. I needed them and they had left me."

Zantigar caught up to Daylen and they continued forward. "Who is to say they are gone? It appears to me that they are with you now more than ever." He looked at Daylen closely. "I see them. They are in your eyes, in the way you carry yourself, in the tone of your voice, and I don't need to be in your mind to understand that they are in your thoughts. They are a part of you. You speak at times, and it is them that I hear."

Daylen reflected on his fallen friends. He could not help to wonder if the same fate would fall upon Zantigar during their adventure together. He suddenly embraced the time at the cottage and he wondered, much to his own dismay, if he would ever find solace by the fireplace, or ever gaze upon the books of Zantigar's library again. It felt uncertain to him. Had he thought that it could lead to the darkest of outcomes, he would have studied more, would have not taken the warmth of the fire for granted. He thought of Zantigar's bizarre, sometimes insane actions, and wondered if his experiences at the cottage all had been a test. Where he was bound, what lied ahead, was surely a test, perhaps the biggest test he would ever face. Zantigar was an enigma, in of himself, a contradiction to all he knew life was capable of, but Daylen was captivated by the game, by the sheer magic of it all. As he travelled beside Zantigar he knew that he would follow Zantigar to whatever end and in this way, he felt he had conquered the worst of his fears and was an example of his growth in acceptance.

They walked in silence for quite some time. There was a shared enjoyment of the fresh air and the sounds of the birds. The cottage had long disappeared into the distance and the day progressed swiftly. They stopped often and Zantigar would silently point out the way the sun's light spilled out onto the forest floor or take time to pick ripe fruit and savor its taste. Zantigar had a way of making each moment memorable, each mundane task insightful.

They stopped at the edge of a cliff. Daylen had not realized just how high from the ocean level they were. The splendor of a valley outstretched below them and across the horizon. The warm colors in the sky were inspiring.

"Dragons used to soar through the sky on such days as these. They would pierce the glowing clouds and fly west over the mountains." Zantigar pointed to a distant mountain range.

It was the first time Zantigar had spoken in quite a long time. Daylen nodded and pondered the thought of a time long past. As he imagined the dragon trailing off beyond the mountains he caught sight of one particular mountain peak that was impressive in size, towering above the others. "That mountain there, look how massive it is."

"Mount Omera," Zantigar said. "It is our destination."

This peaked Daylen's interest. At first, he thought it was a joke, but by the look on Zantigar's face, he knew it to be true.

"Are you sure I am ready for such a feat?"

"I promise that you will be, by the time we get there."

Zantigar stood a moment in silence. The sensitive look on his face was new to Daylen, as if what Zantigar was about to say, and the manner in which he was to say it, was of equal importance. "There is a point in a wizard's training when they confront their inner soul… their true self. They will see their true identity, beyond the mask."

Zantigar paused and took a deep breath in. He slowly exhaled. "Perception; you may have already begun to sense its importance. What is more crucial than the very angle a person decides to view the world around them?" Zantigar did not wait for a response. "Nothing."

Zantigar continued. "To most, the mind will cling to familiar objects, such as a tree, a hill, a bird, the sun. An opinion will be formed, whether conscious or unconscious, and they will feel the emotion it brings, as well as an understanding as to its place and purpose. This we call reality. With this perception, one exists in a world of their own creation. But it is a violent world, and it is a lonely world. Yet, this is an illusion. There is a deeper perception. To see past the mask, you must use this deeper perception. Find your true self and you will find your true voice. Find your true voice… and you will find your spells."

Daylen was intrigued. This was the first time Zantigar had spoken of spells to him.

"The inner voice is who you truly are, a voice absent of mind, yet it is everything. People are so caught up with their external voice, this voice of the mind, that they do not listen to, nor do they even realize, the second voice exists. The true self, if you will, is not fooled by common illusions, for it has no conventional eyes for which to be tricked. It is sometimes referred to as the magic eye, the all-seeing eye. It is, and it encompasses, pure magic. This magic is everything; in the most literal sense."

"The eye of FéLorën," Daylen acknowledged. Daylen looked to the trees around him, trying to see that which could not be seen, trying to hear what could not be heard.

"The true self is not interested in you, the wizardborn. Its focus, its intentions, act on behalf of the world. Although it is your true self, it is everyone. A collective, shared eye. The eye knows no limit of time or space. To connect to it, is to know peace, because this self knows all that transpires is part of a greater, divine design."

Daylen thought about his exile from his homeland. He had hardly ever known a time of peace. They say the land is rid of wars, but the battle rages on inside and interacts with the world in mysterious ways, causing conflict and experiences far from peaceful. Reflecting on the past, as devastating as his childhood had been, he realized that if these tragedies never happened, he never would have found the courage, or the means, to find Zantigar. He wondered if this was the divine design Zantigar spoke of.

Zantigar's voice rose above Daylen's thoughts, as if speaking on behalf of his soul's voice. "The true self is like the sun of our solar system, a massive, bright center, its core condensed with the deepest truths of existence. If one were able to dive deep enough and stand beside the light of one's center, they would be burned and blinded. Our body is but a conduit for this light."

As Daylen stood at the edge of the cliff, with Mount Omera in the distance and the majestic sky before him, he tried to imagine the bright core of existence. He closed his eyes and he thought of Lonely Wood, when he cast that spell he could not control. He had seen a bright burning symbol at the edge of consciousness. It was not in front of him, it was within him. He realized if what Zantigar said was true, then this symbol must have been delivered from his core.

Zantigar continued, as Daylen remained with his eyes shut. "With the awareness of true self, the world we so busily concern ourselves with, melts away, leaving the inner world to take center stage. Too bright to see, too hot to touch, we can only hear it… the voice. Like a whisper, but it shatters through the fragile world of reality with a clarity that is not unlike madness."

Daylen opened his eyes. The light of the world reflected in his eyes.

"No longer aware of objects," Zantigar said, "there is just an overwhelming sensation of feeling."

Daylen allowed a recent memory to enter his mind. He was on Cragel Mountain, kneeling before Rahlen's dying body. Daylen could not remember what the world around him looked like at that point in time, but he could remember the thoughts, the voice, that pulled him to his feet.

Was there a correlation between one's pain, and the path to self-discovery? Daylen thought. Was pain nothing more than the denial, the refusal to accept life's offering? "In Lonely Wood, when I almost died, and the strange light came to my hands…"

"You were forced within," Zantigar explained. "Deep you travelled, and powerful is the sun at your core. You are no wizard, yet, but your true self is, and it always has been."

It was in this moment that Daylen realized why Zantigar had forced him to sit in silence for long periods of time. It was affording him the opportunity to listen, to feel. He had spent his time wondering what he was doing, wondering why he was waiting around, when his boredom in contemplation was of his own design all along. As long as he waited, he would continue to wait. As long as he tried, it would not be enough.

The day he decided to feel and to listen, he would no longer be in waiting. The voice would teach him all he needed to know. As Zantigar had advised, a good mentor would not tell him how to be a wizard, but merely show him the way to becoming one.

Zantigar looked at Daylen with excitement, a knowing glance that revealed he was aware of Daylen's realization. "Take your time. Go deep… go vulnerable… go lightly. The spells you learn will be unique unto you. No other wizard will conceive what you can. And know, that once it is brought into this world, it is your responsibility to bear. Others like you will be able to use what you have created."

Daylen could not help but smile. A shiver ran down his spine.

Staring at the horizon, he studied his environment with a deeper perception, without even trying. He began to see it as the illusion that it was. Trees were no longer trees, per say, but maps to understanding his inner self. He began to realize what Zantigar meant by questioning what it is that he saw. Why a tree? Because he convinced himself it was one. What if it had no name? And why was the birch wood forest of trees back at Zantigar's cottage perceived to be a labyrinth for which to get lost when they were equally a signpost explaining exactly where he was.

Daylen believed he had awhile to go before he would perceive the world as Zantigar did, but he had no problem seeing that his perception influenced his experience. He may not have understood the way home, but he saw the divinity, the life, the magic, coursing through everything he saw, whether it was a living organism, or a lifeless rock. It was clear that there was farther to dive, a deeper layer of the illusion to break. But now, he understood it was a matter of stillness. In the stillness his true self awaited. Behind the wall of illusion lied the spells he craved, but more importantly, it provided the way to FéLorën.

~CHAPTER 19~

When night encompassed the two travelers, Zantigar picked a comfortable, serene spot to set up camp. Daylen started collecting wood for the fire. When he had prepared a large enough mound of kindle, he reached in his pouch for flint and steel.

Zantigar took a seat and placed his hand on Daylen's arm, motioning for him to do the same. "Please, allow me." He placed the tip of his ruby staff on the pile of wood and closed his eyes. A moment later, smoke rose and a fire spawned.

"Shouldn't you conserve your energy, and not needlessly cast your magic?" Daylen asked.

"Yes, absolutely," Zantigar replied. "But do not worry; I did not cast a spell. The staff did." He smiled, and nestled himself on the ground, enjoying the fire's warmth. He clutched his staff close to his body. Before long, it looked as though Zantigar was drifting to sleep.

Daylen had tons of questions, but he shook his head and just marveled at how quickly Zantigar could enter sleep, without a struggle. Daylen would have to be satisfied with the outcome of their day, knowing that if Zantigar was awake to answer his questions it would only generate more. He sprawled onto his back, staring into the stars. He allowed himself to get lost in the expanse of the night sky. After some time had passed, he tossed on his side, unable to sleep. Just when he thought of taking a walk, he heard his name. He would have been startled, even afraid, had the voice not sounded like Ghost.

Daylen rose to his feet. He touched his face, half wondering if he was awake or if he was sleeping. The sensation was real enough. His senses confirmed that this was no dream. "Ghost?" he whispered.

He listened for a sign, anything. Conscious of the noises of the night, he paid attention to the songs of the insects, the rustling of leaves in the wind.

"Daylen," Ghost called.

This time, he was startled, but the voice confirmed his suspicions. Ghost was close, just past his vision, somewhere in the nearby trees. He looked to Zantigar, who was fast asleep. Pausing for a moment to consider waking the old wizard, he brushed the thought aside, afraid that Ghost would be too timid to reveal himself to Daylen if Zantigar was present. He turned to the sound of Ghost's voice and scurried into the trees.

He entered a small clearing where the moonlight shined on the ground. Silhouetted by the moon's rays stood a solitary figure. Daylen slowed his pace to a steady, careful walk, just as he had done countless times in his dreams. "Ghost?"

The figure did not respond, forcing Daylen to move closer. He hesitated and an eagle screamed in the air. He recognized the call and, turning to the sky, his sight confirmed what he had trouble believing. Ayrowen soared overhead. He felt the familiar, yet mysterious bond he shared with the eagle, but he also sensed something more… danger.

Daylen returned his gaze to the stranger, although the stranger was no longer a distance ahead of him. The figure had snuck closer while Daylen's attention had been averted to the sky. No longer was the figure cloaked in shadow. The light of the moon reflected off the visitor's twisted face and lit the broken horns on his head.

Nasavine parted his thin lips into an untrustworthy smile. "Hello, Daylen."

Daylen reached for Sylver, but it was not at his side. His trust in Ghost's voice caused him to neglect making sure he had protection. Once again, his perception and lack of understanding had put his life into danger. Daylen was angered by this betrayal, unsure how Nasavine could have tricked him with a vision that was sacred, believing Ghost only existed in his own mind. "What are you doing here?"

"You came on your own accord."

"Liar!" Daylen shouted.

"Who did you think I was?" Nasavine wondered, his eyes narrowing in suspicion.

Daylen ignored his question. "You just happened to be resting here?"

"Of course not," Nasavine said. "Don't be mad at me. I… was following you. I'm not here to hurt you and besides, it is not I that you should fear."

"I don't need to hide from my fears," Daylen informed. "Your charms and trickery are not needed here."

Nasavine shook his head. "You will wish you had listened, when you come face to face with the Dark One."

Daylen remembered Nasavine had mentioned that mysterious name before, when he first encountered Nasavine in Whispering Falls. Was it possible that

Ghost was the Dark One? "Who is this Dark One? If he is someone that I should fear, then why does he hide? Why won't he show himself to me?"

"In time, Daylen," Nasavine snickered, receding into the shadows. His eyes glowed with malice, and he whispered the following verse:

"With a black hood and matching cape,
Dwelling in the shadows of infinite space,
He hunts without mercy his cane at his waist.
Black as the night, cold as the rain,
He brings death and suffering in the sharp shape of pain.
A mage has a nightmare, it goes by a name,
It is He, the Dark One, a mortal wizard's bane."

When the last line escaped Nasavine's lips, Daylen lunged toward him. He was prepared to strike him with his bare hands. Nasavine was too quick for Daylen's swing, his little goat legs sprung him backward, far out of range. Nasavine laughed and Ayrowen called out from high in the air.

Daylen looked up, and saw Ayrowen circling, as if she intended to strike Nasavine, herself. Nasavine looked up, sensing the danger. He continued to laugh, but his voice trailed off as his little goat legs carried him far into the woods and out of sight. It was apparent, all at once, just how cold he was. Shivering, it was apparent that something evil was waiting for him. Even though he wanted to pursue Nasavine, he had the strong sensation that if he followed the imp's laughter into the darkness, he might not ever see Zantigar again. If he had learned anything from this unpleasant distraction, it was that he was not prepared to tackle the shadows of the world alone. Not yet. He wanted nothing more than to return to the campfire and warm his bones.

Ayrowen called out again. The appreciation for the eagle's return made him realize how important Ayrowen was to him. She was a proven guide and also gave him courage. It was Ayrowen who led him to both Rahlen and Zantigar. They shared common loss and common experience. Perhaps, they were both in search of the same thing. After Daylen's discussion with Zantigar, he considered that perhaps their connection was whatever he perceived it to be. Whatever the case, he cherished their bond.

Ayrowen led him back to camp and Zantigar was still sleeping. Laying down for bed and closing his eyes, sleep came easy. However, as the last waves of consciousness drifted into dreamland, Daylen's final thought of the evening was of the Dark One, and the awareness that this entity now lived in the deep recesses of his mind.

~CHAPTER 20~

It felt like as soon as Daylen fell asleep Zantigar was standing over him, waking him up. He groaned and rolled over, not wanting to be bothered.

"Here," Zantigar said, bringing a handful of berries close to Daylen's mouth. "Eat these. You will need the early energy. We have quite a distance to cover."

Daylen smelled the berries next to his nose. He opened his eyes and grabbed them. He ate them slowly, using the opportunity to fully awaken. When Zantigar pressed him, he stood. He looked for Ayrowen, but she was nowhere in sight. He suppressed his gut instinct to tell Zantigar what transpired the night before. "Okay, let's go."

Zantigar grabbed his staff and stood with the help of its weight. "Today we enter the Cragel Valley. The valley will bring us closer to our destination."

"Okay," Daylen said. "And what exactly is our destination?

"FéLorën," he responded.

Daylen chuckled. "Of course it is."

Zantigar was not oblivious to Daylen's tone. "You find that funny? I'm glad you can be so amused in the face of death."

"Death?" Daylen repeated.

"That is right. But don't be alarmed. We die every day. Die and are reborn. Reinventing ourselves. You should keep it in mind as we embark on this journey to your essence, to bring out the true wizard within you."

Daylen never really got an answer as to where they were going, not in the traditional sense. The trail was vigorous, leading down and across a steep hillside. By midday they had reached the bottom of a deep and narrow valley. Here, Zantigar suggested to rest.

Zantigar appeared more distant than normal, preoccupied. He scanned the valley, as if searching for something.

"Something wrong?" Daylen asked.

"We are not alone," Zantigar responded.

Daylen looked around. "I don't see anything," he whispered.

"That is right," Zantigar said. "No Pluckatees," Zantigar explained.

"Plucka what?"

"They are a species of bird native to the Cragel Valley. They are not intelligent, not good hunters, but they have an extraordinary survival skill."

"They hide well?" Daylen suggested.

"No, they breed and breed and breed. On a normal day like today, you would see hundreds flying around and resting on the mountain ledges."

Daylen nodded. "Hmm, no Pluckatees."

Zantigar nodded. "No Pluckatees."

The statement had new meaning and was a warning of something unknown. Daylen looked down the valley. What do you think scared them away?"

Zantigar shrugged, "It makes no difference. We should travel on."

Daylen walked at Zantigar's side; his steps cautious. It came as no surprise that when they entered the center of the valley, the presence revealed itself. A sharp whistle rang out, echoing off the rocks. Daylen, instinctively, reached for his sword. Zantigar, carried onward, without hesitation.

A man appeared ahead, from behind a boulder. He wore tattered articles of clothing, and mismatched armor, most likely pieced together from things he had found, or more likely stolen. His dress was reminiscent of Echo and her companions, but there was something untrusting about this man, a darker intention. As his whistle echoed through the valley, seven other men emerged. One by one, they descended from above, on either side of the valley. They did not bother to conceal their swords or hide their ill intent.

"Well, well, well," the man from behind the boulder said, stepping into the center of the valley, just ahead of Daylen and Zantigar. He pushed his brown, leather cap from his eyes and bore a smug expression. "What do we have here?" He studied Zantigar, his extravagant robe and bright, ruby staff. "You haven't bothered to hide yourselves. Which tells me you are either morons, or ignorant to these parts, unaware that to travel this valley you must pay the price of admission."

Zantigar stopped, a safe distance from the man before him. "Yes, well, it was not our plan to hide ourselves from anyone."

The man in the brown cap turned to the surrounding companions and gave a deep laugh. "Is that so, old man? Well, that works out well for us."

Zantigar nodded. "That is just fine, then, stranger. Now, if you don't mind, we are in a bit of a hurry."

"Hold on, old man. You've surely been around awhile; you know how this goes. Pay up."

"Ah, well, you see, I'm afraid I can't help you there. I am without a single coin and as I mentioned, I am in a hurry. There is an essence to discover, a wizard, is in need of finding his true self, you see."

"Is this a spirit journey? Like the Cragel villagers undertake? Ingest some local poison, connect with the land, and such?" The man in the brown cap moved closer, extending his hand, with amusement on his face. "Please, I am no stranger. The name is Gron."

The name peeked Daylen's interest. He had heard that name, from a story Zantigar told when he first made it to the cottage. "Zantigar, thank goodness, you know this man."

Zantigar waved his hand to Daylen, motioning for him to stay silent. He mumbled, "I have never met this man in my life." Raising his voice in Gron's direction, he stated, "Yes, of course you are. The name is fitting for your kind."

Gron raised a brow. His hand still extended. "My kind?"

Zantigar coughed, clearing his throat. "Yes, you are a member of the Balton clan, are you not? The embroidery on the cuff of your tunic, the design on the hilt of your sword, and your, shall we say, short physique; is a dead giveaway."

Balton's were a race of people who tended to be a foot or two shorter than most of the other human tribes. This was the joke of many traveling bards that had led Balton's forming a complex about it. Gron's companions giggled, humored by the old wizard's bold observation.

"Pardon me if I don't shake your hand, I'd rather not," Zantigar added.

Gron's eyes narrowed. Short as he was, he was clearly the leader of this pack of ruffians. His companions hushed immediately after feeling his glare. "The time for pleasantries is over. You slight me, so casual, by refusing my hand. You amuse us with your knowledge, at my expense. You are clearly insane. Yet, I was never one to take pity the crazies. You know so much about me, old man, so let's find out what you are made of."

"Correction," Zantigar said, with a deepening voice. "It is time that you understood that it is 'old wizard,' not 'old man.' Let it be clear and let it serve as proper warning."

Daylen grew uneasy. He recognized Zantigar's tone. He felt his palms begin to sweat and he itched to grab Sylver, sensing the conversation was reaching a point from which there was no backing out. With a bit of luck, there was a chance his mentor's keen mind could manage a peaceful resolution.

Gron and his companions were laughing, amused by Zantigar's brazen ways.

"Are you not a bit far from your homeland, Gron?" Zantigar questioned. "If I am not mistaken, the Balton's reside due south, two days travel from the other side of those mountains out there."

"Correction," Gron said, mocking Zantigar. "I reside here, in the valley."

"I see," Zantigar said. "That must make you an outcast, unfit to live with your people. So, you come to the valley, perhaps looking to live off the possessions of travelers with your band of… likeminded rejects."

Gron's followers groaned in protest.

"Careful, old man." Gron intentionally refusing to call him a wizard. The subtle insult did not go unnoticed.

"This wizard has a name. I am Zantigar." He pointed to Daylen. "And this is a Seeker, his name is Daylen."

Daylen would have preferred to stay out of the conversation and didn't much care to grab the attention of Gron's stare. He nodded, nonetheless, unable to look Gron in the eyes.

"Pleasantries are at an end, old man." Gron insisted.

"Just as well," Zantigar said. "I have run out of patience. Now, it is time that my companion and I were on our way. So, if you please…" Zantigar proceeded forward.

Gron stepped in front of Zantigar, and his seven companions closed in. "Not without payment."

"You may be the leader of men, but do not attempt to control a wizard."

"Payment," Gron demanded.

"Or else?" Zantigar asked.

"Or else we will force it from you," Gron said. "You have made me and my men laugh, old man, so I don't want to have to kill you over something so petty. You pay the gold, I let you go."

"It seems you are confused as to who, and what, you control." Zantigar said. "As soon as you step aside, I will consider whether or not *I* let *you* go."

Daylen placed his head in his hand, hiding his grimace.

Gron noticed the look in Zantigar's eyes and took a step back. "I have no doubt that your magic is strong, but you are old and feeble, and travel without your spellbook. You think I have not noticed these things? You think you can intimidate me with your fancy staff and your finely woven robe? Enough with the bluff, already."

Daylen gripped Zantigar's arm.

"If you are without coin, then hand over your staff."

"I am afraid I cannot give you this," Zantigar countered, in a calm tone. "You see, if you touch the staff, then it will burn your flesh to fragments of ash. The pain is most excruciating, I assure you."

Gron looked into Zantigar's eyes, attempting to perceive the lie in his words. He raised his voice, "You think I would fall for this ridiculous banter?"

"I really don't have time for this," Zantigar spoke over him.

Gron, his patience worn out, yelled, "Give me your staff, or I shall take your life! You are surrounded!"

Zantigar sighed, his muscles relaxed in Daylen's grip. "Yes, I have been surrounded by the likes of you for far too long. You may take it." Zantigar held the staff out before him.

Gron, without hesitation, reached forward and grabbed the staff. As he clutched it, a searing heat shot through his hands and up his arms. His eyes widened in horror, as his hands caught fire. The pain paralyzed him, his face contorted in agony, unable to remove his grip.

Gron's companions were momentarily stunned, shuffling nervously, watching Gron scream out. They looked to each other as if waiting for the other to do something. All at once, they pressed forward.

Zantigar, slammed the butt of the staff to the ground, with Gron's hands still stuck to it, and the valley shook in a violent tremor. Daylen could not believe what he witnessed. He had disbelieved the power of the staff, himself, uncertain if its power was true. Now, he was witnessing its strength, firsthand, as he struggled to keep his footing on the swaying ground.

Gron's companions were struggling for balance, themselves. Streaks of electricity traveled through the staff and Gron began to shake with convulsions, as electricity coursed through him. The sky grew dark, and swirls of storm clouds appeared directly overhead, lightning surging within as flashes of thunder rang out.

Gron's hand had melted away, reduced to bones and his grip finally released, sending him to the ground as waves of electricity coursed through his body. He twitched in convulsions until death overtook him.

A streak of lightning plummeted down from the clouds and hit the staff with a resounding boom. Daylen fell to the trembling ground at Zantigar's feet, unable to maintain his balance. Zantigar was unwavering and the staff was pristine, absorbing the lightning strike as if soaking up its energy. Daylen clutched at Zantigar's robe and screamed out above the crashing lightning.

Zantigar was unreachable, lost in a trance, and fueled by a fury beyond Daylen's understanding.

Several of Gron's companions changed course in retreat, realizing they were no match for the force at Zantigar's command. Unable to find their footing, they crawled like animals toward the mountains.

"Stop!" Daylen called out. His voice trembling in unison with the ground. "Zantigar, you must stop this madness!"

Zantigar stared down at Daylen. His eyes were wild with rage. "Is this not what you wanted? To see the power of a Legionnaire?"

Daylen shook his head, pleading. "You must stop!"

Zantigar was poised to carry out untold destruction and appeared intent on doing so. He stood with the forces of chaos at his beck and call, the divine power of the universe. Whatever he willed, would be.

Daylen, uncertain of how far Zantigar would go, shook his head. "No, Zantigar!"

Zantigar looked away from Daylen, the thunder above blocking out the sound of Daylen's voice. Electricity rose from the ground, circling the staff, as lightning bolts rang down from above, encircling Daylen and Zantigar, just as the remaining three of Gron's companions managed to get their footing and courage to advance. Swinging their swords, they clashed in the electrical field. The shock sent them backward, collapsing to the ground.

Zantigar swung the staff in a wide arc. The look in his eyes was a reflection of the turbulent winds that surrounded him. His hair blew in the air like white flames, the point of his staff lowered in the direction of the three fallen men. Three rays of lightning shot from the staff with precision, making contact with each of the fallen foes. A continuous stream of lightning from the tip of the staff pumped into their bodies, the impact raising them into the air, the electrical burns frying them to a pulp. When the streaks of lightning seized, their bodies collided in a mangled heap against the rocks.

The four remaining thieves who had crawled away were now on their feet. Though from a distance, the horror on their face after witnessing the fate of their companions was clear. Frozen for just a moment, they turned and ran for their lives, dispersing in different directions. Zantigar watched them scurry like rats.

Daylen, seeing Zantigar's intent as the staff was swung down in their direction, called out in defiance, as a bright flash of lightning blinded him, forcing him to close his eyes.

A bolt of lightning was sent from the staff in each direction the thieves ran. As the lightning struck them, their bodies tightened, their backs arched, and they shook violently before falling dead to the ground.

The dark clouds of the sky vanished, and the circling of electricity seized. The wind settled, toppling Zantigar's hair, to rest disheveled across his face. The land became still and the fury in Zantigar's eyes diminished. Despite the calm that returned to the landscape, Daylen still clung tight to Zantigar's robe.

"What do you control, now?" Zantigar said in a sobering breath.

Daylen opened his eyes, released his grip from Zantigar's robe and stood, dumbfounded at the carnage around him. Zantigar stood like a storm god above the remains of his charred victims. He turned to meet Daylen's gaze and lowered the staff to his side.

"What have you done?" Daylen asked.

Zantigar was in no mood to talk, he started to progress through the valley, prepared to leave the moment behind like a distant memory. Daylen rushed to his side. "I asked you a question."

"I taught them a lesson."

"You killed them!"

Zantigar raised his voice, "I warned them!"

"There was a better way..." Daylen suggested.

"I rid the world of my conflicts."

Daylen shook his head. "They were human beings, not conflicts. Your inner conflict is your problem, not theirs!"

"I beg to differ. It certainly proved to be their problem." Zantigar motioned to the charred corpses. "I have been surrounded by fools such as these for hundreds of years. Kings and emperors claiming the land as their own, exploiting its minerals, robbing the world out of self-interest. Who are they? What right do they have to anything?"

"But these were not kings, Zantigar. They were bandits, common thieves. If I'm not mistaken, wizards were once in a position as bad as them. Wizards had turned to thievery to survive when they were hunted as witches."

"Don't compare these fools to wizards, Daylen. Wizards had no choice; they were born with their condition. These bandits chose this life for themselves, despite having everything. They were consumed by greed, which makes them no different."

"You don't know what their lives entailed, what caused them to live this way."

"They were going to kill us, Daylen! Is that what you would have preferred?"

Daylen turned away. "They would not have killed us, Zantigar. Show your power, sure, threaten them. They would have left. And those four, they were running for their lives, and you, you struck them down as if… as if their lives meant nothing."

"Daylen, your compassion will be the death of you, one day. I did not want them to get away. That was the whole point. Their reign over the less fortunate, and any future travelers of the valley, has come to an end."

Daylen gave an insincere chuckle, stricken by the madness of it all. "They were just bandits. What you did, you think it brought justice to the world? It solved nothing. I just expected… I don't know, something different from you." Daylen shook his head. The differences between them sobering him. "Something… higher."

Daylen walked ahead of Zantigar, anxious to get out of the valley.

Zantigar followed. "I am a chaos wizard, Daylen. It is my duty to destroy, it is why I am here. That is my purpose. You want something higher from me? You are looking for something in me that I can't provide."

Daylen closed his eyes. Zantigar's words found a way to crush his spirit. "Who are you to decide who lives and dies?"

"I did not choose to be a wizard, any more than I chose to be a Chaos Wizard. It is my nature. My very being. I came to terms with my role years ago."

Daylen faced Zantigar. "I get it. I guess I am just shocked, I – I never really knew who you were. I mean, I thought I did. What you have done, it is madness to me."

"Madness is trying to control others, trying to control the world. The thieves back there, they were mad. Madness is sitting back and watching, doing nothing about the cruelty; or worse, allowing them to control you. By the gods, I saved them from their suffering. I did them a favor by ending their miserable, misguided lives."

Daylen turned away, the lesson of this test, if in fact it was one, was unknown to him, and he didn't want it to make sense. "Please, let's speak no more about it."

Zantigar's tone shifted, his voice, concerned. "You cannot hide from the reality of this world. Death is everywhere. Without awareness, of the darkness and the light, then you will never awaken to your full potential. Life and death are linked, forever. Violence, it is a part of nature, as it is a part of me. Which makes it a part of you. Look at the world around you. Look to the plants, to beasts. Everything struggling, everything killing in order to live. There is no place in this world for pacifists. Change, inevitable and constant, is violent. Do you understand? It's a fundamental principle of chaos. Every moment of life is a celebrated act of chaos. When I close my eyes, when I hear the voice inside, when I become the voice and I open my mind's eye… I see the chaos. I am the chaos."

Daylen sensed a pinnacle difference between himself and his mentor. He no longer wanted to be like him. Just as Zantigar had predicted, time revealed the stark difference between them. In his heart, he could never perceive the world as a Chaos Wizard did. All of Zantigar's ramblings, his defense for his own being, his own existence, it made it all clear.

Zantigar had taught him to find his own way, his own path. Daylen realized that he had been walking in Zantigar's shadow, when that was never the lesson, never the goal. In Zantigar's shadow, there was sadness and pain, because it led to a loss of self. He did not know himself well, but he was learning, through experience, who he was not. Zantigar, as mad as he was, had been right. Daylen would have to find his own way.

If there was anything that was clear to Daylen it was that in the core of his true self, there was not ever-changing chaos as Zantigar described. There was stillness. It was a level of awareness that to him, felt deeper than that of Chaos, something closer to the absolute truth, the one truth, to the magic eye of FéLorën.

As the two weary travelers made their way out of the valley, Daylen pondered why his life was meant to cross paths with Zantigar, when in fact they were such different people at heart. It occurred to Daylen that this was precisely the point of their meeting. The practice of questioning what he saw, forced him to reconstruct his perspective on everything. And it was working. Zantigar had taught him many ways to find his own personal truth and he was finding it by realizing what he wasn't. Their differences were leading Daylen closer to himself. In this way, Daylen accepted and respected the relationship, and could make amends.

Without sharing another word, deciding never to speak of the battle in Cragel Valley again, they pressed on. It was not until the valley was behind them that Daylen calmed down and could perceive in stillness again. Only then did he understand what truly mattered. They co-existed. They were two different sides of the same core.

~CHAPTER 21~

Vamillion hummed softly, her fingers playing with dark strands of hair. Her hands moved from the hair, to rest on the boy's soft cheeks. Her nails tracing the contours of scars, old inflictions, some of her design, others, self-inflicted. Her hand made its way to the boy's mouth, and her fingertips ran across the wounds on his lips, where string had once been sewn to keep his mouth shut. "Beauty… why did you do this to yourself?"

Beauty raised his head from Vamillion's lap. Unable to speak, his eyes were sorrowful, not unlike a dog. He shook his head and grabbed a pen from his table. On a piece of scratch paper, he wrote:

It wasn't me

Vamillion read the words to herself, and then faced Beauty with concern. "Not you? Then who, my child? Who else could have done this to you?"

Beauty pointed to a painting on the wall of a jester, a playful clown.

Vamillion looked to the painting of Popi on the wall. She narrowed her eyes. The love she had projected was all at once absent in her dark glare. "Beauty, it is time you grew up, quit playing these silly games. There is no one else here, but you, child. There is no one by the name of Popi, do you understand that? Popi is what I called you when you were a baby. You were my sweet little Popi, and I used to hold your delicate body in my arms, so innocent, so pure."

She gave a look of disgust. "Not unlike this perverted, ugly man before me now. This crazy fascination of yours, it must end at once. You are my Popi, you always have been. And this clown you speak of, it is just in your head, a memory."

Vamillion continued, but her voice softened. "On your fifth birthday I brought a clown to see you, do you remember that? It made you so happy. You laughed and laughed like I had never seen. And what did mommy do? I made you a little clown doll and you played with it and played with it, day after day. It was your favorite toy of all."

Beauty turned away and cowered to the floor where his bed lay.

"I know, I know. I threw the doll away, but don't even think that you didn't deserve it. You were such a brat, sometimes!" Vamillion lowered herself to the floor, to sit at Beauty's side. "I know I have done things to you, punished you, but all that will change, now. We can put all that behind us. Now that I know that Zantigar is alive. I will find him, and I will destroy him."

Beauty's eyes widened in horror.

"I remember what you told me days ago. I know you expect him to be your savior. But you are wrong, your mind is playing tricks on you, like this jester you conceived. There is no need to worry. Zantigar will die and then you will be free of any pain, as well as any false hopes or dreams. We can be close again, like we used to be. But you will have to do me a favor, okay? Forget the jester. This Popi is nothing more than a figment of your imagination, an alter ego of your creation that punishes you more than you deserve. The sooner you accept this, the sooner we can be happy again."

Vamillion placed her hand on Beauty's shoulder. Her touch made him cringe. "My little Popi. I need you well, and your mind must be clear."

Beauty shook his head in denial and shuddered at her words.

"I will see you tomorrow." Vamillion rose from the floor and left Beauty in his chamber, in a room full of darkness. The last sound he heard was the clanking of the locks from the other side, as it sealed him from the world above.

*　　　*　　　*

Vamillion made her way up the tower steps. There was much work to be done. She entered her study and closed the door behind her. A voice spoke to her from the darkness. It was a voice she had longed to hear, the voice of many voices, speaking in unison.

"You have done well, Vamillion."

She turned from the door and dropped to her knees. Her eyes trying to adjust to the darkness. "Dark One?"

"I am here," he confirmed.

Vamillion shuddered, for the voice was not in her head, but before her. A shadow flickered on the opposite side of the room, in front of her curtain, where no shadow had a natural purpose being. She could not recognize any discernable shape or form. The Dark One was nothing more than a changing mass of darkness, like a thick, impenetrable fog, slithering and swaying with a life of its own. She trembled, because to be visited by the Dark One, in person, was to meet Death, itself. "Oh, Master," Vamillion begged, like a slave. "Do not kill me, I beg you. I am too close. We… are too close."

"Calm yourself," the eerie voice sprang from the dark mass. "I am not here to kill you."

Vamillion sighed. "To what do I owe this honor? To see you… in person?"

"You see but one aspect of me, Vamillion," the Dark One said. "Do not fool yourself into thinking you have earned the honor of seeing my true form." The voices rose together, in a collective sense of urgency. "I have come for another… Zantigar."

Vamillion rose to her feet. "Oh, Dark One, help me have faith. Beauty has unfolded his prophecy. I fear it is too late. Zantigar will be taking him from me, won't he? I can't bear the thought. He must not, he cannot! Everything I have built, all that I am, will crumble before my eyes. All our plans will be forever lost."

The dark mass floated forward, stopping inches from her body. The closeness of his presence was like standing before an eternal void. "Zantigar will not take Beauty from you."

"Tell me it is true! Tell me, despite it being written in the pages of destiny. Without Beauty, I will never claim the portals."

"You place too much faith in Beauty. I can strip him of his power as quickly as it was given to him. No man controls destiny, it is the gods that control the fate of mankind."

Vamillion wiped tears from her eyes. "Then prove Beauty wrong, just this once." She raised her fist into the air. "Kill Zantigar!"

"It will be done."

"You know where he is? You know where to find him?"

"He is high in the Cragel Mountains, traveling to where minds touch the heavens… Mount Omera."

"Mount Omera," Vamillion whispered in reflection. She was perplexed at the news of this, wondering why he would be on a spirit journey. "His death will save Vixus and forever make me indebted to you, my Lord."

"Consider it done." The Dark One vanished, as the multitude of voices faded away.

Vamillion closed her eyes and took a deep breath. A knock came at the door. She was still pressed up against the door when she felt it push open. She stepped aside, allowing the door to swing ajar. "Diamus!" she called at the sight of him. "I am so glad you are here." She placed her hand on his chest and proceeded to tell him all that had transpired.

Diamus looked concerned. "I hope your Dark One is as powerful as he says. Zantigar is no ordinary rogue wizard. He is a Legionnaire, a graduate of Hendor Academy. Who knows the power at his fingers? He, too, could be a god. I mean, how else could someone live so many years?"

Vamillion turned away, not wanting to believe that her faith was unfounded, even though Beauty's prophecy was, in fact, proving her wrong. "I have seen the Dark One, Diamus. He has come to me and spared me. Me, alone! He is everything the rumors say about him… mighty, dangerous… and real. If Zantigar is some kind of god, then we shall see who is greater!"

Diamus nodded. "Indeed, we shall. Either way, the future is kind to us." Diamus pulled several pages from his robe. "I have news from the north. Our forces have entered the desert lands with orders to stop Mullen's advancement by whatever means necessary."

Vamillion moved to the window of the Moon Tower and stared out across the territory of Vixus. "We have done it, Diamus. Queen Abigail has done what was asked of her. She has done her duty and convinced the masses that our attack is in the best interest of the kingdom."

"Yes, but at your suggestion, acting upon your will," Diamus reminded. "You are the genius who made this a reality."

Vamillion smiled with pride. "She is a mere pawn in my hand."

"You truly are the true ruler of Vixus, now."

Vamillion could not contain her excitement. "We are so close to our dreams becoming a reality. The people of Vixus will be safe, and our kingdom strong. The citizens will be proud again, like they once were. War is but a small price to pay for the security of our kingdom."

Vamillion sighed, her shoulders tight with tension. It was a heavy burden to rule a land, to protect and preserve so many lives. She wondered if one day the violence would stop, if she would be able to relax and enjoy the world at her command. Perhaps, when the power of Glazahn's spell was in her hands, perhaps then she would know peace. She could enjoy the remaining days of her life with the certainty that all she had done, she had done for the benefit of her people.

However, in the days ahead, there was uncertainty, death and violence. Harsh experiences in a harsh land would be brought to light. Would the Dark One prevail, and prove his divinity? In her gut, she feared she would be fighting for the rest of her natural life to hold on to what was hers, to defend all that will be acquired.

Diamus took her hand in his and she allowed him to pull her close. "One day soon, the Desert Portal will be ours and all the mysteries within shall be revealed. The world will never be the same and you and I, we will go down in the pages of history. We will live forever, in songs and in books." He kissed her and she wrapped her arms around his neck.

In her younger years, Vamillion had longed for love, especially in turbulent times. She romanticized the chance to let go, to allow another to carry the weight of her troubles, and it was tempting when it was so justified. However, she could not lie to herself. She could never trust another. She could never love another. She would also never allow another to carry her troubles. Yet, there was plenty to be gained from Diamus. She could not complete her dream alone and there were pleasures of the flesh that could be satisfied, and it could be used to control him. She would keep him close, allow him to stand at her side, but would never give in to him, never allow him to take her place. She would kill him before she would let that happen.

Diamus grabbed her waist, and he pulled her body closer still, to rest tight against his.

Vamillion gave a devious smile. She wiggled the shoulder straps down her arms and Diamus tugged at the strings at her waist, loosening her dress until it dropped to the floor. Her skin glowed, pale in the light of the moon. He kissed the contours of her neck, while pulling a blade from his robe. He brought the edge of the blade to her breast, her nipples responding to the cold metal against her skin. She leaned her head back, eager for the release from his cut. They stumbled back, to her desk, where he pressed her against its surface. Her arms outstretched behind her, she searched for the feel of her whip and finding its tough leather grip, brought the whip out before her with a resounding crack.

Their eyes met and their lips came together as they slid from the desk and to the floor. Locked in a passionate embrace.

* * *

Far to the north, Vixus knights were marching with malicious intent. With clear, unmerciful orders, they would advance upon the unsuspecting citizens of Mullen, who were moving their families into the desert lands, unaware of the judgement that awaited them. The first act of war to grace the planet of FéLorën in two hundred years was about to begin. The cogs of time pressed onward, and nothing could change its course.

Beauty sat in the darkness of his chamber feeling the pain of the world, helpless to stop the ensuing bloodshed. He cried, the tears passing down his scarred face. His thoughts traveled to his savior, the wizard who could set him free, the only hope that was left to him. "Hurry, Zantigar," he thought. "Please hurry."

PART IV

MOUNT OMERA

Who is to say we are dreaming when we are dreaming? After all, it is conceivable to dream of interpreting a dream, while we dream. So who will be so bold as to assume we are now awake?

Only after the grandest awakening we will understand that this was all part of the grandest dream – a dream of a dream within a dream, within a dream, within a dream...

-Erramond the Wise from Proverbs of FéLorën

~CHAPTER 1~

The advisor to the Empress of Xyntharia, Qui, lowered his hood as he approached the door to his room. He brought his smooth, elven hand to the handle and upon contact, a voice invaded his mind.

"Tonight..."

Qui pulled his hand away and looked down the vast, empty hallway, his eyes following the long purple carpet and the rows of chandeliers lighting the hall. Despite the stillness, a presence felt near. Turning back to the door, his hand was trembling as he grasped the handle. He opened the door and entered the darkness of his bedroom.

He moved to a lamp as the door closed behind him.

"Tonight..."

Qui's heart fluttered, having difficulty sparking a flame with his shaking hand. His heart pounded in his chest, amplifying each failed strike. At last, the flame spawned. He protected it with the shield of his soft, fragile hand, and brought it to the wick of the lamp. He sighed in relief, as the room basked in a soft, orange glow. The comfort of light was diminished by the figure behind him, a silhouette that the light could not penetrate.

"Turn around," the voice whispered in his mind. When he did, he felt a sharp blow to the head. He fell to the floor on his hands and knees. Blood spilled down his face, blinding his eyes.

"Death has come for you," the Dark One spoke, in a voice of many voices.

Qui reached out, trying to see with blurred vision, his head pounding in excruciating pain. He felt a cold staff press against his forehead. A moment later, he choked on his screams as his soul was ripped from his body.

*　　　　*　　　　*

Vi-Lir Zyraxyvarye stood over her advisor's lifeless body. At either side of her, were two elven women of nobility, Zyraxia and Vyrona. They stared at the crime scene, the lifeless body, the bludgeoning on the forehead.

"The blow to his head would not cause his death," Zyraxia said, in a soft, somber tone.

"His face," Vyrona added, "is transfixed in a state of horror."

"Heart attack?" Zyraxia suggested.

The Empres kneeled before her advisor's lifeless body, turning his head left and right in keen observation. The head wound was still fresh. The only additional abnormality was that his eyes were void of color. She rose from the floor. "The Dark One."

Zyraxia gave her empress a questioning stare. "How is that possible?"

"His soul was robbed from his body. Where once there was life, there is none, like the color that had been drained from his eyes," Vyrona quoted. It was a statement written in the ledgers of a wizard hunter's report, upon finding the remains of one of the Dark One's victims.

The Empress remained reserved in her expression; her poise unfaltering. Yet she could not hide the concern in her voice. The implications of this murder, more poignant and more meaningful than the loss of a trusted advisor. "Send notification to the kingdom of Vixus. Tell them that Mullen will not make its way across Xyntharia River. This madness must be stopped before it gets out of hand. If handled with grace, resolute in its execution, this whole mess can be resolved before war can even be declared."

"Shall I call our troops into formation?" Vyrona asked.

The Empress shook her head. "There is no need to bloody our hands in this matter. Word of our involvement will only fuel the desire for war. The Din Naqui can take care of this matter for us. We need only alert them as to Mullen's intent and they will take care of the rest. They will be discreet and swift, and we can put this matter to bed."

Vyrona bowed. "As you wish, so shall it be." Vyrona exited Qui's room, quick to carry out her empress' demands.

Vi-Lir Zyraxyvarye returned her gaze to her dead advisor. She was aware of the extent of the human god's power, now. The threat was real, even for her own life.

Zyraxia placed her hand on her empress' hand, in an attempt to comfort her, as if she understood what her ruler was feeling. Vi-Lir Zyraxyvarye turned to Zyraxia and smiled softly. She embraced the hand that was offered to her and Zyraxia rested her head on her empress' shoulder. With fear in her voice, Zyraxia said, "the Dark One managed to infiltrate the most sacred of houses with the greatest of ease, leaving no trace behind. He murdered Qui without the slightest struggle."

Vi-Lir Zyraxyvarye turned to face her troubled noble and wrapped her arms around her in a warm embrace. Their bodies entwined, Zyraxia sighed heavily. "I know, Zyraxia. I know." The Empress ran her hands through Zaraxia's hair to soothe her troubled heart. She looked about the room, wondering if somehow, someway, the Dark One was still present, watching from another realm like a witch with a crystal ball. Hoping as much, she spoke into the darkness. "Your reign shall come to an end, Dark One. It is only a matter of time before we find a way."

~CHAPTER 2~

Diamus awoke in Vamillion's bed. He rolled over and his hand rested on her arm. With the touch of her skin, he opened his eyes. She was staring at the ceiling. He kissed her arm. "What troubles you?"

She turned toward him. "Beauty… his prophecy."

Diamus took a deep breath, "You don't need to worry. You said yourself, that the Dark One will kill Zantigar."

Vamillion looked troubled. "And if not?"

Diamus lay in silence a moment, reflecting on the Dark One's words. "Do you believe him?"

"I must, I fear the consequences. Believing in him, is to believe in his word. However, I should still have a plan, as I may have an opportunity to stop Zantigar, especially if the Dark One has destined for me to play a part. This feeling inside, this need to act is too overwhelming to ignore."

"That would be too dangerous. You could not stand up to Zantigar. However, you could do something about Beauty if all other options are lost to us."

"Do something? Are you suggesting I kill him?"

Diamus explained, "Don't sound so alarmed. Would you allow him to live a life away from here? In the control of another? I know you are capable of doing what must be done, if it came down to it."

Vamillion sat up. "You are right."

"Beauty is crippled and broken, and hardly able to communicate at all at this point. Maybe he has outlived his use. Perhaps, it is his time. Just think of it. You could go downstairs, and you could kill him right now. You would no longer have to worry about Zantigar."

Vamillion narrowed her eyes. "The Dark One will not fail." Vamillion took a deep breath. "There is so much more that Beauty could help with, despite his wounds. There is Oryahn, Brownstone, and Glazahn's spell. So many moments of time lost to us if I were to kill him now. I can't take that chance"

"Even if it meant you, alone, changed the course of history? You have to admit, it is tempting."

"Yes, but is it enough to lose sight of the future?"

Diamus scooted to the edge of the bed, removing the sheets he placed his feet on the ground. "Which will make us no different than any other living being on the planet. We must accept whatever the future holds, even if that future is unclear to us."

Vamillion reached out and placed her hand on Diamus' back. "I keep thinking about Oryahn, about Brownstone. Thinking he roams the land, undead." She shifted her body up against Diamus, the sheets falling away from her body. She wrapped her arms around him. Resting her chin on his shoulder. "Do you think he can be found?" She whispered. "Do you think he will help us?"

He glanced back at her. "It has been prophesized, has it not? Beauty's portrait of Brownstone proves it."

"It is just a portrait, it does not prove he will assist us, nor if we will even find him." Vamillion tightened her grip on him. "Who can we trust? Who has the courage to cross the vast sea, to enter the domain of the dead?"

Diamus looked down to his feet, wiggled his toes, and broke free from Vamillion's embrace. He stood and looked to the window. "I will do it. I will set out for Oryahn. I will take Rasatharian with me."

Vamillion sank back down into the sheets. "What if I lose you? And Rasatharian? You are the last living Necromancers on Valice."

Diamus turned back toward the bed and crawled onto it, positioning himself over her body. "You need not worry, my love." He stared in Vamillion's lucid eyes. He smiled at the sight of her vulnerability, enjoying the physical edge over her. "I will go, and I will return with Brownstone at my side. I do not need Beauty's prophecy to reassure me."

"So be it," Vamillion said. She leaned up and kissed his lips. He grabbed her wrists and pinned her arms above her head. Her submissive position did not deter her from matching the piercing look in his eyes, nor did it silence her. "I do not want you to leave until we know, for sure, that Zantigar is dead and Mullen's advancement into the desert has been stopped."

He kissed her. "Okay."

"I want you to take Lord Shyn with you, and as many Knights of Brownstone required. It is only fitting. They were named after him, it's as if they are meant for this."

"Yes, my love." He kissed her again.

She pulled away. "And I will instruct Queen Abigail to have an armada, fit for a king, at your disposal. I will not allow-"

Diamus kissed her deeply, silencing her. "As you command."

~CHAPTER 3~

Zantigar raised his arm and extended his index finger toward the horizon. "Mount Omera is there, just at the edge of our vision."

Daylen observed where Zantigar's finger directed. An enormous mountain, on the horizon, blocked a portion of the sky. It dwarfed the land below.

"It is the largest mountain on all of Valice. A magical mountain, once home to a mighty dragon, long ago. Its treasures still waiting to be discovered, to those brave enough to enter the catacombs. However, it is not its depths that call to us, but the mountain's top, our final destination."

Daylen pondered all that was implied by reaching this final destination. What would be revealed, what he would learn, was unimaginable. The trek to the top would be long and vigorous. As they made their way to the mountain's base, he thought he best keep an open mind and set his fears aside as best he could. "How many weeks will it take to get to the top?"

"Not weeks, Daylen. Months. There is an acclimation process, as the body must get used to the altitude, the thin air. It is a process which will require a series of ascending and descending, as well as days at a time spent camping. The climb will be taken with respectful consideration of the majesty of this natural wonder. There is no need to hurry and there is nothing to fear along the way. There are shelters and resting grounds already established, which house food, supplies, and tools. I will help you survive the elements, so this is not where your focus should lie. You, on the other hand, will have to concentrate on the trials of the mountain. Your focus, your energy, will need to be concentrated on the trials. When you confront them, you will have to face them alone."

"Is it entirely necessary I do the trials alone?" Daylen questioned, intimidated by the thought.

"It is essential. You will find out, once and for all, who you are and all you can be."

Daylen nodded. If anything would give him the courage to proceed, it was this promise. He anxiously pressed on toward the mountain's base.

Zantigar held out his arm and stopped him, grabbing Daylen's attention. "This mountain is sacred ground. Those who did not respect the mountain, those who did not take the trial seriously, died. Stay true and you will live to see the mountain's top."

"I am ready," Daylen said.

"After you." Zantigar lowered his arm, allowing Daylen to proceed. "Where the trail bends up ahead, you will come to the entrance. You will wait there for my instruction. Now go, onward and upward."

Daylen followed the narrow trail. As Zantigar informed, he came to a stone arch with runes carved into it. The stone was like no stone he had seen. It was bluish in color and did not match the stones of the mountain besides it. As a result, it looked like a foreign structure, out of place, looming over the trail like a mysterious, ancient guardian.

Zantigar came up from behind him. "The Gate of Awakening," Zantigar whispered. "No one was aware of its meaning, until Erramond found the text of FéLorën and decoded its scripture. This is one of three sacred structures on the continent of Valice that is left standing from the original people of FéLorën, from a time before our modern, recorded history. The other two structures are better known as portals. If you stood before the portals, then you would notice a similar structure and the same ancient runes." Zantigar pointed to the top of the archway, directly overhead. "The all-seeing eye."

Daylen looked at the symbol of an eye at the top of the gateway arch. Rays of light were carved in the stone, as if emanating from behind it. "The eye of FéLorën."

Daylen's gaze was locked on the symbol. If that stone eye could see, then it would have witnessed the passing of ages and kingdoms, and now, it would be noticing him. "Does that mean, Zantigar, that this is a broken, deactivated portal?"

Zantigar shrugged and shuffled passed, breaking Daylen from his daydream. "I doubt that it is broken, it seems to me that it is functioning just as intended and it would do you good to see it as such. Worry not about it being a portal, though, at least as you define one to be. All who pass through are likely to return."

Daylen stayed close to Zantigar, never taking his eyes off the archway, until he had passed through to the other side. He half expected the world to look different, but it was all in his head. The monument to a long-forgotten time was now behind him, but not forgotten. Its ancient presence alluding to the mystery that lay ahead. "What shall become of us?"

Zantigar placed a smooth, black stone in Daylen's hand. "The dream is almost over."

"The dream?" He looked down at the rock that was placed in his palm.

"The dream of every waking moment you have known before this day." Zantigar folded Daylen's fingers over the stone. "Keep this stone with you at all times."

Daylen felt the weight of the stone in his clenched hand. "A stone?"

"Not just any stone. It is a spirit stone. As long as you hold this stone you will know where you are. You will know that you walk the mountain path, beside me. No matter what you see, you can believe, so long as this stone is with you."

"No matter what I see?" Daylen tightened his grip on the stone.

Zantigar did not answer, but continued forward, ascending the mountain trail. He closed his eyes and inhaled a deep breath of the mountain air, his knuckles whitened around his ruby staff. After a moment of concentration, his eyes opened, and he faced Daylen.

Daylen felt an unsettling force of uncertainty. "When will the trials start?"

"Your first trial will begin in a moment."

"Are you going to leave me already?"

"All you need to know is that mountain trail is a path to truth. In a moment's time, the illusion of your reality will be stripped from you. The rock in your hand is there to remind you, and in this way, it will guide you. Close your eyes and feel its weight in your hand."

Daylen felt his heart beating in his chest. He took a deep breath and closed his eyes. "What truth?"

"The truth inside you."

Daylen heard Zantigar's voice, but it did not come from beside him. The voice came from his mind. Startled, he opened his eyes. Zantigar was gone. The mountain, gone. He stood on a vast empty desert and all that was left of the reality he once knew was encapsulated in the weight of the spirit stone that weighed heavy in his hand. He trembled. "Zantigar," he whispered in a plea. The desert wind blew past his face, the sun, blinding. "It was a mistake coming here. I am not ready."

~CHAPTER 4~

Daylen scanned the desert and the sky above him. Hues of brilliant red made the sky surreal. His environment shifting so drastically produced a whirlwind of questions in his head. He struggled to get his bearings, every direction he faced revealed the same vast expanse of desert. No buildings, no change in landscape, no landmark of any kind confronted him no matter which way he faced. He tried to focus on the thought of Zantigar, Zantigar's words. He clung to the thought of illusions, tests, courage and truth as tightly as he clutched the spirit stone in his hand. Never lose sight of the truth, Daylen thought, the stone is your truth.

He opened his hand and stared at the stone in his palm. It was the only physical reminder of the world he knew. "The stone is still in my hand. Zantigar is still beside me and the world before me is just another illusion. Or, was the world I left the illusion?" Is this the truth that Zantigar spoke of? Daylen wondered. "Where are you?" He spun to look in all directions and threw his hands in the air. "Where am I?"

Daylen felt alone. With this realization, his mind quieted. His thoughts coming together with abstract thought. "I am alone. The truth is I am alone. Yes," Daylen thought aloud. "I must acknowledge what is."

He waited for something to happen, but nothing happened. He thought this fundamental realization would allow him to find his way. He questioned his understanding of the known world. "I am alone, but is that the truth? It is my truth, but it is not the higher truth."

He felt the beat of his heart quicken, as awareness, like pieces of a puzzle, fell into place. "I am on the mountain right now." He looked down at his legs planted in the sand. "I may be moving up the mountain trail as I speak." He closed his eyes and imagined his place. "I am on the mountain; I am on my way to the top. If being alone is not the truth, then the truth is that I am not alone." His eyes widened with a powerful awareness. "The reality before me is a direct reflection of my assumptions. I feel alone, therefore I am alone."

The ground beneath him rumbled and a fantastic shift in his surroundings occurred. A dark pit opened up in front of him. He crept toward the edge. A stairway descended into darkness, leading into a foreboding crypt. He stepped away and looked toward the sky. "Why did it have to be down? I want to go up!" He inched back to the edge of the chasm.

There were just two possibilities available to him. Stay on the desert, or go down, wherever it led. This left no choice in the matter. He clenched the stone in his hand and placed his foot on the first step. He tested its stability, satisfied by the weight of stone step beneath him. With his next step, a cold breeze rushed past him. A stark contrast to the heat of the desert. Step by step, he descended until his body was submerged in darkness, into the cold. There was moisture in the air and the stench of death. The steps came to an end and the ground was sticky and wet like mud, causing him to slip. He fell forward. He placed his hand out in front of him to stop his fall, his hand submerging in the moist ground. When he stood and brought his hand to his face, what he thought was mud was blood. It smelled of rot and decay, which reminded him of the smell that greeted him on his way into Juniper, when he had walked over the remains of townspeople and goblins.

"Goblins," Daylen said with regret. His heart sank at the thought of the devastation they had caused. Their indiscriminate violence and hunger killing so many, including Hogar. He could hear the sound of swords clashing, the cries of battle. It rang in his head as a vivid memory, until the sounds of war became louder. The sounds were not in his head but approaching from behind him.

He walked, quickly at first, until the sounds of war closed in on him. He began to run, deep into the tunnel, away from the advancing carnage. He was unable to outrun that which chased him. A hand grabbed his arm. He screamed and jerked his body free from a goblin's grasp. He felt more hands grabbing, clawing, and scratching. The tunnel was filled with the grunts and growls of goblins as panic took hold. Daylen ran, as fast as he could go. He ripped past flailing goblin arms and saw flashes of angry goblin faces from the corners of his eyes, gnashing their teeth with hungry eyes.

He felt the darkness closing in, as the likelihood of his survival diminished. As he ran, he noticed the walls of the underground passage were shrinking, the tunnel growing narrow. The goblins were behind him now, he could hear their scurrying feet behind him, trying to keep up with his frantic pace. The tunnel became too low to stand within, he dropped to his knees and crawled, desperately hoping it did not close in around him. On his hands and knees, he pushed through the mud and the blood, the thought of a dead end bringing him to tears. The stone was still clenched in his fist, he had forgotten about it, forgotten about the intensity that the illusion could conjure. If he died at the hands of the goblins, would he die for real? He wondered. Would his fear of a dead end cause the dead end to appear? He was shaking, afraid more of his own mind then the goblins, themselves.

The tunnel became too narrow to crawl, but the only way was forward. He squeezed through the narrow passage, wiggling forward, the grasp of goblin claws inches behind. His body covered in blood, his face contorted from the stench, and with hope fading, the walls tightened around him. Failure appeared eminent. In that moment, a voice stronger than a thought came to him, a voice he believed to be the wizard within. It was foreign, yet familiar at the same time. Not an unknown voice, but a voice in which he was remembering, having forgotten as a child. It was loud and it was commanding, and it said to him, "Do not hope for an exit; trust in an exit."

There was an exit, Daylen thought. Suddenly, he could see it. A light appeared ahead. A piercing ray of daylight, salvation. Yet as he found himself at the light, the hole was too small to fit through. He would have to claw his way out if he wished to live. Without doubt, but with trembling hands, he tore at the opening.

With all his might he broke through, just as a goblin claw reached for his foot. With the entire weight of his body, he collapsed into the light, covered in mud and blood, the stench of death still upon him. He stood, trembling, consumed in shock. Having traveled through a personal hell, he struggled to stand on his weak knees. He wiped a mixture of blood and sweat, mud and tears, from his face. Swinging to look behind him, the tunnel was gone.

He found himself in the center of what was once a large cathedral but was now an ancient ruin. Roofless, the walls had caved in and it was consumed by vegetation. The only intact wall was the front of the cathedral, which still framed a stain glass window, pristinely kept, and untouched by the marring of time. The bright sun was a welcome blessing, but it blinded his unfocused eyes. Glimmered through the window, it filtered colors light around him and on the floor.

Between rows of broken pews and columns lay tattered armor, broken shields and shattered blades. Large claw marks were a clue as to what led to the abandonment of the ruined structure many years ago. As Daylen wondered what sort of beast could be so large and so strong as to wreak such havoc, a monstrous roar echoed through the cathedral. The passage of time had not rid the area of beast which haunted it. The sun descended closer to the horizon in an abnormal quickening of time. The sun's rays no longer pierced the stain glass window. A foreboding shadow spilled across the floor. Without the glare of the sun, the design of the stained glass came into view. Daylen's eyes widened in horror. It was a winged lion, made of glass, a replica of the image found in Zantigar's book of history.

Another roar rang through the cathedral. The roar was so loud, he could feel its vibrations reverberate in his chest. He shook his head, knowing all too well what made the noise. He cursed in silence. He had told Zantigar he wasn't ready, but he had not listened. With such thoughts, he felt like he had already failed Zantigar. His attention was drawn to the dead weight in his hand. The spirit stone: a reminder that he was still on the mountain. There was no comfort in knowing this.

Daylen was all too aware that his thoughts had always been his enemy. The third roar caused the cathedral to shake. He fell to his knees. He spread his arms out before him, his hands outstretched, the spirit stone resting in his palm. He breathed deeply. He did not trust what he saw, any more than he trusted his position. He closed his eyes, blocking out the world around him and looked to the realm within.

In the darkness of his closed eyes, he saw light. The core of his being. When Zantigar had stared at the winged lion in his book all he had seen was light. "Light."

Daylen opened his eyes.

A winged lion was standing before him. It growled as it stared into Daylen's eyes.

"It's all an illusion," Daylen said. "It's just light."

The winged lion roared. Its warm breath blew against Daylen's skin, and it felt as real as he knew himself to be. He was afraid. Zantigar had told him that acceptance of what he felt was all he needed. Knowing himself was all the preparation required. He acknowledged his fear, and he knew that he must face that fear, even if it meant death. The loss of his body could not compare to the death of his spirit, and he, alone, was responsible for that.

The lion's tail slithered with anticipation. It's beautiful, yet frightening eyes narrowed on its prey. Daylen's eyes locked with the beast's eyes, and he focused his entire being on manifesting his courage. A memory came to him of when he locked eyes with the wolf in Lonely Wood. This time, he would not falter, he would not remain afraid. He faced the lion as an equal. No, he was not the lion's equal, the truth was far greater. There was no difference between them. The fear disappeared.

In the blink of an eye, he was no longer staring at the lion, he was staring down at himself. He felt the powerful muscles of his legs and outstretched his mighty wings. He saw the world filtered through the eyes of the beast. Raising his front paws, the young wizard before him was just a small creature, consumed by his mighty shadow. Yet, the wizard was steadfast, unwavering against his prowess. Such a little thing, such a small and insignificant person before him. The wizard stood like an offering, and the urge to devour him took hold. He lunged forward and took the wizard's body in his mouth, devouring him. As the wizard entered his mouth, Daylen was shrouded in darkness, consumed by the mouth of a mighty winged lion. There was nothing that separated him from that which ate him. He felt the lion's teeth plunge into his flesh, felt the core of his body crush within its might jaws. His body was whipped through the air and slammed to the floor, his bones shattering like glass.

Daylen was conscious of his human form for only a moment as his skull was split open, but the moment was stretched across time. He felt the searing white heat of the spell he cast in Lonely Wood, but unlike that day, the spell consumed him, not the lion. As the contact of his head to the cathedral floor splintered his skull into pieces, he felt the warm light of the spell embrace him and the final thought that crossed his mind was that it was no illusion, it was all too real, as if in death he was finally alert to pure consciousness.

There was only awareness, without form. A sense of pure being occurred in a realm beyond time, beyond all worldly forms, both material and ethereal. In the stillness was abundance, in want of nothing. Acceptance, of all that was and wasn't. Surrender, in understanding.

THE WINGED LION
G.G.

~CHAPTER 5~

Daylen woke in a fetal position. There was the awareness of the cold, the harshness of the elements and the sound of howling wind. He felt the spirit stone in his hand and was not certain, until opening his eyes, whether or not he was still lost in a world of illusion. He saw that he was on the mountain, his eyes sensitive to the light. It was then that he realized, with absolute clarity, that he was alive. He rose to his feet.

Zantigar stood to the side of the mountain trail, supported by his ruby staff. The wind was lashing at his red robe. He was looking at Daylen, but he did not say a word.

Daylen wrapped his arms tight around his chest, exposed. He looked around him. He was high on the mountain path, much higher than he ever expected to be. They were standing above the clouds, and a clear, massive expanse of sky surrounded them. He was overcome with peace and saw the miracle of life unfolding before his eyes. The world, all of it, was made of magic. Daylen picked up a handful of dirt and let it run through his hand. "The world has changed." As he stared down at the rolling clouds, they flowed like fields of cotton. He realized a deeper truth. "I have changed."

Daylen could feel an abundance of life. Before now, life was hardly more than a word, a description which separated the living from the dead. Now, life was energy, awareness, an immense source of passions. It was not separate from death, it included death. The dirt on his hands and the fresh smell of the air sparked sensations that before he could not even imagine possible. "I feel as though I am seeing for the first time."

"Not for the first time, but once again," Zantigar said.

Daylen nodded. "I am timeless. I am bound to repeat this experience, bound to forget and to see again." He noticed how close to the top of the mountain they actually were and, had he not experienced what he had just been through, he would have questioned how it was possible. Where did the time go? "I thought I had died."

"You did," Zantigar said. "At least one aspect of yourself."

Daylen concentrated on the enormous weight that had been lifted from his shoulders. "There is no more fear."

"Only light," Zantigar said.

Daylen looked into Zantigar's eyes. He recognized a wisdom in them that was familiar to himself. He smiled, aware of how they were one and the same, connected. "Only light." Compelled, he stepped up to Zantigar and hugged him tight. "I feel so much energy."

Zantigar returned his embrace and then pulled away to stare with pride at Daylen's progression. "You feel the spirit of the land… the spirit of FéLorën."

Daylen closed his eyes to savor the moment. He felt the pulsating strength of the world, the strength of himself, the power of his own perception. Thoughts flew through his mind like a soaring wind, he could not hold them all. He let go. Over and over, he let go and he let the focus of this mind rest with the space between thought, where abundance and peace were most strongly felt. When he opened his eyes, all was gone. The mountain, the clouds; Zantigar. Confusion hit him at first, and sorrow followed. He sunk to his knees and was surprised by his feeling of despair. It was as if the entire energy of the universe was within him, but there was nowhere to channel it, no other to experience it with.

It was up to him to create something with all that he had learned, with all that he knew. Madness was just a thought away. He took slow deep breaths and then the world returned to him, like oxygen into his brain. "What is happening to me?"

"You are no longer held hostage to your environment, no longer trapped by your mind's illusions. You see the world as it truly is, an abundant source of energy, a sea of magic from which you are a part of. Now that you are aware, you are ready to learn the unique spells inside you."

Daylen knew that which Zantigar spoke of. All that he saw, all that he felt, the rocks of the mountain and the breeze through the air seemed to be speaking a language, whispering secrets that held the power to unlock his full potential. He was connected to the world in this way, stronger because of his connection to the land. It was just a moment ago, but how was it, he wondered, that he could ever have felt alone?

They continued further up the mountain. "It is shocking that we have already traversed most the mountain. How was it possible?"

"When you were tired, we rested. When you faltered, I held you upright. When you were hungry, I fed you and when you were fresh out of energy, we slept."

"Slept? How many days did we travel in this way?"

"Many days," Zantigar responded.

Daylen nodded. His prior self would have been unable to believe it, would have found it impossible, but this was only because he would have compared the experience to his limited understanding of time, and of his mind. Now, he knew first hand that both time and his mind were two concepts that were beyond definition. Perhaps, they were two abstractions that did not even exist. It was the lack of understanding that made him wiser. "It was the desert," he whispered. "I was on the desert for longer than I care admit."

Zantigar listened, allowing Daylen to come to whatever conclusion he needed to come to terms with what he had experienced.

"And when I thought I had died…" Daylen continued, softly. "I found myself in eternity. It all seemed so fast." He smiled at the thought of his own feeble attempt to grasp eternity and how it could ever be quick, or what it even meant in the realm of planetary time.

When daylight sunk behind the horizon, they found themselves at a campsite. Nestled into the side of the mountain was a shack, big enough for them to sleep in and housed supplies and bedding for a comfortable night's sleep. Zantigar used his ruby staff to start a fire and Daylen gravitated to it for its warmth. Zantigar took a seat beside him.

"I did die back there," Daylen said. "I could swear it. For a moment, it did not matter if I ever came back."

"There have been those who did not awaken. Some choose to die. Some simply lose their way. I knew you would return."

Daylen was not entirely certain how he had awoken. He laughed out loud, realizing the spirit stone was still in his hand. He stared at it in his palm. "This stone gave me courage, hope, when I had believed there was none."

Zantigar leaned forward, requesting to have a look. "May I?"

Daylen nodded.

"Yes, a miraculous entity, is it not? Strange to think I found such a smooth rock just lying on the ground." Zantigar handed the stone back to Daylen.

Daylen twirled the stone in his hand, rubbing it with his fingers. After a moment of reflection, he smiled. "You just found it on the ground?"

"Well, where else would a rock reside?"

Daylen understood the stone was no 'spirit stone' in any more than the cabin he found himself in was a spirit cabin. The stone was no different than any other stone, except for the fact that his perception made it so. The power he accredited to it was the power of himself.

Zantigar appeared to know Daylen's thoughts. "Just as you hold the power to make that stone a spirit stone, you already possess the skills necessary to be as great of a wizard as you so desire. Similarly, the spell power you so desperately want to acquire is already within you."

Daylen stared off into space. This is what made Zantigar so important to him. It was not Zantigar, but his perception of him. If Rahlen had handed him the stone, then it would probably have disappeared, like everything else had when the trial began. "It is hard to explain the way I feel. Understanding the world around me, I feel the world around me. The awareness of my connection to all things, it, feels amazing, but…"

"Tell me," Zantigar said, anxious to know.

Daylen shook his head. "It's hard to explain. It's overwhelming." Trying to explain his experience, he struggled to find the words. "I am happy, I am alive, I am… overjoyed, really. But…" he shook his head.

Zantigar placed his hand on Daylen's hand. "There is nothing you can feel that you should be ashamed of, nothing you feel that can be wrong. It is okay."

"There is sadness," Daylen said. "I wasn't expecting that. I can't really explain it, maybe I am seeing something wrong, but I don't think so."

"Did you expect that with awareness comes happiness?" Zantigar asked. "Awareness is no easy burden to bear."

Daylen nodded. "I just thought, when I was clear of mind, there would be only happiness. That sadness and anger were emotions of an inferior state of being. I get how foolish that was."

To always be happy, to desire only happiness, would be a grave mistake and a profound misunderstanding of life. How limited your experience, how limited your perception, should you only ever feel happy. You are a wizard, gifted with the ability to see what others do not. Never mistrust your feelings, never bury them. The sadness is there to guide you, to show you the way, just as much as your anger."

Daylen looked into Zantigar's eyes and could see the very sadness which he was experiencing. Perhaps, it had always been there, and he never realized it until he too could feel it. He was used to recognizing Zantigar's power, his truth, his madness, but never a tenderness, never did he recognize so much pain. Staring into Zantigar's eyes, he saw more than he wanted to see and more than he, admittedly, wanted to understand. He turned away.

"What is the matter, Daylen?"

"It isn't me." Daylen faced Zantigar. "It's you… something is troubling you."

Zantigar smiled. It was as if Zantigar knew exactly what Daylen was uncovering. "You are perceptive, young wizard. You are seeing as a Master sees, long before it was expected."

"Will you tell me what is troubling you?"

Zantigar ignored Daylen's request. "You are going to be a powerful wizard. You will make me proud, one day."

Daylen lowered his head. Zantigar was not ready to share what troubled him, and it was okay. It would have to wait. He knew better than to persist.

"It is time to sleep. Another long day tomorrow, and the next day, and the next. We have not reached the mountain's top, yet," Zantigar said, lowering himself onto his bedding. "And your trials are not over. You will need all your strength for what lies ahead."

~CHAPTER 6~

The wheels of the carriage were carved from the finest wood. The metal that reinforced them was forged by an experienced, expert blacksmith. The quality of their craftsmanship was confirmed as they were tested against the rough terrain of the desert. Turning over rock, pebbles and sand, the wheels held up to all adversity. They creaked and cracked revolving on strong axles, benefitting from the technology of dwarven artisans. Grinding over the trail, conquering nature's uneven terrain, the carriage shook and rumbled. The royal horses pulled the carriage forward with determination.

From the carriage window, King Mullen III stared out at the vast expanse of desert. The shade of the carriage offering little protection from the heat. He closed his eyes to the grating sound of the carriage wheels, the repetitive rhythm a reminder of the caravan's slow march. With his mind set on the future, his heart was heavy with the burden that only a king could know. Beyond the carriage window, moved a vast migration of his people who depended on him for their future.

The poverty in his kingdom had reached devastating levels. It was a price that was paid for competing with neighboring kingdoms for strength and stability. Wealth distribution had, for years, been allocated to military defenses. Walls, moats, turrets and outposts. Laborers were required to construct them, troops were required to maintain them, along with the necessary weapons and armor to protect them. A wealthy king was an admirable king, a strong kingdom, was a safe kingdom. A safe kingdom was a happy kingdom, or so King Mullen III believed. His father and his father's father built his wondrous territory, made it what it was, and taught him how it was to be maintained, if he were to be proud of that which he inherited.

For a time, it was enough. The kingdom grew, the population expanded, and it was a measure of their success. When the food shortage came, when trade expenses were shifted to greater taxation, the burden on the peasants was great. Harsh life conditions led to crime which in turn led to harsher punishments. Squeezed by the forces which existed to protect them, the peasants rose up in defiance.

At the start of the troubles, a few critical rebels were silenced in order to set an example. This only gave attention toward their grievances and larger communities of dissidence emerged. The first revolt was quelled, and those of royalty celebrated the battle as a victory for the kingdom. However, the peasants cried out at the massacre and would not be silenced. The second and the third rebellion, were greater in number and, in turn, greater in casualties. The problems for King Mullen III were growing in scale, the cost was unbearable, and there was no end in sight to the violence.

King Mullen III was faced with governing a society which he did not understand. Despite misguided priorities that conflicted with the will of his people, the ends which he sought; harmony and unification, was a common desire. He turned to his new advisor, Kallogar, a graduate from Mullen Academy for advice. Kallogar was recently bestowed the title of Legionnaire, after playing an integral role in stopping the latest rebellion. Kallogar, while an obedient servant to his kingdom, and murderer of many revolutionaries, understood the revolution taking place and knew that force was not the way to bring resolution to the rebellion. Kallogar explained a shift in governing practices had to be implemented.

Kallogar introduced a plan to use the king's wealth to combat the growing prices of goods from trade. In return for lower priced goods, the people would take up work in helping with the kingdom's expansion into the Desert Lands. Their willing servitude was required to cultivate and irrigate, and to create housing. The plan was twofold. First, it would unify the peasants under a common cause, a purpose other than rebellion. Second, it would lead to greater wealth as a sound investment. If expansion was a success, trade agreements could be modified, new internal and external wealth created, which would in turn, create an economy ripe for increased taxation.

King Mullen III realized that an end to the rebellion depended on the success of their migration. If he failed to provide space for his people, failed to feed their starving mouths, he would be overthrown, devoured by his own. Yet, pressure did not only come from below. The royal line, his extended family, including the royal guard, were fearful of losing their station and would, in turn, just as easily devour him, should their way of life be threatened.

There were the interests of the Socialites, those of wealth and influence, who looked to the Portals. King Mullen III's highest ranking officer, Sir Manzer, was a knight with close blood ties to the Socialites and was influenced heavily from their desires. Manzer had pressed his king to make a move to claim the Desert

Portal before others, specifically Vixus, claimed it for their own. While Manzer was a gifted militant with expertise in combat, his ambitions provided unwanted pressure. Unbeknownst to King Mullen III, a Vixus spy was within the ranks of Socialites, and was the reason why suspicion of Mullen's intent in advancing into the desert found its way to Vamillion's ear.

King Mullen III wiped sweat from his brow. As he thought of the intricate web of influences, he thought about what transpired at the High Council of FéLorën, of Vamillion's threats, and he feared he would have to plan his moves carefully if he were to prevent a war. All that interested him was the preservation of his throne and his life. Somehow, someway, he had to please the peasants and the elite, by taming the desert lands and claiming the portal. Both feats had never been accomplished, but protecting his throne depended upon his success.

King Mullen III fidgeted with the rings on his fingers and looked to his companions in the carriage. His trusted advisor, Kallogar, was beside him and across from him, Manzer. At Manzer's side was Lord Wen, commander of the Mullen knights, Manzer's superior. They were the very heads of influence that pulled at King Mullen III's strings. They traveled in silence, each in concentration, with the weight of the urgency of migration on their minds.

King Mullen III had not desired to personally lead the migration into the desert lands, but understood the importance. His presence was a sign of his commitment to his people and was great for morale, amongst peasants and the royal guard, alike. The peasants had placed their lives in his hands and conquering the desert was not going to be an easy task. The expansion would take years before it would reap any tangible reward. Troops were required to tame the region, the desert being home to many wild beasts. The very best of the kingdom's engineers and farmers were needed. Technological advancements allowed for channeling water, of making the desert into a man-made oasis.

Occasionally, carriage passengers discussed the goal of expansion, debated the details of The Oasis; its potential and its hardships. Upon The Oasis' completion, it would be a wonder of the world, a symbol of King Mullen III's ingenuity and strength. It was thoughts such as these that drove the king and excited him. The Oasis would result in harmony and unification, of which all those in his kingdom could agree, regardless of class.

There was a tapping on the carriage door. Manzer looked to the king and receiving a nod, opened the door. A Mullen knight on horseback trotted beside the carriage. "An army has been spotted, approaching from the East."

"Stop the carriage at once," Mullen said.

Lord Wen put his head out the carriage and shouted, "Stop the royal carriage!"

The servants did as instructed, pulling the reins of the stallions until the carriage came to a halt. Manzer swung the double doors to the carriage open and jumped to the sand. Servants rushed to the door with a step stool while horns sounded in the distance, informing the caravan to come to a halt.

King Mullen, using the stool provided him, stepped from the carriage. Kallogar followed in his footsteps. Lord Wen exiting once they both had exited.

"An army?" King Mullen questioned.

"Vixus," Kallogar suspected.

The knight on horseback confirmed. "They carry banners of red and blue."

Manzer and Lord Wen shifted with unease, they looked to their king. Turning to address the knight on horseback, King Mullen III said, "Bring the scouts to me, immediately."

Before the knight could gallop off, King Mullen III turned to address Lord Wen. "We will soon be informed as to their size and their current position. Assuming the unthinkable, that Vixus has brought an army to prevent our advance, we must make protection of the people our priority."

"Understood, Your Majesty," Lord Wen confirmed.

King Mullen III narrowed his eyes with anger. "We must expect the worst."

"It would be war between us," Kallogar said. "Is Vixus prepared to have the land of Valice against them? I agree we should prepare for the worst, but let us also be optimistic. The act of war would unite the world with us. In light of this, Vixus must be willing to negotiate. There is no reason to believe they could be so reckless."

Lord Wen returned with the scouts. Dropping from his horse, the platoon leader bowed. He pulled out a map from a pouch on the side of his horse. He spoke with urgency. "Your Majesty, Vixus approaches. At their current speed of advancement, they will divide us from our citizens, here." He pointed to the position on the map that split the migration. As he continued, he referenced the map. "There were also flanking units spotted, heading north, here and here, to engage the head."

"We should prepare our tents for negotiation," King Mullen instructed.

The scout lowered his head, appearing uncomfortable with the news he had to share. "Your Majesty, the front of their army is lined with cavalry units. Heavy infantry are fast behind, with ample archery units. Thousands approach. There carry no tents. They carry no white flags."

"They have no intention to negotiate," Kallogar surmised.

"An ambush?" King Mullen III turned to his advisor and was met with equal shock.

"They will divide our forces and leave the citizens vulnerable to slaughter. Kallogar explained.

"This is war," King Mullen III whispered in disbelief. "By the gods, that lunatic of a Queen has waged war. Is there another way?"

"Assuming we wished to change course, there is not the time to achieve it," Lord Wen said. "Any attempt will leave us to slaughter. Our forces must maintain and defend our advance, but you, Majesty, should consider escaping."

"And leave my people to fend for themselves? We must halt their attack! We can stop them! Tell me, Kallogar, tell me we can stop them."

Kallogar shook his head. "Even if we're capable of fighting them off, the losses would be so great it would not bode well for us. The best way to mitigate our losses is leave a portion of our troops to fight so that we may make our escape, saving as many lives as possible."

King Mullen III was deep in thought. "There must be another way."

'We can all stand our guard and end this madness today," Lord Wen suggested. "Whatever the cost, we could make them pay, and we will win."

"There is another option available to us." King Mullen looked to the scout. "There are thousands of citizens who are just beginning their migration. Take your scouts and hurry to Mullen, warn them to stop their advance and to stay in the safety of our kingdom walls."

The scout bowed, "Yes, Your Majesty."

"Now go!" The king ordered.

"Tell me, my king, how may I best be of service?" Manzer said.

"You and Lord Wen will both accompany me, along with a force just large enough to guarantee safety and speed in our travels."

"Where to, My Liege?" Kallogar asked. "What is this alternative you speak of?"

"If we try to flee, Vixus will surely cut off our forces and pin us," Lord Wen said.

King Mullen III shook his head. I do not suggest we flee. "We travel southwest."

"Southwest?" Lord Wen said in panic. "To elven land?"

Kallogar nodded, placing his hand on his beard. "Yes, southwest, to Xyntharia."

"We ask the High Elves of Xyntharia to aid us," King Mullen III said. "Surely, they would not wish for Vixus to destroy us. With their assistance, we could fight the Vixus army off with minimal losses."

Lord Wen brightened with agreement. "The rest of our forces can hold out until we return with elven reinforcements."

"Ask the elves for help?" Manzer questioned. "This will make us indebted to them."

"We will not sacrifice everything we have built for the sake of our pride," King Mullen III announced. "We must look past this battle and see this act for what it is. War is upon us. If we were to sacrifice all, then we will be playing into Vixus' hands. They are hell bent on obtaining the portal and it is clear the extent they will go to acquire it. If they succeed, our kingdom has no future, no hope. The desert will be blocked from expansion, and by the time the people are successful in their revolt, I will already have been assassinated by my peers."

"With Xyntharia on our side we will surely have the support of the High Council. If we can pull this off, the Vixus attack will reach the ears of the surrounding kingdoms. All the kingdoms of Valice will be behind us."

"It is settled," the king proclaimed.

They entered the royal carriage and directed their sights to Xyntharia Forest, on the quickest path to the High Elves. Behind them, thousands of men, women and children would look for protection from the Mullen soldiers who stayed behind, knowing the sacrifice of their servitude.

~CHAPTER 7~

Elven eyes stared through the leaves of the trees at the loud caravan of Mullen knights, accompanied by a royal carriage, which traveled at a reckless speed. Camouflaged by their tattooed skin and forest-colored garments, the elves were invisible to the untrained eye, their presence, unknown, despite their large numbers. Hidden on the forest floor and high in the treetops, they waited, patiently, for the call to strike.

A Din Naqui elf turned to his companion. In their native, elven tongue, the Din Naqui spoke to one another.

"I thought we were attacking an army. I thought we were preventing a war."

"We will wait."

"And if no other forces arrive?"

"Then justice shall be swift. Their slaughter will send a clear message to their king that war will not be tolerated."

*　　　　　*　　　　　*

There was a feeling of relief when King Mullen III's carriage made its way into the shade of Xyntharia Forest, assured that he had successfully fled the clutches of Vixus' army. By no means was he happy, as his heart was troubled by the fear of the fate that was in store for those left behind. There was little capacity for thoughts on his well-being and safety, but he did notice that the forest of Xyntharia was quiet and was thankful that they had been granted safe passage through the elven realm.

Kallogar sat beside his king and appeared to share his feelings in the overwhelming tragedy. "Vixus will suffer for this betrayal, but the world of FéLorën, itself, will also suffer. The gods look down upon us, and are no doubt pained by the behavior of humankind."

King Mullen III nodded. "Peace had been sustained for two hundred years. What has happened to the natural laws of FéLorën? Do they exist any longer? Did they ever exist, or have we just prolonged the inevitable course of our violent ways? Have we been fools to let our guard down? To trust in humankind? To assume that people could adhere to such a strict, moral code?

Lord Wen sat across from his king. He leaned forward. "Leave questions such as those for the Elders of the High Council to ponder over. We have a duty to our kingdom."

Manzer shifted in his seat and turned to address his king. "Perhaps, it is not in our nature to live as holy beings. We should have seen this day coming, just as Vixus has. We could have been the ones prepared to strike, instead of being the victim to the will of another brave enough and wise enough to see what was coming. What has peace brought us? Our people have suffered, greatly, from the chains of peace. Unable to advance, to enrich our lives, the people have turned on us, turned their natural aggression inward and forced us into this predicament."

"I have listened to your concerns," King Mullen III said. "I know the delicate balance of peace that has existed for so many years was fragile. I am no fool. We would have made the move to claim the Desert Portal, when the time was right. It would not have been as haphazard as our Vixus neighbors, but their act of war is an act of desperation, no more desperate than our attempt to advance into the desert lands. We are all to blame for this tragedy."

"Do not say such a thing, Your Majesty," Kallogar said. "Do not think you are as evil as Vixus? You would never have stooped so low."

King Mullen III nodded in understanding, but sighed with the thought of a thousand regrets. He stared out of the carriage at the large, glorious trees of Xyntharia Forest as it made its way toward the river. "I should have contacted the High Council of FéLorën sooner. I should not have believed that we could manage our needs without outside assistance. If we are to truly be a unified land, then we must be of a unified mind."

A battle cry rang through the air. The unique sound could only be the voices of the Din Naqui. The horses startled and before the traveling caravan could get its bearings, arrows plummeted from the trees. The knight that rode beside the carriage was struck in the neck and a series of arrows buried into the carriage walls. The Din Naqui elves swarmed from the forest and collided against Mullen's unprepared troops.

Leaning out the window, King Mullen III looked to the head of the carriage and noticed no one was guiding the horses. The knights who traveled in front of the carriage had fallen to arrows and the carriage trampled over their bodies. "No one is guiding the carriage," he yelled. "We must get out!"

His cries came too late. The carriage continued, out of control, the wheels struggling to carry over boulders and plants on the forest terrain, as the horses panicked and headed forward, blind, off the cleared trail. The carriage became lodged on a ledge and the horses broke free, the wheels splitting beneath the carriage, before toppling over into Xyntharia River.

The carriage filled with water from the roaring river. King Mullen III tried to escape. He pulled Kallogar through the carriage door as Lord Wen and Manzer attempted to slip through the adjacent window. Lord Wen managed to squeeze through the tight space, but Manzer was caught with the bulk of his armor. The carriage spun onto its side from the rapid current, blocking the only exit for him as the carriage slammed against the rocks of the river floor. Pinned underwater, all Manzer could do was watch his companions swim to the surface as he lay imprisoned in the carriage. His life faded, as the ice-cold water of the river filled his lungs.

On the river's surface, Lord Wen called out to his king, "Let the current of the water carry you!" His voice was barely audible over the turbulent current. "The river will guide us!"

King Mullen III managed to swim to Lord Wen's side, with Kallogar on his back.

"I cannot swim," Kallogar screamed. "Let me go and save yourselves!"

King Mullen III refused his advisor's request. He grabbed hold of Lord Wen's outstretched hand and linked like a chain, they let the rapid current carry the three of them downstream.

Back on land, Mullen's knights were no match for the surprise attack of the Din Naqui and suffered a brutal massacre. The Din Naqui showed no mercy, sparing not a single Mullen life and suffering little to no casualties of their own.

King Mullen III ducked under water to avoid arrows flying overhead. When he came up for air, he felt Kallogar's body slide from his back. He clutched his advisor tight, until he noticed an arrow protruding from Kallogar's face. He hollered, in horror, then let go of his dead advisor, the body taken by the river until it was lodged against protruding rocks. The arrows continued to rain from above and the river ahead was barricaded by Din Naqui forces.

Aware of their fate, Lord Wen grabbed hold of the river's edge, his arm entangled in roots. King Mullen III was able to pull himself out of the water and Lord Wen followed. They were greeted by a gathering of Din Naqui. King Mullen III stared into their elven, unmerciful eyes.

The Din Naqui elves shared words amongst each other in their native tongue, words which King Mullen III could not understand, but it was apparent they were uninterested in keeping any hostages. Lord Wen screamed out loud in rage and swung his sword at the nearest Din Naqui in a final act of desperation. Three spears entered his chest simultaneously, before his sword could find its mark. A Din Naqui reached out and grabbed Lord Wen's head and pushed his thin, elven fingers through Lord Wen's terrified eyes. His screams were suffocated by his own blood, as the elf pushed him to the ground. Lord Wen shook in spasms until the remaining life drained from his body.

King Mullen III faced his aggressors. "I am King Mullen III, ruler of the kingdom of Mullen. Show mercy, if not for me, then for the land of Valice."

A Din Naqui swung his sword through King Mullen III's neck, decapitating him.

~CHAPTER 8~

Daylen stood on the mountain path, feeling the abundance of energy flowing through all things, and was conscious of the invisible force that held the secrets of creation. Zantigar had told him that this energy was magic, itself; and that his perception of this energy would help him discover his spell power. Through awareness, he would uncover the magic that resided within him.

He found himself at a graveyard, a plateau on the mountain ascent where a series of tombstones had been erected. Old, weather-beaten tombstones marked the graves of a long forgotten people, from a long forgotten time.

"Peculiar to find a graveyard all the way up here," Daylen said.

"There have always been people who have scaled the mountain to acquire wisdom and to feel a connection to the world. Many of which were non-magic wielders, who still felt the magic that surrounded the mountain. These graves mark the remains of such a clan of people, a people known as Jeverites. They had given up on what you may refer to as 'civilized' life, in order to live in harmony with the land. They were by no means saints, but they devoted their lives toward something more. They sought spiritual strength, instead of worldly goods. They sought harmony, in body and mind. It is said that the Jeverites were the last known race of people to speak the ancient language of FéLorën. Many of the words Erramond deciphered from the ancient language was obtained from the Jeverites and their writings." Zantigar paused, and pointed to a cliff, where characters were carved in the stone.

Daylen approached the ancient, foreign writing and placed his fingers over the etchings. "Do you know what they say, these writings?"

"No, I'm afraid not. I know some of the language, but not all, and these carvings are so old, it makes it near impossible for me to decipher. Erramond had written about the Jeverite people and their culture, and he remarked that most of their scriptures were descriptive passages of their visions and the insight found on the mountain." He moved back toward the graves. "Do you remember when I asked you who you are, when you first came to the cabin?"

"How could I forget?" Daylen commented.

"At first, you told me you were Daylen; naturally."

"Yes, I remember."

"Truth be told, the word Daylen has a specific meaning. Your father had given you a FéLorën name."

Daylen's eyes widened, hopeful for another clue as to any indication as to who his father was, as a person. "Explain."

"It means, 'of the way,' or more precisely, 'the way of FéLorën.' See, your father must have been a follower of FéLorën. I imagine he wanted you to follow in his steps."

Daylen nodded, filled with satisfaction. All was not in vain; his father would have been proud. It all made perfect sense. Knowing that his father was hunted, knowing that he would have a child, Donovan gave his son a name that could carry the legacy, the destiny that Daylen would one day embrace. He was 'Of the Way of FéLorën.' Daylen realized in this moment, with absolute clarity, that he would become just that.

Daylen now had the confidence and strength necessary to think clearly, to live purposefully. If he could see his reflection in a sparkling pool, he would notice that his eyes reflected this awareness- a peaceful, knowing gaze.

Zantigar had continued moving up the mountain and Daylen followed. Daylen was surprised to see just how far the graveyard extended, passing grave after grave, in a series that seemed to have no end. He felt an uncanny connection to the deceased. He could sense the lives these people lived. He seemed to feel their pain. It was not long before he felt as if he walked beside himself, somehow a spirit of the Jeverites, entering the lives the dead once lived.

"I would love nothing more, when I die, than to be buried on this mountain," Zantigar confessed. "I think I would have loved living with the Jeverites, as they had. It was an incredible honor to be buried on the mountain, for those closest to you to make the journey to the highest site and lay you to rest."

Daylen listened, in silence. He wondered if Zantigar would ever die, and if so, what miraculous age would it be in? By the day's end, he had passed many graves, experienced many thoughts outside himself. He felt a heavy weight on his shoulders and looked to Zantigar. He felt himself leave himself and enter Zantigar, just as he had done with those that lay buried under the tombstones, and not unlike entering the winged lion in his vision. He could see, feel and understand his companion like never before. He was taken back, for Zantigar appeared to be studying and listening to Daylen in the same fashion.

"Do you feel okay?" Zantigar asked. "You are stretching yourself far."

"I… don't know what is happening to me, I see things now. I know things. There is so much sadness in the world. So much suffering."

Zantigar had a somber look on his face that Daylen recognized well. "Do not make other people's sadness your own. You do not know what their experience was. The pain you feel is filtered through your own narrative. It could have been nothing of their personal experience. The trials have opened your eyes to a world larger than yourself. The experience can be exhausting. If you carry the burden of others, if you only accept the suffering, you will never be able to help others."

Daylen looked within and felt that he had been such a fool, so blind. He could not stand who he had been all his life. He was self-centered, concerned only with his small insignificant problems. He was quick to accept his past, what he had been. And it made it easy to move on, to let that old self die. He realized he was exactly who he needed to be now. "The pain is my pain," he whispered to himself, understanding that a duty for his life, a purpose, was slowly manifesting itself.

Zantigar seemed to be watching Daylen's actions very carefully as they walked. "As I told you when you first came to my cottage; there is no separation between you and the world. The mountain path, is good at opening your eyes to this fact."

"I don't know if I can handle this feeling much longer," Daylen sighed. He wondered what the world would be like when he returned to ground level. He pondered over Vixus, his homeland, and held an image of his mother in his mind. He did not know that his homeland was braced on the brink of war and the stability of the High Council of FéLorën, which instilled peace on the world for hundreds of years, had been discarded like yesterday's thoughts- but he sensed something was wrong. Something had always been wrong. Somehow the feelings of overwhelming sadness were connecting him to a chain of events occurring around him. Daylen placed his hand on the hilt of his sword and wondered, "How could I draw my sword on another living creature, after realizing they are a part of me?"

Zantigar led Daylen to a cliff. His thoughts went to Brunhylde, which was once his home. He thought of his childhood friend, Glazahn, and the lone tree; the tree which Glazahn could hear the voice of. Glazahn's voice came into his mind, a distant memory surfacing, "What you carve in me will be carved in you." He wondered where Glazahn was now.

Daylen did not notice Zantigar was beside him, until he heard his mentor's voice. "Close your eyes. Listen now to the inner voice of yourself, the voice of what you have become."

Daylen did as he was told. He sat on the cliff, his eyes closed, until he forgot he was sitting. He continued, until he forgot where he was. Forgetting where he was, he forgot who he was. All that existed was energy and he was a part of it. He saw visions emerge from the darkness of his closed eyes. A symbol flashed before him. He recognized it. He thought of Lonely Wood. A wolf entered his visions. It barked and it howled, but there was no fear, only a sublime connection. The symbol returned and a whisper accompanied it. At first the light was blinding, but after a moment, the vision became so clear that he was shocked out of his meditation, and he opened his eyes.

"Ghost," Daylen whispered. He had not dreamed of Ghost in a long time, it seemed. Daylen gave a deep sigh and looked around. Zantigar was nowhere to be found. He was no longer certain just how long he had been sitting. He had just come from a place where time did not exist, the pain of standing made him realize he had sat for a while. He called out for Zantigar but got no response.

Daylen would have considered waiting, but he saw a figure far ahead of the mountain path. The figure appeared to be transparent and was visible only in waves. He was stunned, certain it was Ghost and his heart raced with anticipation. Somehow, someway, the figure had entered his conscious space. Here on the mountain, anything seemed possible. It was no trick, he could see the figure with his own eyes and with the awareness, the figure turned and headed up the trail, leaving him alone as it turned up the bend of the mountain pass.

Daylen followed. Reaching the bend, he could see Ghost far ahead. Ghost seemed to sense Daylen's presence, for it turned as if looking over its shoulder. Daylen halted, cautious, for he knew that Nasavine had tricked him once before. He narrowed his eyes, attempting to identify the figure's face. Nasavine's face emerged in the transparent figure. The image stayed long enough to startle Daylen, but then Ghost's face became transparent again.

Daylen did not believe Ghost was Nasavine. A stronger feeling overcame him, a feeling that Ghost was communicating with him, aware of Daylen's thoughts. Having thought of Nasavine, Ghost became Nasavine. He was experiencing his next trial. With this realization, Daylen continued to follow, no more afraid of Ghost then he was of his own mind. Daylen did not feel the urge to rush, he knew he was being led, and Ghost was a safe distance in front of him. Perhaps, Daylen was still in meditation, sitting in quiet reflection. The thought passed as quick as it came to him. It did not matter, either way.

Ghost rounded another bend. Daylen followed and found himself on a strange plateau, where wildlife grew in thick patches, where wildlife had no purpose being. The atmosphere was thicker, too, abundant in oxygen where it had once been thin and sparse. Large, lush bushes and trees blocked a stone structure from view. Daylen stepped closer with curiosity. A figure moved from behind the shrubbery. Approaching the plant life, he parted the leaves with a wave of his hand, no longer obstructing his vision. Expecting the figure to be Ghost, he was surprised to see Zantigar standing over shattered fragments of glittering red rubies.

~CHAPTER 9~

Daylen found himself before a fountain. It looked like a mystical shrine, surrounded by stone pillars and covered in overgrown ivy. Shards of glimmering rubies lay at his feet. Ghost was nowhere to be found. Looking closer now, it was apparent that the rubies were broken fragments of Zantigar's powerful staff. Daylen moved forward, trying to grasp the totality of what he was witnessing. "Zantigar?"

Zantigar was startled by Daylen's voice. He stumbled away from the fountain. "I was hoping you wouldn't have to see this."

Daylen shook his head. "I was following some… thing. What are you doing?"

Zantigar stood tall. "I am fulfilling my duty."

"Your staff… what have you done? I thought the staff was your life?"

"Was my life; yes. That is an appropriate analysis. Not any longer. I have destroyed it; the staff is no more. No longer will I be controlled by its existence." Zantigar raised his arms into the air. "I am free; at last."

"Free?" Daylen questioned.

Zantigar dropped his hands back to his side. He was shaking. "I can die, now. I can be at peace."

Daylen took a deep breath, trying to interpret what he was witnessing. "Is this a test?"

"No test, Daylen. The tests are over. You have what it takes to cast magic. I have shown you all that you needed to see."

Daylen shook his head in defiance. "How can you say that? I haven't even learned a spell."

Zantigar's face narrowed. "You fool, you still don't know a thing, even when it flashes right before your eyes."

Daylen thought to the symbol that had, literally, flashed before his eyes while he was meditating. Zantigar seemed to sense Daylen's sudden awareness. All he had to do was look into Daylen's eyes and he knew everything.

Zantigar nodded. "Yes, you see it, now." He stood like a crazy old man, his wild, white hair blowing in the fierce mountain winds. His words shocked

Daylen to the core. "You are no longer a Seeker, but an Initiate. Soon, you will be a fantastic wizard, the likes of which the world has never seen. You are everything I had hoped you would be, and more."

Daylen walked over to the fountain. All he had to do was call upon the symbols in his mind. He knew it would take some time to fully understand what the spell was that he had created. A spellbook would be necessary to catalogue the symbols and define them, until it became second nature to him. However, he was too worried about Zantigar's state of mind then with his own powers. Zantigar's life force, his staff, was in pieces on the ground and Zantigar looked as if the rising winds would blow him off the mountain and into the clouds below.

"It is not over yet," Daylen insisted. "You cannot leave, not now."

Zantigar laughed, in an attempt to make Daylen feel foolish. "Come now, Daylen. You know as well as I that you cannot be attached to others." He grabbed at his robe and patted his chest in awareness of his physical form. "You cannot be attached to the physical objects of this world. Do I need to teach you the importance of separation? About the power of nonattachment?"

Daylen looked within himself. His intuition was not driven by fear of loss. "It doesn't make sense that you would choose this now."

"It makes perfect sense!" Zantigar yelled. "The staff is gone and soon I will feel the reality of what it is to be a two hundred- and fifty-year-old wizard. I expect the pain of dying will not last long for me. My body should give out as quickly as a fleeting breath."

"When?" Daylen wondered.

Zantigar shook his head. "I… do not know." He laughed at the realization. "I have never experienced this before." He seemed excited and smiled at the thought. A moment later, his face became somber again. "I have seen too much, Daylen. I have felt too much agony. Meeting you was a blessing. My curse has been lifted and I can finally be at peace."

"Why? Why must you die because of me?"

I knew when I met you that you held a gift beyond magic. You were innocent, pure, and good at heart… everything I am not. I have recaptured, through you, what has been missing from my life."

"My innocence is your death? How is that right?"

"Your rebirth is my death. We are connected, Daylen. Just as I live in you, you live in me. I have learned from you, just as you have learned from me."

"You learned from me? What have you learned?"

"More than you know. In my mind, you have been the teacher and I the student."

Daylen shook his head. "Impossible."

"You know that isn't true. Impossible only with a limited perception. The truth is, you no longer need me, and I no longer need you; not in this form, at least. The final experience before you and I can both be complete… loss. I lose my life and you lose a mentor. Yet fear not, Daylen. We both live on, in our own way, transformed… in our own way."

Daylen stared at Zantigar in a long moment of silence, searching for something more behind his words then what he let on. "So this is it? What about the mountain top?"

"This is the top, Daylen. It is all around you." Zantigar motioned for Daylen to look behind him, through the vegetation surrounding the fountain.

Daylen walked through the trees, past the leaves and the shrubbery and observed the scenery before him. Below them and around them storm clouds coursed with energy and the air was charged with electricity. "I was on the top and didn't know it. I was too busy, trying to catch this mysterious figure…"

Zantigar was not listening. He was chanting words that seemed to call upon the storm clouds, exciting the energy within them. Thunder roared and lightning shot through the sky. He lifted his arms to the sky and shouted to the heavens.

Daylen watched Zantigar and noticed the world begin to blur. He was uncertain whether his eyes deceived him or if the world around him had actually begun to bend and sway. Colors filled his vision and dizziness seized him.

Several yards away, Ghost stood staring at Daylen. The ground was wobbling, and it prevented Daylen from being able to balance himself. He looked to Zantigar, to call out and show the wizard that Ghost was real, but Zantigar was caught in an ancient ritual, dancing like a tribesman through some chaotic, life altering spell.

Daylen stared into the distorted world and could see the energy that he had been feeling since his rebirth. In the fields of energy were symbols, once foreign, but now were as clear as his own language. In the midst of the chaotic display of Zantigar's spell, Daylen realized that Zantigar was trying to show him something. There was one last lesson to learn, after all. Through the chaos was a way to peace. The symbols, dancing before his eyes, pointed the way toward understanding. If he could break the code of the chaos before him then he could seize the order necessary to reach Ghost, who still stood, a transparent figure, several yards away. He closed his eyes to block the chaos, but it only blinded him from the symbols he needed to see. He opened his eyes again and witnessed the symbols come together with uncanny order and he spoke the message aloud, intuitively. They were pieces of a greater symbol and when they realigned and came together he recognized the symbol as that of the one in Lonely Wood. It was the same symbol he saw moments before while meditating, and he stood, transfixed, and spoke as if in a trance. What came from his mouth were words he had never spoken, never knew he understood, as if he was remembering them from a previous existence.

By the command of his words, the world silenced. Daylen stood, wide-eyed, for he had cast his first spell. He had calmed the chaos, stripped the illusion of Zantigar's magic by countering Zantigar's spell. The student had overpowered the teacher.

Zantigar fell to the ground from his trance like dance and Daylen thought Zantigar had fallen dead. He rushed to Zantigar's side, relieved to see the old wizard was still breathing. Zantigar coughed. The spell he had cast had weakened him. Oddly enough, Daylen was not weakened from the spell he had cast. "Your magic is strong, indeed. You have calmed the chaos. You have calmed my spirit. Thank you."

Daylen helped Zantigar to his feet. Zantigar was looking past him and Daylen remembered there was a presence that was waiting for him. Noticing Ghost, Zantigar motioned for Daylen to turn around.

Daylen turned to where Ghost was standing and saw his father. He had never seen his father before, of course, but it was not necessary. It was his father, standing before his eyes, in flesh and blood, as certain as Daylen knew himself. "Father?"

Donovan smiled but did not speak. His face expressed pride and it was all that Daylen ever hoped to see.

"I will walk the way of FéLorën, father."

Donovan moved toward Daylen and outstretched his arms. Daylen met him halfway, and with tears in his eyes, reached forward to embrace his father. However, instead of a warm embrace, Daylen's arms went through him. Donovan was nothing more than a spirit, which entered Daylen's own. Daylen closed his eyes and felt complete, a feeling of total peace. The mysterious darkness within him had been illuminated and the emptiness he had felt had vanished.

After a moment of reflection, Daylen turned to face Zantigar. Zantigar looked older, on the verge of death. Daylen felt sadness and happiness in a vast well inside him. "It was my father, Zantigar. Ghost was my father."

Zantigar shook his head, but he was smiling. "Daylen… Ghost was yourself."

"It was my father, I saw him."

"You saw exactly what you needed to see in order to embrace your own self."

Daylen looked away. Zantigar was right. He had failed to see it, but Zantigar had not. That was the reason why he felt he still needed Zantigar. There was always more to understand, always further to dive. He was sad to see the old wizard, dying before his eyes.

Zantigar approached Daylen. "You saw what you needed to see. And now? What do you see?"

"You are dying, Zantigar. And yet, there is more I need to understand about this world."

Zantigar nodded and Daylen knew what Zantigar was going to say before the words ever left his mouth. "Your journey toward understanding will never be finished."

There was a sparkle of sadness in Zantigar's eyes and it seemed far greater than Daylen's own sadness. No one understood the eternal learning process better than Zantigar, having lived so many years. "I am not afraid, Zantigar. If you need to… go; then you can go."

Zantigar shook his head. A dim glow radiated from his faded eyes. "I, too, had a vision. Now is not the time for me to die, there is one last thing I must do."

PART V

THE DARK ONE

G.G.

Consciousness is all; existing to discover itself.
All is vibration. All is music. All is singing, "Creation."
Close your eyes and know the creator; Open your eyes and create.
-Daylen of the Light; 237 A.F.

~CHAPTER 1~

Daylen brushed his hair from his eyes. He felt the brilliance of the sun's rays and the brisk air sweep across his skin. He looked to Zantigar, who was slumped over a natural wooden cane, in sharp contrast to the magnificent staff that used to support him. He was in need of the aid of a walking stick now, more than ever, as he followed Daylen down the mountain.

During their descent, Daylen wondered just what kind of experience Zantigar had on the mountaintop. "Your vision, what was it?"

Zantigar seemed to know the deeper question. "You wonder if it includes you."

Zantigar's suspicion was true enough, but Daylen's dependency was not like it had been in the past. He was confident, assured. He knew, deep down, as sure as he knew his own name, that a piece of Zantigar existed inside him and would be there forever. "Well, I know what I need to do; for once in my life."

Zantigar smiled. "Without fear, the path becomes clear. And what does the future have in store for you, do you mind me asking?"

"I am going to Brunhylde, to set my mother free."

Zantigar nodded. "You will. I do not doubt it."

"And you? You avoid my inquiry. Why?"

Zantigar stopped and waited until he had Daylen's full attention. "It is a simple matter, really. What is in store for me no longer involves you, but you can accompany me all the same, if you like."

Without even knowing the destination, he was quick to respond. "It would be an honor." He did not have the spell power of his companion, but he had learned his first spell. When he found the opportunity to make his own spellbook, he would craft it with care. "I am ready to make my spellbook, now. I will bind it with a sturdy cover. Do you know what I will carve into its surface?"

Zantigar gave a curious glance.

"A winged lion," Daylen announced.

Zantigar raised his eyebrows in surprise. "Really?"

"Yes, who knows, maybe it will scare anyone who thinks about opening it!"

For the first time in a long while, they shared laughter. As the day progressed, so did their descent, and they spoke of kind musings and of simple pleasures. However, Daylen recognized that Zantigar had to stop for his breath often. His energy was diminishing quickly, and by the end of the day, Daylen had grown concerned. "How do you expect to carry on? You are growing weaker."

"I can still fulfill my duty."

"Is that so?" Daylen pressed, the curiosity in Zantigar's plan intriguing him.

Zantigar did not respond. He stood up with the help of his walking stick and continued down the mountain. Daylen looked to the road ahead and his thoughts dwelled upon the present moment.

A dark cloud filled his mind. He saw a dark apparition with a pair of glowing red eyes. He was overcome with sadness and pain, and he felt as though his journey would lead him toward immense suffering. That instant, he thought of what Zantigar would one day have to face and wondered if his fate was the same. "Your mission… you are going to the face the Dark One, aren't you?"

Zantigar stopped on the path and lowered his head.

"What troubles you?" Daylen said.

"I was hoping that you would never hear that name."

"Why?"

"So you would never be cursed."

Daylen believed that he was getting quite good at interpreting Zantigar's riddles, but this behavior stumped him. "Nasavine had told me about his presence, but I don't know much else."

"And you should keep it that way," Zantigar replied.

"Well, I think it is important for me to know."

"No!" Zantigar snapped.

"I cannot be left naïve about something, or someone, as powerful as Death."

Zantigar walked a moment longer in silence, as if determining the best way to approach the subject. "What do you know about the Dark One?"

"I know he takes the souls of wizards," Daylen said.

Zantigar nodded. "I was hoping you would never hear of him, at all. That way, he would not be able to find you. The Dark One only has power over a wizard when a wizard becomes aware of his existence. Once you know he is real, then you are doomed to die by his command. In this fashion, the Dark One is Death. He grows more powerful, has more dominance over this world, the more that wizards fear him."

Daylen questioned Zantigar's position on the matter. "What is there to fear? Can't you simply decide not to believe in him?"

"You cannot dispel him any more than you can convince yourself that you will never die."

"So, the Dark One is real?"

"To those who know him." Zantigar bore a tired look in his eyes. "To feel him is to suffer."

Daylen had felt capable of facing the Dark One, until now. His ignorance led him to accept the Dark One, to trust in those final moments of his life, even if it was at the will of one so mysterious. Yet, he did not expect to hear Zantigar admit defeat about anything or to anyone.

Daylen studied Zantigar with probing eyes. "Is your death to be at the hands of the Dark One? Is this your duty?"

Zantigar remained silent.

Daylen wondered about Zantigar's private demons but was hesitant to ask about the dark memories locked in Zantigar's mind. Daylen thought of Nasavine. It seemed that it was that little imp's sole purpose to tell him about the Dark One. Daylen had grown perceptive, and he trusted his instinct, now, above all else. "The Dark One has plans for me, too. Nasavine was intent on possessing my mind in order to curse me with a similar fate."

He looked to the path below his feet, but his mind was somewhere else, battling his inner darkness. "We must do all the good that we can, now, while we are free to choose, while we still live. We know not when our time comes, so we are to live our lives now, the only time that exists. The only time that matters. Now. We would be foolish to spend our time on any other moment. In this moment there is life, and in this moment, alone, we have the power to act. I suppose if it is our fate to confront the Dark One, then it will be in that moment our choices will be revealed to us, and there is no good dwelling on it any more than that."

~CHAPTER 2~

Zantigar's health was deteriorating at a rapid rate, his strength depleting as they came closer to the bottom of the mountain. Daylen did not have the luxury of being on a spirit journey like on the ascent, where time seized to exist. Day after day descending the snowy peak took its toll on him and it was clear it was taking an even more devastating toll on Zantigar. At times, Daylen had to support him. At other times, he had to force him to rest and in the harder moments, Daylen helped him eat and drink. Daylen could feel an uneasy force, as if the Dark One was closing in. The wind cried and the air was cold. Daylen pushed Zantigar onward in hopes that they could reach the bottom of the mountain before he became too weak to travel. At the bottom of the mountain the land was sure to be feeling the blessings of the Season of Bloom, the weather warm and life abundant and flourishing.

Zantigar had grown distant. It was as if a darkness was consuming him from the inside and working at an alarming rate. It was not long before Zantigar was babbling to himself, speaking in words that Daylen could not make out. It reminded Daylen of Zantigar's weaker moments at the cabin, when he was heard yelling to himself.

Daylen feared the worst. "We should find another place to rest."

Zantigar shook his head in defiance but fell to the ground. Daylen attempted to stop the old wizard's fall, but it only made matters worse, as Zantigar shoved Daylen away instead of allowing him to help.

"You will not get me," Zantigar spat.

Daylen realized Zantigar was not speaking to him but conversing with his inner demons.

"Face me now; I am not afraid of you!" Zantigar's eyes filled with a blend of rage and hopelessness. When his eyes met Daylen's, his stare softened. The site of Daylen pulled him back from a place of darkness. He shook his head back and forth and placed his head in his hands.

Daylen kneeled and placed his hand on Zantigar's forehead. "It is the Dark One, isn't it? The Dark One speaks to you. Talk to me, tell me what he is saying, tell me what I can do."

Zantigar rolled on his side, content to rest in the middle of the path.

"Zantigar…" Daylen pleaded.

Zantigar's face filled with rage. "You cannot have me!" He rose to his feet, pushing Daylen back. He was consumed with chaotic strength, his temper commanding him forward. "I hate this world… I didn't ask to be here. Choices… strings on a marionette are all we are! I will not be controlled… I am a Chaos Wizard!"

Daylen placed his hand on Zantigar to comfort him. Zantigar attempted to shoo Daylen away, but Daylen swiped Zantigar's frail arm to the side.

"Damn you, boy, don't you know who I am? I could crush you!"

With his hands firm against Zantigar's body, Daylen spoke a short phrase of foreign words. His hand glowed with a radiant light and a moment later, Zantigar's nerves had calmed, his eyes lowered, and his body settled into a passive state. He dropped to one knee and then softly to the ground, resting his head on the dirt.

"Your spell," Zantigar whispered. "It did not cause you pain to cast it."

It was true, that unlike most wizards, the spell Daylen cast did not seem to affect him physically. Daylen ignored Zantigar's observation and reached into a pouch on his belt and handed Zantigar a few berries.

Zantigar accepted the food. "I hope I did not hurt you, Daylen. I… I am not feeling very well."

"It is the Dark One. He has a strong hold on you, and he is trying to break your will."

Zantigar outstretched his arms. "Your spell is a blessing. This peacefulness was needed." Zantigar stared off into space and his body relaxed. "There is a healing quality to your spell, did you know that?"

Daylen placed his hand on Zantigar's forehead and felt the burn of a fever.

Zantigar seemed to be remembering something from his past. His eyes were distant, stuck in a time long ago, as if remembering something once forgotten. "When I was a young wizard, before I was old enough for the Academy, I lived on a ranch with my older brother, Thamus."

"You had a brother?" Daylen took a seat on a nearby rock, pleased that Zantigar was resting.

"Yes, I had a brother," Zantigar's voice cracked. Sweat was dripping down his face. "He was intolerable most the time, like all brothers can be, but I could depend on him. He was much different than I. He was a gaming man, built like a barbarian, and possessed no magic potential, whatsoever. He loved to sword fight. He would play with the squires in town and dreamed of becoming a knight. You could say we were opposites, he and I."

Zantigar paused and repositioned himself, leaning up against a bolder. "I will never forget the day he encountered the king, face to face. We lived in poverty, so it was never expected to be graced by His Majesty. Thamus was like a little boy, so excited and full of energy, and he could not wait to tell his story to me..."

* * *

"Zantigar! Zantigar, you will not believe who I saw today!" Thamus yelled, running into the house in search of Zantigar.

Young Zantigar sat at his desk, as he usually did, his face buried in books. He was deep in study, with quill in hand. "I am busy, brother, this better be important."

"Oh, but it is!" Thamus exclaimed.

Zantigar looked up and could see Thamus' face filled with joy. He sighed and placed his quill on the table.

"I saw the king today! He spoke to me!"

Zantigar assumed that his brother was playing a practical joke on him, so he said, with sarcasm, "Oh really? What did he say to you?"

Thamus' eyes widened, failing to catch the sarcasm, or simply ignoring it. "I was playing with my sword, out in the fields, you know, just minding my own, when the king approached from out of the woods, not far from the windmill."

Zantigar raised an eyebrow in suspicion. "I find that hard to believe, Thamus. Walking from the woods, alone, the king?"

"I know! That is what is so amazing. He was with no guards, no knights, nobody."

"And you are certain it was the king?"

Thamus nodded with certainty. "When he came closer, I noticed that he was bleeding from several large wounds. He had been in a battle with some type of beast. I didn't know what to do, so I fell to my knees. Then he said to me," Thamus lowered his voice to mimic the voice of the king, "Stand up, boy, stand up. Let me see your sword." Going back to his normal voice, Thamus continued, "So, I handed him my sword and he told me he was going to take it."

"You let him take your sword?" Zantigar hissed.

"Well, of course. Wouldn't you?"

"Well," Zantigar said, "I suppose I would, considering I don't have much care for swords in the first place. But you… you worked for years to afford that sword."

Thamus adjusted his posture in protest, standing tall. "I gave it with honor. Just imagine, the king asking me for a sword. It's not like I had a choice, anyway."

Zantigar began to suspect what this story was all about. Thamus was out playing and lost his sword, and this was all some elaborate lie that he would use on his father to be spared a beating. The thought of Thamus being punished for his stupidity caused Zantigar to smile with guilty pleasure. Perhaps, Thamus would be whipped, that seemed a suitable punishment. He begged Thamus to continue, for humor's sake. "Why did the king want your sword?"

"That is the amazing thing, brother. His sword had shattered in battle. The king said to me that a real champion never travels without a sword. By giving him my sword, he could keep his honor."

Zantigar laughed. "Well, I guess that just shows that you can never be a champion, now. Your sword is gone for good, and you will never be able to afford another!"

"True, I will never see my sword again…" Thamus pulled a crumbled piece of parchment from his pocket. "But he gave me this."

"Let me see that," Zantigar snatched the parchment from Thamus' hands, eager to see the lengths at which Thamus would go to tell a lie. However, Zantigar read the words with amazement. "By the gods, Thamus, this has the royal seal on it. The signature, it is none other than the King's!"

Thamus smiled. "I know. I have been trying to tell you…"

Zantigar shook his head. "Look here, he says you can visit the castle and pick any weapon you see fit from the armory and keep it for yourself!"

Thamus bore a smile that spread the width of his face. "Jealous?"

"Yes," Zantigar exclaimed. "In fact, I am. Of you, of all people! You lucky bastard, you." Zantigar handed the parchment back to Thamus. "What I wouldn't give to walk the king's palace halls and pick a staff of my fancy."

"Did you read the rest? I have been offered a role as a constable. Do you see the potential? Once a member of the royal guard, I could become a knight!"

Zantigar nodded in agreement. This could change everything for their family. Zantigar may have a way into the king's good graces yet, all on account of his bumbling brother.

* * *

Zantigar paused from telling his story. His eyes filled with tears and when they fell down his cheeks they blended with the sweat from fever. It appeared his memories had led to a darker time. Daylen sat motionless, waiting for Zantigar to explain, wondering why the tale of his brother affected him so much.

"Thamus had been ecstatic on that day. You should have seen the sparkle in my brother's eyes. I will never forget it. I think about his happiness that day, often, and I thought about it when I watched him fall."

"Fall?" Daylen asked.

Zantigar sat in silence, as if he did not hear Daylen's question.

"Are you okay, Zantigar?"

"I am fine, Daylen. I am fine."

Daylen was not convinced. The sadness in Zantigar's eyes was the same sadness that he had seen often in the old wizard. He felt that he was moments away from an unsettling key to Zantigar's past, but he did not push for this knowledge. "Is the Dark One with you? Is he still in your head?"

"Always," Zantigar sighed. "He has always been here."

Daylen shook his head, unable to imagine the turmoil. He had prepared himself to hear the voice of Death call his name. Curiosity drove him. Yet, he understood the implications and the dangers of playing with such a mysterious fire.

~CHAPTER 3~

The bottom of Mount Omera was close. The accomplishment brought a feeling of triumph to Daylen, but it was overshadowed by Zantigar's condition. Zantigar's mind was still in turmoil and when Daylen's calming spell would wear off, he would return to maddening rants, only to be placed under Daylen's spell again.

Zantigar hesitated before proceeding with the final steps toward the foot of the mountain. Overcome with exhaustion he took a seat on a nearby rock. Just around the next bend was the arch, the gateway to Mount Omera. It felt like a lifetime ago that Daylen passed through it. "The bottom of the mountain is just ahead."

Zantigar shook his head, as if he didn't want to hear about it. "I have not spoken of my brother, Thamus, to anybody… since his death."

Daylen worried over Zantigar's failing mental state. "Why are you bringing this up now? We need to save our strength, both physical and emotional."

Zantigar turned away. "There is something I want to say… before I die."

"There is still time," Daylen said.

Zantigar had no interest in moving. "I killed my brother, Daylen."

Daylen was quiet a moment. The feeling Daylen had on the mountain, the sadness he saw in Zantigar that he could not place, was bubbling to the surface. "I'm sure you did no such thing,' Daylen comforted, brushing dirt off Zantigar's robe. "You are confused."

Zantigar slouched forward. "Thamus… I killed him. He was about to fall. He needed my help, all I had to do was reach down and pull him up, but I didn't."

Daylen struggled to make sense of the fragmented memory. "Because you couldn't, Zantigar. If you were able then you would have. Don't be hard on yourself."

"That's right. I couldn't. I could not save him because several feet away my staff was also about to fall. It was lodged, ever so fragile, on roots projecting from the cliff side. The gentlest of winds, would send it into the abyss below." A look of horror filled Zantigar's face, his hand outstretched as if reliving the delicate memory. "I chose the staff over my brother. I told Thamus to hold on, despite his pleas. I called him a moron, told him he did this to himself, and that he must suffer the consequences."

Zantigar broke down into tears. "I didn't want him to die, I just wanted him to wait. The winds were picking up and there wasn't anything I could use to reach the staff. I tried to hurry, I tried to find a branch or something."

Daylen shook his head. "The Dark One is telling you lies; you must not listen."

"I wish it were all a lie. For over two hundred years I have wished. The staff was more important than anything else. Don't you see how the staff was a curse, how my life, my power was afforded to me at the expense of all that truly mattered? The staff had kept me alive to feel the pain."

"You said yourself you did not want Thamus to die, you were just too late. You thought he could hold out, you thought you could do it all." Daylen consoled.

"I couldn't find a branch, but there was Thamus' sword. The sword he earned from the king, the one he chose for himself in the armory. It was sheathed on his belt and if I had the sword, I could reach the staff. Thamus was hanging by his fingers, he couldn't hand me the sword. So, I leaned over the ledge, stretched until my hand reached the sword's hilt. My body, pressed against my brother's until he screamed out, unable to hold on any longer…"

Zantigar paused, his mouth drooping. "I saw his face, saw the look he gave me when he realized I was not reaching for his hand, but for his sword. I think he gave up then. In that moment, there was nothing worth holding on to. I watched him fall, as my only thought was to grab the hilt of the sword before it was too late."

Zantigar clenched his hand into a fist. "I grabbed it just in time, it slid from his sheath as he plummeted." It took him a moment to continue, as if the words to follow were too painful to speak out loud. He paused as if waiting for the courage to say the truth. "My only thought was relief; relief that I had grabbed the sword in time."

Daylen yelled, "It's not true, Zantigar! The Dark One is trying to break you. You would have saved him if you could, you cared about him, or else you wouldn't have felt so much pain all this time."

Zantigar did not appear to be listening. "Why didn't I just help him up first? The wind never came. The staff could have waited."

"Regardless of whether it is true or not, it is all part of the past and you have redeemed yourself. You saved the world from the Dark Knights of Omnias, you spread the word of FéLorën. You have broken the staff, now. You have lived a life full of legendary deeds that will be remembered for all time. You, of all people, told me to live in the present moment, and your brother's death was over two hundred years ago!"

Zantigar looked up to Daylen. "You don't understand. The staff is what gave me the power to do those legendary things. I shouldn't have had it; they never should have happened. I should have saved my brother and then maybe, just maybe, the staff would have fallen from a gust of wind and freed me of my enslavement. Instead, I chose power, nothing more. How could I ever forget, how could I look to the present, when the past was my reason for existing?"

Daylen sighed. "Then you have suffered enough for a thousand deaths. You are forgiven. You cannot collapse on me, now, when we are so close. When the Dark One is so near."

Zantigar sat in silence, but Daylen knew that Zantigar's mind was anything but silent. He could only imagine the chaos swirling through his mind. Zantigar was an easy prey for the Dark One, already falling victim to his power.

"Rise to your feet, Zantigar."

Zantigar, much to Daylen's surprise, did as he was told, as if he was unable to think for himself. "Tonight, Daylen. Tonight."

Something about Zantigar's voice and the cold, distant look in his eyes chilled Daylen. "What about tonight, Zantigar?"

Zantigar shook his head, as if to break a spell of dizziness. "Tonight… we must get plenty of rest."

"Yes, I agree, but the day is just getting started and we have to cover a lot of territory. Your cabin is not much further. We must press on."

~CHAPTER 4~

The sun made its descent, the land had grown quiet. A cold sweat covered Zantigar's forehead. He had not spoken a word since the retelling of his brother's death. He just stared, vacant. He brought his arm up to his face and wiped sweat onto his sleeve. "Daylen, do me a favor, would you?"

"Anything."

Zantigar pointed to the west. "Just through those trees you will find a pond of crystal fresh drinking water, the most refreshing water in the known world. We cannot pass that up, my friend. My knees, they are weak."

Daylen nodded. "I understand, I will get some for us. Just wait here."

"I'll get started on a camp for the night," Zantigar explained.

"Not without your ruby staff you won't. No spell casting for you. Just wait until I get back."

Daylen walked into the trees, in the direction that Zantigar had suggested. As he disappeared from the trail, his instincts told him something bad waited for him. So, he moved with cautious steps, checking back often, until Zantigar was well out of sight. After a significant distance was between them Daylen began to question whether or not a pond even existed. Just before turning back, the noticed the pond. The water was not as clear as Zantigar suggested, but it was refreshing. He knelt down and submerged his hands in the water and brought his cupped hands to his lips. Daylen found that the water was not nearly as remarkable as Zantigar suggested. In fact, it was impossible to differentiate it from any other pond he had frequented in his travels. Surely, Zantigar had made a mistake.

Daylen lowered his waterskin into the pond and realized Zantigar had lied to him. Zantigar wanted Daylen to be far away. In that moment of realization, his reflection in the water was covered by the face of another; a one-eyed man, his mouth sewn shut. Daylen stumbled backward, almost screaming. He brought his hand to his face then realized the face in the reflection was his own again.

Behind him, a loud explosion could be heard. Not far from where he had left Zantigar, flames of a wild fire rose above the treetops. He faced the pyrotechnic display and heard Zantigar's raging voice call out.

Daylen ran back into the trees. When he was close enough, he saw Zantigar standing between towering flames. In the middle of the path, Zantigar stood amidst the destruction of his own spell and a dark mass swayed, like an apparition, before him. "The Dark One," Daylen whispered to himself. His body froze, taken by a mysterious paralyzing force, and all he could manage to do was stare, his body locked in time.

The dark shape shifted and morphed into a figure cloaked in black. A hood shadowed the Dark One's face, and the deep shadows gave the illusion that he bore no face at all. However, two red, beady eyes radiated from the depths of the cap's shadow. Daylen could feel his heart pounding in his chest. He was witnessing the manifestation of a god and was helpless to act, wondering how it was possible for him to have become immobilized.

Daylen could only watch, as Zantigar fell to his knees. He must have been famished from the spell he cast, which had no effect on the Dark One at all, despite the surrounding trees scorched and in flames. Zantigar fell into a fit of coughs. Old, and tired, blood sprayed from his mouth with each hacking fit.

The Dark One pulled a thin silver staff from his cloak. At the top of the staff, a cloud of gray gasses spilled from an onyx stone. Cries filled the air. The spirits of all the Dark One's victims moaned in torment, radiating from the stone's center.

Daylen could not stand to watch but was forced to bear witness.

Zantigar lowered his head, bowing as if begging for death to come quick.

The Dark One spoke, it was a voice of many voices, speaking in unison. "You thought you could save Beauty, didn't you?"

With a wave of his hand, the Dark One placed his staff against Zantigar's forehead. "You will now die, and there is nothing you can do about it, despite even the will of Destiny, itself. And do you know why?"

Zantigar reached inside his robe and grabbed a small dagger.

"Because I am a god. Destiny has no control over me. Beauty will stay locked beneath the Moon Tower until I command otherwise. His prophecy to be used by Vamillion, alone."

Daylen was frozen in time, but his mind was not. His thoughts were reeling in a desperate attempt to make sense of what he was hearing. Vamillion, the Moon Tower, something about lost beauty. The meaning was unclear, but the path forward was not.

"Let this be your final thought, as your soul becomes mine," The Dark One concluded.

In one final act, Zantigar sprung the dagger from his robe and shoved the blade forward, burying it into the Dark One's chest. The Dark One appeared unfazed by Zantigar's action. It seemed the last fighting attempt of this mighty Legionnaire was pathetic, hopeless cause. The staff the Dark One wielded tugged at Zantigar's soul. He fell to the ground.

Daylen was dumbfounded. The Dark One stepped back, reached into the darkness of his cloak and pulled out the dagger. It was dropped to the ground where Zantigar's body had collapsed. Then, the Dark One returned with a blur into a shifting mass of shadows and disappeared from sight.

Daylen felt his shock recede and his anger subside as the spell that disabled him came to an end, freeing him from his captivity. As soon as his legs could move, he ran to Zantigar's side. He turned Zantigar's face toward him. Zantigar's eyes were clear orbs, each eye as empty as a crystal ball. His face was stiff in a terrified moment of agony. Daylen ran his soft hands over Zantigar's old face, relaxing it so that it bore the look of serenity.

Through tear-stricken eyes, Daylen turned to a shining object resting by his feet. He lowered his eyes, recognizing the mysterious dagger that Zantigar had kept secretly in his robe. It defied all reason, but the dagger was coated in blood. He reached down and picked up the dagger. He ran his finger across the flat edge, collecting the blood between his fingers.

Daylen stood and processed his newfound awareness. A soft chuckle of laughter could be heard. He turned in the direction of the laughter and saw Nasavine standing before him. Fueled with a passion he believed only Zantigar was capable of feeling, he raised the dagger toward Nasavine and glared into the imp's yellow eyes. "Where is he?"

Nasavine's laughter was silenced the moment he met Daylen's glare. He looked to the dagger and took a step backward. "Don't do anything foolish. I am innocent."

'It was you, wasn't it? You paralyzed me!"

"I could not let you face the Dark One." Nasavine's voice was coated with insincere sympathy. "For your own sake, young wizard. He would have destroyed you... and life has other plans for you, young wizard."

Daylen spoke between a series of deep breaths. "Tell me where I can find him!"

Nasavine challenged Daylen's glare. "What do you think you are going to do… kill the Dark One? No mortal can accomplish that. There is nothing you can do except count the days before he comes for you!"

Daylen was not deterred by Nasavine's empty threats. "I have seen though the illusion and I do not believe your lies." Daylen held the dagger out before him, revealing the blood collected on its surface. "The Dark One is no god. He has fooled the world with his magic, but he cannot fool the world any longer. I know the truth."

Nasavine's face distorted with disgust. "What truth?"

"That the Dark One is flesh and blood. He is nothing more than a Mageslayer, a common hunter. His prize is the soul of wizards who fall to his trickery. I want those souls set free."

"You do not have the nerve," Nasavine spat.

"I have the truth." Daylen struggled to believe it, even as he said the words. The Dark One was a powerful enough trickster, a powerful enough Illusionist, to plague every wizard's mind and fool the greatest Legionnaires. The Dark One was mortal, indeed, but he was still dangerous, the most dangerous person that Daylen could imagine. The Dark One knew how to let the power of a wizard's own mind destroy them.

"How do you kill a god?" Daylen asked.

Nasavine shrugged. "You can't."

Daylen smiled. "When no one believes he exists. All I need to do is spread the truth about the Dark One's fallacy and he will no longer have power over wizards. They will disregard his voice as a mere pest in their mind. His power will be stripped, and his life will be worthless, just like the lies he spreads."

"You underestimate the Dark One's power, boy. Your efforts will be worthless. What do you think, that by defeating the Dark One you shall conquer death? There is no escaping your inevitable doom."

"You are right. I will not escape death, but I have conquered the fear of death, and so shall all wizards of FéLorën. And as for the Dark One… well, he will fade away, to be forgotten with time."

"You won't live long enough to see the day. You think the Dark One won't stop you? He may be mortal, but he is still more powerful of a wizard than you will ever be!"

"We shall see about that. If you are so certain, then tell me where I can find him. Is it the Moon Tower? What does Vamillion have to do with all this? What beauty requires saving?"

"Not what, but who," Nasavine said. His face contorted with an unexpected realization. "You don't know about Beauty."

"Beauty is a person?"

Nasavine laughed. "You are more lost than I thought possible. He is not just any person, he is a prophet and the son of-" Nasavine stopped abruptly, wishing to say no more.

"Beauty is a boy?" Daylen's eyes widened. "A prophet… and the son of who?" He realized Nasavine had said too much and would no longer speak of it. Yet, Daylen had all he needed. Fate would take him to his homeland with new cause. He would travel to the heart of the Vixus kingdom, to the Moon Tower; home of Vamillion, the woman who had taken his father's life.

Daylen lowered the dagger to his side. "You tell the Dark One I am waiting. I'm sure he will know where to find me. I am not afraid."

Nasavine's face wrinkled. "The Dark One has no plans to kill you, not yet. Regardless, you should watch your back, young wizard. The road ahead is paved with the shroud of a poisonous cloud." He turned away from Daylen and sprang into the forest with his quick goat legs.

Daylen stood alone, looming over Zantigar's lifeless body. His thoughts fell upon the recent chain of events. If not for Zantigar's final resistance to death, the truth about the Dark One would not be evident. The Dark One spoke of an unfulfilled prophecy. Fitting the fragments of the story together it suddenly fell into place. Beauty, a prophet, had said that Zantigar would save him. Beauty was locked beneath the Moon Tower.

The Dark One killed Zantigar to stop the prophecy from coming true. Daylen closed his eyes and breathed in deeply. The rising anger passed over him and left like the wind. In the moment beyond the emotion, in the space between thought, a vision came to him. Perhaps, Beauty's prophecy would come true, after all. Zantigar was going to save Beauty, one way, or another, but not as any would expect or see coming.

Daylen took another deep breath and turned toward Mount Omera. For reasons unknown to him, Nasavine confirmed the Dark One had no intention of killing Daylen any time soon. There were forces at work, like the hands of a puppeteer, drawing him toward an inevitable, unknown future. He focused on the present moment, returning to the task at hand. He was drawn back to the mountain, to the graves of the Jeverites, and to fulfill Zantigar's wish to be buried amongst them. The time and the effort it would take to traverse the mountain again was of no concern.

Daylen learned that beyond mountains were more mountains. One does not overcome a mountain to enter the land of no mountains. No matter where he stood, no matter what his pursuit, there would always be a mountain to overcome. He leaned down and picked up Zantigar's frail body and turned back toward the gates of Mount Omera.

~CHAPTER 5~

It was a long climb back up the mountain, but the second trip was different. The hardship of travel was no dreamlike journey. It was harsh and grueling of a physical nature. Time, as strange as it flowed on the mountain top, was now a great obstacle to overcome. His trials were of patience, service, and duty. He had time to reflect on everything in his life, alone, in silence.

Reflecting on his training, Daylen knew that Zantigar was dead only in body. Zantigar was within him and Zantigar was all around him. An intelligent, dangerous, chaotic flow of energy was everywhere. It ruled the surface, material world, manifesting through the lives of all people as challenging life situations, obstacles and hardships, as well as fortune, blessings and happiness. Chaos was the master of unpredictability and change, all things temporal, which would always fade.

Travelling up the mountain, chaos manifested as Zantigar, himself, appearing like a guide. Daylen had ways of calming the chaotic tides and used these tools to carry out his duty. For Daylen's inner eye did not exist on the surface world, where Chaos ruled, he existed under the surface, where a deep stillness lied, which was master to all that was constant and eternal.

He would not be weakened by loss, for everything lost was only so on the surface. All that manifested on the surface was rooted, eternally, in the deeper world of stillness, where nothing could be lost, and nothing was gained.

Daylen buried Zantigar at the Jeverite gravesite. Placing the last rock over Zantigar's grave he stood a moment in silence. He would carry the memory of him as long as he would live, and he was ready to carry through with his plan to free Beauty from captivity.

By the time Daylen reached the bottom of the mountain again, the Season of Bloom was over, and in the midst of the Season of Flourish. It would not be long before the Season of Wither returned, and the cycle began anew. He passed back through the gate to Mount Omera and stared at the world around him. He already felt as though he were home. He reflected on the destruction that had occurred in his life, but understood what light had grown from the ashes of death. At one time, Daylen could not have imagined ever reaching the bottom of the mountain, or even the mountain's top, for that matter. Now that his feet graced the forest floor, for the second time, he was aware of all he had become and aware of all the potential that Zantigar had seen in him.

The Wanton Land was vibrant with life. Birds sang and animals scurried. The foliage was thick, the fruits ripe, and the rivers flowed with fresh, clear water. The land celebrated with abundance. Deeper than just the change of the season, the land was different. The mountain's teachings had forever changed him. He walked with sure steps. No longer devoured by his surroundings, he was his surroundings. Although he walked alone, he was not alone. He embraced the world and the people as a world of magic, undivided.

A cry came from the sky. Daylen looked up to the bright clouds. Beneath them a dark silhouette of an eagle swayed and circled with outstretched wings. Daylen raised his arm into the air and the eagle swooped down to him and clenched its talons into his outstretched arm. Ayrowen had returned. Daylen knew that she had never really left. He stared into Ayrowen's piercing eyes and saw himself staring back.

~CHAPTER 6~

Beauty sat in darkness. With a paintbrush cradled between his three fingers, he painted a sun on the stone floor. To break the monotonous sound of silence, he hummed a nursery rhyme. He felt a presence and tilted his head, listening for a familiar voice.

"Don't be alarmed, Beauty, it is just me."

Beauty felt the hairs on his neck stand on end. He mumbled the name with a tongue-less mouth. "Popi?"

"Who else could it be?"

Beauty placed the brush to the ground and shifted to the corner of his room.

"I understand how you feel. I have not been very kind to you, but you must realize that all I have done has been for your own benefit. It has been crucial for you to remain silent, and I only did what I had to do."

Beauty could make out the faint image of Popi in the darkness. He was sitting on Beauty's desk, as he often did, his legs dangling inches from the ground, swaying in an anxious rhythm. Beauty pointed to the portrait of Zantigar.

"Zantigar?" Popi hopped from his seat on the desk. "You know as well as I do that Zantigar is dead. The Dark One got em'. Got em' good, he did."

Beauty shook his head.

"You may find this hard to believe, but I am your friend. I have been, and always will be, thinking of your best interest. Vamillion certainly won't. And don't cry to me about your mommy. You know, and I know, she is not your real mother. Liana was your mother, remember? It is a shame you never had the chance to know her. Having left you, I am all there is to protect you. I always have been."

Beauty pointed to Zantigar again, the words he tried to say indistinguishable without his tongue.

Popi giggled like a playful clown and pointed to his head. "Perhaps, the candle in the attic has burnt out. Perhaps, the wick is gone and there is nothing left to burn." Popi gave a deranged laugh and crept toward Beauty. "Zantigar is dead! Now, tell me, what good are your prophecies if they cease to come true?

What will keep Vamillion from ending your life when you are no longer of use to her?"

Beauty looked to the floor.

"What will you do to convince Vamillion your prophecies are accurate? Take my advice, from one friend to another. Now is the time to tell her what you know, what you have been keeping from her, or she will no longer see a reason for keeping you alive." Popi pointed to a mural on the wall. "Tell her…" he said, as he stepped away and was consumed in shadow.

Beauty looked up to where Popi had pointed. It was a painting of the Desert Portal and of a lone figure emerging from it.

* * *

Vamillion stared out the window of the Moon Tower and reflected on her recent success. Mullen's expansion was stopped dead in its tracks; King Mullen III assassinated, and Vixus troops were positioned to seize control of the mysterious Desert Portal. They only waited for Vamillion's command. The Dark One had promised a reward for claiming the portal. The thought of what treasures lied within the portal gave butterflies to her stomach, even if she was uncertain how to extract them. Time would tell, and so would prophecy. Until then, there were many pressing matters to attend to, and commanding her expansion would require diplomatic finesse.

She was hard at work on her relations with the neighboring kingdoms, spreading propaganda and lies of Mullen's true intentions. She even convinced herself that she had done everything in her power to avoid full scale war and she was filled with nothing but pride and admiration for all she had done to protect the strength and stability of her kingdom.

After all, Vamillion's plans had single handedly destroyed the fear of a Mullen invasion that plagued the minds of her people. Never mind the role she played in creating that fear. Her actions would have pleased King Averath, had he still been alive; had he still been the man he was many glorious years ago. She sighed, wondering what had become of the world. Life used to be easier, but now, violence was the only way to ensure protection, to acquire what her kingdom needed.

The door to her chamber opened and Diamus entered. Vamillion swung around with a child-like smile. "Diamus, my love."

He moved to her, their hands came hands together, their fingers intertwined. He squeezed tightly and he watched her smile grow. "Priestess…"

"Shall I pour some wine?"

"Please," Diamus said, freeing her hands. He helped himself to a cushioned seat beside her desk and watched her pour two generous goblets of wine. "Everything going according to plan?"

"Better than planned, Diamus. Much better." She handed him a goblet. "I spoke with the Dark One yesterday. Zantigar is dead."

"Unbelievable." Diamus smiled at Vamillion and raised his goblet for a toast. "The Dark One has proven to be all that he says he is."

Vamillion tapped her goblet against his, the impact splashing a bit of each other's wine into the other's goblet.

Diamus brought the goblet to his lips without hesitation and sipped the full-flavored wine. "Who would have thought that our strike against Mullen would bring about the death of King Mullen III? I just couldn't believe our luck. From what I hear, Mullen had no son to be heir, the kingdom left in the hands of his only daughter, who days ago was dreaming of being married off to another kingdom and is now left with the enormous responsibility of running a kingdom she never wished to inherit."

"There are many to thank for our success," Vamillion said. "Vision, alone, is never enough. We have outstanding war generals, exceptional spies, courageous knights…" she leaned forward after a long sip of wine, "You. All of whom have risked their lives to achieve what I have envisioned."

Diamus raised his goblet again. "Beautifully, I might add."

Vamillion smiled from the corner of her mouth and raised her goblet to him. "To Vixus."

"To us," Diamus said. He placed his goblet on the desk. "What news of the Dark One?"

"He feels his power growing just as much as I feel my own power growing. It's as if we are linked in a cosmic alliance. However, he grows anxious. He desires the portal and wonders why it is taking so long to please him."

Diamus' expression changed to one of suspicion. "He is pressured? Perhaps, he knows something that we do not."

Vamillion became uneasy at the thought. "Such as?"

Diamus chuckled, before saying, "I was hoping you would know."

Vamillion shook her head. "He tells me only what I need to know, and what I know brings no reason for alarm. He is only impatient, as am I, eager for what awaits."

"You must keep the Dark One satisfied until I return from Oryahn."

Vamillion took a deep breath. Since Beauty's silence, Diamus' trip presented an unknown outcome. "I don't want you to go."

Diamus took her hand in his. "I must."

"I know, but I need reassurance that your trip will be successful. I keep looking to Beauty's paintings, but they reveal nothing of your trip, as far as I can tell." She blushed and tried to hide a nervous smile that Diamus immediately noticed.

Diamus leaned forward. "What is it?"

"I will be Queen of Vixus, one day."

Diamus leaned back in his seat, a look of surprise on his face. "Queen? When did you prefer the spotlight over the shadows?"

"Since there is no royal blood left to take the throne, if an illness should befall upon Queen Abigail, the politicians will come together like hungry dogs to decide the future of the kingdom. In just a few years' time, I will have secured this kingdom as the ultimate power on the continent. They will have no choice but to hand the throne to me. The people will see me as their savior. With the Dark One's help, and the paintings of Beauty, I could accomplish all I desire."

"There are a lot of unknown variables in your plan, Vamillion. Can you trust Beauty to help, after his prophecy was proven wrong?"

"He was only wrong because the Dark One intervened. We have both of them on our side and no reason to believe Beauty no longer has the vision. The Dark One, himself, has desired that I be the Queen. He will help, in every way that he can." She looked into Diamus' eyes and leaned forward close enough to kiss him, but she refrained. "If I am ever Queen, ask for my hand in marriage. I will accept."

Diamus leaned back. "That would make me King. You would hand the keys to the kingdom over to me? What motive is there for this?"

"Does there have to be a motive, Diamus? I am in love with you." She shrugged and leaned back to stare out the window. "Besides, you are the only person I trust."

Diamus was speechless.

Vamillion knew that love was not enough to convince him. In fact, it weakened her case with him, but it was more than enough to excite the people of Vixus. "Of course, there are other benefits. The wedding will secure the future of the Necromancers. A new world order could be brought to the land, a world of wizards unlike any other. What could cause the people of Vixus to celebrate the birth of the first School of Necromancy on the land of Valice if not with the power of love?"

~CHAPTER 7~

On his way back to Vixus, Daylen stopped by Zantigar's cottage. The birch woodland that had once caused him to get lost was no longer an obstacle. The home had a closed in smell and light through the window spilled into the small living area, revealing thick patches of dust floating through the air. A haunting quality filled the quiet cottage, as if buried amongst the books and between the melted candles some form of Zantigar still lingered.

Memories played out in his mind as he moved down the empty hall. He went to Zantigar's room and could remember the shrill screams from many sleepless nights. Daylen caught sight of Zantigar's spellbook. He went to Zantigar's closet and pulled out Zantigar's ceremonial robe that was used for graduation from Hendor Academy. The fabric was thick and soft, crafted with care. The robe was off white colored, and the cuffs were embroidered with gold lace. On the back of the robe was the seal of Hendor's School of Chaos. He folded the robe up gently and placed it under his arm, then grabbed the spellbook and carried it into the living area, along with several pages of blank parchment. He took a seat by the window, placing the pages on the table where he used to drink his morning tea.

Turning to the first blank page, he wrote down the spell he had learned on Mount Omera, transcribing the symbols he had envisioned. On the top of the page he wrote the spell's simple title: Calm. He was feeling overwhelming inspiration, the desire to travel inward, to discover aspects of himself aching to be known. He sat on the floor and closed his eyes in meditation. He practiced removing the thoughts from his mind, quieting his head, focusing on his breath until no thoughts remained.

A voice entered his mind. It was the voice of many voices, speaking in unison. "I know your plan," the Dark One whispered.

Daylen listened intently but did not falter in his meditation. The words entered his mind and left as swift as they came and instilled no fear in him.

"Speak nothing of my secret and Beauty shall live."

Daylen felt the cold quality of the Dark One's voice entering his mind, invading the precious space he had believed was his own. He kept his eyes clothes, breathing, concentrating on the voice.

"Come to the Moon Tower. Come, and confront your destiny."

The Dark One's voice faded from Daylen's mind and only the silence remained.

Daylen entered deeper into the silence. His mind wished to keep him back, but Daylen let go. He felt the magic of the world and he felt his connection to all things. He heard a voice, a voice that reminded him of Zantigar, but he knew that it was more than that, it was the voice of the world of stillness, recognized as his inner voice.

Symbols appeared in his mind. The voice accompanied them, speaking the language necessary to bring the symbols to life. His body became light, and he felt as though he were a pillar of energy, channeling magic throughout and around him. He was no longer conscious of his physical body, as if he had manifested into a form beyond the constraints of his physical shell.

The symbols came together, just as they had at the top of Mount Omera. Visions of cells brought together, tiny particles behaving as one, like a hive mind, building and brightening, lightening with the symbols of magic. A new spell came to light. He did not create the spell any more than he had discovered it. It was as if it had been buried like a fossil in the recesses of his mind. He was conscious of his body again. He opened his eyes and reached for his spellbook and his quill. He understood the spell's function and was quick to scribe it in his excitement. It was a life changing revelation, a spell that could change the world and his purpose in it. He named it "Life Light."

He rose from his seat, placing the two spells of his creation into his robe. He placed Zantigar's ceremonial robe in a bag and tossed Zantigar's spellbook in with it. He took one final look at the cottage, breathed in the air, and then left to fulfill his destiny.

~CHAPTER 8~

When the hooks penetrated the skin on her back, it was met with relief. The sharp pain of penetration was synonymous with divine connection, and as she was raised from the floor and brought, chained, to the wall. Her enslavement was her freedom from the physical world. She waited with anticipation for her god to appear, as warm drips of blood inched down her body.

Vamillion closed her eyes.

The Dark One spoke, his voice the voice of many voices. "There is a small matter which you must not to interfere with, no matter how much you want to."

"I have always done what you have asked of me."

"A stranger will be coming to the city. He will be asking for access to the Moon Tower, and you will let him in."

Vamillion opened her eyes. The Dark One was standing before her, a dark mass of cloud. "A guest?"

"Yes. The business he brings is not for mortal eyes. For our future, for your safety, you will not be in attendance. Do you understand?"

"He must be important for our cause."

"Indeed, he is, Vamillion. Very important."

"Who is it?"

"You will know, in time."

"How will I know when he has arrived, if I don't know who it is?"

"He will come for Beauty and will tell you so."

Vamillion's eyes widened at the threat of losing Beauty. She could not fathom how another could even know of his existence.

"Beauty is going nowhere. Our guest will make a most useful pawn when I am through with him. A solitary guard will escort our guest to the Moon Tower. You will wait at the castle until you are called upon."

Vamillion felt the limitations of her power like a wall of stone, as real as the chains that bound her to the wall. She was helpless to her god's commands. "Your will is my command."

~CHAPTER 9~

Daylen travelled across the Wanton Land and Ayrowen followed, flying with the grace of the wind. The journey was long but was not arduous as it once was. The insights discovered on the mountain, the experience of his connectedness and loss of fear, remained with him and his awareness impacted his surroundings. In this way, his travel was not much different than it had been on Mount Omera. The Wanton Land became an extension of his newfound perspective and there was no separation. The gift of the mountain top, the closeness he felt with the world, had lasting ramifications on every new experience. Connected to the planet, identifying with all aspects of life as aspects of his self, he knew that his individual identity was nothing more than a construct of language, a label. Just as the flowers depended on the sun, waters, and the bees, it was an entire ecosystem of interrelated parts, and he was not separate from it. It was a grand orchestra of connected life. No one conscious entity of greater importance than the other.

Ayrowen flew overhead. She scoured landscape, her eyes observing her surroundings. To Ayrowen, the world was her home. Daylen shared this belief and had learned to understand her experience as one learns a language. He learned to use the eagle's keen eyes to benefit his own survival. Able to observe things far and wide, his perception travelled beyond his field of vision. The land was now their shared domain.

Daylen understood why Ayrowen had been such an invaluable friend to Rahlen. There was insight in understanding her. With Ayrowen at his side, he travelled steady through the thick wilderness. With careful attention to his companion, Ayrowen pointed out where water could be found, and led him to fruits to keep nourished and warned of dangerous creatures and travelers.

With his mind no longer clouded with fear, he was able to reflect about his companions, the ones who had carried him across the land he now travelled alone, with ease. He was grateful for what they provided and instilled in him. Their contribution to his own identity did not go unnoticed or unappreciated.

Rahlen had taught Daylen much about the land. Thanks to Rahlen, fires were easy to start, campsites easy to prepare, and food easy to spot. He could feel Rahlen's presence in the trees, recalled the tales of his adventures in the wind, and understood the wisdom of Rahlen's mind through his relationship with Ayrowen. Feeling the guidance of Rahlen in this spiritual way, the Wanton Land was not as threatening as he first experienced it to be.

Hogar had taught him the importance of humility amidst incredible strength. Hogar's kindness and his selflessness had been a valuable teacher. Reflecting on what he admired most about his friend, he saw the value in art, in being a force of creative energy rather than destruction and his thoughtfulness and skill was apparent in the wood carvings he had created and shared with Daylen.

Bolinda, with her compassionate heart, solidified the selfless requirement that is required to be a person of respect and virtue. Having been a leader of Twilight, a person respected amongst those worth earning the respect of, proved what was possible from humble beginnings and against the odds. Having been a half elf, shunned by the society she was born into, these things did not become a reason to give up. Her way of life, the way of life of each of Daylen's fallen companions, lived now within him. Like planted seeds, their virtue grew in him and Daylen valued these things as much as the spell power within him.

Thanks to his thoughts, it felt as though Daylen emerged from the Wanton Land sooner than expected. He entered Lonely Wood and stopped before Hogar's cottage. Sadness passed through him like a wave, following the memory of his old friend. What he felt he must do would be difficult. Yet, no matter how bad or seemingly undesirable a situation became, Daylen knew he had the opportunity to practice virtue, to use the situation as an opportunity to be his best self. Despite his magic power, and newfound awareness, he knew he was unable to control when things got hard, when difficult situations were required, but he was in control of how to respond to them. It was the things that tested him, the trials, that made him who he was. In this way, he was driven to knock on the door.

Hogar's elven wife, Trishka, opened the door. In her arms she gently bounced her baby in a comforting motion.

Daylen bowed to her. "I am Daylen of Brunhylde. I traveled with your husband, Hogar, into the Wanton Lands."

"I know who you are, Daylen of Brunhylde. I remember when you first came to twilight. Smaller, more timid then the man who stands before me, now. Would you like to come in? There is food to eat."

"I accept your hospitality, but I do not hunger." Daylen shifted into the cottage; his somber mood was not disguised. Trishka was no doubt wondering why Daylen travelled alone.

"Hogar… is no longer with us," Trishka said, perceptively.

Daylen nodded. "That is correct, my lady." Daylen paused, noticing her eyes swell with tears. He continued, "He died outside of River Ale, defending me from an army of goblins. He did not go down without a fight. During our brief time together, Hogar accepted me into his life and opened up to me about his past. He was a wonderful human being. He may be best known for his strength, and courage, but to me I will remember him best for his kind heart. He was a hero of mine, when I needed one most and he saved my life." Daylen paused, swallowing back his sadness. "It is best that you know that Rahlen died, too; soon after, at the hands of a giant."

Tears ran down Trishka's face, but she did not breakdown. She was steadfast in her resolve and met Daylen's gaze with tenderness and heartache.

Daylen looked to the ground. "Hogar died for me, to help me find a wizard. You can blame me for his death, if you want. I won't disagree."

"You aren't to blame for his death, Daylen. You didn't force him to do anything, you didn't slay him with your hand. He was free to do as he does and if it wasn't for you, then it would have been for another, sometime, someday." She shifted her baby from one arm to the other so that she could take Daylen's hand into hers. "Thank you for telling me. It won't make life any easier, but I can heal, now."

Trishka let go of Daylen's hand. He reached into his robe and he pulled out a wooden talisman that looked like an elongated star, multi-sided like a gem, "Hogar gave this to me. I want you to have it."

He placed the talisman in her hand.

"I remember when he made it. The seed of Ophelia."

"That's right," Daylen said.

"He gave this to you?" Trishka looked up at Daylen, her eyes dry, but red.

Daylen nodded.

Trishka leaned forward and hugged him. "You must have meant a lot to him, Daylen. Thank you."

Daylen moved back to the door and nodded. "I expect to visit Twilight now and again. If you would have me, I would be obliged to check in on you from time to time. See how you and the little one are doing."

Trishka smiled. "Sure, Daylen. You can do that."

"Until next time, then." Daylen left the cottage, turning back to check on her. When she closed the door, he scaled a nearby ladder leading to Twilight.

After taking in the surroundings of the place he had long held in his mind, and often wondered if he would live to see again, he came to a door and knocked.

Nilderon answered, his face beaming at the sight of Daylen. "By the gods, my boy. You have returned! Come on in, come in, please." He waved his arm enthusiastically, beckoning Daylen to enter.

Nilderon closed the door behind him and walked to a nearby table. "Have a seat, please."

Daylen took a seat and looking to Nilderon, felt overwhelmed with joy to be back. He smiled. But his joy was met with equal sorrow. His eyes watered and before he knew it he was crying.

Nilderon stood and placed a hand on his back. "There, there. It's alright. Let it go."

Daylen regained composure as soon as his body would allow. The feelings that swelled had been too overwhelming to ignore and were held in for too long. The release afforded him the opportunity to stand face to face with Nilderon and look him in the eye.

Nilderon moved to a pot. "Let me get you some tea. The warmth with cheer you up."

Nilderon handed Daylen a cup.

Daylen spoke plainly, "Rahlen and Bolinda are dead."

Nilderon nodded his head. He took a seat and leaned back, continuing to nod as if trying to accept the news. He had no words. He sighed a heavy sigh, and his eyes were misty.

Daylen continued. "Bolinda was poisoned in the Wanton Lands. Rahlen was with me until the end, as far as the Cragel Mountains. He is no longer with us, but he did what he set out to do; he got me there."

Nilderon looked up, slowly. "You found Zantigar?"

Daylen nodded. "I did; and he accepted me."

Nilderon's face changed to match the relief that coursed through him. This news was greatly needed after the heartbreaking news of his old friends. The happiness was sweeter with the hollowness he felt inside. "Thank the gods."

Daylen leaned forward, "We travelled together to Mount Omera…"

As Daylen spoke, the mood shifted, and the time flew by. Daylen's accounting of the adventure he took captivated Nilderon and for Daylen, it allowed him to see the fruition of all that was accomplished. All the fortune and all the plight that was experienced could be seen in totality for the overarching grandeur that it was.

After telling his tale, Nilderon commented on the unsurmountable suffering that Daylen must have experienced, with so much loss. He was concerned if Daylen had doubts, anger at what had transpired. Whether the loss of his companions, or the loss of Zantigar.

Daylen shook his head. He looked about the room, trying to find the words. When he caught glimpse of the wall outside the window, he saw ivy growing up it. He walked over to the window and beckoned Nilderon to follow.

"Look there, at the ivy. See how it clings to the wall dispersing in chaotic direction, a seemingly confused rambling. On closer examination it becomes apparent that the ivy is always seeking the light. It sticks to the wall because the wall allows it to reach higher. The fact that it goes left, or right is not a matter of right or wrong, good or bad, it is only a representation of its intentions; to always seek the light. All deviations are part of the process. It's all part of the same movement, the purpose never wavering in its eternal pursuit of the light. In the process, it discovers itself, its being. In this way, one cannot look back on life and see it as a series of right and wrong, but a movement, a flow toward the way."

Nilderon nodded. "You perceive much, Daylen."

"I have seen many things, but these things are relevant in the moment in which it is perceived. I have learned enough to know I know nothing. When I started my journey, it was with the desire to control the world around me, my place in it, and my destiny. I craved the ability to wield spells for this reason. I realized the falsehood in this approach. My pursuit has changed, not to control the outcome of life situations, what I call the chaos of the surface world, but how to live in accord with it."

"The deaths of Rahlen and Bolinda were not in vain. You are becoming a wizard of great wisdom, and I foresee you living a life of incredible significance. You can be a hero, just as Rahlen was. Greater still, you can be a leader and start the revolution that he had dreamed of."

Daylen turned away from the window, uninspired by the notion. "I have no desire to be a leader. A leader proclaims to know the way and asks that others follow behind him. I do not know the way for others, and I will not claim to know.

"As for being a hero, this does not serve our cause and is of little relevance to me. The idea that one person can save us is dangerous. The world is too big and moving too quickly. Who has the nerve to claim they know the way that is best for all? The only pursuit that is relevant beyond bettering oneself is to work toward social justice. Wizards are slave to the Academies; the peasants are slave to kings; the troubles of the world are vast. A hero, alone, can't bring about the change that is needed, as much as we may wish it were true. As long as the world keeps waiting for this hero to come, things will never change. No, what the world needs is not a hero, but a heroic community, and this means the masses must not look to one person for the answers, but look to one another, as a collective."

Nilderon spoke with excitement. "What you say proves there are other kinds of leaders, Daylen. You don't need to ask others to follow you, but you can remind people to look to each other, so that no one is left behind. Encourage everyone to make decisions that are for the good of everyone. Freeing all and providing for all, so there is stability and opportunity for all."

"I can find solace in that. So long as I can be more or less invisible, not to function as one wanting to correct others, but to simply be a good listener. That's what I can provide, and all that I should. In fact, the more I can refrain from saying 'I' the better. What I want, is of little importance."

"You speak in the voice of FéLorën, Daylen. You are living up to your name. The past has been dark, but in the future, there is light."

"It is all light," Daylen reminded. "Just as the path of the vines, even in darkness. It always has been the light, and it always will be."

Daylen moved to his bag and pulled out Zantigar's spellbook. "I want you to keep this in Twilight. Protect it, just as you do the book of FéLorën. It is Zantigar's spellbook and it contains all the Chaos spells from the school of Hendor, transcribed hundreds of years ago."

"My goodness." Nilderon carefully took the spellbook into his hands, his eyes widened with fascination. "I will guard it well, as you requested."

Nilderon set the book on the table and was curious for what the future had in store. "So, you are planning on freeing Beauty from the Moon Tower? A prophet will be a great asset to our cause."

"Assuming it is what Beauty desires. He will be free to do as he pleases. I am not convinced just yet, if Beauty needs to be saved, or even wants to be."

"I see," Nilderon said. "When will you leave for Vixus?"

Daylen returned to the window. He gazed out past the treetops and to where the sun was setting on the horizon. "Tomorrow morning."

"Is there anything I can do to help?" Nilderon asked.

Daylen shook his head. "What I must do is dangerous, and it must be done alone. The Dark One, he is expecting me to be alone. I would very much enjoy having your company, though. Setting Beauty free is just the beginning. There are many that need to be freed from captivity, if not from their chains, then from their minds. I expect it will take most of my life, but it all begins with a single step."

Daylen went to the door. "Meet me in Brunhylde, two days from now. There is a hill, where a lone tree stands. You will know it when you see it. I'll be waiting for you there."

~CHAPTER 10~

Daylen stepped into Vixus territory with a strong sense of nostalgia. He had left as a victim, scurrying headfirst into exile, running from Vixus as if it were a giant intent on crushing him. Now, he felt like a giant, whose influence and strength was limited only by what his mind could fathom.

Having spent his childhood in Brunhylde hiding, he had never been to Vixus City. He was shocked by its majestic size and the inner workings of the community. Feeling like a giant was soon diminished as he was dwarfed against the expansive buildings and wide cobblestone streets. People, from all walks of life, all classes and professions hustled by on their daily duties. The city was like a living, breathing organism, a monster of sorts, due to its intimidating complexity. The city had the propensity to drown out the individuality of its citizens in a collective conscious that thrived on production and consumption. Taking those first steps onto the cobblestone streets was like stepping into a sea of minds as he blended in with the crowds. His destination felt like the den of a mighty dragon, its horde of gold buried beneath the castle at its center.

Ayrowen left Daylen's side, choosing the comfort of nature over following Daylen beyond the city gates. Amidst a crowd of citizens, swaying like a sea of humanity, Daylen made his way toward the castle. Peddlers hollered above the commotion in the streets and merchants beckoned to draw the masses to their shops. Constables marched passed, breaking through the waves of people, steadfast in their determination with little concern for the wellbeing of those they parted in their advancement.

Daylen placed the hood of Zantigar's ceremonial robe over his head and buried his hands in his sleeves, knowing that academy wizards all bore a branding on their palm which he did not possess. If anyone were to notice that he walked without one, he would be arrested. The punishment for being a rogue wizard was death, by hanging, and it would occur in a street not unlike the one he now walked. The towers of Vixus Castle dominated the sky, the banners of blue and red waving in the turbulent winds above. He walked straight through the front gate of the castle. The open doors felt as inviting as walking into a hungry dragon's mouth. Yet, just as he had been devoured by the winged lion, he was resolute and without fear.

* * *

Vamillion was asleep at her desk, her face buried in a series of pictures Beauty had drawn, when pounding came at the tower door. She quickly travelled the spiral steps to the ground floor and opened the door.

A knight stood before her. "High Priestess Vamillion, Queen Abigail requests an audience with you, at once."

"Whatever for?"

"It appears there is a visitor here for you, a wizard by the name of Zantigar. By order of the Queen, Her Majesty, you are to report to the main hall at once."

Vamillion struggled to hide her disbelief, as visions of Beauty's prophecy unfolded in her mind. Her heart pounded and she struggled to keep her composure. Her mind racing at the thought that Zantigar was still alive, curious if the Dark One had lied to her. If Beauty had been right, all along, then it would mean his prophecy was stronger than the will of her god and that Beauty would be taken from her. She choked on her thoughts and stood, dumbfounded, before gaining the nerve to speak. "Of course; lead the way."

Vamillion was led to the main hall of the castle. Queen Abigail awaited her there, sitting in her jeweled throne. Lines of knights stood at attention on either side of the hallway. Standing before the Queen was a figure in an exquisite white robe, bowing on one knee. Vamillion moved to the Queen's side, her eyes fixated on the stranger, unable to make out the identity of the man shadowed by his oversized hood.

Queen Abigail turned to address the High Priestess. "Vamillion, this wizard claims to be Zantigar."

Vamillion narrowed her eyes with suspicion, stepping closer.

Queen Abigail's voice rose, unable to hide a growing anger and frustration. "Do you know what else this wizard has proclaimed? That he has been sent to release Beauty from captivity!"

Vamillion stood in silence. She remembered what The Dark One had said, about a visitor wanting to see Beauty. The Dark One's instructions were explicit. She was to grant the guest passage to the Moon Tower. Her faith was tested in ways she did not imagine possible. The Dark One said nothing of Zantigar arriving and had told her Zantigar was dead.

"Do you know what this means?" Queen Abigail continued with a flurried temper. "Who dares enter this castle and utter such forbidden words?!"

Vamillion's mind continued to race, imagining all the ways she had to make this wizard speak, to bring him to his knees. She knew she would need to act quickly. If anyone were to realize that Beauty lived, that the rightful heir to the throne was alive and well, all of Vamillion's hopes would be crushed by the very empire she lived to protect. She would be hung, and Queen Abigail would be hung along with her. "Remove the hood from your head, stranger."

Daylen pulled the cloak back from his head and raised his eyes to greet the High Priestess' bold glare.

Vamillion looked at Daylen with confusion and then relief. It wasn't Zantigar, after all. At least not the one she was expecting, and her fears of betrayal by the Dark One diminished at once. However, she could not help but feel a sense of trickery, unaware of how she was being played, the strings the Dark One manipulated were expansive and the threats this stranger imposed were unnerving. She had no choice but to obey the will of her god, as much as she wanted to get her hands on this mysterious guest. "Zantigar, is it?"

"That is correct," Daylen said, his voice calm and certain.

Vamillion studied the robe in which he wore. The dress marked a high, sophisticated class, one that did not fit Daylen's age. The robe also was decorated in a fashion that did not match any known Academy she was aware of. It did, however, fool the guards into granting him access to the Queen. "Where are you from?"

*　　　*　　　*

Daylen did not take his eyes off of Vamillion. He took a moment to absorb the feeling her presence evoked. Before him was the murderer of his father. She was strikingly beautiful, mesmerizing as only a sorceress could be. Yet she was cold, and her eyes were uninviting in ways far more potent than he could have expected, even for a murderer. He knew in an instant, that he was dealing with a woman that could not be trifled with or taken lightly. The ability to reason with one this dangerous was not likely to occur. He stared into those eyes of hate and bitterness and wondered how she could call herself a priestess and maintain her integrity.

Daylen could see through to her soul and was aware that she was a slave to power, and her servitude had robbed her of her magical gifts. Her want of power proved that she had been easily bested by common illusions. Her actions were those of one who was desperate to control all that she could not. As a result, she was the lesser, and not prepared to confront the son of the man she had murdered in cold blood. She would regret all she had done, he would see to it.

"You will answer the priestess!" Queen Abigail demanded. "Or you will suffer the consequences."

"My home is where I stand," Daylen announced, "my servitude is to no specific kingdom, other than the kingdom of FéLorën. Please, High Priestess, inform the Queen that I require passage to the Moon Tower. I carry a message for the Dark One, alone." Daylen faced the Queen with unfaltering eyes. "If the Queen so wishes to prevent my passage to Beauty's cell, then I shall call upon the Dark One to silence her."

"Speak no more of your purpose, and do not utter the forbidden name," the Queen advised.

Vamillion, despite her anger, bent her head to the Queen's ear and whispered to her. Daylen could not make out the words but studied the flabbergasted expression that filled the Queen's face. The Queen appeared to hear enough and jerked away from Vamillion in detest. She directed her question to Daylen. "You wish to visit the Moon Tower?"

"Yes."

The look on Vamillion's face confirmed that it must have pained her to submit. "I will have a guard escort you to the Moon Tower. However, before you go, you must relinquish your weapons."

"He already has," Queen Abigail informed. He carried a short blade and two spells written on parchment. Nothing more."

Vamillion was pleased with this outcome and was confident that the Dark One could easily dispose of this helpless stranger if need be. "Very well, then. You will find what you seek below the tower floor." She waved to a guard to escort him.

Queen Abigail addressed the escort. "When all is said and done, I want him here at my feet." She turned to Daylen. "I want an explanation as to everything before I will allow you to leave."

Vamillion averted her attention to Daylen. "Make no mistake, Your Majesty, this wizard will not be leaving."

The guard stepped forward.

"Show Zantigar to the Moon Tower," Queen Abigail ordered.

Vamillion was still staring at Daylen as he lifted the hood of his robe back over his head. She descended from her position beside the throne and stood before Daylen. She followed him on his way toward the door and she leaned close, until her lips were inches from his ear. "I do not know who you are, or where you are from, but you best pray the Dark One shows mercy on you or I will gladly strike the head from your body, myself."

Daylen looked to Vamillion from behind the shadow of his hood. He stared into her cold eyes and felt sadness for her. "High Priestess of Vixus, I have nothing to hide. I have but one mission, and it is to save Beauty from captivity and take him to safety. That is what I have come to do, and it will be done."

Vamillion grabbed his arm, halting him from passing through the door. "The Dark One will never allow it."

Daylen, upon being grabbed, averted his attention to Vamillion, half expecting her to try and stop him.

Vamillion reluctantly placed a silver key in Daylen's hand. "This key will grant you access to the Moon Tower, and to Beauty's chamber. The Dark One will be waiting for you there."

Daylen was freed from Vamillion's grip. "Thank you, High Priestess. What is to be done, shall be done. When Beauty and I are gone from here, I hope it causes you to reconsider where you place your faith."

Daylen turned away from Vamillion, looked to the key in his palm, and walked out of the room. He felt Vamillion's stare burning into his back as he followed the guard out of the castle and across the courtyard. He was led to the Moon Tower that stood isolated from the rest of the castle. It loomed above all other castle towers, its top hidden above the clouds on a moonless night. Daylen looked up to its dizzying heights and almost lost his balance. They came to an iron door, rusted and aged with years of wear.

"The Moon Tower," the guard announced, positioning himself beside the door.

Daylen nodded and stared up at the tower for a moment. The wind howled, as if responding to his arrival. He returned his gaze to the door and placed the key into the keyhole. A vision of two red, beady eyes flashed in his mind. He did not falter. With a faint click, the door unlocked and opened with an agitated moan.

~CHAPTER 11~

Queen Abigail was displeased. "What in the name of the gods is the meaning of this?"

Vamillion paced back and forth within the Queen's study, her temper high and her breath, erratic. "I do not know, but for the first time, I feel like I am being mocked, my power nothing more than a paper dragon, worthless when it matters most."

"What could the Dark One possibly be thinking?" Queen Abigail said.

Vamillion pointed at the Queen. "Be careful what you say," she insisted. "Don't you realize that the Dark One is listening to our every word? Ow dare you question his judgement!"

Queen Abigail rolled her eyes in disbelief. "Can you explain to me what is going on? I do not like being surprised by all of this, being left in the dark."

Vamillion shook her head. "I do not have any control over this, I will admit. The Dark One said that a stranger would arrive and that I should let him through. There is nothing I can do about it."

"Well, we must do something. If word gets out that Beauty is alive, this kingdom will fall apart beneath us. The true heir to the throne is locked away like a monster in your study!"

"Do not worry, my Queen. We have no reason to distrust the Dark One's motives. He has proven to be a loyal ally to our cause time and again."

Queen Abigail shook her head. "What makes you so sure we can trust anybody? What if this wizard who strolled so casually into the Moon Tower without supervision has performed some kind of trickery? He is a wizard, after all."

Vamillion's eyes widened with realization. "He had spells on him, didn't he?"

Queen Abigail scoffed at the notion. "Yes, he had two scribbled pages of nonsense, nothing more than a rogue's meanderings. Hardly anything worthy, I'm sure."

"How can you be sure?" Vamillion asked.

"You think you will be able to read his spells? The chance is slim to none. You are a priestess, a Holy Wizard, and this stranger is no priest. You will never understand the code."

With the look of her eyes, she insisted. "There is a great deal more to be learned from a wizard's spell beyond how to cast it."

Queen Abigail called to a guard, who came quick-footed to her side with the Daylen's belongings. Vamillion threw the sword to the ground and grabbed the parchment with eager hands.

Queen Abigail continued to sneer at the futility of Vamillion's intentions. "You think you will determine his identity from its pages? It's not like he signed it with his name."

Vamillion stared at the pages and shook her head in denial of what she saw. "By the Dark One above, I knew it! I could tell by the look in his eyes." She flipped to the second page, understanding each and every symbol. Daylen was a Holy Wizard, a priest, just as she was; or had been, before losing her gift with the loss of her ways. There were just two spells, one of which was alarming in its ability. She perused the symbols, checking its authenticity. "Life Light…" she whispered, lowering the pages to her side.

Queen Abigail looked over Vamillion's shoulder. "What does it mean, is it dangerous?"

"Hardly, but equally as incredible." Vamillion wished she had not lost the ability to cast spells. What were the chances the students of the Academy would ever derive a spell of this caliber? It would take years, lifetimes to discover. The spell would fit nicely in the Academy collection. As she tucked the pages in her belt she looked to the sword on the ground, which had slid from its sheath. Her face turned pale.

The hilt was red and blue, an older model sword from her kingdom. The shiny surface of the blade revealed the inscription: SYLVER. The name was one she could never forget. "Donovan Sylver," she whispered.

Vamillion picked up the sword and held it in her hands. Her mind raced with confusion, as to how this mysterious, nameless wizard could have obtained the sword. The memory of Donovan Sylver coming to her in waves... His servitude, his loyalty, his friendship with King Averath, and the order for his execution, his head eventually planted on the end of a pole.

As Vamillion reflected on the young wizard's face, the familiar eyes, it struck her at once. "Donovan had a son. The wizard is Donovan's son!"

Vamillion shook from a reeling series of paranoid thoughts. The truth was out there. Surely, Donovan's son knew what Vamillion had done and had come to get revenge! The seat of the throne, the truth of Donovan's death, was all at stake. Suddenly, lost in irrational thought, Vamillion cringed.

Queen Abigail asked the same questions that Vamillion was already reeling from in her mind, her voice rising with each subsequent inquiry. "Why is the Dark One speaking to him in secret? Are they in collusion? Are we being played, to be overthrown?"

"Stop, it!" Vamillion ordered, madness consuming her. "They have all the evidence they need to bury me!" Vamillion spat.

"There is no logical reason for their secrecy!" Queen Abigail screamed.

Surely, there was a devious plot in the works. It was the only explanation for their secrecy, a plot that either led to her demise, or a plot that would impact her greatly. Either way, she could not allow ignorance to prevail. She needed to know, demanded to know. Vamillion stormed from the castle still clutching Sylver in her hands as she made her way to the Moon Tower.

LIFE LIGHT
G.G.

~CHAPTER 12~

When Daylen entered the Moon Tower he was met with stark cold air and darkness, only offset by a line of torches spiraling up the Moon Tower staircase. There was a dampness that was heightened by a feeling of isolation and gloom. The low firelight reflected off condensation on the stone walls and the silence was broken by the monotonous dripping of water. The methodical tapping of droplets heightened the awareness of time and loneliness. Daylen noticed the outline of the trap door at his feet.

He bent down and inserted the key into the lock. He then unraveled the chain that held Beauty locked in his prison. The trap door swung open, and a dark descent led the way to a soft glowing light. When he entered Beauty's cell a lone candle lit the room, revealing a man hunched over a writing desk. With careful steps, he approached. Beauty turned to face him, his one eye widening with enthusiasm. The face was the same as the face he saw reflected back at him when he stared into the pond, moments before Zantigar's death.

The sight of the man was hard to bear. His face was inflicted with numerous scars. His suffering must have been unimaginable. His hair a chaotic mess of dark curls, his pale, boney face and one fake eye made him look like a monster, a freak fit for the circus, for those who bear witness to be aghast at the sight of.

"Beauty," Daylen said.

Beauty smiled, his bruised lips parting. The blistered, split lips of his smile expressed his happiness for but a moment, before the pain prevented him from expressing his true joy in Daylen's arrival.

Daylen moved closer, slowly. Looking to the darkness, he was certain the Dark One was hiding close by. The Dark One did not make his presence known. When he got close to Beauty's side he spoke softly. "I am sorry that Zantigar could not be here. I am here in his place, to finish what he had started. To save you."

Beauty motioned for Daylen to stand over his shoulder, to see his writing table. There were many writings, some of it poetic, others narrative, some in the form of letters. He pulled a blank piece of paper and with quill between his three fingers he scribed, "I have been waiting for you, Daylen of Brunhylde."

Daylen wondered how Beauty knew his name, and the origin of his birth, but if Beauty's abilities were true, then how could he not? The words also confirmed that it was not Zantigar he had been waiting for. Daylen realized that Beauty had no tongue, no way in which to speak. He was overwhelmed with empathy. Before he considered responding he placed his hands on Beauty's face. Beauty closed his eye at Daylen's touch. His hands warmed with a calming heat. Daylen closed his eyes and concentrated on the symbols that came to his mind. In a foreign tongue he spoke the words of his newest spell, "Life Light."

Under Daylen's hands, the wounds on Beauty's face closed and the scars disappeared. His skin regenerated at an alarming rate. Daylen could feel the pull of magic from his own life force, and his hands glowed with a blinding light. The scars from when Beauty's mouth had been sewn shut closed and his tongue returned. The fake, ivory eye fell out of his socket, as the tissue behind it rejuvenated, his eye returning, growing as if from birth, until it was renewed.

When the magic completed its course, Daylen stepped back and opened his eyes.

Beauty smiled, as if the healing of the outer scars were equal to the healing of his inner ones. He was handsome, his skin flush with life. He was the embodiment of all you would expect from a future king. His eyes flickered with an all-knowing light. Smiling, he opened his mouth to speak, and his words were spoken in pristine clarity. "Thank you for coming."

Daylen felt the urgent need to understand many things. "Zantigar was never meant to save you?"

Beauty shook his head softly, still smiling in gratitude. "I am sorry for what happened to Zantigar. We all have our part to play."

Daylen stepped forward and extended his hand. "I will save you."

Beauty's eyes were filled with compassion. "It is not your destiny, Daylen."

Daylen was alarmed and was disheartened that Beauty did not accept his hand. He took a step back. "Then… why am I here?"

Beauty pointed to the wall, to a painting of the Desert Portal and of a figure emerging from it.

Daylen studied the painting and tried to understand its meaning, he shook his head in disbelief as the answer came to him.

Beauty confirmed what Daylen now knew to be true. "This is where your destiny lies."

A voice rose from behind Daylen. It was the voice of many voices, the voice of the Dark One. "And so it is, just as I suspected."

Daylen spun to his rear. A newfound light was emanating from a candle. Holding it, was a figure dressed in black, his face shadowed by his hood.

"Dark One," Daylen said.

"It is I, naturally," he spoke, his voice becoming surprisingly gentle.

"I am not afraid of you."

"You do not need to be, Daylen," The Dark One said with sincerity. "The problem with my profession, is that I never get credit for my genius. People see me on the streets and they do not know who I am. They treat me as a common peasant, but they do not know, they never can know; the truth." The Dark One removed his hood, and the light of the candle met his face, exposing a grey-skinned Elf, with small, emerald eyes. "As you can see, the legend built around me is far greater than the reality. I am nothing more than a humble Grey Elf…albeit a wizard of particular cunning."

"An assassin," Daylen reminded. "A murderer of your own kind."

"I never realized that Zantigar had a companion. He had been alone for so many years, a hermit, protected from my magic by his ruby staff. Who would have thought the Portal Walker would be his companion? It is a small world, so they say."

"Portal Walker?"

"Yes, this meeting confirms it. You are the Portal Walker from Beauty's paintings. Ever since I laid my eyes on the mysterious figure depicted exiting the portal I have scoured the known land looking for you, unsure who it was. I should have known that I need not try so hard. Fate has its way, does it not?" The Dark One walked forward and stood between Beauty and Daylen.

Daylen spoke plainly. "It is my plan to take Beauty from here, Dark One. I don't have any intention of letting you stop me."

"Yes, so it seems. The best-laid plans, or so the story goes." The Dark One pulled the onyx staff from his robe.

Daylen jumped back.

The Dark One gestured for him to relax, and placed the staff on the table. He slowly revealed a sword and placed it beside the staff. Patting his body, he confirmed he had no weapons to hide. "I have no intention of hurting you, Daylen. In fact, I have a proposition for you."

"I'm not interested in anything you have to offer."

"Don't be so quick to decide, until all the facts are in," The Dark One advised. "Imagine, Portal Walker, slipping into the Desert Portal, discovering its secrets, its treasures, and walking back through to tell the tale. I have spent my life trying to be a god, but you, fine sir, you will be a god. The day you return, you will be worshipped like none who walked before. Erramond the Wise, included."

"Gods are only as relevant as the servants who follow them," Daylen remarked. "And I don't care for servants."

The Dark One nodded, a sly smile on his face. "Then a king you will be. King not of Vixus, not even of Valice, but of the world."

"It is my pursuit to be king of nothing, just as I prefer to be slave to no one."

The Dark One laughed, half amused, but with an underlying growing frustration in his voice. "You seem to be missing the point. Power. It starts here, the three of us. You, me, Beauty. My followers at our disposal, Vixus already under our grasp. A mighty army just waiting at our beck and call. Beauty, his prophecy, allowing the future to be our guide. Always one step ahead of the game. And you, Portal Walker, the future of our legacy… world domination."

Beauty shook his head. "My visions, I can no longer see them."

"What is this you say?" The Dark One inquired.

Beauty looked to Daylen. "Your spell, it healed my scars and regenerated my cells, but it did more. I no longer experience the mental pain that I always accredited to spawning the visions. I don't know if I can say for sure, but I think my prophecy days are over. I can feel it, inside, a void, a darkness once filled with images of the future."

Daylen looked to Beauty with concern. "I am sorry, Beauty. I… did not know."

"Be sorry for nothing, Daylen," Beauty replied. "On the contrary, you have set me free, and I am eternally grateful."

The Dark One was left perplexed, unable to speak.

"What do you say to that, Dark One, how will you rule without your prophet?" Daylen remarked.

The Dark One shrugged, upset, but tried to hide it. He made a sharp glance to his weapons on the table, and it did not go unnoticed. "So be it, just the two of us then."

'Popi!" Beauty exclaimed, looking to the Dark One. "Don't say such cruel things. Would you be so quick to discard me, after all we have been through?"

Popi's emerald eyes sparkled, and his thin lips parted in a devious smile. He repeated what he had said to Daylen moments before. "Fate, has its way, does it not?"

Movement caught Daylen's eye, as a shadow crossed the stairwell. "And Vamillion? What plans do you have for her?"

"I have heard enough," a loud voice exclaimed, turning the heads of Popi and Beauty.

Vamillion lowered herself from the stairs and approached with Sylver in hand. "Popi? The Dark One? This… this… pathetic Grey Elf standing before me?"

The distraction was all that Popi required. With Vamillion's awareness of his identity, there was no longer a use for her, or anyone. In an instant, he sprung for his sword and swung it at Beauty, the blade slicing his throat. Beauty collapsed, instantly, blood spilling down his chest.

Vamillion screamed and lunged for Popi, her rage drowned out his voice as she plunged Sylver into his chest. Popi cried out in agony, bewildered by how it could all come to an end this way. He had killed Zantigar, and thought his future was clear. But he had been deceived by shadow prophecy, the very suggestion he gave to Beauty was used against him. To make Popi believe that Zantigar would free him was the perfect suggestion for Fate to play its course.

Vamillion's eyes were filled with a violent rage. She withdrew the sword and plunged it into Popi a second time, this time the blade drove through his heart. "You vile creature! You ruined everything! Everything!" She withdrew the sword and brought it down on his body in a repetitive motion, hacking his body repeatedly, long after it had stopped moving.

Daylen grabbed Vamillion's arm as it descended on Popi's bloody corpse. "Enough!"

The room began to glow in a bright, brilliant light. He placed his other hand on her face, and they locked eyes. Her eyes were wild, not unlike the glare of a hungry wolf. He saw himself in her eyes. Her rage was his rage, it was a feeling that he understood. They were one, locked in magnetic opposition. She was light, only light, just as he was.

Daylen began to chant. Vamillion tried to wrestle free from his grip and cut him with his own sword, but the heat already began to radiate from his hands. She heard the words roll from his tongue and she was powerless to stop it. Light radiated around her, frightening her at first, but this emotion was quickly snuffed out as a feeling of calmness consumed her. The spell echoed in the mind, the one mind they had become.

"Calm… calm… calm…" It echoed, over and over in the language of the Holy Wizard.

The hand pressed against Vamillion's face glowed. Her grip weakened on the blade; her body softened in acceptance. A loud clatter broke the silence, as

Sylver slipped through her fingers and ricocheted off the stone floor. "Calm yourself," Daylen said. "Calm yourself," he repeated.

Trapped under Daylen's spell, she was powerless to refuse, just as Zantigar's chaotic force had been tamed. All the wild passions that drove her to madness had dissolved away. Her eyes lost their fury, and the calming spell enveloped her body until she collapsed, dumbfounded and limp, lost in a serene haze.

Daylen waited until every muscle in her body had become still, until only the soft beat of her heart and the soft breath from her lips remained. He stood over her body and grabbed the spell pages that were tucked in her belt. "I believe these are mine." He leaned over and whispered in her ear. "Remember your place in this world, High Priestess, and you may live to regain the powers of priesthood you once revered. The Dark One's chains have been stricken from you and you are free from your prison. Forgive the world for its cruelty and injustice, as I have forgiven you for yours. Be humble on the path toward your ambitions. Gracious when successful and resilient when you fail. Treat all people of the world with kindness and fairness and see that in them that is no different from yourself. You can be the person that you wish had been there for you. The choice is yours."

Daylen took a step back and stared at the carnage before him. The Dark One was dead. The myth of this great being ended with a motionless body of an emerald-eyed, grey-skinned elf lying dead in a chamber of darkness.

He knelt down to Beauty. Lifting his arm, he felt for a pulse that did not come. The life that was waiting to be lived at last, was taken before it even had a chance. Beauty's face was pale, but he bore a serene expression on his handsome face, having finally found peace, in a world of everlasting stillness.

Daylen grabbed the Dark One's staff from the table. Upon contact, spells entered his mind, a language encoded into the staff that spawned the ability to lose his physical form, displace the souls of any he chose to touch with the staff and to teleport to any destination his mind could fully conceive at the speed of light, by breaking his being down into light, itself. When he thought of Vamillion's chamber at the top of the Moon Tower, he was taken there. After he scoured her room, he thought of Brunhylde, to the lone tree on the hill, and was taken there.

As soon as he found himself by the tree, he raised the staff with both hands above his head. With all his might, he swung it to the ground. Upon impact with a large rock, the staff snapped in two. The onyx stone, affixed to its head, cracked and with a grand release of magical energy, freed the souls of every wizard that had been trapped inside with a shockwave that spread across the sky.

~CHAPTER 13~

Vamillion stared from the Moon Tower window. Her eyes fell upon the majesty of the moon.

Diamus was rummaging through the desk drawers, slamming them shut and tossing papers to the side. "Daylen was up here. He took your Vixus seal and a branding symbol for Vixus Academy."

Vamillion was not listening.

"Can you believe it? The rogue can now brand himself and fit in amongst the world as if he were a wizard of the Academy. And with the Vixus seal, well, he can forge any document he sees fit and proclaim it is to be the decree of the Queen"

Diamus threw a pile of books to the ground. "Are you even listening? Do you even care? Oh, why bother? He took no items of wealth. He could have done much worse. You should consider yourself lucky that is all he took."

Diamus saw Vamillion had not moved from her place by the window, staring vacantly into space. He rushed to Vamillion's side. "You really aren't listening, are you?" He placed his hand on her waist. "Are you feeling okay?"

The touch of Diamus' hand against her body woke her from her self-imposed trance. "I am in hell," she said. "I have turned my back on Glaven, my god, to follow an entity that didn't even exist. In the process, I have been stripped of everything I once held dear and I am left with nothing but the thought of failure, the bitter sting of defeat."

Diamus ran his hand through her long, black hair. "Darling, you must not be so hard on yourself. You still have much to be thankful for."

"Thankful? The word bears no meaning to me. My faith in happiness died with the Dark One." Vamillion grabbed hold of Diamus' hands. "There is just emptiness, now."

Diamus looked into her eyes. "And what shall you do to fill that emptiness?"

Vamillion studied his glare, reading into his soul. She smiled. "Power; I will fill the emptiness with absolute power."

Diamus returned a smile of his own. "We have a mighty army at our command. We have an armada, ready to set sail for Oryahn, and forces to the north, waiting to claim the Desert Portal."

The light of the moon reflected in Vamillion's eyes. "The Desert Portal."

Diamus nodded his head. "As far as I am concerned, the only thing which you have lost is the illusion that the gods play a role in our lives. The truth is, as long as we are alive, the world is ours for the taking. No more trust in false gods, no more reliance on destiny. The Dark One and Beauty both held you captive. Now, you are free. You have all the power you need, right within your grasp."

Vamillion clenched her hands in Diamus' hands. Her emptiness was filled with imaginations spawned by Diamus' words. "Keep speaking, Diamus."

"All you need to do is ask yourself what you long for… and take it! That is the fortunate position you have in this world. So ask it; what do you want?"

Vamillion licked her upper lip and lost herself in the light of the night sky. "The moon, Diamus… I want the moon; and everything beneath it."

~CHAPTER 14~

Daylen stood beneath the lone tree in Brunhylde. The onyx staff lay destroyed at his feet. The Season of Whither was upon the land, just as it had been when he last departed. The storm clouds loomed overhead and any day now, the rains were expected. The vibrant, crisp smell of the pre-rain air filled his breath. Just as in his youth, memories came back to him. Memories of innocence, and of Glazahn filled his mind. He wondered what Fate had in store for his old friend, and if he was living a life of fulfillment and peace.

Standing by the tree again, Daylen felt his bond with it. But it was a different bond then he previously felt. Before, his bond was of loneliness, for Daylen had known nothing else as lonely as the tree but himself. Now, he did not believe the tree was lonely. Its roots were embedded deep in the soil. It was grounded, connected to the world with a strong foundation. The bare limbs were not reaching, in desperation, as once he believed, but rising to praise the glory of existence. The sun's rays beamed down upon it, constantly connected. Forever nourished, forever loved.

Without knowing it at the time, Daylen had carved something into the tree. He had carved a perception of loneliness. He was a mirror of that loneliness. Now, knowing the power of his thoughts, he projected his perception on the tree, again. He perceived a vision of unity, and so it was that he felt that unity.

He closed his eyes to savor the touch of the cool breeze on his face. Ayrowen soared from above and landed on a limb of the tree.

Nilderon moved to Daylen's side, also appearing to appreciate the cool breeze. As he stared down at the village below, catching his breath from the climb up, he brushed wisps of his long grey hair from his face. "Is this home?"

Daylen's eyes followed the slope between the valley where the grass ceased to grow, and the mud devoured the ground. He saw small cottages, not unlike the cottage from his childhood, set between new, large stone structures that blew thick clouds of black smoke into the air. The citizens were hard at work, laboring for the training knights who were learning the art of warfare. Brunhylde was much different than it was when he was last here, having evolved into an instrument of war, but it also had characteristics which had not changed, components of its nature that technology could not destroy.

Brunhylde was living up to its historical name. Long before his time, Brunhylde was a stronghold that defended Vixus from the wild frontier land and bred experienced warriors who sought to change the world through force. It was the days of Heldon, prior to the unification of the Final War. The cycle continued, a territory ensnared in a cycle of violence and perpetual poverty. It was clear the Final War would need a new name, as it was certain there was no such thing as the final anything.

"This is no place for a wizard of your potential," Nilderon remarked.

"Maybe; or maybe this is where my potential could best be put to use," Daylen said. He turned to Nilderon and smiled. "However, this is no place for a wizard's mother."

Daylen hurried down the hillside. Nilderon followed close behind. The streets were in dire condition and caused grief in Daylen's heart. He could not recognize the people, but he recognized their suffering and he felt it as if it were his own. There was a time when he felt he had no purpose, a time when he was blind. Now, the amount of help he could provide, the duty that presented itself to him, provided more purpose than time allowed.

The air had the stench of pollution, the clatter of smiths hard at work on armor and weapons destroyed any opportunity for silence. They were met by a wagon at the side of the road. It was piled with lifeless bodies. Workers who tired during labor and could not keep up, only to end up dead and in piles like garbage. No care or respect for the divinity of life that once emanated from their being. Lying lifeless amongst the piles of the dead was a humanoid creature with goat legs and a fancy embroidered vest.

Several peasants approached them and averted Daylen's attention. They were covered in mud and rags, attracted to Daylen's extravagant robe. "Please, wise one," a peasant exclaimed, reaching out. "Spare me a portion of your wealth."

Daylen reached for the leather pouch at his belt and removed a handful of berries. The peasant fumbled at his side, grabbing the berries with trembling, eager hands. As modest as the berries were, they were not local to Brunhylde and were accepted with gracious, hungry mouths. Nilderon produced a loaf of bread from his bag and tore a chunk of it off to share with a nearby peasant. Soon, a horde of peasants had dropped the weights of their labors and surrounded them. Reaching out in desperation, they fought to grab hold of the strangers' charity.

Daylen moved through the crowd, sharing what he could. A forceful citizen stripped the loaf of bread from Nilderon and it floated above a sea of hands, pinching at it, taking what they could before the bread disappeared in the crowd.

"What is all this commotion?" a strong voice rang above the gathering. "There is work to be done."

The crowd dispersed in fear, separating in every direction. A Vixus knight stood before Daylen and Nilderon. He wore dark sheets of spiked armor, a spiked whip lowered at his side. "What business do you have here, wizard?"

Daylen responded, his face concealed under the hood of his cloak, his hands hidden in the cuffs of his long sleeves. "I am a Vixus priest and wish to speak to the Lord of this lot."

The knight studied Daylen, and by the sight of his robe, took him to be a wizard of imperial status. "Follow me and follow close. We can't afford any disruption, not with so much work to be done."

Daylen and Nilderon were led to the manor house. They were escorted to a large dining hall, where Lord Shyn awaited them. A large plate of food was before him, every inch of the table covered in the abundance of all matter of food and drink. Lord Shyn picked chicken from his teeth, disposing of a small bone with the flick of his finger and waved a hand for Daylen and Nilderon to join him.

"Come in, come in. Please, have a seat. Help yourself to whatever strikes you."

Daylen and Nilderon took a seat and Daylen removed his hood. "My name is Daylen Sylver. I am a priest from Vixus Academy." He raised his arm; his sleeve fell back from his hand, revealing the brand of Vixus Academy on his palm.

Lord Shyn called for a slave, who before being addressed was standing unnoticed against the wall. Lord Shyn extended his mug and the slave proceeded to fill it with mead. "Is there some way I can be of service to you?" Lord Shyn said, addressing the Vixus priest.

"I am looking for a slave within your company by the name of Claudia. Do you know her?"

"I do," Lord Shyn replied.

"May I speak with her?" Daylen said.

"That depends on what you want with her," Lord Shyn said, shewing the slave away who filled his mug.

"She belongs to me," Daylen said.

Lord Shyn yelled to the servant. "Our guests! Don't be rude, they are thirsty and have traveled far!"

Daylen waved his hand. "Please, I am fine, thank you."

Nilderon shook his head vigorously.

"Be gone with you, then!" Lord Shyn yelled to the servant. "Expect a whipping, later, for your inhospitality."

Daylen could not help but assume that all the servants of the manor were treated in this despicable way.

Lord Shyn redirected his attention to Daylen. "What did you say, now? I'm sorry, but these servants are so rude. You train them and you beat them, and they still never learn, no matter how hard you try."

"I said Claudia belongs to me."

Lord Shyn choked on what he heard and jerked forward in his seat. "You must be joking. She belongs, here, in Brunhylde. I need all the help I can get. There are deadlines, expectations; surely the Queen is aware of this. She, herself, commanded it."

Daylen pulled a scroll from his robe. He unraveled the parchment and handed it to Lord Shyn. "Not anymore."

Lord Shyn snatched the parchment from Daylen's hand. "Another demand from the Queen? It is just like her to target Brunhylde. She has mistreated this town from the beginning. She doesn't understand the hard work my soldiers have put into this place. No respect, even now, even after the army I have created for her use!"

Daylen leaned across the table. "This demand is coming from High Priestess, Vamillion. As you can see, by the seal on the parchment. Any and all orders are official and approved by the queen. She has promised me a slave of my choosing. Claudia has a son, who is a slave on my estate. If they could be reunited, it would please me, greatly."

"Lucky me," Lord Shyn said in sarcasm. He narrowed his eyes. "You should be careful of forming emotional attachments to slaves, wizard. It may not serve you well, in the long run."

Daylen leaned away from the table. "It will serve you well to do as you are told. While it is not required of me to inform you as to the reason for this decision, I am inclined to educate you on the fact that a happy slave is a hardworking slave. Keep in mind, that while the efforts of Brunhylde in fulfilling the Queen's demands are appreciated, the war front is in need in all territories of our kingdom, and our success does not rest on the shoulders of Brunhylde, alone."

Lord Shyn lowered his head. "Well, of course not. I have no choice in the matter, be as it may." He threw his napkin to the table. "A happy slave or not, Claudia will not be of much use to you."

"Why is this?" Daylen asked.

"Claudia is sick with fever. She has been for many days now, can't snap her out of it."

Daylen rose from his seat. "Where can we find her?"

* * *

The room smelled of sickness and feces. On either side of the room, makeshift cots held the bodies of the sick, dying and injured, the majority of which suffered at the hands of brutal labor and malnutrition. Flies buzzed overhead. He moved down the aisle, studying the faces of each bed ridden individual until he recognized his mother.

She was lying with her back turned away from him. He stood over her and placed his hand on her leg. She did not move. "Mother…"

When she did not respond he turned her over and saw that she was dead.

Nilderon placed his hand on Daylen's arm.

Daylen did not move, he studied her face, tried to imagine the last days of her life. She was dirty, but she was not bruised. Her lips were dried and cracked.

"Daylen, I am sorry," Nilderon said.

Daylen placed his hands on his mother, and he closed his eyes. He chanted the words to the Life Light spell and experienced the swelling of energy that accompanied him when he healed Beauty's scars and regenerated his eye and tongue. His hands grew warm and glowed with a brilliant light. Claudia's body was surrounded in an aura of healing energy. Daylen repeated the words, like a mantra, over and over. The energy intensifying, the heat in his hands growing hotter and the room illuminated in a bright light.

Daylen was transported to a realm of deep meditation, where time stood still and flowed as a channel of energy, his body nothing more than a conduit. His mother awakened, as if from a dream. She rose from the cot where she lay and embraced him in a long hug. She told him over an over how proud she was of him; how much she knew he would succeed in becoming a wizard.

He did not notice Nilderon's hand squeezing his arm, did not hear Nilderon call his name. He was uncertain how much time had passed. He thought to open his eyes and he felt fear in doing so. When he recognized the fear, he opened his eyes, and was brought back from his dream to face reality.

When his eyes focused and he perceived the world through his magical eyes, they came to rest upon his mother's lifeless body. His spell did not have the power to bring her back to life. Her reanimation, and encouraging words, were only in his mind. He felt his hands grow cold and the light that radiated from them subsided, darkening the room.

Nilderon let go of Daylen's arm and turned to leave. "I will meet you outside. You need some time alone."

Daylen stood over his mother. He let the emotions pass through him. They were stubborn and strong and did not want to pass. He breathed deeply, focusing on his breath, in and out. Tears ran down his face. He leaned over and sobbed into her. He did not hear Nilderon leave as the door closed behind him.

When Daylen finally exited the medical building, he met Nilderon at the side of the road. "Daylen, I am sorry."

Daylen started up the road and Nilderon followed. "You need not be sorry for what you had no control of."

"But your loss," Nilderon said. "First Beauty, and now your own mother…"

"I did not go to save Beauty because I thought I would succeed. I did not come to Brunhylde because I thought I would be my mother's savior. I chose these paths because it was virtuous. It was the pursuit that mattered. The outcome does not change that, nor does it question my trust in Nature."

Nilderon scurried to keep up with Daylen's brisk walk. "What will you pursue now, now that Beauty is gone? And your mother, too?"

"It has not changed anything."

"What may I ask, is your pursuit?"

Daylen stopped in the middle of the road. The question forced him to recollect upon the culmination of all he had been through, to rest upon that pursuit that never faltered, was always there regardless of whether he was consciousness of it or not. "What it has always been… FéLorën."

~EPILOGUE~

aylen stood before the Desert Portal. At the top of the gate was carved the eye of FéLorën. Etched in archaic stone, it lacked emotion in its eternal stare. Within the portal's frame, the world swayed like a reflection on the ripples of a lake.

"Here we are, at last," Nilderon spoke. In his voice was the relief afforded by a quest's finale, but also was tainted with sorrow and uncertainty of what was to follow.

Daylen turned to face his wizard companion, and the followers who accompanied him to the Desert Portal. Villagers of Brunhylde, citizens of Twilight, and those he met who were moved to accompany him along the way, had lowered themselves to their knees, and clasped their hands in prayer, bowing their heads.

Nilderon's face reflected the concerns of all those who attended. He spoke in a low voice, ashamed to have any doubt. "Beauty's prophecy could have been wrong, or misinterpreted. You may never return, just as the others haven't... Must you go? Must it be?"

Daylen nodded.

"I will wait for you, for as long as required," Nilderon assured.

Daylen shook his head. "Do no such thing, my friend. Do not wait for a moment you are uncertain of. All the other moments will pass you by. In this moment, you are the master of your pursuit, where opportunity is your companion. As you just conveyed, I may not return. So use this moment, and every moment you have the privilege to experience, as an opportunity to live wisely."

In panic, a villager shouted, "How can we be wise?"

Daylen could sense the fear and desperation in the villager's voice and nodded in understanding. He closed his eyes and remained in silence long enough for the answer to arise, like a spell. "Know, in the deepest core of your being, that one day you will die. It is all that is required to bring attention to this present moment, the only moment that truly matters. Let that awareness of your own death be the catalyst for living fully. Let it conjure appreciation for all you experience and all that exists beyond your own experience. Let that shape the choices you make and the reasons for them. Let it guide your ability to appreciate others, and the precious, brief life that they, too, have. In this realization, you will become aware of a life beyond your own self-interest, to those of your relatives, your community, to all of humanity. In turn, you will understand the importance in treating each other fairly, and you will realize our shared experience makes us one. This will help you live with courage, which is necessary to living a life wisely, and to follow the way of FéLorën. So, the answer is simple: Know that you will die."

A citizen of Twilight rose to their feet, "What are we to do without you?"

"You fear that I will not return. Whatever awaits me will be. And whatever will be, should be as it is. But no matter the outcome, whatever happens to this body, you will not be without me. I am more than the limits of my skin, and the thoughts in my head, as are you. So, trust not in my return. Trust in life."

Nilderon stepped forward to embrace Daylen.

Daylen placed his forehead against Nilderon's and closed his eyes. He echoed, in a whisper, "You will not be without me."

Nilderon stepped away, receding into the crowd. The people rose to their feet as anticipation of Daylen's entry into the portal grew near. Nilderon raised his hand into the air. Others followed. Hands that were once clinched into fists in resistance and fear, opened along with their hearts, as they found acceptance. When all who attended had their hand raised to the sky, Daylen turned to face the portal.

"Let my action be my message," Daylen said, then stepped through the gate.

ABOUT THE AUTHOR

With Quill in hand, hunched over a desk by candlelight, Galemine chronicles the history of a world long forgotten. Empowered by the teachings of modern and ancient philosophers, he channels inspiration and insight, encouraging a positive outlook in the midst of adversity. To truly live takes courage, to achieve your dreams takes discipline. This work is intended to ignite the spark of creation within each of us. Let the flame of your being illuminate a corner of the dark. Amore fati.